For Loyall Solomon. Who gave me my first newspaper job.
And changed everything.

THE
ECHO
KILLING

As a crime reporter, Christi Daugherty saw her first dead body at the age of twenty-two. There would be many more, when she covered murders in cities like Savannah, Baton Rouge, and New Orleans. Her work eventually took her to England, where she wrote the Night School series of thrillers for young adults under the name C. J. Daugherty. That series was an international bestseller, and has been translated into twenty-four languages. *The Echo Killing* is her first novel for adults. Find out more – and win free books – on her website: ChristiDaugherty.com

@CJ_Daugherty

/CJAuthor

THE
ECHO
KILLING

CHRISTI DAUGHERTY

HarperCollins*Publishers*

HarperCollins*Publishers* Ltd
1 London Bridge Street,
London SE1 9GF

www.harpercollins.co.uk

First published by HarperCollins*Publishers* 2018
1

A catalogue record for this book is available from the British Library

ISBN: 978-0-00-823878-0

This novel is entirely a work of fiction.
The names, characters and incidents portrayed in it are
the work of the author's imagination. Any resemblance to
actual persons, living or dead, events or localities is
entirely coincidental.

Set in Sabon by Type-it AS, Norway

Printed and bound in the UK by CPI Group (UK) Ltd, Croydon, CR0 4YY

MIX
Paper from
responsible sources
FSC™ C007454

This book is produced from independently certified FSC™ paper
to ensure responsible forest management.

For more information visit: www.harpercollins.co.uk/green

Chapter One

It was one of those nights.

Early on there was a flicker of hope – a couple of stabbings, a car wreck with potential. But the wounds weren't serious and the accident was routine. After that it fell quiet.

A quiet night is the worst thing that can happen to a crime reporter.

With an hour to go until her midnight deadline, Harper McClain sat alone in the empty newsroom with no story to write, doing the one thing she despised most in the world – a crossword puzzle.

On the far wall, tall windows reflected back a dark image of the huge open room with its white columns and rows of empty desks, but Harper didn't notice it – she was glaring at the paper on her desk. Smudged and scratched-out letters glared back, like an accusation of failure.

'Why would anyone know an eight-letter word for "reckless bravery"?' she grumbled. 'I've got a seven-letter word for "bravery" – it's called "bravery". I don't need a longer word...'

'Audacity.' The voice soared across the newsroom from the editor's desk at the front.

Harper looked up.

City Editor Emma Baxter appeared to be focused on her computer screen, a silver Cross pen glittering in one hand like a small sword.

'Excuse me?'

'An eight-letter word for reckless bravery.' Baxter spoke without shifting her eyes from the monitor. 'Audacity.'

Baxter was pushing fifty at varying rates of speed. She was small and wiry, and that only made her look better in a navy blazer. Her angular face had a permanent look of vague dissatisfaction, but somehow that suited her, too. Everything about her was precise – her perfectly even short nails, her stiff posture, and you could cut your hand on the razor-sharp edge of her straight, dark bob.

'How the hell do you know that?' There was no gratitude in Harper's voice. 'In fact, *why* the hell do you know that? There is something fundamentally wrong with anyone who could answer a question like "What's an eight-letter word for bravery?" without first wanting to off themselves with a ...'

At her elbow, her police scanner crackled to life. 'This is unit three-nine-seven. We've got a signal nine with possible signal sixes.'

Harper's voice trailed off. She cocked her head to listen.

'I'm willing to forgive your insubordination on this one occasion,' Baxter said magnanimously. But Harper had already forgotten all about audacity.

On her desk, her phone buzzed. She picked it up.

'Miles,' she said. 'You heard the shooting?'

'Yep. Slow night just got busier. Meet you out front in five.' His Tennessee accent glided over each word, smooth as warm honey.

Harper gathered her things with quick efficiency and hooked

her police scanner to the waistband of her black pants. Sweeping a light black jacket off the back of her chair, she shrugged it on. A narrow reporters' notebook and pen were shoved into one jacket pocket. Press pass and phone in the other.

Moving fast, she headed across the room.

Baxter cocked an enquiring eyebrow at her.

'Shooting on Broad Street.' Harper talked as she walked. 'Possible injuries. Miles and I are heading down now to find out more.'

Baxter reached for her phone to alert the copy desk.

'If I need to hold page one,' she said, 'I have to do it no later than eleven thirty.'

'Tell me something I don't know.'

She turned out of the newsroom into a wide, brightly lit corridor that opened directly onto a staircase leading down to the front door. Her editor's final words floated after her.

'When you return, we can have a talk about your attitude.'

It was Baxter's favorite threat. Harper knew better than to worry.

The sleepy-looking security guard at the reception desk didn't even glance up from the small TV on his desk as she hit the green exit button with hard impatience and hurled herself out of the building into the steamy darkness.

June had arrived a couple of weeks ago, bringing blistering days with it. Nights were better, but only a little. Tonight, the air was velvet soft, but so thick you could stick a fork in it and expect it to stay standing up. This wasn't the usual Savannah humidity – this was like breathing under water.

Summer rain in Georgia is no minor threat – it can wash away your car, your house, your hopes, your dreams, and Harper glanced up at the gray clouds scuttling across the sliver of moon

3

as if they might tell her when the water would fall, but the sky had no news to give.

The newspaper's offices were in a century-old, rambling four-story building that took up half a city block on Bay Street, close enough to the slow-moving Savannah River to smell its green river scent and to hear the giant engines of the massive container ships rumble as they rolled slowly out to sea. The neon words 'DAILY NEWS' glowed red from a rooftop sign that must have been one of the last things the sailors saw before the great Atlantic Ocean opened before them.

Down the street, the ornate city hall's gilded dome gleamed, even at this hour, and through a break in the buildings, Harper could see the cobblestone lanes leading down to the water's edge.

She'd never lived anywhere except Savannah, so it had been a very long time since she'd paid much attention to its landmarks and antebellum architecture. To her, like the verdant town squares and endless monuments to ill-fated Civil War generals, it was all just *there*.

She didn't spare any of it a glance now as she waited, one leg jiggling impatiently. Her scanner crackled on her hip. Ambulances were being called out. Backup was being sent.

'Come on, Miles,' she whispered, turning her wrist to see her watch.

It was quiet enough for her to hear the faint wail of sirens in the distance, as a gleaming black Mustang rounded the corner and roared straight towards her, headlights blinding. It stopped in front of her, the motor revving.

Harper yanked the door open and leapt in.

'Let's go,' she said, strapping on her seatbelt.

The tires spun as they sped off.

Inside, the Mustang was alive with voices. Miles had one

4

scanner on his belt, one mounted within the dash where there might otherwise have been a radio, and a third hooked up behind the gear shift. Each was set to a different channel – one monitored the main police frequency, another was set to a side channel the cops used for chitchat. The third monitored ambulance and fire.

It was like walking into a small, crowded room where twenty people were all talking at once. Harper was used to it, but it always took her a second to make sense of the cacophony.

'What've we got?' she asked, frowning.

'Nothing new.' He kept his eyes on the road. 'Ambulance en route. Waiting for an update.'

Photographer Miles Jackson was tall and lean, with dark skin and neat, short-cropped hair. He'd been a staff photographer until a few years ago, when all the photographers were let go. Since then, he'd been freelance, doing whatever paid the most. He could be found shooting a wedding on a Saturday afternoon and a murder later that same night.

If it pays it plays, he was fond of saying.

He had a cool sardonic smile and liked driving fast. He was doing about twice the speed limit as they roared around the corner onto Oglethorpe Avenue, sending the car fishtailing.

Swearing under his breath, Miles wrestled the wheel.

'Doesn't this thing go any faster?' Harper deadpanned, hanging on to the handle above the door.

'Very funny,' Miles said through gritted teeth. But he quickly regained control.

As they raced past Forsyth Park, where a huge marble fountain poured a hoopskirt-shaped arc of water into a stone pool, she cocked her head, listening to the scanner.

'They know where the shooters went?' she asked.

Miles shook his head. 'Lost them in the projects.'

As he spoke, the scanner for the police chitchat channel lit up. A grave-deep voice growled, 'This is one-four. Unit three-niner-seven, what are we dealing with here?'

Miles and Harper exchanged a look. Fourteen was the code number used by Lieutenant Robert Smith, head of the homicide division.

Miles turned down the other scanners.

'Lieutenant, we've got one fatality, two going to hospital,' the officer on the scene responded. Excitement sent his voice up an octave. He talked so fast Harper got a contact high from his adrenaline. 'Gang-banger party. Three shooters, all MIA.'

Not waiting to hear the rest, Harper pulled out her phone. Baxter answered on the first ring.

'It's murder,' Harper said without preamble. 'But it could be gang-on-gang.'

'Damn.' She could hear the editor tapping her silver pen on the desk. *Taptaptaptap.* 'Call me as soon as you know more.'

The line went dead.

Shoving her phone in her pocket, Harper leaned back in her seat.

'If the dead guy's a banger, the story goes inside.'

'Well then, we'd best hope our victim is an innocent housewife,' Miles observed as they turned onto Broad Street.

Eyes on the road ahead, Harper nodded. 'We can dream.'

On early maps of Savannah, the city is a perfectly symmetrical grid of straight lines, OCD neat, with Broad Street forming the eastern border. In all directions, everything outside that grid is dark green emptiness, its contents identified with the words *'Old Rice Fields'* in the nineteenth-century cartographer's precise handwriting.

Today, that orderly grid remains largely unchanged, save for the rice fields, which are long gone, replaced by unlovely sprawl. Broad Street forms a speedy direct line between gorgeous, picture-postcard old Savannah and the parts where Harper and Miles spent most of their working nights.

As they headed west, the grand old houses fronted by trees draped in the gray lace of Spanish moss gradually disappeared, replaced by peeling paint, overgrown yards and cheap metal fences.

No leafy squares broke up the dense housing in this neighborhood. No fountains poured beneath oak trees. Instead, battered apartment buildings stacked people on top of each other in cramped and ugly conditions fronted by broken sidewalks and illuminated by the garish signs marking out fast-food chains and discount shops.

Out here, the streets were busy – drug dealers did good business at this hour.

Miles' hands were steady on the wheel, but his eyes – scanning the buildings around them – were alert.

He was older than Harper – in his forties. Photography was his second career. Years ago, back in Memphis, he'd had another, very different life.

'I was an office guy,' he'd told her once as he took his camera carefully to pieces. 'Pushing paper. Made good money. Had the big house, the pretty wife, the whole nine yards. But it wasn't for me.'

He'd always loved taking pictures and he knew he had an eye. One day, he signed up for a photography course. Just, he said, for something to do.

'After that, I had the itch.'

As far as she could tell, within a year of taking that course, he'd quit his job, left his wife, and started over.

He'd visited Savannah for a business convention and it always stayed with him, he said. The slow way of life. The silky, sweet beauty of the place. The long curve of the river.

He said it felt like a fairytale. So he came here, to live the dream.

They'd both started at the newspaper the same year. Harper as an intern. Miles as night-shift photographer.

Even after seven years, he still saw the city with a stranger's eyes. He loved the homey cafés and the waitresses who called him 'sweetie'. He liked driving out to Tybee Island at sunset, or sitting on River Street, watching the ships pass by.

Harper couldn't remember the last time she'd done any of that. She'd spent all her life in Savannah. To her, this was simply home.

Ahead, swirling blue lights lit up the street like a deadly disco.

'Here we go,' Miles muttered, hitting the brakes.

Peering into the glare, Harper counted four patrol cars and at least three unmarked units.

An ambulance rumbled up behind them, its siren blaring, and Miles pulled to the side to let it pass.

'Better leave the car here,' he decided, killing the engine.

Harper glanced at her watch: 11:12. She had eighteen minutes to let Baxter know if she had to hold the front page.

Her heart began to race in that familiar way.

She had a thing for murder. Some people called it an obsession. But she had her reasons. Reasons she didn't like to talk about much.

Miles gathered his equipment from the trunk, but Harper couldn't wait.

'Meet you down there.'

Leaping from the car, she took off, notebook in one hand, pen in the other, running toward the flashing lights.

Chapter Two

On the street, the warm, humid air smelled of exhaust and something else – something metallic and hard to define. Like fear.

In the dark, the flashing lights were blinding. It wasn't until Harper got beyond the police cars that she saw the body in the road.

If people get shot while they're running, they fall hard. Legs at unnatural angles, hands above their heads, clothes fluttering around them – for all the world as if they've tumbled from the sky.

This guy had been running when he was shot.

Pulling out her notebook, Harper jotted down what she saw. Blue jeans and Nikes, baggy T-shirt riding up over a lean, dark-skinned torso. Large bloodstain forming an uneven circle on the pavement beneath him. The face was hidden from view.

Nearby, the ambulance was parked with its back door open, sending light flooding out onto the street. A team of paramedics was working on the two living shooting victims – plugging them into fluids, stopping other fluids from leaching away.

They were a bit late with that, though. There was blood everywhere.

Both wounded men looked like teenagers. The one closest to her still had baby fat in his cheeks.

They were dressed like the dead guy – T-shirts, jeans, matching Nikes.

Harper made notes, but kept her distance. Trying to be invisible.

Miles appeared across the road, crouching down on one knee to get a shot of the body. He had to be careful – the paper wouldn't use it if the dead guy looked *too* dead. So he angled himself to get a shot of the guy's hand, one finger pointing out, reaching for something now lost forever.

Movement in the distance caught Harper's attention and she looked up to see two men in cheap suits, their eyes focused on the ground, walking with slow deliberation. They were both listening intently to a uniformed patrol officer who was pointing and talking animatedly.

Detectives are easy to spot, once you get to know them.

Taking care not to step in the blood, she made her way toward them, sticking to the edges of the road.

She knew both men from previous crime scenes. Detective Ledbetter was short and portly, with thinning hair and a kind smile. The other detective was Larry Blazer. Tall and thin, with dark blond hair going artfully gray, he had cheekbones to die for and eyes as hard as copper pennies.

All the TV reporters had a thing for him, but Harper found him cold and self-aware, in the way of men who are handsome and know how to use that as a weapon.

Absorbed in their work, neither man noticed as she navigated the shadows until she was close enough to eavesdrop.

'The shooters came up from the Anderson Projects. The victims won't say how they knew each other, but this wasn't random,' the uniformed officer was saying as she walked up. 'Someone wanted these guys dead.'

He was green. This could even have been his first shooting. His words poured out in an excited rush.

By contrast, Blazer's questions were delivered at a slow and deliberate pace; trying to communicate calm and hope it was contagious.

'You say the vics told you the three shooters ran off together. They give any idea where they went?'

The officer shook his head. 'All he said was, "that way".' He pointed roughly towards the building in front of them.

Ledbetter said something Harper couldn't hear. She took a step closer.

In the dark, she never saw the empty forty-ounce beer bottle in the gutter, but the rattle it made when she kicked it was hard to miss.

She winced.

All the cops looked up. Blazer spotted her first. His gaze narrowed.

'Careful,' he said. 'Press on scene.'

Stepping back, Harper waited warily, hoping Ledbetter would be lead detective on the case.

But it was Blazer who walked towards her.

Crap, she thought.

'Miss McClain.' His voice was cool, with an oddly flat intonation. 'What a surprise to see you standing in the middle of my crime scene. I don't suppose you're a witness?'

He was tall, over six-one, and he used that height to intimidate – looming over her. But Harper was five-eight, and she wasn't easy to impress.

'Sorry, Detective,' she said, her tone a cultivated mixture of contrition and respect. 'There's no crime tape. I didn't mean to get in your way.'

'I see.' He studied her with distaste. 'And yet you are standing where no journalist belongs. Shedding DNA all over the place.'

Who was he trying to kid? They weren't going to collect that kind of evidence at this scene. The cops cared no more for a dead gangbanger than Baxter did.

Harper blinked innocently.

'I know you're busy,' she said, all sweetness, 'but could you give me a little information for the morning paper so I can get out of your hair? Names of the victims? Number of suspects?'

'Our investigation has just begun.' Blazer recited the familiar words in a tone that said he saw right through her. 'It would be premature to say anything at this time. We're still identifying the deceased and have not yet notified next of kin. Now, I'm going to have to ask you to step out of the scene immediately.'

Clearly, he wasn't in a giving mood.

Still, Harper gave it one more try. 'Detective, is this part of a drug war? Should local residents be concerned?'

Rocking back on his heels, Blazer studied her with an interest she didn't like.

'McClain, a few small-time scumbags stepped on the turf of some bigger scumbags and they got a lesson in why that's a bad idea. Why don't you put that in your rag?'

She opened her mouth to answer, but he cut her off.

'It was a rhetorical question. I have no official statement at this time. Now, kindly get the hell out of my scene before I have you arrested.'

Harper knew better than to argue. Holding up her hands in surrender, she backed away.

*

When she made it back to the ambulance, Miles was leaning against it casually, checking his shots on the camera screen.

'Blazer's lead detective, so I've got nothing,' Harper announced glumly. 'That man hates me like a canker sore.'

Straightening, Miles motioned for her to follow him back towards the Mustang.

'I shot the lead paramedic's wedding two months ago,' he said quietly, when they were a safe distance away. 'Gave her a cheap deal. She owed me a favor.'

Harper grabbed his arm. 'You got an ID on our dead guy?'

'More than that.' He held up a crumpled piece of paper. 'I've got it all. Melissa had a wonderful honeymoon. She was very chatty today.'

'You hero.' Harper mock-punched his arm. 'What've we got?'

Miles squinted to read his own writing.

'Our dead guy is Levon Williams, nineteen, recent graduate of Savannah South High School – played for the baseball team. Hell of a hitter, I'm told. Also, apparently, an up-and-coming heroin dealer. The two wounded victims are his known associates. Suspects are three black men, slim, two are average height, T-shirt and jeans, one is short and stocky, wearing a bandanna around his neck. All are late teens to early twenties. Suspected members of the East Ward gang.' He handed Harper the page. 'It's all here.'

Harper scanned the paper quickly, seeing nothing that said page one. As soon as they reached the Mustang, she called Baxter to give her the bad news.

'Damn it,' the editor said when she'd heard the rundown. 'Get back here and write it up for page six. It's better than nothing.'

Miles started the engine as Harper ended the call.

'Page six?' he guessed.

Harper folded the paper and put it in her pocket.

'Buried in the weeds.'

He shrugged. 'You win some, you lose some.'

Turning the wheel, he began to pull out of the parking space, before braking hard to let a white van creep by. The words 'COUNTY CORONER' were emblazoned on the side in sepulcher black.

'The iceman cometh,' Miles murmured.

Harper barely looked up. She was scribbling notes for the piece she needed to write when she got back.

When the van passed, Miles turned the car around with neat precision. They'd only gone a short distance, though, when a breathless voice suddenly filled the car.

'Unit five-six-eight in pursuit of suspects from Broad Street.'

Harper's pen froze.

Miles lifted his foot from the accelerator.

They both looked at the scanner.

'Copy unit five-six-eight,' the dispatcher responded calmly. 'Please verify: Are these the suspects from the shooting on Broad?'

'Affirmative.' The man was panting, his voice shook. He was running.

'Three males heading south on foot on Thirty-Ninth Street,' he shouted. 'Two tall. One short with a bandanna.'

In the background, Harper could hear the dispatcher typing the information into her computer, her fingers quick and light on the keys. It was Sarah tonight on dispatch – she recognized the voice. She was good.

'All units. Backup required for unit five-six-eight in pursuit of shooting suspects heading south on Thirty-Ninth.'

Sarah's voice was so unemotional she might have been reading a cake recipe.

Harper turned to Miles. 'That's five blocks from here.'

'Copy that.' He shifted gears and hit the gas. The Mustang responded, tires squealing. A smile lifted the corners of his mouth as he turned towards Thirty-Ninth.

'Let's get ourselves on page one.'

Chapter Three

As they drove through the dark streets to find the suspected killers, Harper stared out the window, tapping her pen impatiently against her notebook. They didn't have much time. Even if this went smoothly, Baxter would have to delay the last edition.

Ordinary people might have been thinking about the victim back at the crime scene – his short life ended in a violent instant. But her mind had already moved on. Now, she just needed to know who killed him.

It had always been like this. Murders didn't bother Harper. They fascinated her.

She knew everything about the mechanics of homicide. She knew what the detectives were doing now, and the coroner's office. How the victim's family would be informed, and how they would react when they learned. She knew how the machinery of government would kick into gear and consume the lives of everyone involved.

She knew, not because she wrote about it, but because she had lived it.

When she was twelve years old a murder had destroyed her world. She could trace her career, her life and her obsessive interest in crime back to that single day, fifteen years ago.

Some moments get imprinted on your mind so thoroughly every breath of it stays with you forever. Most of these are bad moments. Harper could walk through every second of the day her mother died any time she wished. She could place those hours in a mental reel and play them like a film. Watch herself, so small and quick, walking home from school. Utterly unaware that life, as she knew it, was already over.

3:35 p.m. – Twelve-year-old Harper shoves open the low metal gate, closing the latch with a silvery clang.

3:36 p.m. – She dashes up the steps – flinging the unlocked door open and closing it behind her with a resounding thud. God, it's all so bright and warm in her memory; so filled with color. She calls out, 'Mom, I'm *starving*.' No one replies.

3:37 p.m. – She yells up the stairs, 'Mom?' She's not worried yet. Humming to herself, she checks the living room, the dining room.

3:38 p.m. – She steps into the kitchen.

This is where her childhood ends.

There is more color here – not only the yellow of the walls and the tiny vivid jars and bottles of blue and gold and green paint. But red. Red everywhere. Splattered on the walls and counters. Pooling on the floor under her mother's naked body.

Blood-red filling her memories with horror and leaving behind trauma that will never go away.

In her memory film, time has stopped now. It stays 3:38 for a very long time.

In the next frame she's running in slow motion to her mother's side, she's skidding in the blood, losing her balance. She's trying to breathe, but it's as if someone has kicked her in the stomach.

Her whole body hurts and there's no air, no air, as she falls to the floor, blood squelching beneath her skinny knees.

This was the first and only time she was ever afraid to touch her mother. Her trembling hand reaches out to brush the smooth, pale shoulder. She recoils, yanking it back again.

She's so cold.

Someone is sobbing far away. 'Mom? *Mom?*' And faintly, plaintively, 'Mommy?'

She knows now it's her own voice but the her on the memory film isn't sure. She feels far away from her body.

In the next frame, she is scrambling to her feet – still no air to breathe, and she is gasping for it, but her lungs refuse to work – skidding across the kitchen and hurtling out the side door to Bonnie's house. But the Larsons moved away after their divorce, and the new neighbors aren't nice and they're not home anyway, but she pounds on the door leaving bloody marks on the wood, and the pounding echoes in the emptiness.

She's weeping so hard her breath begins to come back, forced into her lungs by tears, as she runs back to her house to find the phone. She picks it up only to see it fall from her nerveless, blood-slick fingers. Then she is sobbing and finding it on the floor, taking choking breaths, making herself slow down. She only has to dial three numbers. She can do this. She *has* to do this.

'OK,' she whispers over and over through her tears as she dials, hands shaking so hard the phone vibrates. 'OK. OK. OK...'

It rings. A distant series of odd, mechanical clicks. A dispatcher answers – and that irrationally calm female voice, so inured to hearing the horrors of the world expressed through the panicked, disembodied voices of witnesses and victims, is a rope she can grasp.

'This is 911. What is your emergency?'

She is trying to speak but her tears and breathlessness make it almost impossible. Only a confused scattering of words make it from her frightened mind to her lips.

'Please help,' she sobs. 'My mom. Please help.'

'What's happened to your mom?' The woman's emotion-free voice is stern-friendly. Stern to help her focus. Friendly because she is a *child*.

Now Harper must say the word. The word she can't even think. A word so distant from her until this moment in time it had no more bearing on her immediate life than Uzbekistan. Her mind doesn't want her to say the word. Saying it hurts.

'My mom... there's blood... I think... someone killed her.'

It is all she has. She is sobbing inconsolably. The dispatcher's tone changes.

'Sweetie,' she says with utter gentleness that disguises the worry beneath it and the absolute tension of the moment, 'I need you to take a deep breath and tell me your address, OK? Can you do that? I'm sending help.'

Harper tells her. She doesn't know then, but she knows now, that as she talks the operator is typing urgent things into her computer, motioning for her supervisor's attention, setting wheels in motion that will turn and turn through her life for years to come.

Then the operator is asking if she's safe, and that is the first time it occurs to Harper that someone very dangerous might be in the house with her. Her levels of fear and panic are off the charts now. And the operator is telling her to take the phone outside, and to stand by the curb and to run and scream if anyone scares her.

She does as she's told, each step wooden and unreal, until she is at the metal gate again with its clanging latch, the phone clutched in one blood-sticky hand.

The dispatcher is saying calming things. 'They're coming, honey. They're three minutes away. Don't hang up, sweetheart...'

In the distance she hears the urgent wail of sirens and despite everything doesn't realize they're coming for her.

When the first police car screeches to a halt, blue lights flashing, she feels even more frightened as the officers climb out of the car with guns in their hands, and run past her into the house.

One of them shouts to her, 'Stay there.'

She stays.

More police pull up and soon she is surrounded by men and women in official uniforms with guns and mace and Kevlar vests.

'Are you OK?' people keep asking her.

But Harper is not OK. Not OK at all.

Then a man, tall, with a deep voice and authoritative air appears at her side. He takes the phone from her hand and hands it to another officer, who places it, strangely, Harper thinks, in a plastic bag.

The man has a weathered face that has seen other children like her, bloodied and frightened. Many of them. There is kindness in his eyes.

'My name is Sergeant Smith,' the man tells her in a deep, soothing voice. 'And I'm not going to let anyone hurt you...'

'Harper.'

She gave a start, blinking hard.

The car had slowed to a crawl. They were on a dark street, surrounded on all sides by run-down buildings with boarded-up windows.

Miles was looking at her oddly, as if he'd said her name more than once.

'We're here,' he said. 'Are you OK?'

'I'm fine.' Her tone was brusque and she turned away, her eyes sweeping the sidewalk for trouble, out of habit.

She was angry with herself. Why had she been thinking about that stuff? It was ancient history.

Right now, she had a job to do.

'Have you seen any sign of them?' she asked, peering into the shadows.

'Nothing at all.' He slowed the car to a crawl, squinting at the buildings around them. 'Looks like we got here before backup did.'

This wasn't normal. Harper frowned.

'What's taking so long?'

Miles shook his head. 'No idea.'

Thirty-Ninth Street was narrower and much darker than Broad, lined on either side by some of the city's most notorious public housing projects. Harper had been here many nights before, but she could never remember seeing it so empty. No one hung out on the steps, or gathered on the concrete drives. There were no pit-bull gangs comparing dogs, no crowds of young men jostling on the basketball court.

Miles gave a low whistle.

'Well, this is unusual.' He spoke softly, as if they might be heard through the windows.

Harper leaned forward in her seat to look up.

'Someone shot out the streetlights.'

'Five-six-eight, what is your situation?' The dispatcher's voice crackling out of the police scanner seemed too loud in the heavy silence.

A long moment passed. All the radio chatter had stopped now, as if every cop in the city was waiting for this one crime to play out.

'This is five-six-eight.' The officer's voice was low now, barely above a whisper. 'Suspects ran into the Anderson Houses. I've lost visual. I'm looking for them.'

'Copy that, five-six-eight,' the dispatcher said. 'Be aware, backup is en route.'

Miles pointed to a decrepit cluster of boarded-up, graffiti-covered three-story buildings at the end of the road.

'Anderson Houses,' he said. 'Been closed a few years now. Great place to hide.'

Pulling the car into an empty space at the side of the road, he cut the engine. The quiet that followed felt unnatural.

In sync, Harper and Miles unhooked the scanners from their belts and placed them on the floor of the car.

Miles looked at her, his eyes gleaming in the shadows. 'This could get messy.'

Harper grinned at him. 'What's new?'

Tilting her head at the door, she reached for the handle.

There was no more discussion. They both knew how dangerous it was.

They jumped out of the car in the same moment, closed their doors carefully and edged down the road toward the boarded-up buildings.

Outside, the humidity hung thick in the hot air and the odd hush felt even heavier. Not one person walked down the normally crowded street. Their soft-soled shoes were silent on the pavement as they moved through the darkness. Still, Harper was conscious with every step of a sense of being watched.

The fine hairs on the back of her neck rose.

'Where is everyone?' she whispered.

Slowing, Miles scanned the ramshackle buildings around them. They appeared empty. But Harper suspected there were people there, behind every dark pane of glass.

'Waiting,' he said grimly.

Across the street, something moved in the shadows.

They both noticed it at the same time but Miles reacted first, grabbing Harper's arm and pulling her behind a parked car.

They crouched low.

Peering into the darkness, Harper could make out three figures about twenty yards away. Two were tall and thin, one was short and stocky. Hidden behind a tall, abandoned tenement, the three didn't seem aware they were being watched. They were staring intently in the opposite direction.

Following their line of vision, Harper at first saw nothing. Then she noticed the glow of a flashlight bobbing at the far end of the long, dusty courtyard.

Her heart sped up. It had to be the cop – Five-six-eight.

The killers were two buildings away from him and he was heading the wrong way. He had no idea where they were. But they knew right where he was.

Carefully, she raised herself up above the hood of the dusty parked Toyota, trying to get a better look at what the men were doing. The small one was fussing with something around his neck. It took her a second to realize it was a bandanna.

The three wanted men leaned towards each other, whispering. They seemed to be arguing.

The smallest one said something that silenced the others. Despite his size, it was immediately clear he was the leader of that group.

The other two dropped back as, with one hand, he tugged the bandanna up over his nose and mouth, like a bandit from a western movie.

Reaching behind his back, he pulled a gun from the waistband of his jeans.

Harper's stomach dropped.

He was going to take the cop out.

In desperation, she looked over her shoulder to the empty street. Where the hell was backup? They should have been here long ago.

But behind them there was only darkness.

A few feet away, Miles had balanced his camera on the very edge of the trunk and was focusing it on the three men. His hands were absolutely steady.

Harper leaned towards him.

'We have to warn that cop,' she hissed.

Miles turned far enough to give her an incredulous look.

She couldn't blame him. She knew as well as anyone reporters at crime scenes were supposed to be nothing but eyes and ears – always observing, never getting involved.

But surely this was different. Someone could die. And there was no one else here to save him.

Before she could make up her mind what to do, the three gunmen stepped out of the shadows.

Harper's eyes had adjusted to the dark now and she could see them clearly as the one with the bandanna raised his gun, leveling it at the bobbing light in the distance.

The would-be shooter was small – no more than five foot four – and so young. He could easily be a teenager.

But his stance was confident. His hand was steady. There was a kind of eagerness to his posture – he leaned forward onto the balls of his feet, the gun thrust out. As if he couldn't wait to kill.

The scene took on a haze of unreality. It was too late to call for help. They were too close, anyway.

Next to her, Miles took his first careful shots. There was no loud click – just a muffled shushing sound, instantly lost in the breeze.

He modified his cameras for silence.

Across the road, the gunman spread his legs, bracing himself to fire. The gun glittered silver in his hand.

Every muscle in Harper's body tightened, preparing for the roar of gunfire. Her hands gripped the trunk of the Toyota in front of her, knuckles gleaming pale.

This couldn't happen. She couldn't sit there and watch a man die. She had to do something.

Closing her eyes she drew a sharp breath. Then, before she could talk herself out of it, she shouted into the quiet night.

'*Police*. Drop your weapons.' She paused, trying to think up something else intimidating to say. 'You're surrounded.'

Out of the corner of her eye, she saw Miles glare at her.

Across the courtyard, the cop's flashlight swung hurriedly in her direction. It blinked once, then disappeared.

The wanted trio whirled toward her voice. The taller two whipped handguns out of their waistbands and pointed them at the Toyota.

Harper and Miles ducked down below the windows.

Squeezing her eyes shut, Harper listened for any sound. Her heart slammed against her ribs. Her breath came in short, tight gasps. She had definitely not thought this through.

'Great.' Crouching next to her, every muscle tense, Miles hissed, 'What's next in your plan? Hit them with your pen?'

Harper didn't have an answer. What *was* the step after yelling? Yell again?

Where were the real police, for God's sake?

Cautiously, she raised her head to look at the men through the dirty car windows. All their guns were pointed directly at her.

With a gasp, she dropped back down. Her ribs felt too tight around her lungs – she couldn't seem to breathe.

If the police didn't get here soon, she and Miles were both going to die.

Swallowing hard, she tried shouting again.

'I said drop your weapons, *now*.'

'Fuck you, five-o,' the tallest of the three shouted defiantly.

She heard a series of metallic clicks.

Her heart stopped.

She heard Miles whisper, 'Oh, hell.'

They threw themselves down flat, hitting the rough concrete as the men fired.

The noise of three powerful guns letting loose was deafening – an almighty cannon roar.

Overhead, the windows of the car shattered.

Her hands covering her head, Harper squeezed her eyes shut as glass showered her.

They were trapped.

Chapter Four

The shooting seemed to go on forever. When it finally stopped, the silence left a hollow feeling in Harper's chest – a curious emptiness.

Her ears ringing, she reached out blindly for Miles.

He wasn't there.

'Miles,' she whispered urgently, hands flailing in the air.

'I'm alive,' he hissed from a few feet away. 'No thanks to you.'

Blinking dust and glass from her eyes, she saw him, crouched by the trunk of the car.

'You dead, five-o?' one of the shooters shouted mockingly.

Before Harper could think of an appropriate reply, a cool voice spoke from behind her right shoulder.

'I am alive and very pissed off,' it said. 'Now drop your weapons or I will *unload* on you.'

Startled, Harper twisted around. A tall, broad-shouldered man stood directly behind her. He had a 9 mm semi-automatic pistol trained on the three suspects.

Luke Walker.

He wore a black T-shirt and jeans. The badge hooked to his belt gleamed. His gun hand was absolutely steady.

'You really are surrounded,' he added, motioning with his free hand.

As if on cue, a line of dark-clad undercover cops poured onto the street. Overhead, a police helicopter thundered across the sky, its blinding spotlight turning the night into cold, white day. Amid the sudden deafening confusion, voices shouted rough commands.

The cavalry had arrived at last.

Caught off guard, the three wanted men were pointing their guns wildly in all directions. But it was too late, and even they knew that.

With slow reluctance, the tallest one dropped his gun. The short one gave him a look of disgust.

But seconds later, as the police shouted commands and threats at him, he did the same.

One by one, they knelt on the ground, putting their hands behind their heads.

As the police swarmed them, Miles left the battered Toyota and ran over to get more shots.

Harper stood cautiously. Her legs were a little shaky.

That had been too close for comfort.

As she turned to face him, Luke holstered his weapon.

'Harper McClain.' He didn't sound happy. 'Why am I not surprised to see you here?'

'Because I'm always this intrepid?' Harper forced a nonchalance she didn't feel into her voice.

She'd known Luke since she was an intern at the paper and he was a rookie patrol officer. At twenty, he'd been earnest and thoughtful. They'd both grown up in the same neighborhoods and they were the same age. So, when her editor assigned her to do a ride-along with him, it was almost inevitable they'd hit it off.

They'd spent three hours racing from one fairly minor crime to another with the enthusiasm of ingénues. She'd written an excited article about his life as a new cop. They'd been friends ever since.

So she knew him well enough to know he was genuinely pissed off as he strode toward her, boots crunching on broken glass.

'Intrepid is not the word I'm thinking of,' he said, a sharp edge to his voice. 'Dammit, Harper, since when do you perform citizen's arrests? You could have gotten yourself killed. You know that, right?'

'What else was I supposed to do?' she asked. 'Backup never showed. Those guys were about to shoot Officer Flashlight over there. I had to do something.'

'You could have *waited for us*,' he said, his voice rising. 'You could have gone to a safe place and called this in. You could have considered your own safety for one minute. You could have done a lot of things, McClain, if you'd just thought it through.'

Harper flushed.

'I did think it through,' she insisted. 'And I decided I wanted everyone to live. Jesus, Luke. Give it a rest, OK?'

She folded her arms tightly across her torso.

His eyes swept her pale face.

'Are you OK?' He took a step toward her, his face softening. 'I was half a block away when they let rip on you guys. I thought...'

His voice trailed off.

'I'm fine,' she assured him. 'They're crappy shots.'

'Not that crappy.'

Across the road, the cops were searching the shooters, emptying their pockets onto the dirty pavement. Fat rolls of money, a handful of tiny plastic bags of white powder, a comb, some change.

Harper had begun to piece the night together. Luke worked on the undercover squad – which meant he mostly handled drug-gang cases. She hadn't seen him in more than a month, which usually meant he was working somewhere deeply unsavory.

'Luke – did this blow your cover?' she asked.

She was relieved when he shook his head.

'I've been keeping an eye on these clowns for a few weeks. Had a tip-off they were making a move tonight against a rival group.' He glanced at her. 'I'm still not sure how you and Miles got caught in the middle.'

'We heard the call that the killers had been spotted,' she explained. 'Came over to see it go down. We didn't realize it was going to go down right on top of us.'

She gestured as she spoke, and only then noticed that glass had cut her hand at some point. A small trickle of blood traced across her skin. Harper stared at it.

'Jesus, Luke,' she said. 'They actually shot at me. Is this what it's like to be you?'

'Every day,' he said evenly.

She rubbed the blood away. 'They don't pay you enough.'

'Tell me about it.'

He fell silent for a second, then suddenly, said, '"You're *surrounded*?" God's sake, Harper. How much TV do you watch?'

'I didn't have time to think of a better line,' she said defensively. 'What do you say in these circumstances?'

He considered this. 'I usually go with "Drop the gun or I'll blow your balls off."'

She gave a short laugh. 'Why didn't I think of that?'

'Next time,' he said, glancing at her.

When he smiled, he looked more like the rookie she'd first met seven years ago. All chiseled jaw and clear blue eyes.

Time and work had done a number on him. His edges had sharpened and all the eager innocence she remembered from back then was gone.

She wondered if he thought the same about her.

In the years that followed the ride-along, their careers had shadowed each other. He'd been promoted to detective the year she became a full-time police reporter. He'd been on a fast-track to sergeant – working homicides at twenty-five.

They'd always had a connection – a holdover from that first night on the road. Whenever she saw him, it was a good night. This wasn't the first time he'd melted out of the darkness at a crime scene to check on her.

Then, abruptly, eight months ago, everything changed. Luke left Homicide and joined the undercover squad. He'd refused to tell her why.

It didn't make sense. Undercover was a lateral move – and a tough one. The work was dangerous and hard. When Harper first heard about it, she'd tried to find out why, but he ducked the question, refusing to be pinned down. Still, she could sense something was wrong.

Since then, she'd seen less of him. He disappeared for long stretches of time. He changed his appearance regularly and dramatically – and he kept his distance. On the rare occasions when she did see him, he didn't seem happy.

'How've you been?' She shot him a sideways glance.

'Busy,' he said, looking away.

Across the road, the three handcuffed men were now on their feet, watching the police with identical expressions of dull disinterest, as if everything were happening to someone else.

By now, crowds of gawkers had appeared on the sidewalk

– manifesting as if from thin air. In malevolent silence they watched the police walk the men to the van that would take them to jail.

'Luke!'

Another undercover cop waved for him to come over.

Luke raised a hand in acknowledgment.

'Wait here,' he told Harper.

She watched him go, his stride long and unhurried. Like him, the other cop was in jeans and a plain T-shirt. He wore his badge on a chain around his neck.

The two conferred in low voices, looking at something taken from the suspects. After a minute, the cop left, holding a plastic bag of evidence.

When Luke returned, he stopped on the far side of the car and motioned for Harper.

'Come here. You need to see something.'

She walked over to join him, her shoes crunching on the glass.

What she saw made her breath catch in her throat.

The car was *destroyed*. All the windows were gone. The spray of bullets had left an uneven pattern of jagged holes in the doors and hood. Some of the gunshot holes were bigger than quarters.

'I wanted you to see how close you came.' The humor was gone from his expression. 'Seriously, Harper, you've got to be more careful. One of these days you're going to get yourself killed.'

'Come on, Luke,' she said. 'I was doing my job.'

'Getting killed is not your job,' he said sharply. 'It's *my* job.'

Harper stared. Before she could think of a good response, Miles walked up to join them.

'Our hero,' he said, holding out his hand to shake Luke's. 'Thanks for the rescue, man.'

'Miles, don't tell me you agreed to this.' Luke gestured at the car.

'As God is my witness, I had no idea she was going to do that,' Miles said. 'All I ask is that you don't arrest her until after she files her story.'

Turning to Harper he tapped his watch. 'On that note, and as pleasant as this evening has been...'

Harper checked the time. It was ten minutes to twelve.

'Shit. We've got to get back.'

Whirling, she ran towards Miles' car. At the last minute, she turned back.

Luke still stood by the ruined car, watching her.

'Thanks for saving my life, Walker,' she called to him. 'I owe you one.'

'Damn straight you do.'

Something in his voice told her he was serious.

Back in the newsroom, Harper wrote the story with Baxter leaning over her shoulder.

'Change "ran" to "fled",' she said, tapping the screen with a short, unvarnished nail.

Harper corrected the line without argument.

'Good, good, good,' Baxter murmured, whenever Harper wrote something she liked. She smelled faintly and not unpleasantly of Camel Lights and Chanel Coco.

It was twelve thirty when the article was finally sent to layout. Miles' stark photo of the three suspects, one with a bandanna disguising his face, gun pointed right at the camera, dominated the front page beneath the headline, **Suspected killers arrested in dramatic shootout.**

Baxter stretched her arms up, loosening the kinks from her shoulders.

'Why can't criminals be more thoughtful about our deadlines?' she asked.

'Because they're assholes?' Harper suggested.

Barking a laugh, Baxter headed towards the copy room.

'Go home, Harper. You've caused enough trouble for one night.'

When she was gone, Harper switched off her computer and tucked her scanner in her bag. But she didn't get up. She sat in her chair, staring at the computer's dark screen.

She kept seeing those blank-faced young men pointing their guns at her. Hearing Luke's voice in her head: '*One of these days you're going to get yourself killed.*'

On some level, she knew he was right. She liked getting close to danger. It drew her.

Tonight she'd been too close. Other people could have been hurt.

She and Miles always took risks but tonight she'd pushed it. Tonight she'd tried to be a hero.

At the other end of the room, Baxter bustled in, interrupting her thoughts.

'Are you moving in?' the editor barked. 'Go home, already.'

Harper straightened.

'I'm going,' she said, reaching for the phone. 'I need to make a call first.'

She waited for Baxter to pick up her bag and head out the door. Then she dialed a familiar number.

'LIBRARY,' a voice shouted impatiently.

In the background Harper could hear the normal Tuesday-night chaos at the bar – loud voices, guitars, clattering glasses, laughter.

'Hey, Bonnie.' Harper leaned back in her chair.

'Harpelicious! Where are you? Why isn't your gorgeous ass making my bar prettier right this very instant?'

Bonnie's always husky voice was rougher than usual after a night of shouting to be heard above the din.

'I'm still at work,' Harper said. 'I was thinking of coming down.'

'Come. I'll make you a mai tai. With extra cherries.'

Harper laughed. Mai tais had been her favorite drink when they were teenagers, sneaking into bars with fake IDs. She hadn't knowingly consumed one in years.

All of a sudden it sounded wonderful.

'I'm on my way.'

Chapter Five

It was nearly one as Harper pulled her car into an empty spot beneath the wide-spreading branches of an oak tree in front of her house. Spanish moss hung so low it brushed the top of the car, soft as cat paws.

Miles wasn't the only one who liked a muscle car. But while his was sleek and new, hers was a fifteen-year-old Camaro. It had 103,000 miles on the clock, but the engine *purred*. She wasn't about to park it anywhere near a bar, especially in June. Summer tourists had begun pouring into town a few weeks ago, a river-over-the-banks flood of them, and they were all drunk on that intoxicating mixture of vacation, warm sun and three-for-one happy-hour specials.

She could walk from here.

She was preparing to climb out when she caught a good glimpse of herself in the rearview mirror. Her face was a freckled, shiny oval. Mascara had left a black smudge under one wide hazel eye. Her skin was blotchy beneath a tangle of auburn hair.

How long had she looked like that?

With a sigh, she slid back into her seat.

'Great, Harper,' she muttered, rummaging in her bag for a brush. 'You fail at being a grown-up, again.'

She fixed her hair hurriedly and, in a burst of inspiration, applied a coating of the red MAC lipstick Bonnie had given to her for her birthday.

'All I ask,' Bonnie said at the time, 'is that once in a while you actually wear it.'

When she was satisfied that she looked less of a mess, she got out of the car and stood for a moment, gazing up at the house across the street.

For the last five years she'd been renting the garden-level apartment in a converted two-story Victorian on East Jones Street not far from the art college. Her landlord was a jolly, self-made redneck named Billy Dupre. He mowed the lawn and fixed things when they broke and never raised her rent. In return, she kept an eye on the grad students who rented the upstairs apartment and did a bit of painting now and then.

It was a good arrangement.

The blue house had a high, peaked roof and a stained-glass attic window that glowed amber and green on a sunny day.

All the windows were dark tonight, save for one light which shone reassuringly in the entrance hall. The door was solid. She'd had the locks changed to a high-security brand shortly after moving in.

It was safe. She'd made sure of that.

Satisfied that all was well, she threw her bag over her shoulder and headed out on foot.

The houses lining Jones Street were not the grandest in town but they had their charms. During the day, their tall windows overlooked tourist buses and students carrying portfolio bags as they hustled to the art school. At night, though, it was a quiet lane, plucked from history. Cast-iron streetlights cast dancing shadows through the graceful arching oak tree branches.

The moon had disappeared now, and the clouds were thickening. It was still uncomfortably warm and the humidity hung in the air so thick she could almost see it.

As Harper turned left at the first corner the sky vibrated with a threatening, low rumble of thunder.

Nervously, she quickened her pace, casting a quick glance over her shoulder at the empty street behind her.

The shooting had thrown her off-kilter. A spiky remnant of adrenaline still coursed through her body. She kept having the same feeling she'd had at the shooting scene – the feeling she was being watched. But whenever she turned around, there was no one there.

By the time she reached busy Drayton Street she was glad of the lights.

Here, even at one in the morning, the atmosphere was buzzing. As usual, Eric's 24-Hour Diner – with its vivid, 1950s neon sign promising: 'Fresh burgers and frozen shakes' – smelled tantalizingly of fried things.

As Harper threaded her way through the crowds, the first fat drops of what looked to be a fearsome storm began to fall.

Half-running, she turned off the main drag. She could hear The Library before she reached it – music and laughter poured out the open door through the crowd of smokers. Harper inhaled the spicy scent of clove cigarettes as she hurried inside.

'Hey, Harper,' the bouncer said. 'Back from another successful night fighting crime?'

Well over six feet tall, he had a scraggly beard, a huge beer belly and the unlikely nickname of Junior. Harper had once seen him haul three men out of the bar at the same time, without breaking a sweat.

'It's a dirty job, but someone's got to do it,' she said, holding up her fist for him to bump.

When he smiled, Junior revealed an array of teeth so mismatched he might have stolen them from other people.

'Bonnie's waiting for you. Said something about a tequila sunrise.'

'Mai-tai,' she corrected him, raising her voice to be heard above the cacophony as she headed into the crowded, dimly lit bar.

As the name implied, the bar was tucked inside a former library. The space was all wrong for a bar – the old reading rooms were small and inevitably overcrowded, but somehow it worked.

Harper liked the place, not only because Bonnie was a bartender here, but also because there was almost no chance of running into anyone she worked with. It attracted a twenty-something crowd who sat around smoking fake cigarettes and arguing loudly about Nietzsche and politics. The cops wouldn't be caught dead in here, while the reporters favored Rosie Malone's, an Irish pub near the river where local politicians tended to hang out.

The Library was Harper's place.

She liked that the walls still held the original built-in bookcases, stacked with paperbacks, and that there was a 'take a book, leave a book' policy. The only rule was displayed on a sign by the door, which read: 'NO PORN PLEASE, WE'RE CHILDREN'.

The main bar had been placed where the librarian's desk had once stood, in the middle of the largest room. Harper weaved through the crowd toward it.

The air was steamy and smelled of sweat and spilled beer and the rain blowing in through the open door.

Bonnie was easy enough to spot – she'd recently added magenta streaks to her long, blonde hair, and she glimmered in the dimness like a beacon.

The shocks of color perfectly suited her leopard-print miniskirt and cowboy boots. But then, with that figure, she could get away with wearing anything.

The two of them had been friends since childhood. Their relationship had always been more that of sisters than friends.

Like Harper's mother, Bonnie was an artist. Since there was no money in that, she bartended four nights a week and also taught a few classes at the local art school – making, from all of her jobs, just about enough for rent on a cheap apartment in a dodgy neighborhood.

When Harper walked up, she was pouring five tequila shots at once and talking a mile a minute. A goateed guy in a neat, button-down shirt was waiting for his drinks and wistfully watching her every move.

When Bonnie finally paused for breath, Harper leaned over the bar and pointed at the shots.

'Thanks, but I'm not that thirsty.'

Whooping, Bonnie shoved the shots at the startled goatee guy and launched herself over the bar, pulling Harper into a full-body hug.

'I can't believe you came. You hate going out in tourist season.'

'The lure of a tropical cocktail never fails,' Harper told her.

'If that's true, I'll make you a mai tai every night.' Bonnie's eyes scanned her face. 'How's it going? Nice lipstick, by the way.'

'It's been a weird night.' Harper shrugged off the question. 'And this is your lipstick.'

'Knew it. I have amazing taste. You should let me choose your shoes.' Jumping back onto the bar, Bonnie swung her legs around and leapt down, landing neatly in front of a long row of glittering bottles. 'Stay there. I'm going to get you that drink and you can tell me about your weirdness.'

Just then, though, a group of laughing drinkers shoved their way to the bar, credit cards clutched in their hands.

Bonnie shot Harper an exasperated look. 'First, I have to get rid of all these fucking people.'

In no hurry, Harper pulled up a bar stool and settled in.

Despite the volume and the chaos, being here made her calmer. Bonnie was the only person in the world who knew everything about her, and Harper could never fool her about one damn thing. Tonight, she needed someone who could see through her.

The two of them had met on Bonnie's sixth birthday. Bonnie's family had been living on Harper's street for a few weeks by then. She'd seen the new little girl next door many times, with her long, covetable blonde hair, roaring up and down the sidewalk on her tricycle, a handful of brothers in tow. It was impossible to miss her.

Although their modest, post-war bungalows were nearly identical, Bonnie's noisy, crowded house was the opposite of Harper's. Harper was an only child. Not in a tragic, poor me, lonely kid way. More in the indulged, loved way.

Her mother was a painter and art teacher. Her father was a lawyer who traveled a lot for work. Her memories of her childhood were a blurry watercolor blend of jazz flowing from the speakers, and color – color everywhere. The kitchen was lemon yellow, the sofa was cherry-red. Harper's room was aquamarine, and her mother's vibrant oil paintings covered the walls.

On sunny days, her mother set up her easel in the kitchen, where light poured in through wrap-around windows. When Harper was young, she'd often set up a tiny easel for her, too, so they could paint side by side.

The day of Bonnie's birthday party, Harper was sitting quietly on the back porch with a coloring book when, on the other side of the fence, Bonnie appeared holding a can of Silly String.

Setting down her crayons, Harper watched as, with careful deliberation, Bonnie made her way across the grass to the wire fence. Her bright pink dress and white-blonde hair gave her a jaunty, elfish appearance. Harper expected her to say hello. To ask what she was coloring. Instead, without warning or provocation, she'd pointed the nozzle at Harper and covered her in sticky pink threads.

Harper had stared at her in disbelief.

'Why did you do that?'

Scratching her shoulder, Bonnie considered this.

'Because you look lonely,' she pronounced after a second. 'And because I thought it would be funny. Come to my party.'

Harper, who had already clocked the balloons tied to the front fence and the BONNIE IS SIX sign on the door, and who had watched other children arrive for the event, played it cool.

'I didn't know it was your birthday,' she lied.

'It is,' Bonnie assured her. 'But I hate my cousins. And my brothers are assholes. I want you to be there instead.'

Harper didn't flinch at the obscenity.

'Why? You don't know me.'

Bonnie gazed at her with a look of beatific confidence.

'I like your hair. Go ask your mom if you can come over and I promise I won't spray you anymore.'

Inexplicably satisfied by this explanation, Harper had removed the Silly String from her clothes and gone into the kitchen to seek permission from her mother, who waved an approving paintbrush from behind her easel.

'Have fun, honey,' she'd said, eyes still on the canvas. She was painting a field of daisies in the sunshine – each petal so real you could almost touch the cool silk of it. 'Be sure and say thank you to Mrs Larson.'

From that day forward, for reasons Harper never fully understood, she and Bonnie were inseparable.

Their friendship had endured the trials of primary school and the grim anarchy of middle school. It had survived first boyfriends, Bonnie's parents' divorce, the pain of the Larson family moving away from the house next door. And worse.

Much worse.

Bonnie was the one reminder of Harper's childhood that she allowed in her life. The only one who'd known her *before*.

The only one who understood.

Harper waited patiently until the bar gradually emptied out. At around two o'clock, Bonnie handed her the third unfathomably pink cocktail of the night, topped with a tiny paper umbrella and four maraschino cherries impaled on a long toothpick.

'Carlo's taking over for a while,' she said, waving a beer bottle at the muscular, dark-haired guy behind the bar. 'Let's go talk.'

Feeling much better about everything by now, Harper held her drink up to the light to admire its atomic shades.

'This is my very favorite drink.'

'There's so much fruit juice and rum in that baby, it's diabetes in a glass.' Bonnie stretched her arms above her head with a groan. 'Man, this has been a long night. I've got to get a real job.'

At this hour, only the most determined drinkers remained, wrestling their demons one glass at a time. The music had been turned down and the air felt cooler.

They found one of the side rooms completely empty. It was largely dominated by a pool table.

Motioning for Harper to join her, Bonnie lifted herself up onto the green felt top.

'Get up here and tell me what's going on.'

Harper climbed up next to her, less gracefully. Bonnie had put a lot of rum in those drinks.

'Nothing's going on,' she said, stretching out her legs until her toes brushed the far edge of the table. 'It's all good.'

'Harper.' Bonnie shot her a look. 'You've been sitting in my bar drinking pink drinks for over an hour without saying a word to anyone. In tourist season. Something's going on.'

Harper smiled. Bonnie always could see right through her.

'There was a shooting.' Harper made a vague gesture with her drink. 'I got a little too close.'

Bonnie took a sip of beer, studying her narrowly.

'How close is too close?'

Thinking of the windows shattering above her head, Harper held up her hand, finger and thumb two inches apart.

'That close, I think.'

Bonnie's eyebrows winged up. 'What the hell, Harper? You're supposed to write about crime. Not get yourself shot.'

'It was fine,' Harper insisted. 'I wasn't in danger.'

'Bullshit,' Bonnie said bluntly. 'It scared you. I heard it in your voice on the phone. I saw it on your face when you walked in the bar. Don't lie to me.'

Pulling the tiny paper umbrella from her glass, Harper furled and unfurled it absently. While she'd been waiting for Bonnie, she'd had a lot of time to think about what had happened. And to question her own motives.

Through the protective haze of alcohol, she found herself asking a question she would normally never have said aloud.

'Tell me the truth. Do you think I'm self-destructive?'

Bonnie hesitated too long.

'Come on,' she said, finally, her tone softening. 'You know you have good reasons for what you do.'

It was true. But it also wasn't a no.

Out of nowhere, Harper thought of Luke, standing on the street like the god of justice, looking at her in a way he never had before. Like he was worried about her.

She'd had some time to think about him, tonight, too.

'By the way,' she said, 'I think I might have a crush on a cop.'

She could sense Bonnie relaxing as the serious moment passed.

'Well, hell, honey.' She nudged Harper's shoulder. 'Get yourself a piece of that law-and-order action.'

Harper shook her head. 'I can't. I write about cops. I'm not allowed to have crushes on them. It's a…' she sought the words from the drunken recesses of her mind, '…conflict of interference. No.' She blinked. 'Interest.'

'Really?' Bonnie looked doubtful. 'Come on. What can they do?'

'He could get demoted for it,' she assured her. 'Cops take this stuff seriously.'

Bonnie made a derisive sound.

'Since when do you give a damn about rules, Harper? The police don't have cameras in your bedroom. Actually, I've been thinking for a while now you needed to get laid. When was the last time you had any?'

Caught off guard, Harper found she wasn't sure of the answer to that question.

'Last year? That California guy, I guess?'

Bonnie stared at her as if she'd announced she liked doing it with cats.

'Harper, that was nearly two years ago. This can't be. I'm going to get Carlo to do you right this instant. Carlo!'

She half-turned toward the bar, raising her voice. Carlo, who was stacking glasses in the dishwasher, looked up enquiringly, muscles bulging through the sleeves of his black Library T-shirt.

'Ignore her, Carlo!' Harper yelled hastily. 'It's nothing.'

Laughing, she tugged Bonnie's arm. 'Behave yourself.'

'He'd do it,' Bonnie assured her. 'I know he thinks you're cute.'

'I'm *not* cute.' For some reason, Harper found the assertion outrageous. 'I'm introverted and I never remember to wear makeup. I've seen the women Carlo hangs out with. I am definitely not his type.'

Bonnie waved her beer. 'Everyone is Carlo's type. But if he's not yours...' She looked around the mostly empty bar. 'There's always Junior.'

'Will you stop?' Harper pleaded. 'Look. I promise, I'll sex someone up. Soon.'

'Do the cop,' Bonnie ordered. 'You like him. What's he like? I'll bet he's all Texas Rangery. Tall with lots of muscles; not much of a man for words. Takes command of the situation.'

'Shut up.' Harper's face heated.

'Oh my God, I'm *right*.' Bonnie's laugh was delighted. 'I want to meet this guy.'

Harper was starting to feel dizzy. She wasn't sure whether it was the mai tais or the conversation.

'We have got to stop talking about this,' she moaned, lying down on the table. The felt top was soft and she turned to press her face against it. It smelled soothingly of chalk and dust.

'Don't fall asleep on the pool table, Harper. Junior might carry you home and have his wicked way with you.'

Bonnie leaned over her, the tips of her long hair tickling Harper's face.

'Anyway, it's decided. You've got to get busy with this cop. And soon.' She smoothed Harper's hair gently away from her face. It felt nice. Harper closed her eyes.

'It'll fix all that ails you,' Bonnie promised.

Harper thought of Luke Walker standing there holding that gun. And wondered if maybe she was right.

Chapter Six

The next afternoon, Harper arrived at the police station at four o'clock, feeling like a truck had run over her face during the night.

At the edge of downtown on a quiet street, the police headquarters looked like a nineteenth-century jail, which is exactly what it was. Neat rows of small, arched windows marched across the brick walls, all of them overlooking a sun-baked parking lot that was, at this moment, completely full.

Muttering under her breath, Harper found a parking place on the street around the corner and fed the meter before hurrying out of the bright sunlight to take a shortcut through the blessed shade of the Colonial Park Cemetery.

Sheltered by the long branches of ancient oak trees, the old burial ground behind the station was more park than cemetery. Ever since she was a child, she'd loved it. You could read the city's history in its inscriptions:

James Wilde.
*He fell in a duel on the 16th of January, 1815,
by the hand of a man who, a short time ago,
would have been friendless but for him.*

At twelve, she'd been outraged for that man. Today, she would happily have been buried next to him.

Her gravestone could read: 'Harper McClain, died of a hangover. What an idiot.'

She and Bonnie had stayed at the bar after closing, drinking with Carlo and Junior, and playing half-hearted, quickly abandoned games of pool. It must have been four in the morning by the time she got home.

She'd awoken at noon, cotton-mouthed and hammer-headed, to find her cat, Zuzu, lying on her chest like an eight-pound tumor.

'Get off me, you evil fluffball,' she'd murmured, shoving the tabby to one side.

The cat waited until she drifted off, then got back on her again, purring maliciously.

At that point, Harper had given up and climbed out of bed. Four ibuprofen and a gallon of water later, she'd felt able to go to work.

When she pushed open the heavy, bulletproof door and walked out of the heat into the police station's icy air conditioning, she didn't remove her sunglasses.

The front-desk clerk looked up as she approached.

'Harper!' she trilled. 'You look *mysterious* today.'

Barely over five feet tall, with glossy black curls and a curvy figure that tested the buttons of her navy blue desk uniform, Darlene Wilson's skin was so flawless it was impossible to determine her age, but Harper guessed she was in her mid-thirties.

'Please, Darlene,' Harper said pleadingly. 'If you love me at all. Whisper.'

Darlene's booming laugh threatened to split her skull.

'All right, honey. I hear you,' she said, lowering her voice a fraction. 'Were you at a party last night or something?'

'Let's just say drinks with an old friend got out of hand.'

As she spoke, Harper flipped rapidly through the thick stack of overnight police reports.

Burglary, burglary, burglary, public nuisance, DUI, burglary, stabbing ...

She paused, scanning the description of the last one.

At 0400 hours, a 34-year-old male did enter the address and proceed to utilize a sharp bladed instrument against a 32-year-old female identified as his former spouse...

'Male friend or female friend?' Darlene prodded.

Harper turned a page. 'Not the kind of friend you're thinking about.'

Darlene made a tutting sound. 'That's a shame.'

'I would like to know,' Harper said, without looking up, 'why everyone is so fascinated by my love life all of a sudden.'

Arching one expressive eyebrow, Darlene turned to her computer.

'No reason,' she said.

It took Harper about ten seconds to decide against covering the stabbing. Baxter hated domestic violence stories. Today, she didn't have the strength for an argument.

Returning that report to the stack, she flipped through the rest, making a couple of notes. She was nearly finished when Darlene held up her hand.

'Oh, honey, I almost forgot.'

The hint of warning in her voice made Harper look up.

'The lieutenant wants you to see him in his office.'

'Now?' Harper's brow creased. 'Did he say why?'

'Not exactly.' Darlene leaned closer. 'All I know is, everyone's talking about the shooting last night. They say you got involved.'

Her heart sinking, Harper slid the stack of paperwork back across the counter.

She should have known the lieutenant would hear about it.

'How pissed off is he? Scale of one to ten.'

'Oh, you know what he's like.' Darlene busied herself straightening papers. 'He likes having something to complain about.'

For a tantalizing second, Harper contemplated slipping out the door and back to the newspaper, but she didn't want the lieutenant tracking her down. He'd done it before. Once, when she'd ignored his summons, he'd sent motorcycle police to pull her over and escort her back, blue lights flashing.

'Damn.'

Reluctantly, she trudged to the security door leading to the back offices. With a sympathetic smile, Darlene pushed the button releasing the lock.

The shrill buzz it emitted was a sound-blade in Harper's hung-over head, repeatedly stabbing her cerebellum. Wincing, she pulled the door open.

On the other side, a long corridor stretched the length of the building. Windowless and shadowy, it was lined on either side by offices. She passed the 911 dispatch room with its glowing bank of computers. Then several sergeants' offices – each small and crowded, all of them empty at the moment.

She was halfway down the corridor when two detectives in

lightweight summer suits approached her, talking quietly. Spotting her, one nudged the other.

Detective Ledbetter's smile took up his whole, round face. Next to him, Detective Julie Daltrey was grinning mischievously. She was ten years younger and a head shorter than Ledbetter, with dark brown skin and endearing dimples.

When Harper reached them, the two stopped, blocking her way.

'Oh hello, *Officer* McClain,' Detective Daltrey said, as Ledbetter snickered. 'I hear you're joining the force.'

'Oh, fuck me running.' She glared at them. 'Is this how it's going to be?'

'Do me a favor,' Daltrey goaded her. 'Say, "Stop or I'll shoot." I want to judge your technique.'

'No, that's not what she said,' Ledbetter reminded her. 'It was "You're surrounded".'

They guffawed. Daltrey bent over double, clutching her ribs.

Harper had heard enough.

'Will you please get out of my way?' Lowering her shoulder she shoved her way past them with such force they had to jump aside to avoid being knocked down. 'Don't you have murderers to catch?'

'Yeah, but you can do that for us,' Daltrey said. 'We're taking the rest of the day off.'

Their laughter followed her all the way down the hall.

Harper knew this was only the beginning. Nobody on the planet enjoys ridicule more than a cop. They never tired of it. Last night she'd basically pinned a bullseye on her back.

She was grateful when she reached the door at the end of the hall where the name 'Lieutenant Robert Smith' was written on the sign outside.

Taking off her sunglasses, Harper stuffed them in her bag.

Then, letting out a deep breath, she tapped her knuckles against the door.

'It's Harper.'

'Get in here.' The voice was a low, baritone growl.

Steeling herself, she opened the door, already launching into her defense.

'Look, Lieutenant, last night wasn't my fault.'

'I'll be the judge of that.'

Lieutenant Robert Smith was about fifty years old, with thick, graying hair and a square jaw made to take a punch. He was six foot two and, even sitting at a desk, he dominated a room. His charcoal suit looked expensive, as did his dark blue silk tie.

He was one of those men who, even when no cigar was present, looked as if they ought to be holding one.

As she approached the desk, he listed the charges against her in an icy voice.

'So you called out three armed men, while wearing no Kevlar and not carrying a weapon. You then impersonated a police officer when those three criminals threatened you. Am I summing this up correctly? And if I am, how is any of that not your fault?'

'I was improvising.' Dropping into one of the faux leather chairs in front of his desk, Harper pressed her fingertips against her pounding forehead. 'I thought they were going to kill that stupid cop.'

'That stupid cop is an experienced officer of the law.' Smith's voice rose. Harper winced. 'He is trained to carry and use a stand-ard, police-issue semi-automatic firearm, and to defend himself in dangerous situations. He was wearing a government-approved bulletproof vest. You were carrying a *notebook*.'

'True,' she conceded. 'But they were about to blow your highly trained officer's stupid head off.' His face hardened, but she plowed ahead stubbornly. 'Lieutenant, he was looking in the wrong direction. It is true that I could have yelled, "Hey, idiotic cop. They're over here." And they would have shot at me anyway. So I tried to buy time until your inexplicably delayed backup arrived on the scene to keep the residents of Thirty-Ninth Street safe from three wanted killers.' She held up her notepad. 'By the way, do you have any comment on the reason for that delay?'

The lieutenant opened his mouth and then shut it again.

'Dammit, Harper. How do you always manage to turn everything around so I'm the bad guy?'

He still sounded a bit heated, but the edge had left his voice.

Harper flashed him an apologetic half-smile.

'I learned from the best, Lieutenant.'

'Flattery won't help you today, young lady.' He shook his finger at her. 'In all seriousness, you could have got yourself killed. Walker told me everything.'

'That narc,' Harper muttered.

'He is *paid* to narc,' he reminded her tartly.

Before she could argue, he leaned forward, resting his elbows on the desk.

'Why'd you do it, Harper? I try to look out for you. But I can't protect you if you walk into a bullet. You understand that, right?'

There was no more anger in his voice. Harper's defensiveness slipped away.

'I'm sorry, Lieutenant,' she said. 'It all happened so fast. Believe me, I know it was dangerous. I promise I'll be more careful.'

Smith's expression softened.

'I don't want you to get hurt.'

'I know,' Harper said, adding remorsefully. 'And I didn't mean what I said about Luke. He was great out there. He saved my life.'

'Luke's one of my best,' Smith said. 'And he didn't come here to "narc", as you say. He came here because he was concerned.'

Harper said nothing, but the idea of Luke worrying about her was curiously pleasing.

'Well.' Smith's brow creased. 'Were you injured? You look pale.'

'I went out drinking with Bonnie last night.' She rubbed her temples remorsefully. 'Overdid it. I feel like crap.'

'Ah.' His expression changed to one of almost paternal indulgence. 'Were you at that hippy bar where she works?'

'It's not a hippy bar,' Harper said, although it kind of was.

'I hope you didn't drive home.'

She rolled her eyes. 'Of course not.'

It was always like this. He talked to her like she was a teenager and before long she started acting like one.

He picked up his pen from the leather desk blotter.

'Before I forget, Pat's after me to get you to come to dinner.' He glanced at her. 'You free on Sunday? It'd make her happy.'

Harper brightened. His wife was an amazing cook. 'If there's any chance she might make her chicken and dumplings, I think I can be free on Sunday.'

'She'll be happy to hear that,' he said gruffly. 'I always tell her you're fine, but she likes to see you for herself.'

He grew serious again.

'Now, look, Harper, can I tell the deputy chief that the crime reporter from our esteemed local newspaper has agreed to stop impersonating an officer at crime scenes for the foreseeable future? Will you at least give me that?'

'I suppose I can agree to stop breaking that particular law,' she agreed. 'I really am sorry. I had to think fast, and I wanted to keep Officer Dumbass alive.'

The lieutenant's eyes held a look that was equal parts affection and exasperation.

'Well, Officer Dumbass owes you one, and I've made sure he knows it.' He flipped open a file on his desk and put on a pair of wire-framed glasses. 'Now then. Get your pen out. The official statement is as follows: Backup was delayed because they required a helicopter in an effort to locate and isolate the suspects. Officers approached on foot from the first crime scene in an attempt to ascertain the location of the suspects, and in an effort to avoid loss of innocent life. Undercover officers arrived first on scene, but awaited arrival of all parties. Said undercover officers have been investigating the three suspects for several weeks, as part of a project to curtail drug dealing in the area.'

After jotting this down, Harper glanced at him. 'You got enough evidence to throw the book at those guys?'

'Off the record?'

She nodded.

'Oh, yeah. We've got them.' He closed the file. 'That will be all, *Officer* McClain.'

'Oh hell.' Harper stood up. 'I'm never going to live this down, am I?'

His smile told her everything.

'I believe they're having a badge made for you upstairs.'

It was nearly five by the time Harper left the police station, half-running to her car. She'd have to hurry to make it to the newspaper's offices in time to file for the early edition.

But five o'clock is a bad time to be in a rush and, as she pulled out onto Habersham Street, she immediately found herself trapped in bumper-to-bumper traffic.

Swearing under her breath, she hit the brakes and fell into line.

As traffic inched along, she replayed the meeting with the lieutenant in her head.

She wasn't surprised Luke went straight to Smith. He knew how close she and the lieutenant were, and he'd wanted Smith to put the fear of God in her.

Harper's own father wasn't really in her life anymore. They spoke a few times a year, and that was more than enough for her.

Now that he lived up north and had a young family, it was easier than ever to forget he even existed.

Besides, Smith had filled that role for her for many years. Together with his wife, he'd helped her through her teens, fed her when the money ran short and remained close to her even now. She was grateful for them both.

No matter how old she got, Smith still saw her as a child in need of protection. In part because the day they'd met was seared on both their memories forever.

He was the cop who took the phone from her hand the day her mother was murdered.

Chapter Seven

When Harper arrived at the newsroom twenty minutes later, the day shift was already wrapping up their final articles. Editors were making the usual demands, issuing low-key threats. In the bustle, no one paid any attention as she made her way to the battered black office chair and switched on her police scanner.

The familiar crackle and drone of official voices filled the air.

She was turning on her computer when the writer at the desk in front of hers rolled his chair back and swung around to face her.

'Hey.'

Harper glanced at him. 'What's up, DJ?'

David J. Gonzales earned his nickname after announcing that his newspaper byline must include his middle initial.

'It's an important part of my name,' he'd explained earnestly, to anyone who would listen.

At twenty-three years old, and on his first-ever newspaper job, he had no idea why this was so hilarious to the paper's hardened old-timers.

At first they'd referred to him as David J in all circumstances. 'Is David J coming?' 'Have you seen David J?'

Over time, that shrank to his initials, and he'd been DJ to everyone at the paper ever since.

'Baxter's looking for you,' he said. 'Where you been?'

An unruly mop of thick, dark hair overshadowed his glasses and round, jovial face.

'Cop shop.'

'Huh. She said she tried to call you.'

'Oh crap. Did she?' Harper dug through her bag until she found her phone. The message on the screen blinked an accusation.

Ten missed calls.

'Balls. I forgot to turn the ringer on.'

'Again?' DJ shot her a look. 'She's going to kill you.'

'Good. At least that'll give me something to write about,' she said snappishly.

Half-standing, she looked to the front of the room, but the city editor's desk was empty.

She sat down again. 'What does she want?'

DJ shrugged. He'd missed a spot shaving and the dark whiskers stood out against his tawny skin like a fingerprint.

'Dunno. She's on the warpath about something.'

'Yeah, but that's every day.'

'True.' Seeming to notice her suddenly, he took in the dark circles under her eyes and her unhealthy pallor. 'You look terrible. What'd you get up to last night?'

Harper typed her login – a machine-gun rattle of keys.

'Demon alcohol is destroying my life,' she informed him solemnly. 'I need to find Jesus.'

DJ grinned. 'My mom knows where he is if you're really looking for him. She also has an excellent lock on the Virgin Mary's location.'

With that, he shoved his chair forward and around in a surprisingly accurate move that propelled him precisely as far as his own desk.

DJ was only four years younger than Harper, but they were four really long years. When he'd first started at the paper, he was like the kid brother she never wanted, and she'd blamed Baxter bitterly from day one for putting his desk next to hers. He was so needy – constantly asking questions. It drove her crazy.

Gradually, though, he'd got better at his job and, although she couldn't put her finger on when it happened, at some point she'd decided she liked him after all.

Pulling out her notes, she began typing up a quick report of the day's smaller crimes. These would go on page six, in a box unimaginatively called 'The Crime Report'.

'McClain.' Baxter's voice cut across the hum and buzz of the room.

'Present.' Harper lifted her hand.

Baxter marched over to her desk – her hair bone-straight, her angular features set in tight lines. She moved so fast her jacket swung around her thin frame when she stopped at Harper's desk.

'I had an agitated call from the deputy police chief this afternoon,' she announced. 'Seems you got too close to the action at that homicide last night. Is this true?'

As she spoke, the ambient noise in the room dipped subtly.

Harper leaned back in her chair, calculating her chances. Even after years at the paper, she found it impossible to tell when Baxter was really pissed off. The woman had to be a nightmare at the poker table.

'I guess I did,' she conceded. 'That bullet missed me by inches.'

The room was very quiet now. DJ swiveled slowly around to watch.

Baxter's hand dropped onto Harper's shoulder in a movement that could either have been a pat or a punch.

'Good work,' she barked. 'That's what I like to see. Initiative.'

The noise in the room returned to normal.

'Get me another front page like that and I'll give you a raise.' Baxter spoke loud enough to ensure the whole room could hear.

Behind her back, DJ gave Harper a thumbs up.

'A raise? Isn't that one sign of the apocalypse?' Harper heard someone ask in a pseudo-whisper.

When the editor had returned to her desk, DJ slid closer.

'That reminds me. I meant to tell you your story was awesome today,' he said. 'That picture, too.' He shook his head. 'You've got the best beat. I never get to write that hero shit.'

DJ was on the education beat. The most exciting thing he got to write about was a new dormitory at the college.

'The hours suck,' she pointed out kindly.

'True.' He spun around again and returned to his desk.

She didn't know how he could do that so many times a day without making himself puke.

Harper's copy of the day's paper still lay on her desk. Idly, she picked it up. Miles' photo took up most of the space above the fold, with her story running underneath it.

Because of the darkness, and the way Miles had widened the aperture so he could shoot at night without a flash, the photo looked almost black and white. The barrel of the gun was pointed right at the camera. Above the shooter's bandanna, his young, jaded eyes stared at the reader with unconstrained loathing.

It was intimate. Intimidating. It grabbed you by the throat and demanded to be noticed.

'Hell of a shot,' she muttered.

Then she tossed the newspaper aside and got back to work.

Chapter Eight

That night was blessedly uneventful – Harper spent most of it at her desk, listening to the low rumble of the scanner and trying to stay awake.

At midnight, she went straight home and collapsed in bed. She was asleep in seconds.

The next day, she woke after noon, ravenous, the last remnants of the hangover finally gone.

Following a quick shower, and a scan of her emails, she headed out for breakfast. She was sitting alone in a red vinyl booth in Eric's Diner eating one of the 'fresh burgers' advertised in vivid neon out front when Miles called.

Stuffing a French fry in her mouth, she hit the answer button.

'What's up?' she asked.

'I'm at a crime scene on Constance Street. I think you better get down here.' His voice was low but intense.

'What've you got?'

Even as she spoke, she was wrestling her scanner out of her

bag; switching it on. A confusing tangle of police voices hissed into the air.

A man at a nearby table glanced over curiously and she turned it down.

'Looks like homicide,' Miles said. 'A bad one. Everyone's rolling out.' He paused. 'It's a good street, Harper. Expensive houses. Fancy cars.'

She didn't wait to hear the rest. Pulling a wad of cash from her wallet, she dropped some bills on the table and hurried to the door. It jangled cheerfully as she opened it.

'How many vics?' she asked, stepping out of the ice-cold air conditioning into the bright sunlight.

'Unclear,' Miles said. 'Can't get a word with the detectives. They're all inside. And I do mean *all* – there must be six of them in there.'

Harper gave a low whistle.

Two detectives were standard on a normal homicide. Six was unprecedented.

A wall of heat hit her as she opened the door of the Camaro. She dumped her bag unceremoniously on the passenger seat and stuck the scanner in the dashboard holder. Switching her phone to speaker, she started the engine and cranked up the air conditioning.

Hot air hit her face like a punch.

'What's it look like to you?' she asked, putting the car in reverse and glancing over her shoulder.

She'd turned the volume up high – Miles' voice soared above the rumble of the engine.

'It looks like page one.'

When Harper arrived, Constance Street was blocked by crime tape and a uniformed officer waved her away. The TV news crews were already there and their satellite trucks took up most of the available spaces.

Just outside the historic district, this neighborhood had once been affordable. But lately the big lawns and Arts and Crafts houses had been discovered and prices had skyrocketed. The schools were good around here and parents would claw each other's eyes out to get their kids in one of them.

Harper could already see what Miles had observed – this was not the usual place for a homicide.

She backed hurriedly into an empty space around the corner and ran toward the crime tape, straight into the TV reporters, who were blocking the way with the forest of tripods and boom microphones that followed them everywhere.

'Hey, Harper.' Josh Leonard, Channel 5's blow-dried but not entirely offensive news correspondent flashed a blinding smile as she approached the crime tape. 'We were wondering when you'd show up.'

'I can't believe you beat me,' Harper said absently, her eyes on the police activity beyond the crime tape. 'I guess there's a first time for everything.'

'The first time was that car racing accident, actually.' Josh straightened his cuffs. 'But who's counting?'

She raised one eyebrow. 'You are, apparently.'

'Five times.' He held up his right hand, fingers splayed. 'Five times – and I can list each one – I've got there first.'

'Give up, Josh. This is not a fight you're going to win.' Natalie Swanson, the anchor from Channel 12 stalked up to them. In a pristine blue suit and four-inch heels, she looked impossibly regal as she hooked a tiny microphone to her lapel. The sun made her glossy helmet of blonde hair glimmer.

Harper blew her a kiss. 'Looking hot as ever, Natalie.'

The other woman smiled serenely. 'Compliments will get you everywhere.'

'Now, see,' Josh told his cameraman, 'I'd never get away with saying that.'

'Try it. See what happens.' Natalie's voice dripped pleasant malice.

Harper looked down to where police were bustling in and out of a yellow house with a high peaked roof.

'What do we know?' she asked, glancing from Josh to Natalie.

'All I've been told is the victim is a woman in her early thirties.' Natalie lowered her voice. 'The cops are being weird about this one. My producer talked to the information officer and he wouldn't tell her a thing. Never got that before. Anyone got anything else?'

Josh shook his head. 'Everyone's keeping schtum.'

'Miles might have more.' Harper stood on her toes, trying to see through the growing crowd of gawkers, cops and TV cameras. 'I better find him.'

Grabbing her phone, she typed a quick message:

Where are you? I'm here.

When she'd walked as far as the tape allowed, she paused beside a handful of residents gathered in a worried huddle. Most of them were elderly.

That made sense. Everyone else would be at work at this hour.

While pretending to look at her notepad, Harper studied them carefully. Their clothing was perfectly serviceable, but nothing fancy. There was no indication that they could afford to pay half a million dollars for a three-bedroom. They must have bought before the bankers moved in.

This was good. Bankers would know better than to talk to her.

Sticking her notebook back in her pocket, she made her way to the center of the group. She moved slowly, a sympathetic look softening her expression.

'I hate to bother y'all,' she said, thickening her native Georgia accent and keeping her voice hushed.

As one, they turned to glance at her.

'I'm from the *Daily News*. Can anyone tell me what's going on?'

'Oh Lord,' a sixty-something woman in a floral dress said mournfully. 'The newspaper's here, too. Someone's dead for sure.'

A dark-skinned, gray-haired man with a glossy black cane took a step towards her. 'I wish you could tell us. All we know is the police are in Marie's house. They won't tell us anything. Is she dead?'

'It can't be Marie, can it?' The first woman shook her head. 'Or her little girl? Sweet Jesus, not that.'

Gradually, Harper moved closer to their tightly knit circle, making herself one of them. She kept her expression curious but also open and unthreatening.

'Tell me about Marie,' she said, all sympathy. 'Who is she?'

'Marie Whitney,' the first man said. 'She lives in that house.' He pointed his cane at the yellow house. 'Where the police are.'

'She lived there long?' she asked.

The neighbors conferred.

'Was it two years?' someone said.

'It was after the tree fell on the Landry's place,' the first man reminded everyone.

'About three years, I think,' a woman said, after a second.

Harper did a quick mental calculation. Three years ago, prices were already rising. Whoever bought that place had money.

She needed to tell Baxter to hold the front page.

'Is she married?' she asked easily.

'Divorced,' a small woman in a blue cardigan informed her, a hint of excitement underlying her tone. 'Ex-husband lives out of town somewhere.'

She seemed chatty. Harper inched closer to her.

'Do you know if she worked?'

The woman lowered her voice confidentially. 'She worked down at the university. I don't know what she did there, though. She wasn't a teacher, I don't think.'

'And there's a daughter?' Harper asked.

The woman nodded so hard her gray hair bounced.

'Camille is how old now? Maybe eleven or twelve years old?' The woman glanced at the others for affirmation. 'But she should be at school today. She's doing that special program this summer.'

'Not now,' floral dress reminded her. 'It's nearly three.'

The realization sent a shiver through the group like a breeze.

'Oh, it's horrible,' cardigan woman said, pulling her sweater more tightly across her plump shoulders.

'Did anyone hear anything at all?' Harper tried to refocus them. 'Or see anything?'

'I thought I heard a sound.' The voice came from the back of the group. Everyone shifted until Harper saw a woman, thin and pale, her hair cotton white. 'At first, I thought it was a scream but it was so brief. I decided it was a crow.' Her shoulders drooped and she looked around for forgiveness. 'I truly thought it was a crow.'

'No one can blame you,' cane man said gruffly. 'Nothing like this ever happens around here. We all would have thought the same.'

Harper asked a few more questions, then, pulling out her notebook, convinced a couple of people to give her their names. As she'd suspected, this put an end to the discussion.

She was jotting down notes from the conversation when Miles appeared at her side.

'I got a name from the neighbors,' Harper told him. 'Marie Whitney. You got anything?'

'All I know is she was code four when the police arrived.' Glancing around to make sure no one could hear him, he whispered, 'A patrol cop I know told me it's a bloodbath in there.'

'Do they have a suspect?' she asked. 'Neighbors say there's an ex-husband.'

He didn't get a chance to respond. At the other end of the crime tape, the news teams had swung into motion, lenses focused on something happening further down the street.

In tandem, Harper and Miles rushed forward, leaning across the tape to get a better look as the front door of the house opened and a group emerged.

Miles raised his camera and focused, firing off a round of shots.

Harper saw Blazer first – his smoothly carved face and cold eyes were impossible to miss. Nearby, Ledbetter and Daltrey stood at the edge of the group, talking somberly – no mocking smiles today.

A familiar tall figure stood behind them.

Harper's brow creased.

'What's Lieutenant Smith doing here?'

If he heard the question, Miles was too busy shooting to respond.

As Harper watched, the group stepped slowly out of the yellow house. When they reached the street, the cluster parted enough for her to see who was at the center.

It was a girl, about twelve years old. Her thick, dark hair had been plaited into a long glossy braid. Her small fingers held tightly to Smith's big hand. With her free hand, she wiped tears from her cheeks. She stumbled towards a parked car, the stunned look on her face clear even from a distance.

Harper couldn't hear the breeze in the trees anymore. Or the low murmur of the crowd behind her. All she was aware of in that instant was *her*.

This scene was torn from her own tormented childhood. She'd been that girl once, standing in front of her house with Smith holding her hand.

The pen dropped from her nerveless fingers. She took a slow-motion step forward, bowing the crime tape. An official voice barked a complaint at her but she barely noticed.

The girl, her attention caught by the angry words, looked up. For an electrifying instant, their eyes met.

Harper stared at her own twelve-year-old self – pale freckled face surrounded by tangled russet hair, hazel eyes filled with tears.

Then she blinked and the dark-haired girl returned.

Leaning over, Smith said something and the girl turned to climb into the car. Harper knew how it felt to do that – hands so numb it was hard to feel the rough fabric of the seat. Small body moving clumsily, knees suddenly forgetting how to bend.

The lieutenant closed the door behind her.

Seconds later, he and Daltrey got into the car with her, before it sped to the other end of the lane and disappeared around the corner.

Harper let out a long breath.

In the aftermath of this incident, the gathered gawkers were hushed enough for Harper to hear Natalie whisper to her camera operator, 'You get that?'

'What a tragedy,' Miles said, flipping his camera over to look at his shots. 'I hate to see kids at these things.'

Harper, still studying the yellow house, didn't reply.

Miles glanced up at her. Seeing the look on her face, his eyes sharpened.

'Something wrong?'

'It's nothing.' She kept her gaze fixed on that front door. Seeing that girl's eyes.

This was too familiar. The house. The girl. The time of day. The time of year. A woman alone. Murdered.

Something was coming together in her mind. Something unthinkable.

'Miles, I need to get inside that house.'

He stared at her, incredulous.

'Oh sure,' he said. 'The cops won't mind if you step into the middle of their homicide scene. As long as you make it quick.'

Harper opened her mouth and then closed it again.

This was going to be hard to explain.

As far as she knew, Miles wasn't aware of what had happened to her mother. Few people were. It wasn't something she ever discussed. Miles had only lived in Savannah seven years – he wasn't here back then to read about it in the paper, or see smiling pictures of her mother on the TV news.

Still, she didn't need him to understand everything, she needed him to help.

'This is going to sound weird,' she said slowly. 'But I need to reassure myself about something. Literally, I need two seconds in that house.'

Miles still looked perplexed.

'Harper, don't be ridiculous. Every cop in the city is in that house.'

It was true. Four patrol cops stood out front, guarding the door. Two more were on the crime tape, stopping anyone from getting in.

After Smith and the girl had gone, Blazer and several detectives had gone back inside, along with the coroner – whose van was parked in the middle of the street.

She thought for a minute, studying the neighborhood. There had to be some way to at least see what had happened in there.

She'd grown up on a street a lot like this one, with houses lined up, backyard to backyard. Her street had been more modest, but the layout was more or less the same.

'I only need to see in a window,' she said, thinking aloud. 'That would do it. I don't have to actually go inside.'

The look Miles gave her told her he still thought she'd lost her mind.

'What the hell is this about?'

She hesitated. She had to tell him something, but this wasn't the time for long explanations.

'Look,' she said finally. 'I have a hunch. I think I've seen a crime scene a lot like this one a few years ago. A mother dead. A girl coming home after school. I'm probably wrong. It's probably nothing. But that killer was never caught. If I'm right…'

She didn't finish the sentence. She didn't need to. She'd already seen the light dawn in his eyes.

'We could be dealing with the same killer,' he said slowly.

Their eyes locked. Neither of them had ever covered a serial killer before.

'You sure about this?' he asked.

She shook her head. 'Not at all. In fact, I'd be willing to bet if I take a look at the crime scene, it'll be completely different. And I'll come back here feeling like a fool.'

'Why is this so important, then?' Miles asked. 'Why not call Smith and ask what he thinks?'

It was a good question. Smith had been at both crime scenes. He would certainly know.

But this time that wasn't enough. She had to see for herself. To know for certain whether there was any connection at all between this crime scene and the one on that day, fifteen years ago, when her childhood ended.

Because no one ever caught that murderer.

That little girl never got justice.

'Please, Miles,' she pleaded. 'I just… I have to do this. I need two seconds looking through a window.'

He held her gaze, his expression a complex mix of doubt and worry.

Harper thought he'd refuse. His relationship with the police was important to him. Ever since he'd been laid off he'd had to tread a fine line with the newspaper, the police and his work. He did not want her to mess that up.

But then, shaking his head, he held up his hands in surrender.

'Tell me this before we throw our careers away. How do you propose to illegally cross that police line and get into that house without the cops and detectives and their merry band promptly arresting you?'

Harper pointed at the houses peeking out through the trees behind the crime house.

'Through the backyard.'

Chapter Nine

Here's a thing about crime scenes most people don't know: they're boring.

The vast majority of any reporter's time at a crime scene is spent waiting around. First you wait for the detectives, then you wait for the forensics team, then you wait for the coroner. Sometimes, hours will pass before you're even told what you're waiting for.

At a crime scene this high profile, Harper knew she had time to burn. The forensics unit had just begun putting on their white moon suits when she stepped away from the crime tape. Nothing would be announced until they'd had a chance to examine the house.

As she hurried down the street, nobody noticed her departure. Everyone was still focused on the yellow house.

Around the corner, away from the gawkers and journalists, the neighborhood seemed calm and peaceful. But Harper wasn't.

Despite her bravura performance with Miles, she was so nervous her stomach burned. She had to force her hands to unclench.

She'd always pushed the limits but she'd never done anything like this before.

For one thing it was wildly, profoundly illegal.

If she got caught, the police would undoubtedly arrest her. The newspaper would be unlikely to bail her out because breaking the law was not part of her job description. Not overtly, anyway. Oh, they were happy to take advantage of it when she broke the rules and got a good story, but if she were ever truly busted for it, they'd let her hang.

And yet, she didn't stop. She had to know.

In her mind, she kept seeing that girl in her school clothes, standing dazed and shocked in a protective phalanx of police.

She looked so small. So vulnerable.

Was that how *she'd* looked that day?

And Smith – what was he doing there? A single homicide, even in a neighborhood like this, ordinarily merited his oversight from a distance but not his physical presence. She couldn't remember the last time she'd seen him at a crime scene. Certainly not since he was promoted to lieutenant four years ago.

'I'm a paper-pusher now,' he'd told her at the time, pride in his voice. 'I'm off the street at last. Got a chair that cost as much as I make in a week and a great big office, and by God, I'm going to use them.'

He'd been true to his word. Until now.

What if he was here because he had seen this once before?

The next street along was a perfect mirror image of Constance Street. The same brightly painted, over-priced houses with lush gardens behind low fences.

The blue paint on Number 3691 was perfect and its front garden was lavish. Fat, pink roses spilled over the glossy black bars of the wrought-iron fence in a fragrant tumble.

75

It was directly behind the murder scene.

If she stood on her toes, Harper could see the yellow house from the sidewalk.

Given the well-maintained look of the house, odds were ten to one the lawyer or banker who lived here was at work and the place was empty.

Or a trophy wife could be inside, watching cable and doing her nails.

There was only one way to find out.

Setting her jaw, Harper lifted the cool metal latch on the heavy gate and walked with purpose to the door. When she knocked, the sound echoed in the quiet street like a gunshot.

For a moment, she stood still, summoning an excuse, waiting for footsteps.

None came.

Just to be sure, she knocked again.

Still, nothing.

Pulling her phone from her pocket she called Miles.

He answered immediately.

'I'm in,' she said, hurrying down the steps toward the side of the house. 'Do it now.'

There was a long silence.

'You sure you want to do this?' he asked.

'I'm already doing it.'

Without waiting for his reply she hung up, setting the phone to silent before she shoved it into her pocket.

Back on Constance Street, Miles should now be going up to the officer standing guard and demanding to talk to a senior detective. He'd complain about the slow pace and lack of information. He'd get Natalie and Josh involved – it was never very hard to get them riled up about deadlines.

Hopefully, this would keep everyone busy out front, ensuring nobody wandered around to the back while she was there.

That was the plan, anyway.

The really terrible plan.

There was no gate between the front and back garden of number 3691. A narrow walkway led past a ginger hedge on the side of the house to the perfectly manicured back garden.

A patio table surrounded by six wicker chairs sat near the back door. A curving stone path led through lush daisies and climbing bougainvillea to where two pear trees bookended the yard right in front of the back fence.

Ducking behind one of the trees, Harper peered into the backyard of the murder house.

The garden across the fence wasn't at all like the one in which she now stood. The lawn was neat, but unimaginative.

A purple bicycle leaned against the wall of the house near a rusted barbecue grill that looked like it hadn't been used in quite a while.

This was the house of a single mom too busy to worry about gardening.

From here, Harper could see the murder house had big windows lining the rear wall and a back door with three steps leading down to the patio.

The fence between the two houses was about four-feet tall and chain link. That was normal around here – the summer humidity and heavy winter rains destroyed wood so quickly most people didn't bother with it. Harper could make it over the fence easily.

The only problem was, now that she was here, all she could see was that she was about twenty long steps from getting arrested. There was no place to hide in that yard. And the hot sun reflected off the windows, making it impossible to see inside. There could have been fifty police looking out at her and she'd never know.

Biting her lip, she stood staring across the expanse of green grass.

She could turn around. Tell Miles she changed her mind. Go back to the crime tape and do her job.

But then she remembered that girl again – her achingly familiar look of despair.

She had to know what was in that house.

Taking a deep breath, she stepped on the raised roots of the nearest tree for a bit of height then, grasping the top of the fence, warm from the sun, she stuck the toe of one shoe into a chink in the fence and hoisted herself up, swinging a leg over the top and dropping down on the other side.

The jangle of the metal against the support poles seemed absolutely deafening. As soon as she landed, she crouched low and froze, eyes on the house, waiting to see if she'd been noticed.

There was no cover here. If she was going to be caught it would happen now.

Nothing moved. Nobody opened the back door. No one yelled a command.

Adrenaline gave her heart a kick. She had to run.

Keeping low, she sped across the grass.

It was no more than forty feet from the back of the garden to the house, but it seemed to take forever until she made it, pressing against the warm yellow siding between the door and the window.

There, she paused, breathing heavily.

It was strangely quiet. All the sounds of a normal afternoon were missing. No children laughed. No dogs barked. No cars rumbled by. She could hear her heart pounding, and her own rasping breaths.

It took a minute to steady her nerves enough to move again. Gritting her teeth, Harper inched along the wall to the window and stopped.

If this house was like the ones she knew, the kitchen would be here. All she needed to do was look into that window and she would know the truth. One way or another. If there was nothing there – if the murder scene were in the bedroom, or the living room – she was done here.

Steeling herself, she turned and took a sliding, sideways step to her left until she could see through the bottom sliver of window.

A uniformed policeman stood directly in front of her.

Harper jerked back, her heart pounding in her throat.

On the verge of panic, she stood stiffly, forehead pressing against the wall, nails digging into the yellow paint, breathing in the smell of dust and heat and her own fear.

It's OK, she promised herself. *It's OK*.

The cop's back had been to her. There was no way he saw her.

Still, every muscle in her body tensed as she strained to hear what was happening.

There were no sounds of movement or alarm from inside the yellow house. Only the faint murmur of official voices, words too soft for her to make out.

Harper bit her lip hard, trying to decide what to do. A cop was right in front of the window. She was now at one hundred percent risk of getting caught.

But in that brief flashing view, she'd seen the kitchen. And something on the floor.

She couldn't leave now. Not without knowing.

She took a strangled breath, hands clenching into fists against the sun-soaked wall. It took everything in her to slide back to the window and look again.

The policeman had shifted to the left. He was leaning back, his uniform dark against the glass. Harper could see past him on the right-hand side.

It took a moment for her eyes to adjust from the bright sunlight to the shadowy interior.

It was a more modern kitchen than the one she'd grown up with, but not dissimilar – square and spacious. Cupboards – modern and expensive. A designer range, as big and glossy as a Land Rover.

Automatically, she noted indications of a struggle – chairs had been knocked over and the kitchen table had been shoved at an odd angle.

A cluster of men and women in white forensic suits stood over something on the floor. Harper recognized the chief coroner's distinctive short, prematurely gray hair. She was studying something through a magnifying device and talking quietly to Detective Blazer, who crouched beside her, looking where she indicated, a notepad in one hand.

It was only when the coroner straightened to reach for another tool that Harper saw the body.

Her heart stopped beating.

It was her mother's body.

The woman was naked, lying face down on the tile floor in a dark, viscous pool of blood. Against her paper-white skin, the wounds on her back and arms seemed lurid. Harper counted three stab wounds but, with all that blood, she knew there would be more on the other side.

One pale hand was flung out defensively to the side, delicate fingers reaching for something they would never touch. Her nails were painted pale pink.

Harper couldn't tear her eyes away. She knew how cold that skin would feel if she touched it.

The woman's wavy hair had been soaked in blood, making it hard to determine the color. It looked like red with streaks of gold.

The same as her mother's hair.

Harper heard herself make a whimpering noise deep in her throat.

Instantly, the policeman on the other side of the window shifted. Shuffling his feet, he began to turn around.

Panicking, Harper yanked back, flattening herself against the wall next to the window.

Her ribs closed around her lungs.

She closed her eyes against the blinding sun, and images of that day so long ago flooded back. Sliding in the blood. Hands ice-cold and slippery.

Mom? Mommy?

It felt like her chest was going to explode. She had to breathe. She had to get out of here.

Blindly, she stumbled across the back garden, her feet clumsy where earlier they'd been so swift. She was certain everyone on the block could hear her hammering heart. Her choking breaths.

When she reached the back fence she didn't even slow down. Using her forward velocity to propel her, she leaped up, grabbing the bar at the top and vaulting over. The sharp points of metal were blades digging into the palms of her hands and she let go too early, landing badly in the pretty backyard on the other side. Her ankle twisted with a worrying crunch, sending her sprawling into the petunias.

For a moment, she lay there amid the colorful blooms, clutching her leg and breathing in sobbing gasps.

That body. That hand, reaching out.

This was no coincidence. That murder scene looked *exactly* like her mother's murder in every way.

How was that possible?

Chapter Ten

When Harper limped back to the crime tape a few minutes later, the news crews were leaning against their vans, drinking coffee from cardboard cups.

Spotting her, Natalie's eyebrows shot up. 'What the hell happened to you?'

Harper had brushed as much of the dirt from her clothes as she could, but her ankle had begun to swell. She was hot and sweaty, her clothes clung to her back.

'I tripped on a broken curb. Twisted my ankle.' She made a vague gesture that she hoped said would-you-believe-it-what-a-day, and limped over to where Miles stood some distance away, watching this exchange without expression.

'I assume that went as well as could be expected.' His tone was dry.

'It went fine,' she said shortly. 'How about at this end?'

He gave a one-shoulder shrug.

'The TV crews are now very exercised about the lack of information.' He gestured at her disheveled appearance. 'What the hell happened back there? You look like you walked through a snake's nest.'

'I fell,' she said, 'coming back over the fence. That's all.'

He stepped closer to her.

'You got in the crime scene?' His voice was barely above a whisper.

'I got a look,' she said. 'I didn't go in.'

He looked at her with reluctant curiosity.

'What'd you see in there?'

In her mind Harper saw the pale body. The spreading pool of deep red. Her mother's kitchen.

But she made herself think like a reporter.

'The victim's in the kitchen,' she said evenly. 'Looks like it's the mother, as we thought. Seems to be only one victim – the coroner and Blazer were both in the room with her. The forensics unit is examining the body now.'

Miles knew her well enough to know she wasn't telling him everything.

But when he spoke, all he said was, 'She shot?'

'Stabbed. Repeatedly.'

A flare of interest in his eyes.

'Stabbing's a personal crime,' he mused, rubbing his jaw. 'Crime of passion. They'll be looking at the husband.'

'I don't think there is one.'

'An ex-husband then. Or a boyfriend.' He met her eyes. 'You said this scene reminded you of another crime. Is it the same?'

Harper had promised him an explanation but now wasn't the time to get into everything.

'Looks a lot like it,' she said. 'Before I can be sure, though, I need to do some research.' She paused. 'The other crime... It's an old one, Miles.'

'How old?'

'Fifteen years.'

His eyes left hers, sweeping down to the house in the distance.

'Now why,' he wondered aloud, 'would someone kill and then not kill again for fifteen years?'

Harper didn't reply. But it was a good question.

Why *would* her mother's killer be back now? Where had he been for all these years?

Police had investigated her murder for months. Harper's family had protected her as much as they could from what was happening but she'd known.

The investigation had torn her family to shreds. Leaving her with nothing.

And in the end, after all that, the killer got away.

'Tell me about this old murder,' Miles said. 'Who was it? You would have been a child fifteen years ago.'

'Not now.' Harper's reply was sharper than she intended.

When he shot her an exasperated look, she gestured at the crowds around them.

'There's too much going on, Miles. I promise I'll explain. But let me do it later, OK?'

'Fine with me.' His tone was curt, but he seemed more perplexed than angry.

Suddenly, he straightened, hands reaching for his camera.

'Looks like we're about to find out something.' He gestured with his chin.

A cluster of police had left the house and was heading for the crime tape.

Detective Blazer strode ahead of the others, his sharply structured face somber. Two less senior detectives walked behind him, along with a few uniformed cops.

Miles was already shooting pictures as the group ducked under the crime tape. The TV crews hustled to shift camera tripods into place. Josh and Natalie held out fur-covered microphones, like gigantic caterpillars, to catch his words.

Pulling a notebook from her pocket, Harper limped past the neighbors crowding around to eavesdrop, until she stood next to Natalie.

When everyone was still, Blazer spoke in a cool flat tone.

'This afternoon at 3:30 p.m., the body of a deceased person was discovered at 3691 Constance Street. The body has been identified as that of one Marie Whitney, thirty-four years old, resident of said address. Cause of death is still being investigated by forensic units, but the weapon used appears to be a bladed instrument. The case is being treated as a homicide.'

The crowd of neighbors gave a collective gasp and drew closer together – shutting the reporters out. Harper heard someone say, 'Oh, sweet Jesus.'

Glancing up, Blazer frowned.

'The time of death is estimated between eleven hundred and fourteen hundred hours. We would like anyone in the area who saw or heard anything suspicious at that time to contact the Savannah Police.'

He put his notebook away. It was a remarkably short statement, under the circumstances.

'That's it?' Josh looked around the team of detectives.

Blazer's brow lowered. 'Print it the way I said it.'

'I don't *print* anything,' Josh reminded him tartly. 'I put it on television.'

Blazer glowered at him.

'May I remind you a woman was murdered today?' he said. 'Can't you behave with decorum for five minutes?'

'Detective Blazer, please forgive my colleague from Channel 5.' Natalie deployed her most winsome look. 'Could you, perhaps, tell us about the girl we saw earlier? Is she related to the victim?'

Nobody could resist Natalie when she was on her game, not even Blazer. His expression softened infinitesimally.

'All I can tell you is that she is the daughter of the victim,' he said. 'And she's safe and unharmed.'

'Could you tell us her name?' Natalie asked hopefully.

Blazer had clearly anticipated this. 'Her name is Camille Whitney.'

Josh leaned forward, jutting his microphone out. 'Did she discover the body?'

Blazer fixed him with an icy stare.

'I can't tell you any more than that at this time.' His gaze swung back to Natalie. 'I'm sure you'll appreciate this is a delicate situation and we want to keep everyone – particularly children – as safe as possible.'

'Detective.' Harper angled herself forward. 'Have you got any suspects?'

He glanced at her without interest. 'We're not yet ready to divulge that information.'

'Could you tell us more about the crime?' Harper tried again. 'Were there signs of a struggle? Do you suspect a relative?'

Blazer's jaw tightened. 'It's too early for this. Give us some time to do our jobs here, would you?'

'We're trying to do our jobs, too, Detective,' Josh reminded him.

By then, though, Blazer had had enough.

'Thank you for your cooperation,' he said pointedly.

Ducking under the crime tape, he stalked back towards the yellow house, the other detectives following a short distance behind.

'Thanks so much, Sergeant,' Natalie called after him.

As he rolled the microphone cable around his arm, Josh shot her a withering look.

'Kiss ass.'

Natalie smiled beatifically.

'Of course you can kiss my ass if you'd like, Josh. All of Channel 5 can.'

'Seriously, though.' Josh tilted his head at the retreating backs of the police officials. 'What was that about? He didn't give us anything.'

Miles appeared at Harper's side, his phone in one hand. The puzzled look he'd worn since she'd insisted on seeing the crime scene was still there.

'That's all we're going to get out here, today, I reckon. I'm heading back to the newsroom,' he said, distance in his voice. 'Baxter wants you in, too. Says you need the story before six for the website.'

She nodded. 'On my way.'

He paused, staring down at the yellow house. 'That was a short statement, wasn't it? He didn't say much.'

Grabbing her keys, Harper turned to limp to her car.

'He said plenty.'

Back at the newsroom, she wrote up a quick article for the early edition. Miles sat a few desks away from her, pointedly not looking at her as he edited his photos. Harper knew she'd have to give him some sort of explanation for what had transpired out on Constance Street, but there wasn't time now.

Still, the practical work of putting together the scant facts the police had been willing to share steadied her. When she finished writing, though, the article was far too short. She needed to know more.

Pushing other papers out of the way, Harper flipped through her notes from the crime scene. Hadn't the neighbors said Whitney worked at a university?

Savannah had two colleges – the Savannah College of Art and Design and Savannah State University. The art school was downtown, not far from where Harper lived. It was funky and modern, populated mostly by tattooed kids from wealthy northern families.

The university was out in the suburbs. It attracted working-class Georgia kids looking for a smaller school closer to home than UGA in Athens.

Harper wasn't immediately certain which one the neighbors meant.

With quick sure movements, she typed Whitney's name and the name of the local college into the computer. The search brought up a page on the Savannah State University website with an image of a slim, polished woman. Her shoulder-length hair was honey blonde, forming a striking contrast with her warm, brown eyes. She had a wide, Miss America smile.

Under her picture the caption read: 'Marie Whitney, Vice Chair for Development and Enrichment'.

Leaning closer, Harper stared at the image. It was hard to believe this was the same woman she'd seen earlier that day.

Death takes away everything that makes you distinctive. Everything that makes you who you are.

Dead, Whitney had been anonymous. Pale skin on the cold floor – a hand reaching out imploringly.

Alive, she'd looked *electric*. She was almost hypnotically beautiful – cinnamon eyes and flawless golden skin warm and glowing with life.

If Harper was looking for parallels between Whitney and her mother, she wasn't going to find any in their appearance.

Her mother had been beautiful, yes. But Harper could hardly remember a time when she wore makeup. Her long red hair had usually been twisted up and held haphazardly in place with a paintbrush or pencil. She'd favored faded jeans with torn knees and was usually barefoot when she worked.

There was nothing to connect her, physically at least, to this polished woman.

Still, there were obvious elements linking the two. They were both in their thirties. Both were mothers. Both were about the same age when they were killed. Both were stabbed multiple times in their homes in daylight crimes. Both were found naked, on the kitchen floor. Both were discovered by their twelve-year-old daughters after school.

It wasn't enough to go on and Harper knew it. But it wasn't nothing, either.

'Is that her?'

Baxter's sharp voice made Harper jump. The editor had walked up without her noticing. She peered over her shoulder at the image on the screen.

'Uh… Yeah. That's her,' Harper said, clearing her throat. 'I'm trying to figure out what Development and Enrichment means.'

'Money,' Baxter said. 'It's a long-winded way of saying "fund-raising".' She straightened. 'Find DJ and get him to call the university and ask permission for us to use that.' The editor tapped her fingertip against Marie Whitney's face. 'Tell him to get a high-res version for print. I'll let art know.'

She hustled off, her low heels clicking on the terrazzo floor.

When she was gone, Harper didn't immediately search for DJ. Instead, she searched for more information on Whitney.

She was mentioned in a few articles about the college, mostly as a minor player. There was only one piece of any length – an over-excited article in the university newspaper, *The Caller*. It had been written two years earlier and was headlined: **Whitney Brings in Big Bucks.**

Fundraiser extraordinaire, Marie Whitney, 32, is being credited with organizing a campaign that has so far brought a whopping $4.3 million to the school's coffers.

Whitney has arranged gala balls, celebrity concerts and art sales, together with an online campaign. Thanks in large part to her efforts, the school has exceeded its annual fundraising goal of $3.8 million by over half a million dollars.

Ever cheerful, Whitney is popular with other workers in the Development Office, for her bubbly personality as well as her can-do attitude.

'Everyone loves Marie,' her boss Ellen Janeworth said, when interviewed. 'She's a dream to work with. There's nothing she won't do for the university.'

Whitney told us she was delighted by her recent success.

'I loved my time at college,' she said, smiling. 'It was the high point of my life. I want to make sure future students – including my own daughter – have the chances I had.'

The article was illustrated with a candid picture of Marie, standing on the portico of the university's administration building. She wore a white pencil skirt and a blue, snug-fitting top. Her skin was unlined. Her lipstick was a conservative, delicate pink. She was smiling that same perfect smile.

Harper stared at that picture for a long time.

There was so much that didn't make sense. What connected Whitney to her mother? Who would have wanted to kill both of them?

And, if the same person killed them both, what had made him come back now?

Chapter Eleven

Two hours later, Harper walked out of the darkening city through the heavy glass door into the police station. The entrance hall was empty at this hour and her footsteps echoed in the hollow quiet. Her ankle still ached from her fall earlier, but she was no longer limping. The air conditioning felt like ice against her skin.

Dwayne Josephs looked up from the screen of the small TV that sat underneath the top of the broad modern reception desk. Seeing her, his face brightened.

'Harper! I heard y'all got y'allselves a live one,' he said, his tone meaningful. 'Got everyone here in an *uproar*. Like someone killed the *president*.'

Dwayne was dark-skinned and as skinny as daytime receptionist Darlene was curvy. He was six feet tall but his arms and legs still seemed too long for his body, a fact that imbued him with the endearing gawkiness of a teenager, although Harper reckoned he had to be at least thirty-five.

She'd known him for years and she knew how much he loved to gossip. At the moment, she needed information, and she was hoping he'd have something she could use. But she had to play this carefully. As much as Dwayne loved gossip, he also hated breaking the rules. So the trick was to get him to talk without realizing he was saying anything he shouldn't.

Harper tried to strike a note somewhere between interested and not too interested.

'Really? Why are they in an uproar?'

Leaning against the counter, Dwayne lowered his voice conspiratorially.

'Well. Blazer went through here a while ago cussin' a blue-streak,' he confided with breathless reproach. 'F-this and F-that.'

Aware that Dwayne had a close and fervent relationship with his church, Harper shook her head disapprovingly.

'Did he now? My goodness, that's not like him.' It *was* like Blazer actually, but she also knew Dwayne liked to think the best of everyone. 'What was he so upset about?'

'Said the TV reporters were vipers crawlin' all over his crime scene and talkin' the b-word.'

It took Harper a second to figure out that 'talking the b-word' probably meant 'talking bullshit'. She could readily imagine Blazer coming up with that one.

'Really?' She tried to look aghast.

'Said they were tryin' to trip him up.' Dwayne warmed to his topic. 'Make him say something wrong. Get him in trouble. Said there's a killer out there who's a professional and they ought to be worried about that instead of wastin' his time.'

Harper's heart jumped. She had to look away so he wouldn't see the excitement in her face.

'A professional?' She pretended to dig in her bag for something. 'In Savannah? Is he crazy?'

Dwayne didn't notice the tight edge to her voice.

'He ain't crazy,' he assured her. 'Everyone's sayin' it. No fin-gerprints. No footprints. No DNA.'

Harper pulled out her lip balm as if that was what she'd been looking for all along. Her eyes glanced off of his.

'So they don't have any suspects at all?'

It was a step too far. Dwayne paused, biting his lower lip.

'I don't know about that,' he said, suddenly cagey. 'You'd best ask Detective Blazer.'

His brow lowering, he took a step back from the counter.

'Yeah, I really should.' She kept her tone easy, meticulously applying the lip balm and then dropping it in her bag. 'Is he in?'

He shook his head. 'He's at the morgue.'

This was fine with Harper. There was no point in talking to Blazer. He'd give her nothing. But someone else might help.

'What about the lieutenant?' she asked.

Relief suffused Dwayne's features. He hated to tell her no.

'He's in his office,' he said. 'I'll buzz you through.'

She headed for the security door. 'Thanks a lot, Dwayne.'

It was after seven and the long, narrow hallway, busy during the day with uniformed police carrying files, dispatchers heading off to get coffee, and detectives strolling to interview rooms, was quiet.

As she walked, Harper worked through the information Dwayne had unknowingly revealed.

A professional killer? What did that mean? A hitman? Or just someone who'd killed before?

And if it was the latter, why couldn't it be the same person who killed her mother fifteen years ago?

Smith's door was near the end of the hallway. The lights glowed softly through the frosted-glass window as Harper approached.

He wasn't usually in this late. The Whitney case must be keeping him busy.

She knocked once.

'Enter,' he called gruffly.

When she stepped in, she saw surprise on his face. Closing the folder on his desk, he set a paperweight – a heavy bronze golf ball – on top of it.

'Harper.' He didn't sound thrilled. 'I figured you'd be busy writing up that homicide.'

'I am. That's why I'm here. I need to talk to you.'

He gave her a warning look.

'Now, listen, you know I can't help you with an active investigation…'

She held up her hands. 'I know. But still. There's something I need to ask you.'

Without waiting for an invitation, she closed the door and sat in one of the chairs facing his desk and leaned toward him.

'The girl I saw you with today – Camille Whitney – is she OK?'

Some of the sternness left his expression.

'She's fine, Harper. You know we'll look after her.'

She did know. She knew exactly what would happen to Camille now. How police would try to keep her distracted, plying her with soft drinks she didn't want and coloring books she was too old for, until social workers and family could spirit her away to some inadequate kind of safety.

'Is that all you wanted?' Smith asked, when she didn't speak again.

'I just…' she paused, looking down at the notebook in her hand. 'Seeing her today. With you. It was so similar to what happened. Back then.'

Smith shifted the golf-ball paperweight across the folder.

'I thought the same thing when I saw her,' he said gruffly. 'My first thought was it was too much like you.'

'Lieutenant, do you think…' Harper paused, gathering her courage. 'Did it look to you like the same person who killed my mother, killed Marie Whitney?'

An odd look crossed Smith's face then. A kind of visceral shock – as if she'd slapped him.

'What the hell kind of question is that?'

His deep baritone voice was the low, ominous rumble of thunder in the distance.

'Could you answer it?' Harper looked at him pleadingly.

Smith shook his head.

'Harper, no. Trust me – all those two crimes have in common is a girl coming home from school.'

His tone was firm – irrefutable. But she knew that wasn't true at all.

She wasn't sure how to play this. She couldn't explain what she knew without revealing she'd seen the crime scene. And then he was going to want to know how exactly she'd managed that.

But she didn't have much choice.

'Are you sure? Whitney was found in the kitchen, right?' She tried to sound confused but not challenging. 'Naked and lying on the floor. Stabbed repeatedly. Lieutenant, that's exactly like my mother.'

His eyes widened. She could sense him preparing an argument, so she launched into all the questions that had filled her mind in the last two hours.

'What kind of knife did he use? Was it the same kind used on my mother? Have you compared the cases? If it's the same guy, why—'

'Harper *stop*.' Smith's big, craggy face reddened. 'How the hell do you know where the body was found? None of those facts have been released to the press and I'll be damned if Blazer told you. That man would sooner kiss a rattlesnake than talk to a reporter.'

'It doesn't matter,' she argued. 'What matters is whether the same person killed Marie Whitney as—'

'Enough,' he snapped, cutting her off again. 'You don't get to ask the questions. I do. Now, you have somehow accessed information you should not have about a murder case under investigation. As head of the homicide division I am ultimately responsible for that crime scene. And I will know who gave you those details, or I will be on the phone to your editor to get her over here to explain for you.'

Harper swallowed hard.

Now and then she got small glimpses of what it must be like to be a murder suspect interviewed by him. His narrow blue eyes were so steely and penetrating it hurt to look at them. It was as if he could see through her to her soul.

'I saw the crime scene,' she confessed.

Smith rubbed his forehead tiredly.

'Oh, wonderful. And how, exactly, did you manage that?'

'Through the window,' she said. 'I happened to get a quick glance. That's it.'

'*Happened* to get a quick glance?' Smith cocked his head, eyeing her with open suspicion. 'Which window?'

'One of the back ones.' She tilted one shoulder. 'Does it matter?'

'Hell, yes, it matters. Because the only way to see through those windows...'

With a silent apology to Miles, Harper said, '... is with a long-range camera lens from the backyard of a helpful neighbor. Yes. And that is not illegal, Lieutenant. As you well know.'

His mouth snapped shut.

There was a pause as they both sat staring each other down across the vast desk.

Finally, he blinked.

'Harper, why did you do that? This isn't like you.' The anger had left his voice, replaced by weariness. 'You know you've got no business spying on an active homicide investigation.'

This time Harper didn't have to think up a good lie.

'I saw Camille,' she said. 'I saw her standing next to you, and it was like looking at myself. I had to know if the crimes were the same. And they were.'

The lieutenant sagged in his seat.

'It's not the same,' he insisted. 'That girl isn't you.'

'Lieutenant, please.' Harper leaned forward. 'I have to know why this crime scene looked so much like my mother's. I don't want to fight with you. I need to understand what's happening. This is for me, not the newspaper. For *me*.' She pressed a hand hard against her chest. 'Do you think the same person committed both murders? Is my mother's killer back?'

Deep lines scored the skin above Smith's eyes as he studied her with grave understanding.

'I'm so sorry, Harper,' he said gently. 'The same person did not commit both murders.'

Some tiny strand of hope or fear that had wrapped itself around Harper's heart from the moment she first saw Camille standing on the street hours earlier, let go. And she hated to see it leave.

She felt numb. She'd been so sure.

'You're certain?' Her voice was airless.

'I'm certain.' He leaned forward. 'Now, look. I'm not denying there are striking similarities with your mother's case. But there are differences, too, Harper. Significant differences.'

'What differences?'

'The type of weapon used, the angle of the wounds, the force used in the attack – it all indicates a different person committed this crime,' he said. 'This person is taller than your mother's murderer. He's heavier. The wounds were less efficient, more tentative – Whitney had more defensive wounds, so she had more of a chance to fight. This all points to a different killer.'

He spoke with confidence. Evidence was where he was comfortable. It's where all detectives are most at home. Building a case from a hundred microscopic individual strands, like an architect designing a building one pencil-stroke at a time.

Harper couldn't argue with evidence.

'There are enough differences in this scene to reassure me that those superficial similarities are no more than coincidences,' he continued. 'Listen, if you stick around in this business long enough, you get to see the same kind of murder happen again. There are only so many ways to kill.'

Harper tried to think of something to say, but all the fight left her. She kept seeing Marie Whitney – her hand flung out, fingers curled. And her own mother, still and cold.

'Oh,' she said softly.

'Harper,' the lieutenant looked concerned. 'Are you OK? You need something? Some water?'

'No...' she told him. 'I mean... I'm fine.'

It wasn't true. She wanted to ask him about what Blazer had said, about the killer being a professional, and what did that mean but, suddenly, she felt suffocated in this windowless room. She had to get out.

She stood abruptly, shoving the chair back so hard it skidded harshly on the floor. Smith looked startled.

'I'm sorry,' she said, backing to the door. 'I have to get to the newsroom. Deadlines.'

Smith nodded. 'Of course.'

But he stood up behind his desk, as if deciding whether or not to follow her as she fumbled with the door.

In the open doorway she stopped and looked back at him. He hadn't moved, but his eyes were worried.

'I'm fine,' she said. 'Really.' Remembering their agreed lunch plans, she added hurriedly, 'I'll see you Sunday, OK?'

Before he could reply, she yanked the door open and ran out into the hallway, rushing to the security doors and out into the warm summer night.

Chapter Twelve

Five hours later, just after midnight, Harper stood in front of a converted warehouse on a cobblestoned lane at the edge of the river squinting at the numbered buttons in the dark.

The light above the door had gone out two weeks ago and no one had fixed it yet. One of these days she was going to come down here with a screwdriver and replace that damn bulb herself.

Finding number twelve, she hit it hard and waited, staring at the camera above the door. Her right leg jittered with ill-concealed impatience.

Now that she was here, she wanted to get this over with.

'Jackson.' Through the tinny speaker, Miles' voice sounded crisp and cautious.

'It's me,' she told the camera. 'Obviously.'

With a deep, mechanical *clunk*, the heavy steel door unlocked and swung silently inward.

Inside, she crossed a spacious, empty lobby, past over-sized pots holding glossy palms and ficus trees that seemed small in the cavernous space. The owners had kept the original pitted and worn stone floor, polishing it up to make it look a bit more like a home and less like what it had been for more than a hundred years – a giant holding area for crates of cotton and tobacco, sweet potatoes and sugarcane.

Even now, despite all the developer's efforts cleaning and glossing and polishing, she thought she could detect the faintest scent of ancient field dust in the artificially cooled air.

The elevator opened as soon as she pressed the call button. They'd gone for a post-industrial look here, with walls made of sheets of metal that looked like someone had punched it repeatedly until it behaved.

As the lift rose, she leaned back against the wall, closing her eyes. Her stomach grumbled loud enough to be heard above the elevator's pulleys. She hadn't eaten anything since her interrupted lunch at Eric's. There'd been no time.

Once she'd returned from the police station, she'd spent hours putting together a complete news package about Marie Whitney for the final edition. DJ had stayed late to help.

The headline – **Murder Shocks Peaceful Neighborhood** – was mediocre, in Harper's opinion. But it was, at least, accurate.

Miles hadn't told anyone about Harper's behavior at the crime scene. Now, she was here to give him the explanation she'd promised.

On the fourth floor, the doors swept open with a soft shushing sound, revealing a dimly lit, wide hallway with exposed brick walls. The door to number twelve stood ajar.

She walked in, shutting the door behind her. A husky blues singer's voice streamed from speakers.

'Hello?'

The loft apartment had soaring ceilings and a floor made of wide planks of reclaimed oak. Huge windows lined one wall, framing the glittering lights of downtown Savannah and the undulating dark swirl of the river.

The living room, dining room and kitchen were all one space. His furniture was modern – leather and chrome. Most of the lights were turned down low, except in the kitchen, where Miles sat at the table in the bright, clean glow of a pendulum light.

Glancing up at her, he tilted his head toward the fridge. The wire-framed glasses he wore for close-up work glittered in the light. If he was still angry at her, it didn't show on his face.

'Grab yourself a beer.'

He'd spread the internal parts of a camera out on clean, white paper and under a bright light was working with an array of complex tools, meticulously putting it back together.

He did this regularly; said it helped him think.

A police scanner on the counter next to the fridge buzzed and crackled loud enough to be heard above the music.

Harper pulled a bottle from the fridge.

'I'm surprised to see you,' Miles said, as she popped the lid with an opener he'd left on the counter. 'Figured you'd be at Rosie's.'

After the paper went to bed, everyone had headed down to Rosie Malone's for a drink. It was a tradition after a big story. Harper knew Josh and Natalie would be there, too, but she couldn't face the post-mortem chitchat tonight.

'Didn't feel like it.' She pulled out the chair across from him and sat down, resting her beer well away from all the neatly arrayed metal parts. 'New camera?'

'Got it on eBay,' he said, with as much satisfaction as if he was announcing a lottery win. 'Cost about a dollar more than nothing. They said the shutter wasn't working properly and couldn't be fixed.' He gestured at the bits of black metal spread on the table. 'I'm fixing it.'

Using a tiny tool, he chose a mysterious-looking part and placed it back in the hollowed-out camera body with deliberate precision.

'So,' he said, when it was where he wanted it. 'What brings you here?'

He glanced up at her, his gaze as steady as his hands.

Harper swallowed a long drink of cold courage.

'I owe you an explanation,' she said after a beat. 'And I'm here to give it to you.'

'Shoot,' he said.

Harper cleared her throat, bracing herself.

'You wanted to know about the fifteen-year-old murder. The one the Whitney scene reminded me of.'

He nodded at his camera, adjusting something inside it.

'Yes, I did. Seemed like you didn't want to talk about it.'

'I don't. But I will.' Harper worried the label on her beer bottle. 'The crime scene today – it looked exactly the same as the scene where my mother was murdered.'

He dropped the screwdriver, which clattered to the table.

'Your mother was *murdered*?'

He stared at her with open shock.

'Yes.' Harper's voice was calm. 'She was stabbed to death in our kitchen when I was twelve.'

Setting down the camera, Miles reached for the remote control at the edge of the table and turned the stereo down. The blues faded.

Shifting in his seat, he studied her, his brow furrowed.

'You saw that crime scene?'

'I found her body,' she told him. 'Like Camille found her mother today. In the kitchen. Stabbed to death. Naked.'

Miles took off his glasses and set them on the table. He looked bewildered.

'Harper, you never told me a word of this before. We've been working together nearly six years.'

There was a question buried in the confusion in his voice. And there was no way for Harper to pretend she didn't notice it.

'I'm sorry I've never told you. But I don't talk about it,' she said. 'Ever.'

She turned the beer bottle around. The label, with its foreign name, appeared and disappeared.

'They never caught the guy?' he guessed.

Harper shook her head.

'Nope.'

'And you think the same guy might have killed Marie Whitney?'

'I did,' she admitted. 'Until I talked to Smith tonight. He told me flat out he thought I was wrong.'

'Damn.' Miles leaned back in his chair and took a swig of his beer.

'Yeah,' Harper said. 'But I've been thinking about it and I'm not sure he's right.'

Miles gave her a look.

'I saw both crime scenes, Miles,' she said, setting her bottle down with a thud. 'They looked identical. The location of the body in the house. The time of day. The type of weapon used.' She ticked the similarities off on her fingers. 'The specifics of my mother's murder scene were never published and yet the two crime scenes were precisely the same in every obvious way. How could that be a coincidence?'

It was a genuine question. Because she'd had time to think it over and, whatever Smith thought, this couldn't be explained away by knife angles.

'Now, wait a minute. Let's think this through,' Miles said.

'What did Smith say, exactly? Did he tell you how the crime scene was different?'

Harper told him what Smith had said about the size of the weapon and the angle. The way the Whitney killer must be taller and heavier.

He listened carefully, a frown gradually creasing his forehead.

'That's not a hell of a difference,' he conceded, when she finished.

'Yeah, and the more I think about it, the weaker it gets,' Harper said. 'He says this killer's heavier? It's been fifteen years since the last murder. People get heavier. And as for the angle of the stab wounds...' She shrugged. 'What if Marie Whitney was shorter than my mom? That would affect the angle, wouldn't it?'

'Seems to me it would,' he murmured.

'I think,' Harper continued, 'Smith believes it's just too unlikely. All these years have passed and the killer comes back now? Even I don't understand how that works. It doesn't make sense that it's the same killer. But then, it doesn't make sense that it isn't. Do you see what I mean?'

She glanced at Miles hopefully.

'It's a strange one,' he said after a long pause. 'But time doesn't always stop a killer.'

He reached for his own beer and, finding it empty, headed to the fridge for another.

'Smith tell you anything else?' he asked from across the kitchen. 'Anything at all?'

'Not Smith,' Harper said. 'Blazer. Apparently he's telling everyone the killer's a professional. What does that mean?'

Miles walked back with two bottles and handed her one.

'You got me,' he said, sitting down again. 'I sure don't see this being a hit. Who takes out a hit on a single mother who works in fundraising at a small college?'

'Exactly.' Harper leaned toward him eagerly. 'And yet, if Dwayne heard Blazer right, there were no fingerprints, no footprints, no DNA.'

Miles let out a low whistle.

'Well, that's something,' he said. 'In that case, it wasn't a crime of passion. Because if you're caught up in it and you're killing without thinking, you make mistakes.' He picked up his camera again, twisting it around to let the light inside. 'We're talking about an educated man. A trained man.'

'And if it is the same man, why come back now?' Harper asked. 'Where has he been all these years? Was he in prison for another crime? Or is he a roamer, who came here once and ended up back here again?'

'Good questions all,' Miles agreed.

By now, Harper's earlier exhaustion was gone. Her brain was firing on all cylinders. Miles was a cautious man with an encyclopedic knowledge of crime. If he didn't think her theories were crazy, then she really might be on to something.

'I've been thinking about this,' she told him, as he reached for the camera again. 'First, I need to research my mother's murder. See if there's anything I can find to tie it to the Whitney case. Then I need to find out more about today's murder. Put all the pieces together.'

Miles' hand, reaching for a tool, paused.

'Be careful,' he cautioned. 'This is sensitive territory. If the detectives find out you're running an independent investigation, they won't like it. Blazer's a hardass. He'd love to find something to use to hang you out to dry.'

'I'll be careful.'

Harper's tone was blithe. The last thing she cared about was Blazer complaining about her to Smith.

In fact, it was hard to care about anything except getting started. For the first time in her life there was a chance – just a chance – she might find the man who killed her mother. If Smith was wrong, and she believed he was, Marie Whitney could lead her to him.

'You do that,' Miles said. 'I'll poke around a bit, too. See what I can dig up. I've got an old girlfriend in the coroner's office. I'll give her a call. See if maybe I can get my hands on that forensics report.'

Miles had a lot of old girlfriends in useful places. They often came in very handy.

'Thank you,' she told him. 'That would help.'

'Well.' He set down the camera again and met her gaze. 'I've got to say I never imagined any of this, Harper. What you went through when you were a little girl – I can't believe you never told me.'

'I guess everyone has secrets.' Harper picked up her bottle. 'Some are worse than others.'

Chapter Thirteen

The next day, Harper arrived at the newsroom two hours early. Sunlight streamed through the tall windows overlooking Bay Street, giving the rows of desks an ethereal glow belied by the normal daytime cacophony of fifteen journalists typing a hundred words a minute and talking even faster.

DJ did a double-take when she reached her desk, a large coffee in one hand, her scanner in the other.

'What are you doing here so early? Did someone die?' he asked. 'I mean... again?'

'Everyone dies, DJ,' she said, switching on her computer.

He wasn't to be dissuaded, though.

'What's going on? Is it the Whitney case? Did something happen?'

'Nothing happened,' she said breezily. 'I'm doing some digging. For the follow-up. Thought I'd get an early start.'

It was almost true.

After leaving Miles, she couldn't sleep. She'd spent most of the restless night making notes, formulating a plan. She'd dozed off on the couch shortly before dawn, pen still in her hand, tumbling hard into brief, uneasy dreams of blood and pursuit.

When she woke up, it was late morning – sunlight was pouring through the curtains and Zuzu was curled up behind her knees, purring.

In an instant, she'd been wide awake. She didn't want to hang around the house all day, waiting for four o'clock to come. She wanted to get to work.

Now she glanced at DJ, as if a thought had occurred to her.

'Come to think of it, I could use your help again. If you're not too busy.'

Brightening visibly, he rolled his chair closer to her desk.

'Absolutely. Whatever you need. Say the word.'

'You did good work yesterday,' she told him.

It was true. He'd run all over town gathering information for the piece, and worked fast to get it all together early enough to beat the news channels.

'Come on. It was nothing,' he insisted, color rising to his cheeks.

Harper suppressed a smile. The guy had no poker face.

'It wasn't nothing,' she said. 'Baxter was very impressed, too.'

He lowered his voice so the writers at the desks around them couldn't hear.

'Honestly, Harper, today's paper was the first time any of my friends voluntarily read one of my articles. Crime is definitely where it's at. Being on the front page – I felt like a rock star.'

'Well,' she said. 'Let's do it again.'

She flipped over the copy of the newspaper on her desk, pointing at the photo of Marie Whitney. It was the one from the university website, all white teeth, golden skin and shining blonde hair.

'We need to dig a little deeper. Do you think any of your contacts at the college knew her well enough to be aware of what was going on in her life?' Harper tapped Whitney's chin. 'We need to find out who she was dating. Was there someone new? How had she been acting in the days before her murder? Was she anxious? Scared? All of that could be useful.'

Behind his glasses, DJ's eyes widened. 'You're investigating her?'

Harper had to be careful. She couldn't overplay this. The last thing she needed was for DJ to get over-excited and tell everyone that he and Harper were investigating a murder.

'Not really,' she said blandly. 'I just want to see if there's anything to be found. Something we might have missed yesterday. What if it's really obvious? I don't want Channel 5 to get it before we do.'

DJ's face darkened. 'That douche Josh Leonard is probably all over this. I hate that blow-dried frat boy.'

'Exactly,' Harper agreed, although she was pretty sure Josh would never think to ask questions like these. 'If you'd do the rounds over where she worked, that would really help. Find out if anyone knows anything. But don't raise attention. We don't want anyone – even the cops – to know we're looking into this.'

'Subterfuge,' DJ enthused. 'I like it. I'll be Woodward. You be Bernstein.'

He was practically bouncing in his chair.

'Tell you what.' He glanced at his watch. 'I'll head over there now, see what I can find out.'

'That would be great,' Harper said. 'Be sure and…'

Her voice trailed off. Across the room, the newspaper's head editor had emerged from his glass-walled office and was strolling straight towards them.

DJ turned to see what she was looking at.

'Oh shit,' he whispered, sinking back into his chair. 'It's Dells.'

Paul Dells almost never talked to reporters unless they were being hired or fired. Harper had met him the day she was elevated from intern to full-time reporter, and not again until two years ago, when he'd addressed the entire newsroom to announce the first wave of layoffs.

For the subsequent round of layoffs – the one in which Miles lost his job – Dells hadn't bothered to make a speech.

And now, he was walking up to her desk. Smiling.

'Excuse me,' he said jovially. 'Aren't you Harper McClain? I heard a rumor you worked here, but I thought it was a lie.'

Dells had thick dark hair with artful gray streaks. His teeth were blindingly white. He looked perpetually polished and tanned. His suit probably cost more than Harper made in a month.

Still, she had nothing against him personally. Times were tough. No one wanted to pay for newspapers anymore. It wasn't his fault the world had gone crazy. Besides, he never interfered with her work. That was the best thing about him.

She smiled politely. 'Hi, Mr Dells. How's it going?'

The newsroom had gone quiet around them. Harper could feel everyone listening, even as most still stared fixedly at their computer screens.

'Call me Paul, please.' His smile widened, making his eyes crinkle appealingly. 'Everything's fine, unless your presence here at this hour signals some sort of apocalyptic event, in which case, please tell me now so I can head to the bunker.'

Disguising her bafflement at this sudden charm onslaught, Harper forced a dry chuckle.

'No need to hide. Getting a start on today's story.'

Dells held up a copy of the newspaper. Whitney's beautiful, fine-boned face gazed down at Harper.

'Well, I won't keep you. I just wanted to congratulate you on your work. This is a really solid piece. Excellence across the board. You beat every TV station in town.'

'Thanks.' Harper flushed, despite herself.

Behind Dells' shoulder, she saw DJ watching this exchange with open amazement. Quickly, she gestured at him.

'I couldn't have done it without DJ's help, of course.'

DJ grinned like a kid who'd found out he was getting a bike for Christmas.

Dells' smile swung to take in both of them.

'You make a great team. We'll be entering this in awards competitions later this year.' Dells tapped the corner of the paper on Harper's desk. 'Keep up the good work.'

With a parting professional smile, he headed back to his glass office.

Noise levels in the newsroom gradually returned to normal.

DJ stared wonderingly at the editor's retreating back.

'I've been here a year and a half and he has never noticed me before.' He turned to her. 'Harper, honest to God, I will do anything for you. Do you want me to clean your house? Polish your shoes?'

Harper's reply came without hesitation.

'Find out everything you can on Marie Whitney.'

After DJ headed off, more excited than ever to do unassigned work for her, Harper grabbed a notebook and pen and made her way across the newsroom.

When she walked by the editor's office, she could see Dells through the glass, sitting at a sleek designer desk, talking quietly on the phone. He didn't look up as she passed.

Right beyond his office, a set of double doors opened onto a long corridor. These were the guts of the newspaper – there was a staffroom back here, which exuded a permanent smell of scorched coffee, as well as offices for the lifestyle writers and the sports guys. From the latter, an unseen TV burbled a steady stream of incomprehensible chatter about baseball.

A door at the end of the hall opened onto a stairwell. Harper turned into it, her footsteps echoing soft scuffs as she climbed to the third floor. At the top, another corridor stretched down past the mysterious offices for sales and marketing, administration and corporate, whatever that was. She'd never had a reason to go into any of them.

Through open office doors, she could hear the buzz of conversation and the sound of a phone ringing insistently.

Midway down the corridor, she pushed open a plain white door. The only thing identifying the room was a small sign reading: 'Records'.

Everyone at the newspaper called this room 'the morgue' and always had. But Harper guessed putting that on a sign would have been distasteful.

The windowless chamber was plain, undecorated, with dingy vanilla walls and rows and rows of dark metal file cabinets arranged by year. It smelled faintly of old paper and ancient ink.

Starting at the row nearest her, she checked the cards on the front of the file cabinets. Those closest were dated seven years ago.

After the newspaper switched computer systems a few years back, it had never got around to entering older editions into the new servers. It had been planned, but then the layoffs happened and the clerks who would have done the work were let go.

For everything up until seven years ago, only paper records remained.

Harper walked slowly down the row – when she reached the end she was ten years in the past.

Turning the corner to the row on the right, she found she'd suddenly gone back twenty years.

Too far.

She backtracked, turning down the row to the left of where she started and working her way through time, until she reached the era she sought, fifteen years ago.

Each file cabinet within the year was arranged by subject, sometimes capriciously cataloged, and Harper moved one drawer at a time, flipping through files labeled for politicians, tornadoes, football games and university expansions, until she found what she was looking for.

McClain, Alicia.

Above the folder, Harper's hand stilled.

It was disorienting, seeing her mother reduced to another name among thousands in a soulless metal cabinet tucked away in a rarely visited room. Filed by strangers who never knew her. Never saw one of her paintings. Never watched her dance across the kitchen while cooking dinner.

Here, she wasn't Harper's mother. Here she was two words. Two words can't contain a human being. Their smile. Their smell. Two words are nothing more than letters arranged in an order we can recognize.

She felt breathless – sucker-punched.

This was why, in all the years she'd worked for the newspaper, she'd never come up here and looked for these files before.

On some level she'd always known it would feel like this.

Still. She had to do it now.

Shoulders set and resolute, she pulled the thick file out and carried it to a table, and sat down on a cold metal chair.

The air conditioning was set too high for this little room – Harper shivered as she lifted the cover.

Carefully she unfolded the article on top – the newspaper was soft beneath her fingertips.

The picture on the page was of the small, white house she'd grown up in. Seen like this, it was both familiar and incredibly distant – like a house she'd seen on a TV show she used to like.

The headline screamed up at her: **Murder in the Afternoon**.

'Catchy,' Harper murmured, but her voice cracked – she kept staring at the house.

She'd walked up that concrete path to the front steps every day for twelve years. In her memory, she could see herself opening that front gate, carelessly. Pushing up the horseshoe-shaped latch, striding through into her old life.

With effort, she tore her eyes away and began to read.

The article was straightforward – the writing was clear and accurate. Something about it struck Harper and, instinctively, she glanced at the byline: Tom Lane.

'Of *course*,' she whispered.

Lane was the police reporter when Harper first started at the paper as an intern. He'd been in his late fifties then, an old school journalist – working his sources and writing fast. No frills – just the facts. He'd taught her most of what she knew about the crime beat.

Lane never told her he covered her mother's murder. But of course he had. He'd been at the paper twenty years on her first day. He must have known who she was the moment she was introduced to him. Her name was unusual enough, and it had been a massive story.

Yet he'd never said a word.

Always acerbic, he'd made it clear he was less than thrilled to have her following him around. He had little time for women and no time at all for *young* women. But she'd been ruthlessly persistent – peppering him with questions until he finally gave in and told her how things worked.

It was Lane who taught her what to look for in a police report, how to work a crime scene and how to keep the cops sweet so they didn't cut you out, even after you had to write a story that made them look bad.

He cultivated them – constantly building relationships.

The detectives often took their dinner breaks at the Slow and Easy Café on Johnny Mercer Boulevard, so Tom took his dinner breaks there, too. He made himself available, but he also gave them their space, sitting at a table near enough that they could see him, but not so close they felt crowded.

'Sometimes they want to chat, sometimes they don't,' he told Harper one night. 'If they do, I get information. If they don't, the place does a hell of a Reuben sandwich, so…' He shrugged. 'I still get something out of the deal.'

He had, even after two decades in Savannah, a touch of New York in his accent. He always insisted he'd ended up in Savannah by accident – 'I took a wrong turn off I-95 on my way to Florida.'

Harper had soon learned that she couldn't operate the same way Tom did – put a young female reporter in a room of male detectives and you get an altogether different reaction than you do from the presence of a male reporter. She went to the Slow and Easy Café precisely once. A group of detectives sat at their table, craning their necks to look at her, and laughing.

She learned from that.

The lead to the article open in front of her was typical of his straightforward writing style:

A peaceful Savannah neighborhood was shaken today by

news that a thirty-five-year-old mother had been stabbed to death in her home, in broad daylight.

Alicia McClain was found dead inside the house by her twelve-year-old daughter upon her return from school, detectives said. According to police, Mrs McClain had been stabbed repeatedly, and bled to death before the ambulance arrived.

Police say there was no sign of burglary or forced entry. A search is now underway for the perpetrators of this crime…

Harper scanned the rest of the article quickly, finding nothing new. She stopped on one quote:

'A child lost her mother today, in a senseless attack,' Sergeant Robert Smith said. 'We are going to find who-ever did this and bring them to justice.'

She could picture him as he'd been back then – quietly furious about what had happened to her. Vengeful as a superhero. It had taken the police a while to track her dad down that day, and Smith had kept an eye on her the whole time. Bringing her food she wouldn't eat, giving her soft drinks in Styrofoam cups she'd shredded into small, white pieces. He even sent a uniformed officer out to the store to bring back coloring books that were far too young for a twelve-year-old.

When her dad showed up, frantic and red-eyed, to take her home, Harper took those coloring books with her. She'd trusted

Smith to handle everything better than her father, who her instincts had told her even then wasn't all he should be.

Bracing herself, she turned the page.

The next article in the folder was from the following day: 'Murdered Artist Had Real Talent'. Her mother's delicate oval face smiled up at Harper from the page.

Even though she'd expected something like this, Harper's breath caught.

In the picture, her mother sat on the front step of their house, with the sun in her eyes. Her vivid red hair hung loose over her shoulders. She wore an oversized shirt and blue jeans. She looked so young.

Harper couldn't remember ever seeing that picture before. For a moment she wondered how they'd gotten the image, but she already knew the answer.

Dad must have given it to them.

She knew how it would have worked – she'd done it herself a hundred times. Tom would have called, apologizing profusely for bothering her father in this difficult time. In his kindest voice, he would have explained how they wanted to show Mrs McClain in the best possible light, and did he, by any chance, have a photo he would like them to use?

It was hard to imagine her father actually dealing with this. He'd been so lost in the days after the murder. Trying to comfort her, while processing his own shock and grief.

In truth, neither of them had ever recovered from those first traumatic hours.

There was nothing in the article she didn't already know. Harper turned the page.

The next article had been published a few days later. The

headline was an above-the-fold gotcha: **Police Question Husband in Murder of Artist**.

Someone had snapped a picture of her father, ducking into the police station, surrounded by police. He wore a dark suit; his head was down. You could only see the side of his face, unshaven jaw grimly set.

He looked exhausted. And guilty.

Aside from the excited innuendo of the headline, though, the article didn't actually reveal much – police were holding their cards close to their vest back then. There was only one direct quote.

'We are keeping all lines of investigation open,' said Sgt. Robert Smith.

Harper knew much more than Tom Lane about what went on back then. She could have given him a real story.

Police had investigated her father hard. They'd hauled him in for questioning repeatedly. They'd searched their house, turning it upside down. Searched his car. His office. Even though he was, himself, a lawyer, her father had hired the best criminal attorney in the city to represent him.

By then, Harper was living with her grandmother in the rambling farmhouse where her mother grew up. It was in a small town about ten miles outside of Savannah. Everyone had agreed it was the best place for her, under the circumstances – away from the press.

Nobody told her about her father's arrest.

Her grandmother told her tautly, 'Your daddy's helping the police right now, honey. He'll be back soon.'

But everything about her body language – muscles tight, face carved in worried lines – told Harper otherwise. And she had to know the truth.

So she'd become an adept eavesdropper – crouching outside the living room to listen to adult conversations, ear pressed against the door whenever the phone rang.

This was how she learned her father was a suspect. And later, this was how she learned her grandmother thought he might be guilty.

'But where was he that afternoon?' she heard her ask her relatives over glasses of iced tea. 'And why won't he tell the police the truth?'

Their replying murmurs indicated none of them understood.

Harper could still remember the empty feeling in her stomach as she listened to the ice tinkling in a glass when someone she couldn't see took a sip.

'You don't believe he did it. That's not what you're saying, is it, Mom?' Her Aunt Celia had sounded aghast.

'He's a lawyer,' her uncle said then, his tone heavy with meaning. 'If anyone knows how to cover up a crime, it's a lawyer.'

Her aunt shushed him. 'You can't say that. Peter wouldn't hurt Alicia. Would he?'

No one replied.

Now, in the harshly lit room on the top floor of the newspaper building, Harper let out a long breath and turned another page.

Victim's Husband in Love Nest During Murder

This article, published a few days after her father was first questioned about a possible role in the crime, was coldly disapproving. Word by word, Lane explained that, while his wife was being viciously stabbed, her husband was with his lover in a small apartment about a mile away.

Harper had never seen the article before, but the whispers from the living room had told her this, and more.

On the day of the murder, her father wasn't at work – something he didn't tell the police when they first questioned him. His office thought he was meeting with a client. The client told police he'd never seen him.

This was why it took police so long to find him on the day of the murder – this was why she sat at the police station for two hours.

When police realized there had been no client meeting, they brought her father back in for questioning.

At first, he refused to tell them where he'd been – he was protecting his mistress. This silence was why they'd considered him a suspect – he had no alibi.

In the end, he'd come clean, revealing that he'd spent the afternoon with Jennifer Canon, an attractive paralegal fifteen years his junior, at her apartment.

Lane's assessment of this was short and stark: 'Police have verified his account and say that, given this new development, Mr McClain is no longer a lead suspect in the murder, although he may still face charges for filing a false statement.'

Her father never did face those charges. Police were too busy to pursue it. Besides, the DA had gone to law school with him. There would have been a handshake, and then it would have been quietly dropped.

The law forgave him. But Harper never could.

News of the affair ripped the family apart. Her grandmother wouldn't speak to him at the funeral, which was an icy event conducted in the glare of the media spotlight. TV crews filmed them from a distance as they clustered around the open grave in

Bonaventure Cemetery in stony silence, Harper clinging to her grandmother's hand.

From that point on, Harper's relationship with her father was irrevocably damaged. She never could get the idea out of her head that he could have been there that day. He could have saved her mother's life.

It was irrational, of course. If he hadn't been with Jennifer, he would have been at work – it was a weekday afternoon. Her mother still would have been alone.

But her heart didn't care for rationality.

When the media lost interest in the case, her father got a place of his own, and she lived with him briefly, but it didn't last. They argued constantly.

She moved back in with her grandmother a year after the murder.

Her father married Jennifer, the pretty paralegal, relocated to Connecticut, and started over in a town where no one had ever heard of Alicia McClain.

And so it goes.

She turned the page.

The articles were getting smaller. It was no longer a front-page story. Many were only references: a violent robbery on a nearby street was 'believed unconnected to the murder of Alicia McClain...' A stabbing elsewhere in town was, '... not at all like the McClain case'. And so forth.

There was one, though, a few months after the murder, in which the police attempted to explain why there were no leads in the high-profile case after all that time. Harper scanned it, seeing all the usual non-information sentences police liked to pull out when they were stuck: 'Still digging... Working hard... Difficult case...'

She could see right through it. The case had gone cold. There were no new leads. After that, it dropped out of the paper altogether.

Harper opened the last article – from page ten, a year after the murder. It was short – there was no picture. The headline, **McClain Case Remains Unsolved**, was as true today as it was then.

Mostly it was a rehash with a few defensive comments from investigators. Then, near the end, one last quote from Smith:

'The key issue at this point is the sheer lack of evidence. No one saw anything. No one heard anything. The killer left us nothing. It's like Alicia McClain was killed by a ghost.'

Harper tapped that line with her fingertip.

A ghost, she thought. *Or a professional.*

Chapter Fourteen

In murder cases, there are two ways things tend to go – either everything happens very quickly and the killer's locked up in twenty-four hours, or the process slows to a crawl.

After that first rush of information, by Saturday it appeared the Whitney case was grinding to a halt.

The police gave Harper nothing new – Blazer refused her calls and Smith was nowhere to be found. The signs were everywhere that the investigation was losing steam – the scanner offered no new investigations at the yellow house. Nobody was taken in for questioning and police announced no suspects.

The case was growing cold.

Harper's own investigation was moving equally slowly. DJ had found nothing on his first foray at the university – all the staff were at a memorial service for Whitney that afternoon, so there was nobody to speak to.

'I'll try again on Monday,' he promised Harper as he left.

Baxter had saved a chunk of Sunday's page one for the Whitney story. It's hard to fill a front-page slot with a story saying 'No new information', but Harper did what she could.

The editor was not impressed.

'This isn't new, Harper,' she'd called across the empty newsroom Saturday night. 'It's a reminder of everything we knew already. You might as well say, "Read Friday's paper for the latest news".'

'I'm trying,' Harper told her. 'But if the police don't have anything, what can I do?'

Baxter wasn't sympathetic.

'Do the impossible, Harper,' she told her. 'Or the next time Dells walks across the newsroom it won't be to kiss your ass.'

By the time Harper pulled up outside Smith's modern, colonial-style house on Sunday afternoon, she was determined to get him to tell her more about the case.

His house was on the southern edge of the city, in the kind of upscale new development where the front gate bears a made-up name like 'Westchester' in a lavish swirling font.

A long drive curved up to his ostentatious front door, flanked by topiary boxwoods the size and shape of bowling balls.

When he'd moved here from the more modest house where he and his family had lived for a decade, Harper had teased him mercilessly.

'Your valet didn't open the door,' she liked to say. 'You should fire him.'

'I am my own valet,' Smith would reply wearily. 'But if I had a valet, my first order to him would be to refuse to let you in when you're being silly.'

'You know you love me,' Harper would reply, breezing past him.

Today, though, it was Pat who opened the door.

'Harper!' she exclaimed, pulling her into a warm hug. She

smelled of some honeyed perfume. 'Right on time. Come in. Come in.'

Smith's wife was nearly as tall as him but twice as angular, with a broad, appealing smile and bright blue eyes beneath short, practical brown hair. As she walked briskly across the ceramic tile floor she kept up a constant line of cheerful chatter, her voice echoing in the oversized, vaulted entrance hall.

'It's been too long. Where have you been keeping yourself? How's Bonnie?'

'I've been really busy with work,' Harper told her. 'There've been a few big stories. Oh, and Bonnie is fine.'

'She still teaching at the art school?'

'Mm-hmm.'

The closer they drew to the kitchen, the more the rich cooking smells made Harper's mouth water. Pat's cooking was legendary.

'I've made chicken and dumplings with mashed potatoes and collard greens,' Pat told her. 'And the early peaches are out of this world, so there's peach cobbler for dessert. It'll be ready in a few minutes. The boys are all in the living room. Why don't you go say hello, and I'll bring you a glass of iced tea.'

The living room, like the rest of the house, was spacious, with four deep leather sofas arranged around a big central coffee table. Everything faced a wide-screen TV which, at the moment, showed a pitcher, spitting on a baseball.

The walls held mostly modest prints of landscape views in heavy masculine frames. Near the door, though, there was a picture of a younger Smith, shaking hands with the governor, smiling broadly as he accepted a medal for valor.

The image was hung to the right of the real thing who, clad in khakis and a neat, white polo shirt, lounged on a sofa, the newspaper in one hand, reading glasses perched on his nose. His two sons, Kyle and Scott, sat across from each other, staring at their phones.

'Hi, guys.' Pushing Scott's baseball hat down over his face, Harper dropped onto the sofa next to him. 'Stop with all the chitchat, will you? It's exhausting.'

'Doggone it, Harper,' Scott complained, straightening his hat. He was thirteen – all long legs, freckles and early pimples.

At fifteen, Kyle was more self-confident than his brother. He glanced up from his phone to wave, then returned his attention to the device.

'Who's he talking to?' Harper asked, nudging Scott with her shoulder.

'His *girlfriend*,' Scott told her, in a tone that conveyed ridicule and disbelief.

'Shut up,' Kyle said mildly.

'Every time I mention her,' Scott stage-whispered, 'he says that.'

'What's wrong with her? Is she ugly?' Harper stretched out her legs, propping her feet on the coffee table.

'She is *not* ugly,' Kyle said.

Snickering, Scott typed something into his phone and held it up for Harper to read. It said, 'YES SHE IS.'

They exchanged grins.

Smith folded his paper placidly. 'Boys, get along.'

'Here you go, Harper.' Pat appeared from the kitchen, holding a glass of iced tea with a sprig of mint floating cool and fresh on the top.

Taking the glass from her, Harper said, 'Can I help at all? None of these lazy guys are offering.'

'I'd help,' Scott insisted. 'But she says I get in the way.'

'Thank you, Harper.' Pat rested a hand lightly on her shoulder. 'It's all under control.'

The first time Harper ever had dinner with the Smiths was a few months after her mother's murder. Smith had called her grandmother and asked if the two of them would like to come over.

It was an awkward evening – the unsolved murder cast a looming shadow over every conversation. Back then, Pat was heavily pregnant with Kyle. She saved the night by asking Harper's grandmother for baby advice and the two were soon chatting away.

Over time, Harper would learn how like her that was – Pat was a born southern diplomat, calmly diverting tricky conversations, seamlessly stopping squabbles.

Later, while Pat and Harper's grandmother talked softly in the kitchen over cups of coffee, Harper had remained in the living room where Smith had been reading a file from work. He'd put the paperwork aside to quiz her with gentle persistence about school and her life.

'It's fine,' she told him, because she didn't know how to say that school didn't seem to matter to her anymore, and that each day was like swimming through glue to a razor-covered shore.

Smith had missed nothing, though.

'Anyone gives you any trouble, you come to me,' he told her gruffly. 'And maybe you should come over more often. Pat's worried about you, and I don't like her being worried.'

Over the course of the year, she started spending more time with the Smith family. After Kyle was born, she was invited frequently, ostensibly to help Smith watch the baby while Pat ran errands.

Later, she would see these reasons for her visits were contrived so Smith could keep watch over her, make sure she was surviving. Back then, though, it was just nice to feel like she was part of a family again.

By the time Scott came along, Harper was old enough to babysit.

After that, she spent frequent evenings looking out for the two boys when Smith and Pat went out to police functions.

Even now, although her work at the newspaper had created some necessary distance between her and Smith, she still came over once a month or so, to catch up.

'So.' Smith removed his reading glasses. 'I saw your article.'

Instantly alert, Harper glanced at him in surprise. Was he about to open the Whitney conversation himself?

'Uh-oh.' Looking up from his phone, Kyle grinned. 'Did she piss you off, Dad?'

'Of course not.' Smith propped his feet up on the ottoman. 'And don't say "piss" in front of a lady.'

'She's not a lady,' Scott reminded him with an eye-roll. 'She's *Harper*.'

'That fact aside,' Smith growled. 'A lady is what Harper is. As I was saying…' He rattled the paper. 'Your piece on the shooting last night was excellent.'

Harper bit back her disappointment. The shooting last night had been nothing special – page-ten filler.

'Thanks,' she said. 'That scene was messy, wasn't it? You wouldn't think a .22 would make him bleed so much. I thought six people had died when I walked up.'

'A .22 can do a lot of damage,' Smith assured her. 'Frankly, if you know where to aim, you can kill a man with a credit card.'

'Where, Dad?' Putting down his phone, Scott scooted to the edge of the sofa. 'Where do you hit him?'

Harper shot Smith a look but he didn't notice, warming to his subject.

'There is an artery here,' he said, pointing to the side of his neck, 'and another here,' pointing to his inner thigh. 'Hit either of those with anything remotely sharp and the best doctor in the world can't save you. You'll bleed out in minutes.'

'Wow,' Scott breathed, wide-eyed with fascination. Even Kyle looked up from his phone. 'Have you seen people die like that?'

'Well...' Smith began modestly, but he didn't get a chance to finish.

'*Robert*.' Pat's disapproving voice came from the doorway. 'This is not appropriate conversation.'

Smith's brow furrowed. 'I think it's perfectly reasonable if the boy wants to learn about human anatomy and criminology.'

Pat dried her hands too hard on a tea towel.

'He is *thirteen*, Robert. Why can't you argue about politics like normal people?'

'I don't like politics,' Scott informed her.

His mother sighed.

'Well. Lunch is served.' She headed towards the dining room, her espadrilles swishing. 'And blood is banned from the table.'

After the meal, Smith helped Pat with the dishes, while Harper and the boys played basketball outside. She'd always been able to hold her own with them, but these days Kyle was taller than her, and faster.

When he shot his third clean jump shot, catching nothing but net, Harper sagged back against the garage wall.

'When,' she wheezed, sweat pouring down her face, 'did you get so good?'

'I'm on the JV team.' A cocky grin lit up his face. He dribbled the ball from hand to hand. 'First squad.'

'Crap.' Waving for the two boys to continue, Harper backed away from the makeshift court. 'You guys do this. I need to go have a nice quiet heart attack.'

When she walked back into the house, the air conditioning chilled the perspiration on her back, sending goosebumps down her spine.

Everything was quiet. The house – always too new, too big – felt empty.

Her footsteps echoed as she made her way down the corridor to the sunlit kitchen. The gray, marble countertops were spotless. The dishwasher hummed. There was no sign of Pat.

When she backtracked to the living room, the TV flashed images without sound. The sofas were unoccupied.

On the wave of cool air, Harper smelled the sweet, cloying scent of cigar smoke. She turned on her heel, following the smoke around the foot of the stairs to where Smith's study door stood ajar. It was the only room in the house where Pat allowed him to smoke.

For a second, she stood in the hallway, deciding how to handle this.

Then, she tapped her knuckles against the wood and pushed the door open.

'Lieutenant?'

Smith's study was all dark wood and leather furniture. A deer head was mounted above the door. Its glassy eyes surveyed walls holding framed photos of the lieutenant with various dignitaries – the chief of police, the mayor. There were a few black-and-white shots of a younger version of him in uniform at crime scenes, badge on his chest, standing over handcuffed men.

A picture of Pat and the boys grinning at the camera stood on his desk, next to his laptop, which he closed when he saw her.

His cigar waved her in.

'Who won?' he asked, as she perched on one of the leather chairs facing his desk.

'Kyle.' She shook her head ruefully. 'That kid's a ringer. Why didn't you tell me he'd gone pro?'

There was pride in his smile. 'He swore me to secrecy.'

They talked about the boys for a while. How Scott was doing in school. Kyle's new cheerleader girlfriend.

They were laughing about something Scott had said at lunch, when Harper pounced.

'Oh, hey,' she said casually. 'I was looking for you on Friday and couldn't track you down. I wanted to talk to you about the Whitney case.'

Smith leaned forward to tap the ash off the stub of his smoke. When he glanced up again, his eyes were guarded.

'Work talk isn't allowed on Sunday,' he reminded her.

'I know.'

Leaning back in her chair, Harper adopted a look of apology.

'The thing is, the case seemed to go quiet over the last few days. Is everything OK?' Seeing the warning glint in his eyes, she added, 'Come on, Lieutenant. This isn't for attribution. I'm just curious.'

He examined his cigar. '"Just curious" gets people fired.'

With a shoulder tilt that said it was fine either way, Harper reached for a hunting magazine on the low table next to her chair, flipping through it without seeing it.

'Never mind,' she said. 'I wouldn't have brought it up, except Baxter's after me to write a piece about how slow progress is on the case. You know how she is.'

Smith drew on the cigar, blowing out a puff of bittersweet smoke.

'Emma Baxter needs to mind her own business,' he growled.

'Tell me about it,' she agreed. 'I've held her off for now, but when I'm back in the office on Tuesday...'

She made a helpless gesture.

'Anyway, I thought I should warn you.' She turned her attention back to the magazine, which bristled with weaponry. 'Give you time to brace yourself. I think they're planning an editorial.'

From the corner of her eye she saw Smith toying with that stub of cigar, his lips pursed.

'Look,' he said after a second, 'I'm not going to deny this is a tough one. My guys don't have much to work with. None of the neighbors saw a thing. No car was seen on the street outside. No sound of a struggle was heard.' He paused. 'Whoever did this – between you and me – he knew what he was doing. That scene was spotless.'

Harper put the magazine down.

'What about the ex-husband?' she asked, no longer disguising her eagerness. 'Could it have been him? Is he smart enough?'

Smith studied her. There'd been a time when he loved telling her about the cases he was investigating. He'd give her all the background. Get her to guess who he thought did it.

Once she became the official police reporter, that ended. They'd had to find a middle ground between their affection for each other and pure professionalism and, up to now, they'd done that just fine. But this case was different.

Harper was *involved* in this case. She felt part of it.

And Smith knew it.

'The father was at work,' he told her after a second. 'Rock-solid alibi. He was supposed to come in and pick up his daughter from school that day, but he got called in at the last minute.'

'Was there a boyfriend?' Harper persisted. 'Someone she fought with?'

His lips tightening, Smith shook his head.

'Come on, now. You know how much I'd love to discuss this

case with you, but I simply can't give you this information. I honestly wish I could.'

'Lieutenant,' she leaned towards him, 'you have no suspects and yet you're sure this case has nothing to do with my mother's murder? Help me out here. I don't understand.'

'I didn't tell you we had no suspects.' A hint of steel entered his voice. 'I told you the ex isn't one of them.'

'But how could the layout of the crime scenes be so identical?' she asked, the words bursting out. 'Are you seriously telling me that's a coincidence? That both women happened to be naked, and killed in exactly the same way, in the same room, with the same MO?'

'That is what I'm telling you,' he said evenly. 'I know it's difficult to accept, but similar murders happen.' Seeing the look on her face, he held up his hand. 'But you are right – the similarities are striking and I have instructed Detective Blazer to keep both cases in mind in his investigation. Nonetheless, my gut tells me it's not the same guy.'

It wasn't much, but at least it was something. Harper had a feeling that was all she was going to get out of him.

'Please, Lieutenant, if you find out anything about my mother's case – you'll tell me, won't you?'

The silence that followed was heavy with shared memories of bloody floors and slippery hands. Of her real father's failures and Smith's decision to step into his shoes, and be there for her.

'I promise,' he assured her. 'I'll tell you all I can.'

Before she could say anything else, he glanced at the cigar butt in his hand and briskly stubbed it out in the heavy wooden ashtray on his desk, waving away the cloud of smoke that rose around him.

'I better open a window. Pat's going to kill me.' He jumped up to lift the sash. 'Look, give Blazer a call when you're back in the office. I'll tell him to brief you on the record.'

The moment was over.

Chapter Fifteen

On Tuesday, Harper had to race out to a fatal car accident at the edge of town early on, so it was after five when she dashed past a patrol car and ambulance parked outside the door of police headquarters, and hurried across the quiet lobby to the reception desk.

Darlene made a show of looking at her watch.

'Ooh,' she said. 'Somebody's late. I was about to go home.'

Grabbing the stack of police reports, Harper spoke without looking up.

'Wreck on Veterans' Highway with fatalities.'

'Oh, lord,' Darlene gave a slow headshake. 'Why don't people drive like they can die?'

'That is a question I ask myself every day,' Harper replied, still flipping through the files. 'What'd I miss here? Anything new?'

'Mm-hmm.' Darlene glanced over her shoulder, then leaned forward across the desk. 'Everybody around here's up in arms.'

Holding her place in the file with her fingertips, Harper looked up.

'Really? What's going on?'

Darlene lowered her voice to a whisper. 'It's the Whitney case again. Mayor's on the phone. Police chief's yelling. Blazer looks like he's on his *last* heart attack.'

Forgetting about the police reports, Harper leaned against the counter.

'What's everyone so mad about?'

Darlene gave her a look.

'You know. White lady gets killed in her own house in a safe neighborhood in the middle of the day and they don't have a clue.' Her eyebrows arched up nearly to her hairline. 'Mayor's about to fire everyone in this building. Sow the ground with salt.'

So Smith's unworried demeanor on Sunday had been acting. The pressure was on.

Excitement flared in Harper's chest. Maybe she could get somewhere with the case today after all.

'Is Blazer in?' she asked. 'Smith wants me to talk to him.'

The receptionist shook her head. 'He went out in an all-fire rush about thirty minutes ago. Said he'd come back by six.' She lowered her voice again. 'I heard him and the lieutenant had a shoutin' match. Lieutenant told him to find a suspect or else.'

At that moment, the security door behind her buzzed and swung open. The two women both jumped.

Darlene turned her attention to her computer screen as if it was the most fascinating thing she'd ever seen in her life. Harper resumed flipping through the day's police reports, although the information was a blur of burglaries, public sex acts, and alcohol consumption within a hundred yards of a school.

'Hey, Harper!' Grinning, a man in the green uniform of a paramedic emerged from the back offices, a clipboard in one hand. He was about her age, stocky, with short blond hair and guileless blue eyes.

Harper relaxed.

'Hey, Toby. I haven't seen you in ages. What've you been up to?'

His smile faded. 'Got moved to day shift. I hate it. It's so boring. Nothing but car wrecks and slip-and-falls all damn day.'

'Bet Elaine's happy about it, though.' Harper nudged him with her elbow. 'She gets to see you again.'

She'd met Toby Jennings at a shooting scene when he was fresh out of med school four years ago. He was young enough to be a great source of information, and fun enough to hang out with outside of work. His wife, Elaine, a doctor at the local hospital, was one of those women who took one look at Harper and started sending her home with leftovers.

'Yeah,' he conceded. 'That part's good, at least. I'm getting back on nights soon, though. I've already put in my request. How about you? Still chasing the detectives around?'

'Same old, same old.' She glanced at him hopefully. 'Hey, you don't know anything about the Whitney case do you?'

'Oh, hell no, Harper.' He laughed. 'That's about twenty levels above my pay grade. Besides, they don't call paramedics for the dead ones.'

'I was afraid of that.' She shrugged. 'Had to try.'

Glancing at his watch he said, 'Look, I better go. I've got to turn the bus in for the next shift.'

Paramedics never use the word 'ambulance' for some reason.

'Well, it was great seeing you,' she said. 'Give my love to Elaine.'

He took a step towards the door before pausing.

'Actually, are you going to the party tonight?'

Harper and Darlene both looked at him.

'What party?' Harper asked.

'I think you were at the last one at Riley's place? The wild one where everyone started arresting each other? They're doing it again tonight. You should come. I'm planning to drop in for a quick one. Leave before they burn the place down. Elaine might come, too.'

Harper did remember. Riley was a patrol cop who threw all-night parties. The last one had turned a bit messy, and Harper had slipped away when the cops started singing Frank Sinatra and building a bonfire in the backyard.

She hadn't planned on doing anything tonight, but spending an hour or two at a cop party could be useful. They got a bit chatty after a few beers.

'Sure,' she said. 'I might just do that. I don't get off until midnight, though.'

'No one does. Party doesn't start until twelve.' With a jaunty wave, he headed out. 'Seizure later.'

Darlene waited until he was gone to pass judgment.

'Those night-shift parties,' she sniffed. 'Are notorious.'

When Harper returned to the newspaper building, DJ was waiting with obvious impatience.

'I've been trying to reach you.' He spun his chair towards her. 'Is your phone on?'

Before she could reply, Baxter stormed up to Harper's desk in high dudgeon.

'Where the hell have you been? The website is waiting on your wreck story, and we need an update on the Whitney case.'

Hastily, DJ wheeled himself out of the line of fire.

'Sorry.' Harper logged into her computer. 'I got caught up at the station.'

Baxter was not in a forgiving mood. 'The company provides that phone for you at great expense. You are required by your contract to answer it at least occasionally, if only to check that it still works.'

'I didn't hear it ring,' Harper said, reaching for her bag.

'I suspect that will be because you turned the ringer off again.' Baxter sounded exasperated. 'At least tell me you've got something new on the Whitney case. I'm holding the front.'

'Not exactly.' Seeing the look on her editor's face, Harper added defensively, 'I tried, but the lead detective wasn't in.'

'Dammit.' Drumming her fingertips on her desk, Baxter looked away, thinking.

'Work up a story that says the police are still investigating, looking for clues, the usual bullshit. Put some heat on them about why this is taking so long. Mention that cases not solved in the first twenty-four hours are unlikely to be solved at all. Get me a quote from the police or something new from the coroner's office, call the family. Do what you have to do.'

Whirling, she strode back towards her desk, still talking.

'I've got to have something, Harper. An empty front page is not an option.'

'Man,' Harper said under her breath. 'Someone should slip her some decaf.'

Still, she knew when Baxter was serious – and this was one of those times. She had to find something.

DJ turned around to talk, but she shook her head at him.

'I can't now,' she said, grabbing the phone. 'Catch me later.'

Fingers flying, she dialed a number from memory. It rang only once.

'Homicide.' The voice that answered wasn't familiar. It had a thick southern twang and sounded in a hurry. But detectives were always in a hurry.

'This is Harper McClain from the *Daily News*,' she began.

'Uh-oh,' the voice said cheerfully.

Instinctively, Harper added more country to her voice, to make herself familiar. Unthreatening.

'Who'm I talking with?'

'You've got Detective Al Davenport, ma'am. What can I do you for today?'

From the back of her mind, Harper summoned a hazy image of Davenport – scarecrow tall and Ichabod-thin, with a long, narrow face and a slow way of walking like nothing in the distance could be as interesting as what was right in front of him. He'd only been working Homicide a year or two, so she'd rarely encountered him so far. He'd worked mostly on case background.

'I'm trying to track down Detective Blazer,' she said. 'Is he in?'

'I hate to break your heart, Miss McClain, but he's out at the moment.'

Harper paused, considering her next move.

'Detective, I know you're busy, and I don't want to bother you,' she said sweetly. 'But I'm wondering if you can help me out?'

'I'd be happy to help, if I can.'

The merest hint of caution had entered his voice. Harper eased up on the charm.

'I'm looking for an update on the Marie Whitney case.' Before he could argue she added, 'Now, I know you can't tell me much. But Lieutenant Smith did say I should call today. Is there anything you can tell me?'

There was a long pause.

'What kind of information are you looking for?'

There was no mistaking the reluctance in his tone but he hadn't hung up on her, and that was something.

'I'm writing a story on the progress in the case,' she explained.

'I need some very basic stuff. Has anyone been brought in for questioning at this time?'

Another long pause.

'No, ma'am, not as far as I am aware.' The smile had left his voice. 'Miss McClain, I do not wish to be quoted on the record, as I am not heavily involved in this case.'

Ignoring the last bit, Harper prodded, 'But there must be lines of inquiry that Detective Blazer is following? Can you give me some idea of those?'

'I can't say, at this time...' There was a pause and then, with palpable relief, Davenport said, 'The detective is walking into the office now. Can you hold on one minute?'

The phone went quiet.

Harper sat with the receiver in her hand, staring at the scarred wood of the desk. A long minute passed. She could imagine the squabbling going on in that room.

A click and then a *whoosh*, as if Blazer had teleported the phone to his mouth.

'Blazer.' His tone was ice cold.

'This is Harper McClain.' She removed all the smile from her voice. There's no point in trying to charm a viper. 'I'm calling for an update on the Whitney case.'

Silence.

She tried a direct question. 'Could you give me an update on where the investigation stands at this time?'

'I cannot. That information is confidential.'

Pressing her fingers against her forehead, Harper pushed her temper back.

'Detective, I was assured by Lieutenant Smith that I could expect an update from you, today. Was he mistaken? I can call him and ask, if you'd like? As you know, I have his home number.'

Her tone was measured but cutting.

This time, when Blazer didn't reply, she let the silence hang there.

He gave in first.

'At the current time, we are pursuing all possible leads,' he said flatly.

Gritting her teeth, Harper wrote the non-quote down, in case it was all he gave her.

'Have you questioned any suspects?'

'At the current *time*,' he said again, 'we are pursuing all possible leads.'

'Have you received the coroner's report on the Whitney case?'

'I might have,' he said, 'but I'm certainly not sharing it with the press.'

He was enjoying this now. He thought she'd get angry or give up. This was because he didn't know her very well.

'Listen, Detective,' she said quietly. 'My editor's in a crappy mood. She wants me to write one of those articles about how a good woman died in a town that's supposed to be safe and now the murderer's getting away with it. I could call Smith and get him to give me this information. But from what I hear, he's on your back already and you probably don't want that. So I'm asking you one more time.' She took a breath. 'Do you have the coroner's report on the Whitney case?'

It shouldn't be possible to sense how much someone loathes you from the quality of their silence on a phone line. But it is.

'I have the report on my desk,' he said finally. 'And there are several things in it that I cannot share for investigatory reasons.' He paused. 'However, I can tell you that Mrs Whitney was killed with a common household butcher knife – one found in most people's kitchens. No such knife was found at the scene, so we believe the killer took the knife with him.'

His tone was bitter. As if she'd pulled the words out of him with pliers. But she'd take it however she could get it.

Tucking the phone against her shoulder, Harper wrote quickly.

'How many times was she stabbed? How many of those wounds could have caused her death?'

'Mrs Whitney was stabbed seven times,' he said. 'She also had shallow, defensive wounds on her hands and forearms, indicating she struggled with her assailant. One strike with the knife severed her carotid artery, and that is the one that ultimately caused her death.'

'Can you give me any description of the killer, based on the wounds or evidence from the scene?'

'The killer was a man with a knife,' Blazer said sardonically. 'Come on, McClain. How can I describe a man no one saw?'

Harper didn't rise to the bait.

'Does the height or angle of the wounds give you an idea of the height and weight of the killer?' she asked calmly. 'Were any hairs found at the scene? If so, what color hair does he have?'

'We believe the killer was a man, given the depth of the wounds and the strength required. The angle of the wounds indicates a muscular man, at least six feet tall, possibly taller. I have nothing beyond that.'

'Was she sexually assaulted?' she asked.

'There's no evidence of that.'

Harper wrote fast; she kept up with him easily. When he'd finished talking, she leaned back in her chair. She had a feeling this was the last question he'd answer and she wanted to choose it carefully.

'Why is the investigation moving so slowly?' she asked. 'Is there anything you want to tell the public about the investigation? Should they be afraid that a killer is walking around, free?'

'What the hell kind of question is that?' Blazer's voice rose. 'Off the record, McClain, if you think you can do this better, get on it. On the record: The investigation is going smoothly, but the killer took measures to hide his identity. We believe he wore gloves and other protective gear. We are still in the early part of the investigation but there is no need for the public to fear.'

Harper thought of what Smith had told her – that Blazer knew about her mother's murder.

'Do you have any reason to believe this killer has killed before?' she pressed. 'Have there been other, similar murders?'

There was a pause.

'I cannot get into that,' Blazer said.

'But—'

He spoke over her. 'The lieutenant told me to brief you, so I've briefed you. Now, if you don't mind, I'm getting back to work.'

The phone went dead.

It was after nine by the time Harper had finished filing her story and things calmed down enough for her to remember that DJ had wanted to talk to her.

She punched the number of his cell phone. It rang five times before he picked up.

'Hello?' He was somewhere noisy – she could hear voices and laughter, the sound of a television.

'Hey,' she said. 'It's Harper. Can you talk?'

'Hold on,' he said. 'I'll go outside.'

She heard him fumbling around, getting up, then the noise receded and she heard a door open and close.

'Where are you?' she asked, leaning her elbows on her desk.

'At Rosie's. Watching the game with some of the sports guys.'

Harper wrinkled her nose. 'Gross.'

'This is why I don't invite you to things,' he said. 'I'm glad you called, though. What I tried to tell you earlier was I went back to the college looking for information about Whitney. You're going to want to hear what I found out.' She heard the sound of pages flipping – he must have taken his notebook to the bar with him, in case she called.

'Marie Whitney was not a popular woman. Or rather, she was too popular.'

Harper's brow furrowed. 'What does that mean?'

'Basically, a lot of people were surprisingly eager to tell me she was a slut,' he said bluntly.

'You're kidding.'

She could almost hear him shaking his head.

'Husband-stealer. Nymphomaniac. You name it, I heard it today.'

Harper was stunned. Whatever she'd expected him to find out, it wasn't this. She reached for her notebook, but she wasn't sure what to write.

'I don't get it. What does her sex life have to do with her murder?'

'If you ask the professors and grad students at Savannah University, she finally slept with the wrong guy and he killed her,' DJ said. 'They think they've got this thing solved.'

'Well,' Harper said. 'It's not an unusual motive for murder. Did anyone have any names? Someone she was going out with lately?'

'Yeah, about that. When I asked people if she was dating someone new before she was killed, they laughed at me,' he said. 'One grad student said, "She only liked them new." He sounded particularly bitter. I got the feeling maybe he'd been the new one once.'

'Ouch.' Harper was taking notes now. 'Did you get any names at all? It might be good to track some of these guys down.'

In the distance, Harper heard a crowd cheer. Someone must have scored.

'I've got a couple of names,' DJ said. 'But nobody knew how recent these guys were. Seems Whitney liked to date multiple guys at once and she moved through them fast. Some she kept secret. Some were more public. People said she liked to play them off against each other. Make them jealous.' He drew a breath. 'The information I got was consistent. The woman was a player.'

'And none of these guys raised any alarms with anyone? No axe-wielding weirdos among them?' Harper asked hopefully.

'Far as I can tell, it was the opposite,' he said. 'She went out with a few arty types, but mostly she went for men in positions of authority. She liked lawyers, politicians and cops.'

Harper's pen skidded across the page.

'Wait. DJ, did you say cops?'

'Yeah, I thought that might interest you.' She could hear the grin in his voice. 'Apparently she had a thing for guns and the guys who carry them.'

Harper's stomach tightened. Her mind spun through everything she knew about the Whitney case. A clean crime scene. No mistakes. A professional.

A cop could do that.

'Holy shit,' she breathed. 'I need to see those names.'

Chapter Sixteen

Harper almost didn't go to the party that night.

After she got off the phone with DJ, he'd texted her the names he'd collected. She'd rushed to do basic searches on all of them. They were certainly high-profile enough – a former city manager, a state senator, and a CEO.

None of them were cops, but DJ told her he thought there were more names to be gotten.

'Lots more,' he said. 'I'll keep digging.'

Certainly, no one on his list shouted murderer at her. Much less, murderer of two women, fifteen years apart. She ran quick searches on all of them. None of them had criminal records. None had a known history of violence.

She fretted about it all the way home. For a moment there, she'd thought DJ had found what she was looking for. Now, an hour later, she wasn't sure.

It was only when she'd parked and got out of the car that she remembered Toby's invitation.

She wouldn't have even considered going if Riley didn't live eight blocks away.

He was the only cop she knew who lived in the historic district. All the rest lived in the suburbs, as far from the city as possible. But he was different in a lot of ways.

He was vegetarian, incredibly buffed, went to yoga classes, didn't drink alcohol, and threw the most insane parties.

He lived in a cute, turn-of-the-century cottage, and Harper heard the party before she saw it. A low roar of voices, the *thump-thump-thump* of a bass.

Tuesday might seem a strange night for a party, but weekends are the busiest nights for police, and lots of beat cops get Tuesdays and Wednesdays off.

When she walked up the front steps, the door was ajar. It looked like everyone had turned out for it. Music – mostly rap and pop – blared from the speakers. The furniture had been pushed out of the way, and a couple of people were already dancing.

There's something weird about seeing cops out of uniform, being normal people. It's like seeing a priest in jeans. Or spotting your doctor wearing tennis shorts at the supermarket. Even then, it's not the same, because their inherent *copness* is unmistakable. The military haircuts, the rigid posture, the subtle, unspoken anxiety about rules being broken – it's obvious once you're aware of it.

Seeing no one she knew, Harper threaded her way through the crowd across the living room and dining room to the kitchen at the back of the house. It was a long, narrow space, old-fashioned but in an arty way, with glass-front cabinets and one of those trendy pastel refrigerators that look like 1950s ice-boxes.

She found Riley leaning against the wall next to the back door holding a glass of club soda and arguing good-naturedly with

Toby and his wife, Elaine. As soon as he spotted Harper, he cut himself off.

'Hey, Harper!' He waved his beer. 'I didn't know you were coming.'

'Toby talked me into it,' she said. 'Anyway, I love your parties. They're so calm and formal.'

Riley found this hilarious.

'Formal…' he sputtered. 'Yeah. Right. Grab yourself a beer and come set Toby straight. Turns out he's wrong about everything.'

The sink had been filled with ice and beer, and was acting as a de facto cooler.

Popping the top off a cold Corona, Harper walked over to join them.

'What's Toby wrong about today?' she asked.

'I was explaining to the officer that getting a suspect to the hospital when his eyes are rolling back in his head from an overdose of crystal meth might be more important than taking him to prison,' Toby said.

Riley grinned. 'And I was explaining to Toby that one out of every two suspects pretends to be overdosing when we arrest them hoping we'll make this particular mistake. Those hospital beds are more comfortable than the ones in the county jail.'

'Dear God,' Elaine said, turning to Harper. 'Make them stop bickering.'

Elaine was tiny, with wavy brown hair and doll-like features that led some to underestimate how brilliant she really was.

Harper wanted to be her when she grew up.

'Hey,' she said, ignoring the debate, 'I didn't think you'd be here. I thought you were on days.'

'I am,' Elaine said. 'But I've got Wednesday off this week, so I thought, what the hell. I'm hoping this will convince Toby that working normal human hours is not a prison sentence. It's still possible to have fun.'

Toby gave her a pitying look.

'Nice try,' he said.

In the next room, someone cranked up the stereo. Riley leaned in to be heard above the music.

'I can't believe you guys gave up the vampire hours. What's it like being normal people? Honestly. Is it better?'

Elaine glanced at Toby, who raised one eyebrow.

'Look,' she said, 'having regular hours is great. I get more sleep. When I go to the supermarket it's people buying groceries – not a bunch of drug addicts stealing candy bars, which is what it's like at three a.m. And I can go to the gym, go to dinner with friends...' As she spoke, Toby's expression grew more outraged, and she hurried to finish before he could interrupt, resting one hand on his arm. 'But I'm not going to lie, the work is less fun. There's no adrenaline rush when you're doing a pre-scheduled gallbladder removal.' Her tone was wry. 'God, it's so twisted. I never thought I'd miss gunshot wounds.'

'I'm going back on nights,' Toby said firmly. 'I can't take any more normality. Bring on the shootings and overdoses.'

He raised his beer and clinked bottles with Harper and Riley. After a brief hesitation, Elaine raised her beer to join theirs.

'Oh, what the hell,' she said.

They talked for a while by the open door, drinking too fast. The beer went straight to Harper's head, and she was glad. Someone handed her another and she drank that one, too.

After the last few days, it felt good not to think.

When Riley described a case he'd worked the night before in which an elderly woman called 911 because she couldn't find her cat, she found herself laughing helplessly.

'I told her, "I'm sorry, ma'am. Spangles is not an emergency,"' he said, adopting an earnest tone. 'And she said, "She is an emergency until you find her, young man."'

'What did you do?' Harper asked.

'I looked for the damn cat,' Riley confessed to raucous laughter, adding defensively, 'That woman was very persistent.'

At that moment, a song everyone loved came on, and Toby and Elaine ran into the living room to dance. Riley tried to convince Harper to join them but she shook her head.

'I can't let anyone see me dancing,' she insisted. 'It'll ruin my credibility.'

Grabbing her hand, he pulled her close, thrusting his leg suggestively between hers and moving her body in smooth circles with his hips.

'I could teach you,' he said, waggling his eyebrows.

Laughing, she pushed him away.

'Go find yourself a nice rookie to dance with,' she told him. 'You're too good for me.'

He backed away, still holding out one hand.

'Don't pass up on this, baby,' he begged. 'It would be so good.'

When she didn't back down, he gave in to the beat, joining the others bouncing around the living room.

For a while Harper stood watching them, but it was hot in there, even with the windows open, and she felt a little dizzy. She shouldn't have drunk that last beer so fast.

The breeze blowing in from outside felt good – so she slipped out the back door to catch her breath. It was a warm, humid night but, after the crowded kitchen, it felt cool.

A path of pale stone led from the house through the long, narrow garden. The waxing moon cast a pale blue light over the yard.

Harper closed her eyes, letting the breeze dry the perspiration on her face.

'Better be careful,' a voice said behind her. 'I hear there's been a lot of crime in this area recently.'

She spun around.

Luke Walker stood a few feet away, leaning against a tree, watching her with unnerving steadiness.

Harper's heart kicked. She hadn't noticed him arrive.

'I've got 911 on speed dial,' she informed him.

'Yeah, but police response times are shit.' He walked closer. 'I read it in the paper.'

'That rag?' She smiled. 'Don't believe a word. It's full of lies.'

Unlike the others, Luke looked normal in street clothes. In dark jeans and a button-down shirt that showed off a triangle of smooth, tanned skin at his throat, he looked dangerously good.

Something about this moment in the moonlight, with the air soft against her skin, felt inevitable. On some subconscious, instinctive level, she'd known he'd be here.

In fact, hadn't she been waiting for this, ever since that night he'd appeared behind her with a gun like a six-foot-tall guardian angel?

'I didn't see you inside,' she said. 'Were you dancing?'

He gave a dry, sardonic laugh.

'Just got here. Went to the kitchen to get a beer and saw you sneaking out.'

'I wasn't sneaking,' she clarified, unnecessarily. 'I was walking.'

His shrug said it didn't matter.

'Actually,' he said, 'I've been looking for you.'

Her eyes darted up to his.

'You scared the shit out of me the other night,' he said. 'I still don't understand why you put yourself in that situation.'

For Harper, the shooting seemed like a lifetime ago and, while she didn't like being told how to do her job, she really didn't want to argue about it anymore.

'Look,' she said, 'I miscalculated. I got too cocky. Won't happen again.' She smiled darkly. 'You know what's funny? Everyone was pissed off about that except my editor. She practically gave me a medal.'

He nodded, as if this didn't surprise him at all.

'I hear you. The more you risk your life, the more the boss likes it. It's not like they'll have to pay for your funeral, after all.'

His voice was sharp. Harper's brow creased.

This bitter side of him surprised her. Luke had always loved his job. Something had changed.

'Hey,' she said hesitantly. 'Is everything OK with you?'

He looked at her for a moment, his expression hard to read. But when he replied, his tone was brisk.

'It's fine. Same old, same old.'

Still, the way he upended his bottle, swallowing hard, belied his words.

Normally, Harper would have let it go at this point. But the beer made her reckless.

'You know, I still don't understand why you switched to under-cover,' she said. 'You're a good homicide detective. One of the best. It never made sense.'

He studied his beer bottle.

'Office politics.' His clipped tone warned her against asking more. But she decided to push it.

'What does that mean?'

'It means,' he said, 'I don't want to talk about it, Harper.'

'Well,' she said, unperturbed, 'you're wasted, chasing drug

dealers. You ought to be solving murders. Like this damned Whitney case.'

That caught his attention. He tilted his head.

'Why do you say it like that? What's going on with that case?'

'Blazer's blowing it,' she told him, with a sudden burst of righteous anger. 'He's got no suspects. I don't think he has a clue. Smith won't listen. And there's another little girl without a mother, and everyone's looking at it wrong.' She waved her bottle. 'The killer's out there and no one's doing anything about it. It's all slipping away.'

In the sudden silence that followed, she drew a long breath.

'Damn. Where did *that* come from?'

Luke had said nothing all this time – he let her talk, listening with a kind of intensity she found unfamiliar but not unpleasant.

Now, instead of answering her question, he reached for her empty bottle. Their fingers brushed as he took it from her hand. His skin was warm and dry against hers.

'Stay here,' he told her.

He disappeared through the back door, where the *thump-thump-thump* of the music had increased in volume. He was gone less than a minute, returning with two fresh beers. Motioning for her to follow, he led the way to the back of the yard, out of sight of the house, and handed her a bottle.

'Thanks.' Harper pressed the cold glass to her forehead.

'OK,' Luke said. 'I get that you're pissed off at Blazer. But I don't really know why. Tell me your theory about the Whitney case. Start at the beginning.'

Harper bit her lip. Until this moment, she hadn't really considered telling Luke what was going on. And this was probably a diversion to get her to stop asking about what was happening with him. Still, all of a sudden, she wanted to tell him everything.

'This is going to sound crazy,' she warned him. 'I don't have all the pieces yet. It's a hunch, more than anything.'

He waved his bottle impatiently.

'Look, Harper, any cop will tell you every theory about a case starts out as a fucked-up idea. Talking it through is how you unfuck it. You whittle away the crap and get down to the truth. So... Talk.'

Harper drew a long breath – steadying herself.

'I'm looking at two similar crimes,' she told him. 'Fifteen years apart.'

He swung his bottle in an impatient circle. 'The Whitney case and...?'

'My mother's murder.'

Undercover cops learn early how to hide what they really think. The only way she could tell he was caught off guard was by the time it took him to respond.

'What ties them together?' he asked after a split-second too long.

He was calm, interested. But what was most important to Harper was what he *didn't* say – he didn't ask how or when her mother was killed.

He knew already.

The realization jolted her.

She'd always suspected most of the detectives had to know her history. After all, some of the older ones had worked that case.

But Luke was young. It was strange to think that he might have known all along. And never mentioned it.

'Harper?' Luke prodded with unexpected gentleness.

'The crime scenes,' she said, gathering herself. 'They're identical.'

Quickly, she told him what she knew.

'I know how crazy it sounds,' she said, at the end. 'Fifteen years is a long time. But if you could have seen those scenes, Luke. They're exactly the same.'

She paused, wondering how to explain.

'It's like my mother's death made this huge noise a long time ago. And this murder is the echo of it.'

Luke stood staring into the darkness, his jaw tight. The breeze ruffled his hair.

When he didn't speak, Harper decided he thought she was wrong, too. Like Smith and Miles and everyone else she'd confided in. Maybe they were right.

Maybe she really was seeing what she wanted to see.

She took a drink. 'I told you it would sound crazy.'

'The problem I'm having here,' he said slowly, 'is it's not nearly as crazy as I'd hoped.'

Harper stared at him in stunned surprise.

Someone laughed loudly in the house. The sound made them both flinch.

'Don't get me wrong.' Luke glanced back at the house, his brow creasing. 'You shouldn't take it to court yet. But it's worth finding out more.'

Something broke with a crystalline crash. Loud cheers arose.

The party was reaching its peak. Soon, the neighbors would call the police, not without irony, and some night-shifter would come break it up. It would never appear in the stack of police reports on the reception desk.

Blue looks after blue.

Clearly, Luke had come to the same conclusion.

'Listen,' he said suddenly, 'let's get out of here. Do you have your car?'

'N-no,' she stuttered, caught off guard. 'I walked.'

His smile was a flash of white in the shadows. 'I forgot you live downtown. You're as bad as Riley.'

'I'll bet my rent is less than yours,' she retorted tartly.

He gave a low chuckle.

Setting their half-finished beers on a garden table, they walked back to the house.

'This way.' Luke pointed to a shadowy path leading down the side. 'Let's try to get out of here without rumors starting. Cops are worse than teenage girls.'

Just as they slipped away, drunken, mock-fighting bodies tumbled down the back steps behind them.

'They'll be handcuffing each other next.'

Luke whispered the words in Harper's ear. His breath against her skin felt electric.

She suppressed a shiver.

As they walked through the dark, she felt hyper alert – every nerve firing. Something was different tonight. She could sense it – smell it in the air, like smoke. He was closer to her than he'd ever allowed himself to be – their hands were almost touching. He wasn't finding an excuse to leave, as he often did. He was making no effort to put a safe distance between them. To ensure they didn't cross a line.

There had always been something between them – a low unspoken force of attraction. They had always ignored it. Their jobs meant they had to.

But ever since the shooting, she'd felt the strangest need for those barriers between them to fall. Maybe he'd felt that, too.

This felt dangerous. And she liked danger.

They slipped through the side gate and out onto the sidewalk, heading down the silent street. The rambling, historic houses were dark at this hour. Aside from the pair of them, the only movement was a black cat, in the distance, slinking under a parked car.

Harper shot a surreptitious sideways glance at Luke. His hands were loose at his sides and his eyes were focused straight ahead. He had a loping, easy stride, like a cowboy heading back to the bunkhouse.

She made herself look away.

'Look,' he said, when the sounds of the party had faded behind them. 'About the Whitney case. I've heard some things.'

Harper was instantly sober.

'Like what?'

'Like no useful evidence was collected at the scene,' he said. 'Like, everything was too clean to be believable. The killer was professional. Things you already know.' He glanced at her. 'You're not the only one to notice – people are talking. Even outside Homicide. Everyone knows Blazer hasn't got a handle on it.'

'Why doesn't the lieutenant do something?' she asked, frustration ringing in her voice. 'He should take Blazer off the case.'

'Office politics,' Luke said, for the second time that night. 'Smith and Blazer go way back. There is no chance of Smith admitting he has any doubts. Not publicly, anyway.'

That made sense to Harper. Blazer was Smith's second in command. They hung out together outside of work. They often went fishing in Blazer's bass boat in the summer.

'What do you think is going on?' Harper asked. 'Do you think the killer was a professional, like Blazer's saying?'

Luke made a disgusted sound.

'None of it fits. Why would a professional killer murder Marie Whitney? It feels like an excuse for not solving the case.' He hesitated. 'But... Harper, it's extremely unlikely the Whitney case has anything to do with what happened to your mother. You know that, right? Killers don't lie low for decades and then reappear to commit the same murder again.'

Harper turned away.

'I know,' she said. But her voice was tight.

'Hey.' He touched her arm. 'Listen.'

Their steps slowed. His face was serious.

'If it were my mom, I'd do exactly what you're doing. And if I can help from the inside, let me know.'

Harper stared. This offer broke any number of police codes and rules. And it wasn't like Luke to break rules.

'You'd really do that?'

'Sure. I'll poke around, see what I can turn over.' He smiled that cowboy smile. 'I'm between cases. They always make us wait for six weeks before going back undercover again. All I'm doing is running down low-level drug dealers. I've got to do something else to stay busy.'

'Thank you,' she said, with genuine feeling. 'That would really help. If I'm on the wrong track, I want to know.'

Somehow they'd reached her street. As they neared her front steps, they both stopped, looking up at the blue, two-story building with its peaked roof. The students upstairs were asleep – all the lights were off except the one in the entrance hall.

'This is you,' Luke said softly, turning to her.

Their eyes locked.

Harper's chest tightened. She'd been right – something *was* different tonight. She didn't know why, but something between them had changed and they could both feel it.

It wasn't like Luke to offer to break rules for her, and it wasn't like him to show up at Riley's party, or to walk her home. Or to stand here now, looking at her like that.

Like he wanted her.

But he was and she didn't want him to go. And she knew he didn't want to go either.

A muscle worked in his jaw.

Harper thought she could see her own confused longing reflected in his eyes. She felt that look in the pit of her stomach.

With aching slowness, he reached out, brushing a strand of hair from her cheek with his fingertips.

His skin was so warm. She leaned into his touch.

'Harper…' He said her name with soft reluctance. Like he was about to say 'I have to go.' Or 'We can't.'

But he didn't say either of those things. He didn't say anything. The moment had the fragile tension of thin ice.

Harper tried to make herself think clearly. Was this what *she* wanted?

The one rule Harper had never violated – the one she genuinely saw the sense in – was never to get romantically involved with the police. They were her subjects – her sources.

Except now, all of a sudden, she didn't care one damn bit about any of that. She wanted to break that rule, and break it hard.

Was this what she wanted?

Yes.

She could feel the desire coming off him like heat. His gaze was like a held breath.

'You could come in,' she suggested hoarsely. 'I have coffee.'

For a second he stood still, waging an internal battle she'd already lost. Then his jaw tightened, and he grabbed her hand.

They took the front steps two at a time.

Harper fumbled with the key, unlocking the door with feverish impatience. They tumbled into the house. His lips were on hers before the door swung shut.

Luke's body was all hard muscle as he pulled her to him, kissing her with a hungry urgency that made her insides dissolve.

They stumbled over a pair of shoes she'd left by the front door, falling back against the wall.

He caught his balance, holding her close against him.

Everywhere he touched her burned like fire.

His body fit perfectly against hers. She had always known he would feel like this. Smell like this. Taste like this.

'We're not supposed to do this,' he whispered against her skin.

How could she tell him that some part of her had wanted to kiss him since that night in the police car when they were both twenty-one and ready to conquer the world?

Harper ran her hands down his back. Raised her lips to his ear.

'I won't tell if you don't.'

Then they were kissing again, his tongue teasing her lips apart, his breath filling her lungs. He smelled of soap and salt and trouble, and she wanted him to stay the night.

He trailed kisses along her jaw to her ear, and her breath caught as his teeth pressed against the sensitive skin there.

'We could both get fired,' he whispered.

Somehow, everything he said sounded like a promise of the best sex of her life.

She stood on her toes, whispering two words against his lips: 'Worth it.'

His hands slid down her spine, flattening against the small of her back, pressing her body against his.

'Oh, hell,' he said, looking down into her eyes. 'I think you might be right.'

It was all over now. There would be no more fighting it.

His mouth covered hers as he pushed her back against the wall.

She ran her fingers through the soft strands of his hair that she had always wanted to touch.

She was trying to remember if she'd left anything embarrassing out in her bedroom when his phone rang.

They both froze.

The harsh buzzing echoed insistently in the quiet hallway.

Exhaling, Luke pressed his forehead against hers. His eyes were steady, a clear, trustworthy blue that seemed to see directly into her soul.

'I have to get it.'

She brushed her lips against his. 'I know.'

With obvious effort, he stepped back, pulling the phone from his pocket.

Clearing his throat, he said, 'Walker.'

A voice on the phone spoke to him in quick, authoritative sentences Harper couldn't quite make out. Luke listened, his eyes on hers.

'Got it,' he said after a minute. 'I'm on my way.'

He ended the call, sliding the phone back in his pocket.

'It's work. I have to go.' He traced his fingertips lightly under her chin, following the line of her jaw – even that touch raised goosebumps on the back of her neck. 'I really don't want to.'

'Go,' she said gently. 'Catch your drug dealer.'

He pulled her close, kissing her one last time. When he finally released her, she felt colder.

He opened the door and the night poured in.

He glanced back with a wicked grin.

'Harper McClain,' he said. 'You are full of surprises lately.'

Chapter Seventeen

The next day, Harper slept until noon. When she woke, light was filtering softly through the blinds. She stretched languorously. Then her whole body went rigid.

Shit.

She sat up abruptly, dragging the sheets with her, sending the blanket to the floor and making Zuzu, who had been asleep on the end of the bed, leap to her feet.

Luke.

Dropping her head into her hands, Harper replayed the last minutes of the night.

In retrospect, it felt like a dream but, even through the fog of morning, she knew it wasn't. She could still feel his hands on her back, hear him whisper against her skin, 'We're not supposed to do this.'

The memory sent heat rushing through her.

'*Shit.*' She said it aloud this time, for emphasis. 'Shit, shit, shit.'

So much was wrong with this.

She and Luke were friends, and nothing ruins a friendship like skin against skin. Then there was the fact that he could lose his job for it, not to mention, if the police complained hard enough, she could find herself in trouble at work as well.

Her stomach was tight with a contradictory tangle of trepidation and longing.

If she were honest, all she wanted was to finish what they'd started. But odds were, wherever he was right now, Luke was having the same realization she was.

They couldn't take this any further.

The rules in the police force called for no 'fraternization' with the press outside of work hours 'in a manner that could compromise the integrity of police investigations'.

Oh, there were always flirtations between cops and the reporters who covered them – there was hardly a male cop on the force who hadn't hit on Natalie from Channel 12 – but she'd never heard of a cop actually having a relationship with a reporter.

It wasn't only because of the rules. The fundamental mistrust between the police and the press created a hazy no-man's-land between the two. Journalists made a living uncovering the things cops wanted to keep buried. Normally, nobody had to work very hard to keep them apart. They were oil and water.

Except for Harper. She was different.

She'd grown up with the cops. Been part of them, in a way.

After her father left, Harper's grandmother couldn't always pick her up after school. Usually she went to Bonnie's house on those days but, if she couldn't, it was Smith who came to get her. Sometimes he came himself, other times he sent a patrol car to drive her – lights flashing, sirens howling – to the station to do her homework.

When she was there, waiting for Smith to finish working, the cops would vie to entertain her. They brought her drinks and bags of potato chips from the vending machines. The traffic cops used to take her for rides around the parking lot on their motorcycles.

At twelve, thirteen, fourteen – she was their mascot. She was almost one of them.

And yet, despite all of this, and despite her long, close friendship with Smith, she wasn't one of them. Not really.

Luke could get into real trouble.

Suddenly, everything they'd done last night seemed stupid and reckless. Anyone could have seen them together in the garden, whispering. Anyone could have spotted them leaving and put two and two together. They were cops, after all.

She'd gone still for so long, Zuzu yawned, arched her striped back, and strode away stiffly.

'Mind your own business,' Harper called after her.

Dragging herself out of bed, she padded barefoot down the hall, where sunlight bounced off the polished wood floors, refracting off the clean walls.

She kept the place sparsely furnished – neat as a hospital ward. It held only two gray Ikea sofas and a small television. She liked that she could walk straight lines across it without running into anything.

She'd never really thought about why – it was just the way she was.

All the walls were painted the same off-white they'd been when she moved in – it had never occurred to her to change them. The splashes of color came from the art. The wall between the living room and the tiny kitchen held a large, bright canvas featuring a field of yellow and white flowers so beautifully painted they seemed to sway in a breeze. It was Harper's favorite of all her mother's paintings.

Another painting hung above the fireplace – a dreamy,

sun-drenched piece painted by Bonnie years ago. It portrayed a younger Harper in a white dress with flaming red hair, a delicate scattering of freckles on her cheeks, turning away to look into the golden light.

It was ironic that Bonnie had been the one with the art gene, rather than Harper. But Harper had never painted again, after her mother died.

'I always loved watching your mom paint,' Bonnie said when she first started studying art seriously. 'She seemed so happy; so free. No other grown-ups in my life loved their jobs as much as she loved hers.'

Like the rest of the apartment, the small bathroom was orderly, too. Towels hung just so. Soap dish sparkling. Without even noticing she was doing it, Harper straightened the bath mat by half an inch, before climbing into the shower.

Later, clean and dressed, she turned on her scanner and brewed a pot of strong coffee. She listened absently to curt, emotionless discussions of fender-benders and sidewalk falls as she waited for the coffee to finish.

Her kitchen wasn't big, but it had everything she needed, with a window overlooking the backyard, and tall cabinets Billy had made himself. Like the hallway, the walls and cabinet were white.

The black-and-white tiled floor was cool under her bare feet as she carried a mug of coffee to the kitchen table.

Zuzu crouched by the cat door beneath the window, tail switching, then suddenly leapt through it, as if pouncing on the world.

'Goodbye to you, too,' Harper murmured, reaching for her laptop.

Having a cat hadn't been her idea.

Three years earlier, a particularly feckless crew of tenants upstairs had moved out (owing, Billy told her mournfully, two months' rent) and left their cat behind. The skinny gray tabby showed up on Harper's porch one afternoon, staring at her insistently with hungry green eyes.

'No,' Harper told her, heading off to work.

When she returned at two a.m., it was raining and the cat was still there, trying to sleep, with her back pressed hard against the front door.

Harper saw the cat flinch as the rain splashed her fur.

'Oh well,' she'd said to herself when she opened the door to let her in. 'Maybe cat food isn't that expensive.'

It turned out they had a lot in common. Both of them liked their independence. And both of them hated sleeping alone.

Sitting cross-legged, she logged into her email, but she'd only opened one message when her cell phone rang.

'Harper,' she said, still reading.

'It's DJ.'

She could hear the buzz of the newsroom in the background – low conversation, phones ringing.

'Hey,' she said. 'What's up?'

'I've been digging around into this Marie Whitney thing.' He was talking so quietly it was hard to hear him. 'I've found something out. I think you're going to want to hear it.'

'Spill,' Harper ordered, looking around for a pen and paper.

'Yeah... actually...' He sounded anxious, his voice was low. 'Can you meet me somewhere?'

'I could come in early?' she suggested.

'Not here,' he said quickly. 'Is there someplace else we could meet?'

Harper's brow furrowed.

'You don't want to meet at the newsroom?'

'Uh-uh.' He was whispering now. 'How about the coffee shop you go to? The arty one.'

There was an edge to his voice – excitement, nervousness.

He'd found something.

Harper set down her coffee so hard it splashed.

'Pangaea? Sure. When?'

'Half an hour?'

'No problem,' she said calmly. 'See you there.'

By the time he hung up, she was running to the bedroom to finish dressing.

When Harper walked into the coffee shop twenty minutes later, DJ was already there, sitting alone at a table in the far corner under a painting of unidentifiable blue squiggles, a double cappuccino in front of him.

She ordered a large, black coffee and walked over to join him.

'Hey,' she said. 'This isn't usually your place.'

'I thought it would be nice.' His voice was even but, under the table, one of his legs was jittering.

'Uh-huh. Enough already. What's up with all the subterfuge?'

She blew on her coffee, watching him carefully. He was so nervous, she needed to exude calm to keep him from bouncing out of his chair.

DJ's eyes skittered around the room. The place was busy with a lunchtime crowd of twenty-somethings, most glued to their laptops or smart phones, angling their bodies to block the sun pouring through the tall windows from their screens. A bossa nova tune oozed out of the speakers.

'Nobody's paying attention to us,' she assured him. 'You can talk.'

DJ took a deep breath. 'You know how you asked me to go back to the college and nose around, see what else I could turn over about Marie Whitney? Well, I went back over there this morning and talked to some people in her office. They told me more about the guys. About her. I heard all kinds of crazy things.'

He leaned forward, moving his coffee out of the way.

'Colleges are incredibly gossipy places, and most of it's usually bullshit. But, the way people were talking, it sounded like there was something to this. They said she had a reputation for liking danger-ous sex. She particularly liked seducing other women's husbands. From what people were telling me it's like...' he paused. 'It's like Whitney enjoyed messing with people's heads. The impression I got was she enjoyed hurting people.'

Harper watched him closely.

'And you believed them? The people who said this stuff?'

'The women I talked to, they were genuinely emotional about her. It was hard not to believe them,' he said. 'Everything they told me – it was so consistent. Some people were really afraid of her.'

Harper rubbed her forehead. Her image of Marie Whitney, a martyred mother so like her own, was growing hazy, replaced by Marie Whitney, swinging sex goddess. Destroyer of marriages.

'This is so weird,' she said. 'Her whole profile is this together businesswoman. A single mother, raising her kid. Now you're telling me she was this sociopathic man-hunter.'

'She can be both,' DJ pointed out. 'I think maybe she was both.'

Harper had covered many crimes where a jealous ex killed his former wife, or where a betrayed woman gunned down her replacement. But that didn't fit the scene she'd seen in that kitchen.

'Whitney's death wasn't a crime of passion,' she said flatly.

He frowned. 'How do you know?'

'I saw...' She stopped herself just in time. 'I saw the reports on the murder. The crime scene was neat and orderly. The killer didn't leave a single fingerprint. Not even a hair. It was carefully planned and perfectly executed. Passion crimes are a *mess*. Those killers aren't thinking, they're reacting. They trash the place, leave evidence everywhere. They're tantrum killings.'

She paused, seeing Whitney's body. Camille's tearful face. That orderly kitchen.

'This was cold-blooded. Ruthless.'

'Well,' DJ said. 'That's where this other thing might come in.'

Harper's eyes shot up to meet his. 'What other thing?'

'Remember how I heard she liked powerful men?'

Harper nodded.

'I was talking to the receptionist in the office where she worked,' he said. 'She said she saw Whitney holding hands with a guy with a badge a few months before she died. He wasn't wearing a uniform, though. He was in a suit. But he was obviously a cop.' He looked at her. 'Harper, doesn't that mean Whitney was dating a detective?'

Harper stared at him – her pulse began to race.

Nobody – not one cop – had mentioned Whitney was involved with a police officer.

'Wait,' she said, forcing herself to think it through. 'It could be. Or it could be a rent-a-cop. A security guard. Those guys sometimes dress a lot like detectives.'

'I thought about that, too,' he conceded. 'And I said that to her. But she said she asked Whitney if he was a cop. And she smiled and said, "I love a man with a badge."'

'That's not a yes,' Harper said.

'This source, she said it was. She took it as a yes.'

'Damn,' Harper swore. 'I wish she'd said yes or no.'

Under the table, DJ's leg shook anxiously.

'Harper, if it is a cop, this just got really dangerous.'

'Yeah,' she said. 'And *very* interesting.'

'No, seriously, Harper.' He shot her a look. 'These guys aren't going to let you write about a detective who maybe killed someone. And, look,' he shifted in his seat, 'odds are it's unrelated, right? She went out with this guy three months ago, nothing came of it, they broke up. This receptionist told me Whitney hadn't been spotted with this cop in months. But if, say, a cop was involved, and he murdered a woman...' Behind his glasses his brown eyes locked on hers. 'He'll gun for you before he lets you expose him.'

His worry was contagious. Harper swallowed hard.

She pushed back against the nerves.

'Come on, DJ.' She forced a light tone. 'It's not like I'll stroll up to a detective and say, "I know you did it." Give me some credit.'

He watched her steadily, choosing his words carefully.

'I guess you know what you're doing,' he said after a moment. 'But, still. You have to be careful this time, Harper.'

'I'm always careful,' she said. 'Now, what did your receptionist friend know about this detective? Could she identify him?'

'She doesn't know his name,' DJ said apologetically. 'Apparently he never came into the office. She saw him from a distance. Tall – over six feet. In his late forties. Light hair – blond or salt and pepper.' He paused. 'Oh, and she said he had scary eyes. Whatever that means.'

The sounds of the coffee shop receded. The music, the conversation – all hushed.

Harper could think of only one detective who fit that description. And he was investigating Whitney's murder.

Detective Larry Blazer.

Chapter Eighteen

In the newsroom that afternoon, Harper went through the paces of a normal day. She wrote up short pieces on the day's crime for the back pages, and made a few calls. All the time her mind was going over and over the things DJ had told her.

By the time she finished, the newsroom was empty. Baxter was in a meeting with the copy desk. She was alone.

Pulling out her notepad, she sketched out everything she knew about Whitney, Blazer and her mother. It barely filled a page.

Whitney had a complex sexual background, with multiple partners. She was resented by many wounded ex-wives and girlfriends, and the wrecked men she left in her wake. Any one of them could have motive to kill her. She also may have, as recently as a few months ago, been dating a detective who looked like Blazer.

Her own mother, as far as she was aware, had no such sexual proclivities. She was in an unhappy marriage but she seemed loyal.

Seemed.

Harper tapped the pen softly on the notepad.

Her dad had been cheating on her mother when she died – was

she aware of that? Did she consider finding someone of her own, as revenge, or to soothe her wounded pride?

Could that person be the one who killed her?

The idea of Blazer as a roving psychopath on the lookout for lonely, beautiful women in Savannah, fifteen years apart, seemed too much of a stretch.

Still, Harper made a tentative note: 'Did Mom cheat on Dad?'

After a second, though, she scratched the words out roughly. Even writing it felt disloyal.

She'd been so young when her mother died, their relationship was frozen forever at the time when she was twelve. Her father had been away a lot for work, so it was her mother she'd turned to for advice, for help. They'd never had a chance to grow apart; find their independence. Share adult confidences.

For the first time it occurred to her that she actually knew very little about her.

She was so lost in reverie that Baxter's sharp voice jolted her.

'What are you doing? Waiting for the newspaper to write itself?'

The editor stood at the front of the newsroom, looking at her from across the banks of empty desks. Outside, the sun had set while Harper was lost in thought. The windows reflected back her own image – oval face pale, her hair tangled. She looked tired.

Reaching for her scanner, Harper said, 'I'm waiting for the shooting to start.'

Right on cue, her scanner crackled. 'All units, we have a report of Signal Nine at Broward Street and East Avenue. Be advised we've had multiple calls from witnesses. Ambulance is dispatched.'

'There you go,' Harper said. 'First shooting of the evening.'

'You are making this up,' Baxter said accusingly.

'You heard the lady.' Standing, Harper gathered her things. 'They're sending an ambulance.'

'This is witchcraft,' Baxter grumbled.

Ignoring her, Harper hooked her scanner on her waistband and grabbed her notebook, flipping pages until the lines about her mother disappeared.

Somehow the thought of going to a shooting scene was cheering. This was exactly what she needed – something straightforward and immediate. No baggage. Just a gun, a bullet wound and a story to tell.

'Is Miles on it?' Baxter asked.

Harper headed across the newsroom. 'I'll call him from the car.'

The Camaro was parked outside the front door. Harper slid into the driver's seat and put the scanner on the dash. The engine started with a rumble of pure power.

Putting her phone on speaker, she dialed Miles' number. To her surprise, it went straight to voicemail.

Harper's message was terse: 'Shooting on Broward. Baxter wants you there. I'm on my way.'

As she dropped the phone on to the passenger seat, she frowned.

Miles always picked up.

Broward Street was on the south side of town, not far from where the shooting had occurred the other night. In normal traffic you would get there in fifteen minutes. Harper covered the distance at speeds that were not at all legal, and saw the flashing blue lights ahead of her in ten.

Parking the Camaro a block from the scene, she half-ran the rest of the way.

It was an uncomfortably warm night – the pavement had soaked up the sun all day and was still pumping out the last of that heat. The air had a harsh smell of exhaust and overcooked garbage.

Two ambulances were parked at rough angles to the curb, blocking the road; four police cars were clustered in front of them.

A crowd of about thirty onlookers had gathered on the sidewalk, watching the action.

'I said get back,' a sweating patrol officer shouted at the crowd as she walked up. 'Take three giant steps back. Or else.'

Skirting the group, Harper slipped around the side to see what was happening.

Two men lay on ambulance gurneys. Both wore baggy, knee-length shorts and T-shirts, both were young and skinny, and both had the same shocked expression. Like until this moment they simply hadn't believed bullets worked.

Paramedics bustled around, strapping them to tubes and bags, cutting their shirts open to get at their wounds.

'Damn,' Harper heard a teenage boy say in the crowd. 'That's a hundred-dollar shirt.'

Her eyebrows shot up.

Now, the reason a guy would wear a hundred-dollar shirt in a neighborhood where weekly rent was only slightly more than that was pretty clear.

Harper eased her way over to the boy who'd spoken.

'Hi,' she said brightly. 'I'm a reporter from the *Daily News*. Did you see what happened?'

He studied her from beneath a lowered brow. Seeing only a woman holding a pen, he shrugged.

'Everybody saw it. They was fightin' in the street. Then they started shootin'.'

'Who were they fighting with?' Harper asked.

'Each other!' the reply came from three people at once.

Harper looked around the crowd. 'What? Those two guys got in a fight and shot each other?'

'Yes.' A small black woman with gray hair pushed her way through the crowd to reach Harper. 'Those two have been nothing but trouble for months. I called the police and they didn't do a thing. This was bound to happen.'

Her spine was as straight as a dancer's as she peered at Harper through glittering glasses. 'Are you the police? Because we called many times.'

The crowd around her nodded and murmured.

'I'm not the police, ma'am,' Harper said politely. 'I'm a journalist.'

'Journalist.' The woman looked, if anything, less pleased about this. 'From the newspaper?'

'Yes.'

'The newspaper ignored it, too.' The woman announced this condemningly.

'I'm sorry about that,' she said. 'Could you tell me now? Who are they?'

'Boy on the left is Jarrod Jones,' the teenage boy offered before the woman could reply.

'Other one's Lashon Williams,' someone else said.

Harper made quick notes.

'And you say they've been fighting?' Harper looked around, encouraging more.

'They've been fighting for six months,' the elderly lady informed her disapprovingly. 'One says this is his block. The other says it's his. Back and forth. Back and forth. I told the police someone was going to end up dead.'

'Tonight it all kicked off,' the teenage boy explained, with a hint of delight.

This was all Harper needed.

'Thanks very much,' she said, making the last of her notes. 'Could I use your names in my story?'

The crowd recoiled.

'Hell no.' The boy looked so horrified she might as well have asked if she could boil him alive.

'I can't believe you would even ask that,' the elderly woman admonished.

There was something so authoritative about her demeanor, Harper found herself backpedaling.

'I'm sorry,' she said. 'I didn't mean...'

'For heaven's sake,' the woman said, shaking her head.

The crowd of onlookers seemed suddenly less friendly.

'She's trying to get people in trouble,' someone muttered, and the others agreed with growing enthusiasm.

Still muttering apologies, Harper beat a tactical retreat, trying to fade into the shadows. When she'd left the crowd behind, she made her way closer to the crime scene, where the two victims/criminals were being treated.

Standing to one side, she squinted at the scene, cast in sharp relief by flashing blue lights.

On the sidewalk, two bloodstains darkened the paving no more than five feet apart.

The crowd was right – it looked like they'd shot each other at point-blank range.

'Harper!' Clad in green scrubs, a clear, plastic IV tube in one hand, Toby jumped out of the back of the ambulance and bounded over to her like a man-shaped puppy. 'Look at me, back on the night shift.'

She eyed him dubiously. 'Did you hijack the ambulance? Does anyone know you're here? Should I tell the police?'

'No stealing was involved,' he assured her amiably. 'I put myself on the replacement rota and someone called in sick tonight.'

He held up his arms, the tube dangling from his hand.

'I'm beating the system.'

'You're insane, Toby,' she said, but her tone was indulgent.

'Yeah, in a good way, though. Right?'

'Right...' She gestured at the two victims. 'Hey, is it true these guys shot each other?'

'Hells to the yeah,' he enthused, pointing at the gurneys. 'You're looking at a real-life circular firing squad. Genius on the left thought genius on the right was invading his drug territory, so he pulled his gun. Genius on the right already had his gun in his hand. They fired at the same time.'

'Anyone else hurt?'

He shook his head. 'This is what you call divine justice, my friend.'

A paramedic working on the one on the left signaled to Toby.

'Hang on a minute,' he told her. 'I'll be right back.'

Harper stood to one side while he raced over to connect the IV to the cannula in the man's arm.

A minute later, he returned, snapping blue rubber gloves from his hands.

'Is he going to live?' Harper asked.

'Oh, yeah,' he said, shrugging. 'He's leaking now, but he'll stop.'

With dizzying speed, he changed subjects, nudging her with his shoulder.

'Hey, you and Walker disappeared from the party last night.' His tone was arch. 'Is there something going on there that I should definitely know about?'

Harper winced. So, they had been spotted.

'No, Toby.' She kept her tone uninterested, with a touch of irritation. 'We left at the same time. Nothing more.'

Grinning, he nudged her again, harder this time.

'Walker's good people, Harper. You could do worse.'

'I know that,' she snapped, hoping the grumpiness disguised the panic rising in her chest, 'but I'm not *doing* anyone.'

The gurneys jangled as the paramedics slid them onto the ambulances and braced them in place.

'Load up, Toby,' someone shouted at him.

He took a step back.

'Maybe you aren't. But I, for one, hope you are,' he said impishly. 'The man is pure sex. I'd do him myself but I don't swing that way. Besides, I'm taken.'

Jumping up into the open door of the ambulance, he flung out his arms and looked up at the dark sky.

'God, I've missed this.'

Seconds later, the shriek of its siren split the night and the ambulance pulled away from the curb. Its flashing blue lights lit up a group of officers who, up until now, had been hidden behind the emergency cars.

Right at the center of it was Detective Larry Blazer.

Harper's mouth went dry.

Deep in conversation, he hadn't noticed her yet. Taking a hurried step back into the shadows, she studied him with surreptitious interest.

She tried to imagine him dating Marie Whitney. Growing enraged at her. Killing her.

It didn't seem possible. And yet.

Normally, she'd ask him for a quote about the shooting, but tonight she turned and walked away. If there was even a slight possibility that Blazer was involved in the Whitney murder then there was also a possibility he was involved in her mother's murder.

She wasn't ready yet to pretend everything was fine.

She was nearly to her car when she spotted Miles standing under a streetlight, checking shots on his camera screen.

'Hey,' Harper said. 'Where have you been? Why didn't you return my texts?'

He looked up from his camera, unsmiling.

'I finally had a meeting with my coroner friend.' His tone was dark. 'We need to talk.'

'What have you got?' Harper asked.

She and Miles were sitting in the Mustang, a block from the crime scene. The only illumination came from the blue lights of the police cars in the distance. It gave everything a strobe-lit, unreal feel.

Miles hadn't turned on the air conditioner, and it was uncomfortably warm in the car. Harper was conscious of her top sticking to her back.

The scanner on the dash was on, but the sound was turned down so the uneven hum of voices formed a backdrop to their conversation.

'My coroner friend looked into the Whitney case,' he said. 'She told me some things didn't seem right.'

'Like what?'

'The scene was forensically clean,' he said. 'No fingerprints on any surfaces. Everything was pristine. Even Whitney's hands had been cleaned.'

Harper frowned. 'Her hands?'

He nodded. 'Someone had wiped her hands down, even swabbed under her fingernails. Her skin smelled of rubbing alcohol – my friend said it appeared he even cleaned her face.'

Harper didn't know what to think.

'Is that normal?'

He shook his head. 'My coroner friend has never seen it before in her entire career.'

'The detectives are saying it looks like a professional killer,' she said.

'This must be why.' Miles shifted in his seat, turning to face her. 'Get this – Whitney was naked when her daughter found her, but clothing fibers were found inside her wounds.'

Harper's forehead creased. 'What does that mean?'

'It means she was wearing clothes when she was killed,' he explained. 'But the killer took them when he left.'

The skin on the back of Harper's neck prickled.

'Whatever you're thinking,' she said. 'Say it.'

His eyes met hers.

'Harper, as far as I can understand it, everything the coroner would normally use in their investigation is missing. Clothes gone, weapon gone, victim's hands cleaned, nails scrubbed, face wiped. The killer even wore surgical shoe covers so he'd leave no prints in the blood.'

Harper felt oddly calm – like she'd already known this was what he had to tell her. Everything was pointing in one direction.

'No ordinary killer would know what forensics would look for,' Miles concluded. 'This guy knew everything.'

Harper looked down the street at the flickering blue lights.

'Like a cop,' she said softly.

'Like a cop,' he repeated.

She turned to him. 'There's something I have to tell you.'

Quickly, she explained what DJ had learned at the college, including the description of the man wearing a badge. She didn't tell him who that description reminded her of, though. She wanted to see if he would draw his own conclusions.

When she finished, Miles sat back in his seat.

The scanner crackled with ambulance dispatches, police checking in, a burglary on East 27th Street.

'It sounds like Blazer,' he said finally.

Harper was surprised by how relieved this made her feel. She wasn't going crazy.

'Or it could be someone else,' he continued, a cautioning note in his voice. 'We can't draw conclusions. Lots of jobs give you a cheap suit and a badge. It could be a security guard.'

'A security guard who knows to swab her face?' Harper asked, her voice rising. 'To take her clothes? To clean under her nails? To wear *shoe covers*?'

Tension sharpened her tone.

'He would be the best damn rent-a-cop in America today.'

'I hear you,' he said calmly. 'I'm just saying, we can't jump to conclusions. There are a lot of factors at play here.'

Seeing her rebellious expression he held up one hand.

'But,' he said. 'Yes. This looks like a cop. Or like someone who really knows police business damn well. And that is not good.'

'No,' she agreed. 'It's not.'

He stared through the windshield. 'You feel like this is something you could take to your buddy Smith?'

Harper shook her head hard.

'They're friends,' she said. 'They're both cops.'

There was no need to say more.

Heavy silence filled the car like water.

Harper felt lost. Where did she go from here? She'd never investigated the police for something like this. Everything she knew about rogue cops she'd learned from movies – they were dangerous. They were out of control. People got killed investigating them.

'Now that you know more,' Miles said, glancing at her, 'you still think the same guy that killed Whitney killed your mother?'

Harper had been thinking about this all day, and she still didn't have a great answer.

'Maybe.' She could hear the doubt in her own voice. 'I need to know more before I can be sure about anything. All I have are my memories. I need to get my hands on the original crime reports from my mother's case. See how those compare with what we know about the Whitney murder.'

'Most of those records aren't public,' he reminded her. 'You can only see the original incident report.'

'I'll find a way.' Twisting in her seat, she turned until she was facing him. 'But, Miles, what if it is Blazer? I mean...' she paused. 'Let's say it *is* him. What the hell are we going to do then?'

Across the shadowy car, their eyes locked. The worry in his face mirrored her own.

'I don't have an answer to that,' he said. 'But I know this case is very dangerous. Are you ready for this, Harper?'

At the end of road the police were packing up their cars, tearing the crime tape from the light posts, closing the scene. She could see the shadowy figures hurriedly preparing to move on to the next shooting. The next stabbing.

The swirling blue lights switched off one by one.

By the time she spoke, the street was dark again.

'I have to be ready.'

Chapter Nineteen

The next day at four o'clock, when Harper arrived at police headquarters, only a handful of people lingered in the lobby, waiting for appointments.

Her steps felt stiff and careful, but she tried to keep her expression neutral. If she looked strange, no one seemed to notice.

She passed two traffic cops she knew, helmets tucked under their arms, mirrored sunglasses hooked to the top buttons of their dark blue uniforms.

'Hey, McClain,' one said.

She waved and said something pleasant she couldn't remember a second later. It was a hot day, but she felt strangely cold as she slowed her steps, waiting until the two were out of the building before continuing on to the reception desk.

She forced her facial muscles to smile cheerfully when she reached the front desk.

'Well, Harper McClain.' Darlene eyed her with interest. 'What's got you all bright-eyed and bushy-tailed?'

'Oh, nothing,' Harper said brightly. 'I'm just thrilled to be at work.'

'Mm-hmm.' Darlene's voice dripped sarcasm. 'Ain't it great?'

Sliding the police report folder over to her, she leaned her elbows against the desk.

Harper opened it and forced herself to focus on the words in front of her as nerves fluttered in her stomach.

Burglary, burglary, burglary, sexual assault, gunshots reported, gunshots reported, noise disturbance, burglary, burglary, burglary...

Pulling out the sexual assault report and two armed robberies, she busied herself making notes.

'Harper.' Darlene tapped a page with a long, multi-hued nail. 'I've been hearing some gossip about you.'

Harper's heart sank. Still, she kept her head down and her tone dismissive.

'Oh great. What has the rumor mill got on me this time?'

'Something about that murder last week. The lady from the college.'

Harper looked up at her. 'What about it?'

Darlene lowered her voice. 'They're saying you spied on the crime scene with one of those telephoto lenses, and the lieutenant was not happy about it. Even the deputy chief got involved. Is it true?'

The muscles in Harper's shoulders relaxed.

'Now, Darlene,' she chided, resuming her note-taking. 'Does that sound like me?'

'Yes, ma'am.' Darlene nodded.

'Then it's probably true. But it wasn't so much me as Miles, and how am I supposed to control an inspired photographer?'

'That Miles.' Darlene's voice took on a dreamy tone. 'He's a long drink of cool water, isn't he?'

'Mmph.' Harper kept her response vague.

'A *photographer*,' Darlene continued wistfully. 'A true artist. And a gentleman, as well. Every time he's in here he's so polite and patient.'

She stared down the long lobby.

'You should tell him I'm single,' she announced suddenly.

Harper gave this serious consideration.

'I'll do that,' she said.

The conversation took the edge off her nerves. By the time she finished making her notes and slid the blotter back to Darlene, she was ready.

She stopped, mid-move, as if a thought had struck her.

'Oh, by the way, I'm working on an article about old crimes – murders from ten, fifteen years ago. Even older. A kind of retrospective.' She blinked at Darlene hopefully. 'Where could I get my hands on some old crime reports? You know, the big cases. The ones that really made headlines back in the day.'

Darlene, busy putting the folder back in its holder, barely glanced at her.

'Well, those are in the archive, down in the basement,' she said. 'Haven't you been down there?'

Harper had been to the archive many times. She'd worked down there as an intern. She also knew perfectly well that journalists needed approval from the deputy chief to go down there.

What she was banking on was that Darlene didn't know that.

'Oh yeah. How could I forget?' Giving a wry smile, Harper shook her head. 'Could you buzz me through?'

'No problem, honey.' The phone at Darlene's elbow began

ringing, and she reached for it. 'Head on down. Good afternoon, Front Desk...'

Casually, Harper crossed to the security door. She kept her steps unhurried – betraying none of the tension she felt. Like it was any other day.

Still chatting on the phone, Darlene buzzed her through without looking up.

When Harper told Miles she intended to get her hands on the old records, he hadn't pressed her on how she was going to get them.

This was how.

The long, windowless corridor leading past the detectives' offices was busy at this hour. She joined the flow of uniformed cops, detectives and assistants going about their work. She'd been back here many times – there was no reason for anyone to mind.

Still, anxiety swirled in Harper's stomach as she passed the 911 room. One of the dispatchers spotted her through the window and waved, still talking into her headset.

Harper lifted a hand in reply and hurried away, lowering her gaze.

About halfway down the corridor between reception and the lieutenant's office was a wide, utilitarian staircase. Relief coursing through her body, she turned into it and dashed down the stairs.

When she reached the basement level, she paused.

From this point on, she was breaking the rules.

The police department required all civilians to be escorted at the basement level. For good reason. There were holding cells down here, as well as weapons storage rooms. This was a high-security area.

It was often busy. All she could hope for was that the same

dynamic that had just played out upstairs would happen again. Nobody thought of her as a normal civilian.

Squaring her shoulders, she turned right, down the narrow concrete hallway.

Almost immediately, three uniformed patrol officers emerged from the men's changing room right ahead.

Harper's heart began to pound.

She kept her eyes straight ahead, her stride confident. But she knew that wasn't enough. Surely one of them would stop her and demand to know what she was doing down here.

They were deep in conversation, and none of them noticed her until they drew close.

One of them – middle-aged, balding, with a bit of a paunch artfully disguised by his heavily laden utility belt – looked up and caught her eye. His brow creased.

Harper's mouth went dry.

He had the alert, narrow gaze of someone born to be a cop.

'Oh,' the officer said, smiling, 'I'm sorry, ma'am.' Turning, he motioned to the others. 'Make room for the lady, will you?'

They squeezed to one side, waiting for her to pass.

Harper's frozen lips somehow formed a polite grimace.

'Thank you,' she said hoarsely.

But they had already forgotten her.

'You get that same unit again? They fixed the brakes yet?' one of them asked.

'No,' the balding one said, glumly flipping his hat in his hands. 'I think the sergeant might be trying to kill me.'

'Well, just stick a foot out when you need to stop,' someone suggested.

Their laughter echoed as they turned into the staircase.

Harper let out a breath and hurried her pace, hurtling past the changing rooms, from which emanated the faint scent of masculine body wash (chemical pine and something like cloves) and the sound of showers splashing. Then around a sharp corner.

She was half-running by the time she reached the archive room.

The door swung open at her touch.

A vast, warehouse-like space sprawled in front of her. With a concrete floor and rough walls, the harshly lit room held long rows of cardboard boxes stacked on open steel shelves that reached the ceiling.

By law, basic police incident reports are public information. The police are required to show them to the press and any member of the public who requests them. These brief forms were the documents the police kept on the front counter for Harper to look through every day.

Police investigation files are a different matter altogether.

These are lengthy – sometimes dozens of pages long. They contain information compiled by detectives and forensics investigators over weeks, even months of work. They include crime scene photos, interviews with suspects and witnesses, all their research – a play-by-play handbook for each major crime.

These are not shown to anybody.

And they were all stored in this room.

Each box held all that remained of weeks, months, even years of police work. Cases investigated down to the molecular level and then filed away, solved or unsolved, in cardboard boxes in this chilly, ugly, harshly lit room.

All the boxes were labeled with a series of numbers and letters and a barcode. That was it. No names, no dates.

The system was ruthlessly logical and impenetrable.

The box she was looking for would be easy to find... as long as she knew the box number... Which she didn't.

She hadn't dared ask Darlene for case numbers, as that would have raised attention she didn't want. Without a case number, she'd have to open thousands of boxes.

Unless.

At the center of the room, a single computer sat alone on top of a metal desk.

Once upon a time, there would have been an archivist in charge of all these files. That person would have handled locating boxes – making sure everything that was removed was put back. That person would have taken one look at Harper and called the lieutenant.

Luckily, that person got laid off a long time ago.

When she touched the mouse, the screen lit up, and a Savannah PD badge filled the center of the blue screen. The legend beneath it read 'To protect and to serve'. At the bottom of the screen was a narrow box and the command: 'Enter ID'.

Harper put her hands on the keys and hesitated, trying to remember a series of numbers and letters she hadn't used in a very long time.

When she'd interned for the department, she'd been issued a police ID number so she could work in the system. Police computers timed out anytime they went unused for more than five minutes, so she'd had to enter that code about a thousand times a day. It was in her memory somewhere.

What she didn't know for sure was whether or not it would work.

The police IT department was small and over-worked. Issuing new ID numbers and deleting old ones from the system was one of those jobs that tended to get overlooked. In fact, the department often reused old ID numbers from former workers rather than go through the hassle of requesting a new one. That's what they'd done when she worked there. She'd never had a new ID number – instead she'd used the number of some guy who hadn't worked there in years. If she was right, nobody would ever have bothered to delete that ID from the system.

The only problem was, she wasn't sure she could remember it. Also, there was always the chance they might have cleared out the system at some point in the intervening years.

The only way to find out was to try.

Closing her eyes she imagined typing the number without thinking about it. Fingers moving without any planning.

She tried to clear her memory of her work login, her email passwords, her banking passwords – all the clutter of modern computing.

815NL52K1

Holding her breath, she hit 'enter'.

For a second the PC churned. Then the image on the screen changed to a white background fronted by the message: 'Welcome Craig Johnson'.

Harper gave a triumphant air-punch.

Good old Craig.

Her euphoria was short-lived, though. Because, from this point on, she was breaking the law.

It took her a few minutes to remember how the police system was arranged, but it came back to her. Hunched over the computer, she worked with nervous speed, constantly listening for footsteps in the hallway outside or voices that could be heading her way.

After what seemed like a lifetime she found the records section and typed in 'McClain, Alicia'.

Instantly, a folder appeared, the cursor blinking beside it methodically.

Taking a deep breath, Harper clicked on it. The folder opened to reveal dozens of files.

None of the file names made sense, so she started at the top, opening each one. The first few were random bits of paperwork – scanned in notes that had long ago lost their meanings and other routine paperwork.

She clicked on file after file until at last she found what she wanted: 'Official Case Report HOMICIDE McClain, Alicia'.

Pulling her notebook out of her pocket, she read the file rapidly, letting words jump out at her. Deceased. Stab wounds. Assailant unknown. Weapon not recovered. Her old address. She scribbled quick notes, fingers cold on her pen.

Then the screen filled with sickening images – photograph after photograph of her old kitchen. The table where she'd eaten Cheerios for breakfast shoved violently to one side. The chair where she'd sat, upended. A naked, pale body lying face down on the floor, one hand flung out in a silent plea.

Exactly as she'd remembered it. Exactly like Marie Whitney.

Harper made herself look at it. Forced herself to look for anything she had missed then.

She could see signs of herself there – the long mark where her sneakers had skidded in the blood. But there was nothing there – not one thing – that wasn't already branded on her mind forever.

She closed the file.

The next file held more emotionless description of horror, and a mention of herself ('Body found by daughter, Harper, 12').

She scanned it quickly, pausing on two lines. 'No fingerprints at the scene.' And then, a side note: 'Coroner reports clothing removed posthumously.'

Her heart jumped.

She read the words again and again.

Clothing removed posthumously.

That was precisely like Marie Whitney. Precisely.

Surely this was proof?

Somehow, though, the knowledge didn't make the situation any clearer.

What more did the detectives need? How could they say the two cases weren't connected?

They couldn't. It was a lie. They were protecting someone.

Protecting Blazer.

She was clicking through the last of the files when she heard voices approaching the door.

Swearing under her breath, she fumbled with the mouse, rushing to close the files, trying desperately to remember how to log out of the system.

'Please, please, please...' she whispered, as she frantically clicked on everything until finally finding the option buried in the menu.

As soon as the files disappeared, and with the computer still churning, she jumped away from the desk and dashed between the long rows of boxes.

The voices were drawing nearer. A deep male rumble of words she couldn't quite make out over the hammering of her heart.

Pressing herself back into the shadows, Harper searched her brain for an excuse. She'd only come in here looking for a file. She hadn't found it. She was sorry.

The voices were right outside the door now. She dug her fingers into the cold steel shelf behind her.

And then ... they kept going.

Whoever it was walked by the archive and continued down towards the armory. The sounds gradually faded.

Harper sagged back against the nearest box until her panicked breathing returned to normal.

Then she grabbed her notebook and started looking for her mother's records.

Most of what she'd needed had been on the computer, but she had to know everything now. Everything the police knew.

Using the case file number she'd acquired from the computer, she soon found the box she sought on the fourth row at the back of the room, on the middle shelf. Plain manila cardboard, exactly like the others, with no name.

Gingerly, Harper slid it towards her. It was disturbingly light. She'd imagined it filled with the heavy weight of a long murder investigation, but she pulled it from the shelf easily and set it on the floor.

Kneeling next to it, she carefully lifted the lid.

As the lightness of it indicated, it was only half full. Mostly it held papers – originals of the documents she'd already seen on the computer.

Beneath those, a stack of plastic envelopes contained evidence collected at the house.

Harper lifted them out, examining each one. A broken plate, some old envelopes. Unexpectedly, her own white tennis shoes, stained brown with blood.

She'd always wondered what happened to them.

In an instant, she could remember the last time she'd seen them. Sitting on a plastic chair at the police station. Someone kneeling in front of her, swabbing her hands, unlacing her shoes.

Smith had sent an officer out to get a new pair. She'd been in such a daze she'd barely understood what was happening as the unfamiliar shoes – stiff and uncomfortable – were slipped onto her feet.

'Where are my shoes?' she'd asked.

'We have to keep them,' Smith told her. 'But these are better.'

Now, as she turned the plastic bag in her hands she saw that, true to his word, he had kept them all these years.

Reluctantly, Harper set the shoes down and turned her attention to the box. There was only one plastic bag left.

This one held her mother's paintbrushes.

Her throat felt suddenly tight.

They were so familiar. Her mother used only one brand of brushes, with plain, unvarnished wooden handles. She was always leaving them around the house – in the living room. In the bathroom.

They were as much a part of her as her skin, her hair.

Harper held the bag holding the brushes up to the light – two of the brushes had dried paint on the bristles, caked and flaking – vivid vermilion, and pure white.

She couldn't imagine why the police would have been taken these for evidence. Maybe her mother had been using them when the killer arrived. Perhaps she'd dropped them at the scene.

Either way, she hated that they'd ended up here, in a cardboard box, on row four of twelve beneath a cold fluorescent light.

She had to force herself to put the bag aside. But she'd come here to see everything, and she wasn't going to stop looking now.

She dug through the rest of the box, increasingly aware that she was pushing her luck staying in here so long.

At the bottom of the box was a short stack of random pieces of paper.

Kneeling on the hard concrete, her knees beginning to ache, Harper skimmed the pages quickly, her bottom lip caught between her teeth.

Several of them were cover notes that had accompanied forensic evidence from the crime scene to the detectives to forensics. The last one was an official forensics request form that had accompanied blood samples sent for further testing. It was dated one month after her mother's murder.

The terse, handwritten instructions on the form read: *RI-check blood type/DNA.*

The handwriting was spidery and narrow, written with a strong, left-hand slant.

The signature at the bottom was clear and unmistakable: *Larry Blazer.*

Chapter Twenty

When Harper returned to the newsroom half an hour later, it was empty except for Baxter, who was typing furiously.

'You got anything?' the editor called without looking up.

'Nothing much,' Harper said, heading straight to her desk.

She hoped her confused emotions didn't show on her face. The last thing she wanted was Baxter getting curious.

But her editor was too involved in whatever she was writing to notice the stiff set of Harper's shoulders, or the terse tone of her response.

That signature had jarred her. Despite everything, until she'd seen that name, she'd doubted her own theory.

It simply seemed too unlikely that Blazer could be the killer. Or any cop she'd ever met.

Now, though, after everything she'd learned in the last twenty-four hours, things felt different.

Still, she knew she needed to calm down. To think rationally. To make her case.

Pulling out her notebook, she flipped to a clean sheet.

What did she have?

She wrote down:

Murder scene professional – killer knew how cops work
Blazer connected to investigation of both murders
Blazer possibly associated with Marie Whitney before
her death
If true: Blazer covered up his connections to Whitney

Her pen paused above the paper as she tried to summon more facts that might point to Blazer.

There weren't any.

When she wrote it down like that, it didn't look like much. In fact, it didn't look like anything at all. Nothing connected him to her mother – not one thing.

It seemed as if each piece of evidence she found left her more suspicious of Blazer, and yet nothing came together as a cohesive case. There was no killer proof here.

She needed something absolutely solid. And she didn't have it.

In fact, what did she really know about Blazer?

She knew he was a detective, he'd risen through the ranks fairly smoothly, he was close to Smith. Some saw him as next in line for head detective.

Beyond that, though, she knew almost nothing. She didn't know anything about his personal life. Was he married? Kids?

The realization steadied her. This, she could work on.

Logging into the computer database, she searched for his name.

Hundreds of articles came up. Many of them by her, others by the former police reporter, Tom Lane.

Most detectives avoid the glare of media attention. Being an unknown entity is important when you're questioning a killer – the less they know about you, the more dangerous you seem. But Blazer wasn't like that.

He liked being interviewed – particularly by TV reporters. He'd walked right by Harper at crime scenes on more than one occasion, and presented himself to the cluster of TV cameras – hair perfectly combed, tie dead straight.

Most of the articles were quotes about crime cases, brief and to the point. She found nothing personal. Not a word about his background, his age, his education.

For that, she'd need access to police records. And as soon as she started poking around there, word would get out.

Dropping her pen, she raked her fingers through her hair.

Normally, Lieutenant Smith was the first person she'd call on something like this. She trusted him to be honest. But he'd known Blazer for twenty years. How could she tell him she thought his friend might be the psychopath who murdered her mother?

Besides, his reaction when she'd merely suggested the same person killed Whitney and her mother had been so negative, she couldn't imagine him receiving this latest theory of hers positively.

Leaning back in her chair, she turned to the window. Night had fallen. On the river, a container ship sailed slowly by, lights blazing. The ship was enormous, dwarfing the riverfront buildings so completely that, for a moment, it created the optical illusion that the ship was sitting still as the city sailed serenely away.

Out of nowhere, Camille Whitney's tear-stained face came into her mind. She wondered where she was. If someone was taking care of her. If she'd begun to understand how completely her life had changed.

On the desk, Harper's phone buzzed. Tearing her gaze away from the ship, she picked it up.

It held a text message from an unrecognized number:

Seems to me, we have some unfinished business.

Her brow creasing, Harper read the sentence twice.

It could have been from anyone. A source. Someone who read one of her articles in the paper and somehow tracked her down.

After a brief hesitation, she typed: 'Who is this?'

A second later, her phone buzzed again. There was just one word on the screen.

Luke

Harper's stomach flipped.

'Damn,' she whispered.

With the Whitney case occupying her waking hours, she'd mostly pushed him out of her mind. She'd convinced herself that he must regret taking that chance. Risking his job.

And she'd told herself she was fine with that.

Now, though, everything came back to her in a rush of heat – the feel of his body pressing against hers. The clean smell of him. The way his hands felt against her back.

'Damn,' she whispered again, turning the phone over in her hand.

The question was, with everything that was unfolding around her, did she want to get involved with Luke right now?

She was in the middle of a murder investigation – in the middle of something much bigger than she'd ever worked on before. She could be on the verge of solving the murder that had destroyed her life.

And yet.

The whole time she'd been with him that night, all thoughts

of murder and death and corruption had left her mind, for a few minutes.

There'd been nothing but heat and emotion and sensation.

It had been wonderful.

An image flashed through her memory of him, standing on the street, his gun trained over her shoulder at three armed men. A look of cold, protective fury in his eyes.

Heat flooded her body.

Before she could change her mind, she wrote a quick reply.

You know where to find me.

When she walked out of the newspaper building at midnight, some part of her expected Luke to be standing outside, waiting for her.

But the street was empty.

Harper hated how disappointed she felt.

That's why this is a bad idea, she chided herself. *This is a distraction. You have too much to do. There's no time for this.*

She should be thinking about the Whitney case, her mother, and how the hell she was going to do what she had to do.

Not about Luke.

Suddenly weary, she climbed into the Camaro and sat for a moment with her hands on the wheel, staring at the empty road ahead. A full minute ticked by before she started the engine.

All the way home she forced herself not to think about him. She would text him again when she got home. Tell him the truth.

They couldn't do this. She had too much at stake now.

By the time she pulled into her usual spot under the sheltering branches of an oak tree, her mind was made up. Grabbing her bag, she climbed out of the car and turned towards her house.

Only then did she see him.

Luke was leaning against the door of a black sports car. His arms were crossed casually across his chest. He wore jeans and a black T-shirt that accentuated the bulge of his biceps.

All her doubts evaporated like a warm breath on a cold night.

She crossed the street, her feet oddly light.

He watched her steadily. Waiting.

'This is a bad idea,' she told him, but her voice sounded unconvinced, even to her.

'Probably,' he said.

He reached for her hand.

His fingers were warm and strong. When he pulled her closer she didn't resist.

He tilted his head down towards her. His eyes were dark blue and she could see no doubt in them.

'It's the best bad idea I've had all day,' he said.

Then his mouth found hers.

This kiss was more demanding than the other night. More urgent. And she felt that same need in her whole body.

With a sigh, she pushed back against him, her lips teasing the corners of his mouth. Her tongue found the soft indention from some unknown injury, as she explored him without apology.

Her hands slid up his arms, across the hard muscles of his shoulders to tangle in the soft strands of his hair.

His breath hitched, his hands sliding down to her hips, pulling her against him.

The way their bodies moved together felt so natural, so familiar. As if they somehow fit.

Suddenly, Harper didn't care if the newspaper and the police department came down on them with a stack of rule books. If she was right about Blazer, her career in Savannah was probably over anyway. The police would never forgive her.

Smith would never forgive her.

Everything was about to fall apart. She could sense the tremors rattling the foundations of the life she'd carefully built for herself.

Couldn't she have this one thing first? Didn't she deserve this?

She drew back.

Luke searched her face. 'Harper?'

Nobody had ever said her name quite like he did. Like it meant something to him.

Harper's chest ached, like she'd been holding her breath for years. And at last she could breathe.

'Let's go inside.'

Chapter Twenty-one

When Harper woke late the next morning, Luke was gone.

His phone had rung shortly after three in the morning. There was a murmured conversation before he slipped from the room.

She'd been wide awake when he returned a few minutes later, dressed in his jeans, his T-shirt in one hand.

When he bent over to brush his lips lightly against hers she could smell the toothpaste mint on his breath.

'I have to go.'

For a second, she thought that, like last time, it was all he was going to say. But then he seemed to change his mind.

'One of my CIs managed to get himself arrested,' he explained, tracing a fingertip across the bare skin of her shoulder. 'I've got to go see if I can get him out before they lock him up.'

Harper knew how important confidential informants were to detectives. She also knew the fact that he'd told her was a sign of trust.

Stretching up, she pulled his head down until their lips met again, letting the sheet slip down to her waist. The kiss was passionate and lingering. His hand slid up to cup her breast.

'Dammit, Harper,' he whispered against her lips. 'You're not making this easy.'

With slow reluctance, he disentangled himself, crossing the room with a long, loping stride Harper thought she could pick out in a crowd of thousands.

In the bedroom doorway he stopped to look back, lips curving into a rueful half-smile.

'Now we really are in trouble.'

And then he was gone. She'd listened to his footsteps down the hall. The sound of the door unlocking and closing behind him with a muffled thud. A minute later, the rumble of the sports car's engine as it started and then faded away.

After that she'd stretched out on the bed, taking up as much of it as she wanted, and slept like a baby.

Now the sun sent strips of light through the blinds, striating the rumpled sheets.

Zuzu was nowhere to be seen.

With a sigh, Harper padded naked down the hall to the bathroom. While she waited for the shower to heat up, she reached for the toothpaste, only to find it wasn't where it should be.

She looked around the neat space, puzzled. Things had been moved. The toothpaste wasn't to the right of the sink where it always was. A damp washcloth had been put back in a different place from where she usually left it. The soap dish had a bit of water in it.

In the mirror above the sink, her reflection stared back at her – thoughtful hazel eyes with a smoky smudge of mascara beneath them, and tangled auburn hair around a pale, oval face.

Normally, this was the point where she started getting anxious about having someone in her house – someone touching her things. Getting too close.

She'd always been terrible at dating. Men didn't understand her life. Or they felt threatened by the fact that she spent most of her working day hanging out with cops. And she didn't like them in her house – moving things.

It was easier, in the end, not to do it.

There had been odd dates here and there, usually with men foisted on her by Bonnie. But it never came to anything.

There'd been the California graduate student two years ago. He'd charmed her with his surfer looks, all shaggy hair and tawny skin, but their lives had been so different. He taught classes on T.S. Eliot to sleepy-eyed undergrads, didn't believe in owning handguns, and found Harper's job bizarre.

'Show them your scanner,' he'd say, when they were out with his friends. And Harper would have to pull out her scanner so they could listen to the police.

'She's a cop-chaser,' he'd explain with an odd mixture of pride and distaste as they looked at her, wide-eyed.

She'd known he didn't understand her life. When he stayed over it felt like an invasion.

After a while she told him it wasn't working out, and that was that.

She'd never missed him.

Even if she'd wanted to, dating was nearly impossible when you worked from four in the afternoon until one in the morning. By the time Harper got off work, pretty much everyone who wasn't an alcoholic or a criminal was in bed.

Her options were largely limited to other journalists, police and paramedics. The police were (supposed to be) out of bounds. Journalists were hopeless. Paramedics were mostly married.

Which left pretty much nobody.

She'd preferred being alone, anyway. Fewer complications. Fewer distractions. Her job consumed not only her nights but, in some ways, her days as well.

Bonnie, however, disagreed. Vocally and frequently.

'You're not fooling anyone with this loner act,' she'd said more than once.

'It's not an act,' Harper would reply. 'I am actually a loner.'

But Bonnie wouldn't let go.

'God, Harper. There's more to life than work. Tell me you can see that.'

Harper never really had seen it, though.

Privacy mattered to her. It felt weird that Luke had spent half the night in her bed and used her washcloth and toothpaste.

Weird. But, to her surprise, not bad.

This was different.

The way he'd looked at her, with genuine tenderness – that had been real. The things they'd said to each other – the whispered words in the dark – those had been real, too.

Whatever barrier had kept them apart all these years, last night they'd knocked it down.

Luke had always been careful about what he told her – their friendship stopped at the door of the police station. When he disappeared on undercover jobs, it was pointless asking where he'd been.

Still, Harper had secrets of her own – things she chose never to discuss with anyone.

Last night there had been no secrets.

'Where did this come from?' she'd asked, running her fingertips across a long, narrow scar on his abdomen.

It had been after two in the morning and her head was on his chest. His fingers were in her hair. The night felt languid and limitless.

'I made someone angry,' he said. 'That someone happened to have a big knife.'

The only light in the room came through the window, from the streetlight outside, but Harper could see that while the scar was slick and healed, the edges were still tinged with red.

'This is recent.' She raised herself up to see his face.

He was watching her – his eyes dark. Somehow, she sensed he wanted her to ask the next question.

'Where were you? What happened?'

He'd stayed silent for so long she thought he wouldn't reply. But then...

'I was investigating a gang in the county, outside of town,' he said. 'They'd been supplying the projects for a while. Really pure product. Lots of it. I came in as a new supplier, who could hook them up with coke and pharmaceuticals.'

His fingers still stroked her hair gently but, with each word, she could feel him tensing beneath her; muscles coiling inward.

'Did they figure out you were a cop?' she asked.

'No. There was a guy who never liked me. One night he did too much sampling of his own product. Went for me without warning.' He put his hand over hers, pulling her fingers away from the scar. 'Things got hairy for a while. But it's not as bad as it looks.'

An image of him in some isolated farm, surrounded by thugs and bleeding, flashed in Harper's mind, and she shuddered.

'What happened to him?' she asked.

Luke let out a breath. 'The other guys went for him. They pulled him off me. Cut him up.' Seeing the look on her face he brushed her hair back. 'Don't worry – he survived. But barely. He got lucky.'

She touched the scar again. '*You* got lucky.'

'Can't argue with that,' he said.

'I still don't know why you moved to undercover,' she said. 'Do you like the work? Is it better than Homicide? Because it seems really awful.'

'It is awful.' His voice was tinged with self-loathing. 'And I don't like it. I hate it. The things we have to do undercover – you don't know, Harper. We have to live their life. We have to become what they are. It changes you. I think it's changing me.'

'What do you have to do?' she asked, a prickle of worry climbing her spine. 'What have you done?'

He seemed to stop breathing for a long moment, looking off into the darkness.

Then he shrugged, and she felt the moment pass. 'Nothing. I'm just... I'm tired, Harper. I'm not making sense.'

But she didn't want to let it go. Not yet.

'Why do you do it?' She raised herself up on her elbow to see him better. 'Why don't you move back to Homicide? You were so good at it, Luke. You're a natural.'

'It's not that simple.' His voice sharpened. 'You can't always have what you want. That's not how it works.'

Before she could ask what he meant, he pulled her closer.

'I don't want to talk about any of this stuff.' Wrapping her in his arms, he rolled them both over until he lay above her, looking down into her eyes.

'I want to do this.'

He kissed her then with such insistence and hunger Harper let it go.

But as she brushed her teeth, her thoughts kept returning to that moment.

One thing was clear. Whatever happened to him on that last job, it had left more scars than the one she'd seen.

He'd always been a by-the-books cop, so obsessed with rules his nickname among the detectives had been 'Robocop'.

That Luke would never have allowed last night to happen. And he certainly wouldn't have told her what happened on the job.

This new Luke took more chances. He went for what he wanted.

If she couldn't go to Smith about Blazer, maybe she could go to Luke? After all, he'd already offered to help with the Whitney case.

Involving him in her research would put dangerous pressure on what was happening between them. He might feel like she was using him. He would doubt her.

She couldn't tell him yet. Maybe later.

The one person she needed to talk to, though, was Miles.

After her shower, she recovered her own clothes from around the apartment, putting everything back in its place. She had to search for some time before locating her bra deep underneath the sofa.

Zuzu stayed gone until Harper finished straightening, when she slinked in through the cat door, shooting her an icy green glare before heading to her food dish.

'Who are you? My priest?' Harper snapped.

Zuzu ignored this with cool dignity.

When all evidence of last night's activities had been put away and the apartment restored to order, Harper grabbed her phone and called Miles.

'Jackson.' Beneath his terse voice, Harper could hear the rumble of a car on the road.

'Where are you?' she asked.

'On my way to Hilton Head,' he told her. 'Got an assignment from some hotshot agency shooting a golf tournament. They're paying a fortune and all expenses.'

Harper swore under her breath. He'd be there all day.

She didn't want to talk about Blazer on the phone. She needed to tell him in person – see his face.

'When are you getting back?' she asked. 'There's something we need to talk about.'

'Tonight,' he said. 'Late. Can it wait?'

Harper was so impatient, for a fleeting moment she considered driving after him – Hilton Head was only a few hours away. But she had to be at work by four and it was noon now.

'It can wait,' she said reluctantly. 'But call me as soon as you get back. No matter what time.'

'What's going on?' he asked, his interest piqued. 'Did something happen?'

Harper paused, then shook her head. 'I'll tell you later.'

'Everything OK?'

'Everything's fine,' she assured him, although she wasn't sure that was true.

'All right then,' Miles said. 'I'll call you tonight. Man, I hate golf.'

The line went dead.

After her conversation with Miles, Harper couldn't sit still. It was too early to go to work and she felt too antsy to stay home. She needed to be investigating Blazer. But she felt as if she'd gone as far as she knew how to go without talking to Miles.

After dressing quickly, grabbing everything she'd need for work, she climbed in the Camaro and headed to Pangaea.

Before she even walked in she knew Bonnie was there. Her pink, twenty-year-old pickup truck was parked outside the door.

The coffee shop was crowded. Modern jazz flowed from the

speakers and the air smelled so strongly of coffee she got a caffeine buzz from breathing.

She found her sitting in a corner, a sketchpad sharing space on the table with a pot of tea. Most of the pink had faded from her hair now, and she wore it plaited loosely over one shoulder, as she often did when she was drawing. Slim, in an ankle-length skirt with biker boots and countless bracelets on her wrists, she looked ethereal – a blonde, boho, gypsy girl, her charcoal dancing across the page.

When Harper sat down across from her, clutching a gigantic mug of coffee, Bonnie's face lit up.

'Harpelicious!' Shoving the sketchpad to one side, she jumped up and ran over to hug her, bracelets giving an ashram jangle with every step. She smelled of the cool, lemony perfume she always wore. 'You look amazing.'

'Do I?'

'Definitely.' Back in her seat, Bonnie squinted at her suspiciously across the table. 'Something's different about you. You look lush. What have you been up to?'

'Working a big case,' Harper said, sipping her coffee. 'And having sex with a cop. The usual.'

Bonnie set her cup of green tea down with a thud.

'No. Way.'

'Way.'

'Wait, wait, wait.' Bonnie leaned forward so eagerly the end of her braid narrowly missed landing in her cup. 'Is it the one from the other night? The one you told me about?'

'That's the one.'

'Holy shit, Harper. I didn't think you'd really do it!' Bonnie exclaimed, so loudly a bearded hipster at the next table stared at them. She lowered her voice. 'Tell me everything right this minute. Was it good? Do you love him? Can I be your maid of honor?'

Harper made a face at her. 'It was good. But it was once, OK?'

Bonnie was not to be deterred.

'Tell me about him. Would I like him? Is he pretty?'

Harper thought of the way Luke looked leaning against the car in the dark last night.

'Yeah,' she conceded. 'He's pretty.'

'Pretty cops are the best kind.' Under the table, Bonnie tapped her leg with her toe. 'Could he get me out of parking tickets? I've got so many parking tickets and I'm a good person, Harper...'

'He works undercover,' Harper cut her off. 'If you're ever held hostage by a drug gang, he can help. Otherwise, not so much.'

'Undercover?' Bonnie sounded impressed. 'Is he broken by all he's seen, Harper? Do you need to pick up the pieces and make his life worth living again?'

'Stop it.' Harper shot her a warning look. 'Be nice or I won't tell you anything.'

'I withdraw the question.' Bonnie took a demure sip of tea. 'At least tell me his name.'

Harper lowered her voice. 'His name's Luke Walker.'

Bonnie choked.

'Luke Walker,' she sputtered, 'is the most cop name I've ever heard in my life.'

She deepened her voice. 'Ma'am, I'm Officer Luke Walker. I'm here to fix your refrigerator ...'

Harper didn't laugh. Normally, she would enjoy joking about a guy with Bonnie.

Luke was different.

Spotting this, Bonnie stopped. Her smile faded.

'Hold on,' she said softly. 'You really like this one, don't you?'

Harper never could hide anything from her.

'It's a bad scene, Bonnie,' she said. 'I've known Luke for years. I think maybe I always had a thing for him that I wouldn't admit to myself. Now… I don't know how it's going to work.'

'Now that you got his pants off,' Bonnie filled in the blanks, 'you're afraid you won't be friends anymore.'

'Something like that,' Harper conceded. 'Also, like I said the other night, cops aren't allowed to have relationships with journalists.'

'Come on, sweetie,' Bonnie said. 'We're talking about *you*. No one can tell you who to date. Your boss can't pick your boyfriend. Even in modern America.'

'But there are *rules*, Bonnie,' Harper said.

Her anxiety about the situation made her tone more harsh than she intended, and she held up her hands apologetically.

'Sorry, I don't mean to growl at you.'

But Bonnie waved that away.

'Harper, it seems to me you have to make a decision.' She grew serious. 'You can say it's not worth the risk. Or, if you really like him, you say to hell with the rules. And take your chances.'

She tilted her head. Her eyes were vivid blue in the bright sunlight.

'Do you really like him?'

Harper held her gaze.

'I really like him.'

Bonnie shrugged. 'Then, to hell with the rules, Harper.'

Harper thought of how it had felt lying with her head on Luke's chest, his hand stroking her hair.

'Yeah,' she said, as much to herself as Bonnie. 'To hell with them.'

Chapter Twenty-two

'How old is Blazer?' Harper glanced at Miles. 'Late forties?'

'Something like that.'

He was behind the wheel of the Mustang. She was in her Camaro. They'd parked their cars nose to tail, so their open driver's side windows faced each other.

It was after midnight and they were in an empty parking lot at the edge of downtown. It was surrounded by hedges – impossible to see from the street. They'd often met here under other circumstances, to discuss work, gossip, or just hang out when adrenaline made sleep impossible.

But tonight there was no small talk. No jokes.

True to his promise, Miles called as soon as he got back in town. He'd obviously had a long day – he looked tired.

When Harper told him what she'd found in her mother's archive file, he'd gone quiet, replying in short sentences, eyes on some unidentifiable point in the distance.

'So, when he was thirty-two or thirty-three, he worked my mother's case,' Harper said. 'Then, fifteen years later, he dates a woman who happens to end up murdered under identical circumstances. Miles,' she implored him, 'this is no coincidence. You can see that, right?'

He rubbed his eyes hard.

'All I see is you haven't got proof of anything. You've got a cop's name on an old piece of paper. That's a little bit of nothing.'

His tone was cutting.

'But if it was him...' Harper argued.

'It's too early for if,' he cut her off. 'We get into *if*, we're going to lose how and why. Not to mention why not. And there are a thousand members of the why not family.'

He shifted in the car so he was facing her – his expression was deadly serious.

'Harper, you have to be careful here. I don't know Blazer well but I know enough about him to know he's a ruthless son of a bitch. He's got a career plan and he's been courting the deputy chief for the last five years. He's ambitious as hell and, if you threaten him, he has the means to take you out of the picture.'

The truth in that sentence sent ice into Harper's veins.

'Well, what am I supposed to do?' she asked helplessly. 'We both know this case smells bad. But how do I prove it?'

Miles considered this for a moment. In the distance, a freight train whistle blew, low and mournful.

'Seems to me, you're going about this all wrong,' he said finally. 'You've chosen an outcome you want and you're trying to build the facts to match it. You've created your truth and now you're trying to twist everything to prove you're right.'

Harper's cheeks flushed at the injustice of this, but she let him talk.

'You've got to stop that. You need to treat this like any other story you investigate,' he continued. 'You've proven Blazer was involved in both cases. There *is* a connection. Now you've got to find the rest.'

He made it sound so easy. It wasn't easy.

'I'm *trying*,' Harper said, her voice rising. 'But I don't know where to look. I'm at a dead end.'

Miles shook his head.

'Think about it, Harper – if Blazer was the killer, he had to know your mother. They had to have had a relationship. You're looking for the same things the police look for – opportunity, motive and means. We know he had the means. He's a cop. Cops know how to kill. But what about opportunity and motive? Why would he want to kill your mother? What on earth would he stand to gain from that? Could he do it? What was going on that day in his life? Those are the puzzle pieces you haven't found yet.'

He rubbed a tired hand across his jaw.

'Work on motive first. Almost no one kills without it. Find out if he had any connection to your mother. Did he know your family? You remember seeing him around when you were a kid?'

'No.' Her reply was emphatic.

'Then maybe he knew your parents in some other way. Your dad still living?'

Harper nodded.

'Well, give him a call. See if he remembers Blazer. Track down some of your mother's friends, show them Blazer's picture. See if any of them remember him. Parents have lives kids don't know about. Maybe your parents met him through work.'

Some of Harper's despair seeped away. This was practical advice. Things she could really do.

'OK,' she said, nodding slowly.

'But I'm telling you this now, Harper.' Miles' voice turned cool. 'You find nothing? You've got to let this go. You cannot Captain

Ahab this thing forever, you hear me? A vendetta will eat you alive. It won't be Blazer you destroy. You'll destroy yourself.'

Harper turned away biting her lip hard. She didn't want to argue with Miles – he was the only person she had to talk to about this.

But he hadn't been Camille Whitney once, the way she had, and then seen her standing there years later, like a mirror of her own past.

He didn't understand what this was like.

That intransigence must have shown in her posture, though, because Miles gave a weary sigh.

'Do what you have to, Harper. I'll help if I can. Now, I need to get some sleep. It must've been a hundred and ten degrees out there today and golfers don't like shade.'

He started the Mustang's engine. The powerful rumble echoed off the concrete around them.

He had to raise his voice to be heard above it as he issued parting words of advice.

'If you're really going after a cop, you need to treat this case like your own mother was a stranger. Dig into her life. If you can prove Blazer was in her life as well as Whitney's, then you've got something to take to Smith. Right this minute, you haven't got a thing.'

Miles' words followed Harper home that night, and stayed with her over the next few days. Much as she hated to admit it, there was a lot of truth in what he'd said.

After years spent assiduously avoiding her own past, she now had no choice but to immerse herself in it.

Worst of all, she needed to call her father.

She hadn't spoken to him since Christmas, and that was the way she liked it. So she'd put off that call as long as possible.

With Billy's help, she dragged boxes of family papers and memorabilia out of the attic and spread them out on the living room floor. There weren't very many – eight, altogether. But it made her uncomfortable seeing them sitting there. Like rectangular time bombs.

'Whatcha looking for, darlin'?' Billy asked, surveying the dusty boxes doubtfully.

The thick Louisiana accent he'd never lost coated his words in aural velvet.

'I'm researching my family history,' she told him. 'Looking for old pictures. The usual thing.'

'I never do that,' he told her, hands in the pockets of his paint-stained jeans. 'My mama kept pictures hangin' on the wall. Spent mosta my life tryin' to get away from all them dead people.'

Harper gazed at the stack of boxes.

'I keep my dead people in here,' she said.

When the landlord had gone, she tore the tape off the first box and dug through it, unsure of precisely what to expect.

After her mother's murder, they'd never lived in their old house again. Harper's father had packed up their belongings a few months later, and put the house on the market.

When he moved up north, everything belonging to Harper's mother had been sent to her grandmother. After her grandmother died a few years ago and her house was sold, Harper inherited what remained of those boxes.

She'd put them in the attic without opening them. And there they had stayed. She had no idea what lay inside.

The first box turned out to contain old letters, report cards, school papers (B- 'Harper needs to work on her attention to detail…'), and photographs.

After some indecisiveness, she divided the items up into separate stacks – letters, bills, photos, junk.

She could mostly eliminate the letters, which were largely notes she and Bonnie wrote to each other at school, letters when one or the other of them was at camp, long missives from when they briefly went into a diary craze and wrote every single thought down by hand for posterity and exchanged them.

I think Brad likes me, Bonnie had written eighteen years ago, her handwriting sprawling and florid, between margins where she'd drawn elaborate rows of school desks, with tiny students sitting in them. *He smiled at me six times today. SIX. Even when I kicked his ankle in PE, he smiled at me. I don't like him.*

Snorting a laugh, Harper put the page aside to give to Bonnie later.

It was funny how little she remembered of her own childhood. It felt like she was reading someone else's letters. Snooping into someone else's life.

Pulling out another envelope, Harper paused. A gold and white daisy had been painted next to her name. At the sight of her mother's familiar handwriting, each letter perfectly curled, her breath hitched.

I'm glad you're having fun at camp, her mother had written. *But I miss painting together in the afternoons. And I look forward to the time when we can go back to normal...*

She'd written that less than a year before someone stabbed her to death.

Harper held the paper to her nose, but there was none of her mother's scent on it. Nothing of her spirit.

Folding the letter carefully, Harper tucked it back in the envelope.

The rest of the box contained nothing except forgotten memories

– an award Harper won at school, a dried-out pen from Atlanta, a North of the Border sticker.

When she reached the bottom, Harper breathed a sigh of relief and refilled the box, shoving it aside.

One down. Seven to go.

Bracing herself, she tore open the next box.

This one contained more of her mother's things. There was no order to it – it looked like her father had thrown everything in without looking. Old paintbrushes, a flyer for a restaurant, a pair of well-worn winter gloves, an alabaster jewelry box, electric bills and phone bills.

Harper dug through the chaos until she came across a small leather address book.

Hurriedly, she flipped through it to the Bs, but there was no Blazer.

Most of the names were familiar – aunts and cousins, old friends and neighbors. There were a few she didn't recognize, though, and she set the book aside to do more research later.

At the dusty bottom of the box, along with a broken gold necklace and a box of matches, she found a stack of personal letters.

Most were nothing – short gossipy notes from relatives.

The last letter was in a thick cream envelope bearing her mother's name. As soon as Harper picked it up she recognized her father's handwriting. There was no return address, and the postmark was dated two months before her mother's death.

Cautiously, she unfolded the handwritten page. The ink was coal black. It appeared to have been written quickly, every word a slash-mark of anger.

There was no affectionate salutation, merely 'Alicia'.

As Harper read it, her lips parted in shock.

I won't let you get away with this, the letter began.

Your accusations show you've become hysterical.
You accuse me of affairs without any proof at all. I'm
BUSY, Alicia. I've got to support our family, and god
knows your art doesn't bring in anything. How dare
you accuse me of cheating on you? How dare you
threaten my relationship with our child? It's not like
you're pure as the driven snow. If you don't stop this,
I swear you will pay. You always have been a selfish
bitch. Grow up. Jealousy doesn't become you.

It was signed with a 'P', for Peter. Written with such force his pen had gone through the paper.

Harper read it through twice, gripping the letter tightly.

So, her mother had known about her father's affair. And she'd called him on it.

It was so like her father to want to respond in writing – always the lawyer. But the heated tone and fiery language – that was out of character. He prided himself on staying calm and defeating every opponent with infuriating logic. This time, though, he'd lost it.

How dare you threaten my relationship with my child…

Had her mother threatened to leave him and take Harper with her?

She kept coming back to the most threatening line: *I swear you will pay.*

Rocking back on her heels, she stared at the letter in her hand.

Was this proof that her father had motive?

His alibi had come from his girlfriend. She could have lied. The only proof they'd produced that he'd been with her that afternoon was a receipt, dated around the time of the murder, from a gas station near her apartment.

Wouldn't it have been easy for him to get home from the

suburbs, kill his wife and then slip back out again without being seen?

The thought turned her stomach.

She'd always accepted her father's innocence – the police had gone after him so hard, she'd assumed if there was anything to find, they'd have found it. Her anger at him had come from the cheating – not from any suspicion that he might actually be guilty.

But this letter indicated she didn't know anything about her parents' relationship. And she was starting to doubt the police.

Even though it blew a hole through her theory that the same person committed both murders – after all, he hadn't lived in Savannah in more than a decade – she couldn't ignore this.

She had to add her father to her list of suspects. Right under Blazer.

Chapter Twenty-three

The next day, she took her mother's address book to work. Whenever there was a lull, she went through it, calling her mother's contacts, looking for connection to Larry Blazer. After finding that letter, it seemed more urgent than ever to establish some thread from the detective to her mother's life.

Each conversation was unfeasibly long and involved endless explanations. She hadn't kept in touch in recent years and, presented with an unexpected call, everyone wanted to catch up. ('Good lord, girl. We haven't heard from you in a dog's year ...')

Conversations had to be guided gradually around to the questions she needed answers to, and that took time and patience.

Most of the discussions went much like the one she had with an artist friend of her mother's.

'Hello, Mrs Carney, this is Harper McClain...' Pause. 'Yes, *that*, Harper McClain.' Pause. 'Yes, it has been a while.' Pause. 'My dad is fine, thanks. Living in Connecticut.' Pause. 'I *know*. Miles away.' Pause. 'Well how wonderful. A doctor! Hasn't he done well! And in Florida. How nice. I'll bet you have lovely vacations down there.' Pause for a very long time. 'Mm-hmm.'

Eventually, after what seemed like forever, she'd guided her around to a point where it was safe to explain the reason for the call. 'I'm looking for an old friend of my mother's. A police officer. I wondered if you knew him back then. What? His name? Oh, Blazer. Larry Blazer. Does that ring a bell?'

Over and over again, in call after call, the answer was the same: 'No.'

It was late in the evening when Harper reached the Ls. The only name on that list was Larson – Bonnie's mother.

Mrs Larson laughed merrily when asked about the possibility that Harper's mother might have been friends with a detective.

'Oh, Harper, your mother was an unreconstructed hippy. She thought cops were the enemy. Her friends were all artists and musicians. I always thought she was so exotic.' Her voice grew wistful. 'I'm sure she thought I was a boring housewife, with all those kids and no career. But, gosh, I adored her.'

When Harper assured her that wasn't true, Mrs Larson shushed her.

'It's all water under the bridge, now, isn't it, honey?' She'd paused then, a thought occurring to her. 'Now, if you're looking for someone who knew cops, you should ask your dad. He was always hanging out with them, as I recall.'

Harper had been so surprised, she had to work to keep that out of her voice.

'Dad? Really?'

'Well, of course,' Mrs Larson said. 'He was good friends with that young district attorney and his wife – what was her name? The Andersons, that's who they were. Anyway. He went to all those police events – fundraisers and so forth.' She chuckled.

'Your mother hated those parties. She was always complaining about how dull they were. She said everyone drank too much and all anyone talked about was work.'

Sitting at her desk in the mostly empty newsroom, Harper scrawled a quick note to herself: 'Did Dad know Blazer? Did he introduce him to Mom?'

Next to her computer monitor, her scanner had begun buzzing a series of excited messages but Harper barely registered it.

She was close to something here, she could feel it.

She turned the scanner down.

'Did Mom ever mention a detective – a blond guy named Larry? He would have been in his thirties then.'

Mrs Larson considered this thoughtfully. 'I'm sure she didn't,' she said after a while, adding apologetically, 'But maybe I'm forgetting. I'm getting old, Harper.'

They talked about other things then – about Bonnie's work at the college, and how one of her brothers had gotten a job in Dubai and they never saw him anymore but, 'at least he's got a job'.

Eventually, Harper found an excuse to end the conversation. When she'd hung up, she stared out the dark window.

First the angry letter and now this. Everything was leading her to her father.

She'd been sixteen when he moved away. At first, he'd tried to stay in touch – calling her every couple of weeks. But their conversations were uncomfortable and, over time, they called each other less and less.

He and Jennifer had two small kids now – both boys.

Her father came to Savannah occasionally on business; each time he'd take her to dinner and they'd spend a couple of hours in stilted conversation that was most memorable for the things they didn't say.

It had been a couple of years since his last visit.

Every Christmas Jennifer sent a card with a picture of them all, standing on skis on some snow-covered mountain, or splashing in turquoise water, always smiling broadly.

The cards were how she knew her dad had started losing his hair. And that Jennifer looked less like a nubile young conquest these days, and more like a normal busy mom.

She could have tried to get closer to him, as time passed, but she couldn't seem to make herself do it. Her father was a reminder of everything she'd lost. Distance was the only weapon she had.

Now, though, she had no choice.

With slow reluctance she reached for the cell phone and dialed his number.

'Hello?'

Her father sounded brusque. Harper glanced at her watch – it was after ten.

'Dad? It's Harper.'

'Harper?' Puzzled concern filled his voice. 'Has something happened? Are you all right?'

'I'm fine,' she said. 'Sorry to call so late.'

'Oh… Well, that's fine…'

Despite his words, the confusion was clear in his tone.

Why are you calling? I thought you hated me.

'Look, I'm sorry to bother you,' she said. 'It's just… Look. I've been going through Mom's things, and I need to ask you a few questions.'

Silence.

There was no easy way to do this. Gritting her teeth, Harper forged ahead. 'I wondered if you knew any police when you were in Savannah.'

'I knew a few through work.'

A new note of caution entered his voice.

'Did you know a detective named Larry Blazer?'

A pause. She could almost hear him trying to figure out what she was after.

'Harper, what is this about?'

She pressed her fingertips against her forehead. This was even harder than she'd expected.

'I know this is coming from out of nowhere, but I need to know for... something I'm working on. Did you know a detective named Larry Blazer? It's important.'

'No... I don't know. Maybe? I knew a lot of people.' He sounded irritated, confused. But Harper sensed obfuscation as well.

He was hiding something.

Her instincts hummed. She'd interviewed hundreds of people over the years. Her father had no idea how good she was at this.

Relaxing her posture, she made her voice calm. Unthreatening.

'I know you did, and it was a long time ago. No one could blame you for forgetting. So you don't know if you knew him or not?'

'The name sounds familiar,' her father said reluctantly. 'I might have known him.'

Harper's chest tightened. She had to fight to keep the interest out of her voice.

'Through work or... Were you friends?'

'We weren't friends,' her father's voice was dry. 'I remember my friends.'

'Is it possible,' Harper asked with a kind of preternatural calm, 'you might have introduced him to Mom?'

The phone went so quiet she thought the connection had been lost.

Then he spoke again.

'Harper, what is going on?'

His voice was crisp and professional now. A lawyer questioning an investigator.

Looking out the darkened window, Harper bit her lip. Maybe it was time for some truth.

'There's been another murder,' she said finally. 'Exactly the same MO as Mom's.'

'Oh.'

It wasn't a word so much as a gasp. As if she'd punched him with the information.

It took him a few beats to recover.

'Do the police think...?'

There was something in his voice she hadn't expected – grief. And hope. As if he, too, had been waiting for someone to be caught.

She didn't know what to feel.

'The police don't know,' Harper said simply. 'They're investigating.'

'What does this Blazer have to do with it?' He still sounded winded, but he was recovering. Using logic to pull himself to the surface, the same way she did.

'I don't know,' she admitted, bracing herself. 'I'm fishing here – trying to figure out what they think, where they're looking. Blazer's a cop – they don't think it's him. But there are some things about him that make me suspicious.'

'You think a cop might have done this?' He sounded doubtful. 'Alicia was never much of a fan of the police.'

'I know,' she said. 'But she could have met him through you. If you knew him, it might answer some questions.'

'I'll look through my records,' he said, after a brief pause. 'But if I knew him, I didn't know him well enough to remember him. And that probably means Alicia didn't either. Look, Harper, shouldn't you let the police handle this?'

An impatient note had entered his voice. Her call was unexpected and unwanted, and now he was ready for it to be over. She was a nuisance. A reminder of a former life he wanted to forget.

Harper thought of the furious letter she'd found among her mother's things. And suddenly wondered why he'd packed it up for her to find later, instead of throwing it away.

That blew away the clouds of sympathy that had begun to swirl.

'Actually, I'm trying to keep the police away from you, Dad.'

This wasn't true at all, but she needed to hurt him to throw him off balance. Get more truth out of him.

It worked as well as she'd hoped.

'Away from *me*? What the hell— What do I have to do with this?'

He sounded panicked. Scared. His carefully cultivated calm evaporating.

'Nothing, Dad,' she said. 'Except, I found a letter among Mom's things.'

'What letter?' His voice rose. 'What are you talking about?'

'A letter you wrote to her a few months before her murder. She suspected you were having an affair. You threatened her. It looks bad, Dad. If the police got their hands on it…'

Harper was ruthless now. Every word a bullet. But it hurt more than she'd thought it would.

'Harper.' Disbelief filled his voice. 'What are you saying?'

'Nothing, Dad,' she said coolly. 'I'm asking you: do you know a man named Larry Blazer? Have you heard of a woman named Marie Whitney?'

There was a long silence. The scanner on her desk buzzed its unheard message.

'I've never heard of the woman you mentioned.' His voice was so cold it could be carved from stone. 'I've already told you, I can't remember if I ever met a man named Blazer.'

He took a breath and seemed to gather himself. 'If the police need me, they have my number. And I think I want you to stop calling me.'

The phone went dead.

Harper pressed the cool plastic receiver against her forehead and closed her eyes. There'd been precious little love left between her and her father for a long time.

But he was family. And what she'd done felt like betrayal.

Slowly, carefully, she set the phone down and turned to her notebook.

She was now fairly certain her father did not know Larry Blazer. And there'd been no reaction to Whitney's name.

Mention of the note – and the implicit threat of exposing it – had roused anger and hurt. Not cold calculation.

And he'd seemed genuinely upset by the news that there'd been another murder.

He'd batted a thousand.

On her desk, her scanner was buzzing constant messages about ambulances and backup. Harper stared at it blankly, her mind replaying the conversation over and over.

Her dad knew nothing about what was going on here, she was willing to bet on that. So where did that leave her? Aside from feeling suddenly terrible.

Baxter's voice soared across the empty room, shaking her from her reverie.

'Harper! Get over here.'

Harper blinked.

'What's up?'

Baxter was behind her desk, the remote control in her hand, staring at the TV mounted on the wall.

Following her line of vision, Harper saw Natalie Swanson's perfectly formed face on the screen. She was standing in front of a row of police cars, their lights turning her blonde hair a flickering blue.

Harper's stomach dropped.

Shoving her chair back, she tore across the newsroom.

When she reached the editor's desk, the words at the bottom of the TV screen read, *Three shot in southside brawl.*

'Detectives tell us they're looking for two shooters,' Natalie explained somberly. 'All young men. All are considered armed and dangerous. One is possibly carrying an automatic weapon. It's a scenario that's become all too familiar to residents south of Broad Street. And tonight the violence claimed three new victims. Back to you, Bob.'

The image on the screen changed to the newsroom, where the dark-haired anchor shook his head.

'Thank you, Natalie. Stay safe out there.'

Muting the sound, Baxter pointed the remote control at Harper.

'Did you know about this?'

Harper stared at the TV over her shoulder as if it might hold the answer to that question.

'I don't...'

This must have been what was on the scanner. She'd been so caught up in her phone calls, she hadn't heard the codes for shooting, or for sending ambulances, or for backup.

She felt sick.

She'd never missed a shooting before. Not once. How could this have happened? Why hadn't Miles phoned to warn her?

'I'm really sorry, Baxter,' she said finally. 'I didn't hear my scanner.'

'You didn't hear your...?' The editor looked baffled. 'How did you not hear your scanner? It's sitting on your desk. Harper, *I* can hear your scanner.'

'I don't know,' Harper admitted helplessly.

Baxter's expression was thunderous. 'What the hell is going on with you? In all the time you've been at the paper I've never known you to miss anything. Lately you've been coming in late, disappearing for hours, missing stories... I can tell you're not really here. Where are you?'

'I am here,' Harper insisted. 'I've had a lot on my mind. Family stuff.'

'*Family* stuff?' Baxter stared. 'You don't get to have a family when you are on my clock. Miles doesn't have a family. I don't have a family. No one here has a family when there's a triple shooting.'

Harper opened her mouth to defend herself but Baxter wasn't finished.

'You work here eight hours a day – sometimes more.' Seeing the look on Harper's face, she added the last two words hastily. 'All I ask is that for those eight hours you do your job.'

Flipping her wrist impatiently, she looked at her watch.

'I don't have time for this now. You've got a news article to write.' She pointed at the television screen. 'You've got an hour. Get on the phone and get me this story.'

She delivered her final words with icy precision.

'Fix this, Harper. Or don't bother coming in tomorrow.'

Chapter Twenty-four

The next day, Harper made a point of showing up for work half an hour early.

She'd hardly slept. She'd stayed up most of the night, listening to her scanner. Every time the cool voice of the dispatcher sent police to a reported break-in, a stolen purse, a drunk wandering in the middle of a street, she tensed.

By dawn, she was exhausted – sitting on the sofa clutching a cup of coffee like a weapon.

She still couldn't believe she'd missed the shooting.

In the end, she'd gathered enough basic facts about the incident from a few phone calls to police contacts to cobble a story together by deadline.

It turned out Miles *had* called her to tell her about the shooting. Five times, in fact. But she'd been on the phone.

His messages had grown progressively apocalyptic.

'Are you trying to get yourself fired, Harper?' he'd asked at one point, in a message she listened to much later that night. 'Baxter will lose her shit if you miss this.'

Thanks to his pictures and Harper's contacts, no readers would suspect she hadn't been on the street last night, reporting live. But he was right about Baxter.

Harper was quite certain she was going to hear more about it today.

Luckily, the editor wasn't at her desk when Harper arrived. The room was busy, with the daytime crew still filing their last stories. Gray afternoon light flooded in through the tall windows. The room smelled faintly of burned coffee.

She plugged in her scanner, displaying it prominently near her keyboard.

Every move she made was rife with purpose and grim determination. She had her head in the game and she was determined to keep it there. From now on, her mother's case had to be her personal project, done on her own time.

Nonetheless, it had filled her thoughts during the sleepless night.

She'd kept hearing her father's voice: *I think I want you to stop calling me.*

He'd sounded as if she disgusted him.

She was disgusted with herself. It wasn't necessary to be so cruel.

But what was done, was done.

'Harper.' Baxter's voice cut through the newsroom buzz. 'Get over here.'

When Harper looked up, the editor was standing at her desk with a face like a firing squad.

Setting her shoulders, Harper rose to her feet.

She could feel the other reporters watching as she crossed the room, until she stood uneasily in front of Baxter.

Baxter fixed her with a cold stare.

'Last night was a shitstorm,' Baxter told her. 'Missing that story was inexcusable. I've worked at newspapers where you'd be gone already. I know editors who would have fired you on the spot.' Resting her hands on the desk, she leaned forward. 'What's going on, Harper? I have never known you to miss a story. And a triple shooting? That's your bread and butter. What the hell happened? And, if you want to keep your job, don't say "family troubles".'

Harper had spent much of the night preparing for this moment. Now she launched into the explanation she'd crafted in the heavy darkness at three in the morning.

'I got too involved in a story I've been researching,' she said quietly. 'I lost my focus.'

Baxter eyed her suspiciously. 'Which case?'

'The Whitney killing.'

'The Whitney killing?' Baxter frowned. 'Why are you still working on that? Is there something new?'

There was no hint of awareness in her voice that the same story she'd been desperate for a week ago now was deemed uninteresting.

'There are discrepancies in the police reports on that case. I think there's more to it than the police let on,' Harper explained, with the slimmest filament of hope that Baxter might find this intriguing. 'I've been trying to piece it all together. I was working on it last night when I didn't hear my scanner.'

The creases on Baxter's forehead deepened.

'Have you taken your thoughts to the police? Given them a chance to comment?'

'They...' Harper hesitated. 'They don't agree with me.'

Baxter looked confounded.

'If you've been digging into that case for nearly two weeks and nothing has come up so far, you're wasting your time. All your energy should be focused on your day-to-day work. People read your stories because they want to know what's happening right now. Not what happened last week. The Whitney case is history. You got me?'

'Yes,' Harper said meekly. Now was not the time to argue.

The editor leaned forward, her navy blazer brushing the edge of her desk.

'If you miss another breaking news story because you've disobeyed my direct order on this, I won't be able to save your job.' She pointed to a thick file folder she'd placed, with a theatrical flourish, on her desk. 'I've got fifty applications in this folder from hungry reporters dying to do what you do. No one is irreplaceable.'

Whatever she'd meant to say died on Harper's lips. She couldn't tear her eyes away from the folder, and that stack of résumés inside spilling out.

'Now,' Baxter growled, 'get back to work.'

Grabbing a pack of cigarettes and a lighter from the top of her desk, the editor turned on her heel and walked to the door, her steps quick and angry. DJ came in as she went out, and she shoved past him without a word.

He stood watching as she stormed down the stairs, puzzlement creasing his face.

'What's wrong with Baxter?' he asked, when he reached Harper.

'I missed a shooting last night,' she said as they walked back to their desks. 'We didn't know about it until the news came on.'

His eyes widened. 'Both channels covered it?'

'Yep.'

He gave a low whistle.

'You still work here?'

It was a joke, but Harper couldn't summon a laugh.

'Barely,' she said.

She sat down at her desk with a sigh. That had actually gone better than she'd expected, but she still felt scalded. There were enough empty desks in this room for her to believe the editor was serious.

'See, I think your problem is you're too good.' DJ spun his chair around, propelling himself closer to her. 'Everyone else misses stories now and then, but you've never missed anything before. Now Baxter thinks the world's falling apart because you missed one thing.' He leaned back in his seat, folding his arms. 'The moral of our story is, be terrible more often.'

He was trying to cheer her up, but she was in too deep.

'Yeah,' she said dully. 'I guess you're right.'

'That said, how *did* you miss that shooting?' DJ pointed at her scanner, which was crackling out a stream of minor crimes and fender-benders. 'I thought you had that thing wired directly to your cerebellum.'

'I do, normally.' A hint of defensiveness entered her voice. 'I've been busy this week.'

His expression was the perfect mixture of sympathy and pragmatism.

'Look, they shouldn't get so pissed off about one screw-up,' he told her. 'But give them two mistakes and they'll nail you. So... let me know if I can help, OK?'

The thing about DJ was, he really meant it. He would genuinely help.

Harper cast him a grateful look.

'Thanks,' she said.

A crooked grin lit up his face.

'Hey, if you do get fired, though, can I have your stapler?'

Fighting a smile, Harper raised her middle finger.

'Fuck off, DJ.'

Laughing, he spun his chair and rolled away.

Harper logged in to her computer. The newspaper logo came up.

She stared at it blankly.

DJ had been joking, but he had a point. Because of her willingness to work crazy hours, and her connections to the police, Harper had always been untouchable. She got away with more than the other reporters and was given more freedom to take risks.

Something fundamental had changed now, though. She could feel it in the air.

She was on the edge here.

Working for the newspaper was all she'd ever wanted to do. But every word she'd said to Baxter had been a lie. She couldn't stop now. She had to know the truth. She had to understand what tied her mother's death to Marie Whitney. What connected Blazer to both of them. If not her father, then who?

If she wanted to keep her job *and* investigate Blazer, she couldn't do it alone. And Miles and DJ could only help so much. She needed someone on the inside.

Picking up her cell phone, she held it in her hand for a long time.

She scrolled through her address book until she found the name she was looking for. With rapid, determined movements, she typed a message.

Can we meet? I need help.

Less than a minute later her phone buzzed.

Luke's name appeared on the screen.

Meet me at 12:30 tonight. The Watch.

Chapter Twenty-five

The Watch was a narrow crescent of verdant land on a bluff overlooking a sharp river bend to the east of the city. It was a popular place for joggers and dog walkers during the day, but no one went up there at night. It was too dark and too far from the safety of the city.

The perfect place to meet if you didn't want to be seen.

It had earned its name during the Civil War, when volunteer guards kept watch there for enemy vessels that might threaten the town. When those boats finally did come, of course, the poorly trained volunteers were overwhelmed in minutes and the city soon fell. It was a standing joke that The Watch should have been called The Rout, or The Surrender. But The Watch had a better ring to it.

When Harper pulled the Camaro onto the dirt road leading to the viewpoint at twelve thirty that night, it was deserted. There were no streetlights here and no pavement – only a rough dirt parking lot and a long expanse of grass and trees curving gently down to the river.

The car bumped and juddered over potholes she could only

barely see in the thick dark. Muttering complaints under her breath, she pulled over and cut the engine.

The bluff wasn't high, but the sharp angle of the river bend created a sweeping view of the lights of Savannah, stretching out like a diamond blanket thrown over the land. The river was a wide velvet ribbon snaking through it.

When she climbed out of the car, it took a minute for her eyes to adjust to the gloom.

It was cooler here than in town, and Harper tilted her head back as a breeze swept across her skin.

In the stillness, she could hear the low sound of distant traffic and, occasionally, the faint musical clang of a chain as the current shifted a moored boat somewhere in the darkness below.

She turned on her phone to check the time. The blue screen lit up the night – twelve thirty-five. Luke was running late.

Nerves fluttered in her stomach. She folded her arms tightly across her waist.

Whatever this thing was between them, it felt incredibly fragile.

Being with Luke had given her the tiniest glimpse of how it felt when someone had your back. It was like peering through the keyhole into someone else's life.

Someone else's *better* life.

She didn't want to screw this up. But she needed advice now, and she didn't know where else to turn.

The deep rumble of a powerful engine cut through the quiet.

Headlights illuminated the trees as a black car rounded a corner. It moved with slow purposefulness across the cratered dirt lot towards her. It wasn't the car Luke had driven the other night.

This one was bigger, and older.

Undercover cops switched cars all the time – it made them harder to track. They had a whole lot of them to use. It struck

Harper that she didn't know which car belonged to Luke really, or if he even had one.

After the darkness, the light was blinding. Harper raised one hand to shield her eyes. The other hand felt behind her for the door handle.

The car pulled in next to hers, and the engine switched off. For a second, nothing happened.

Then the door swung open and Luke emerged, backlit by the car's interior light.

Relaxing, Harper let go of the door handle.

He walked towards her – those long, smooth strides made her stomach clench.

'What's going on?' he asked. 'Your message sounded urgent.'

She hadn't heard from him since the other night. Neither of them had texted the other. The cautious look on his face told her he thought that was why he was here.

She cleared her throat, which felt suddenly dry.

'I have to tell you something,' she said. 'You're not going to like it. But I want you to hear me out, OK?'

Even in the gloaming, she could see his eyes grow guarded.

'OK...'

She took a deep breath.

'Remember how I told you I was investigating the Whitney murder, and it didn't add up? That it reminded me too much of my mother's murder?'

He nodded slowly.

'I think the murderer might be a cop.'

For a second Luke didn't react. Then he swore softly.

'Come on, Harper. There's no way.'

'It gets worse.' She clenched her hands at her sides, preparing herself. 'I'm looking at Larry Blazer.'

'Oh, goddammit.' He gave her a look of pure disbelief. 'You've got to be kidding me.'

'I wish I was.'

Taking a step back, Luke raked his fingers through his hair.

'This is crazy,' he said. 'It's not Blazer. Whatever you're thinking, you're wrong. The guy's a complete asshole, but he's not a murderer.'

There was such certainty in his voice, Harper momentarily forgot what she'd planned to say. But she recovered quickly.

'Hear me out first,' she said. 'Then you can tell me I'm wrong.'

Talking fast, she told him what the receptionist at Whitney's office had seen, and the name on the piece of paper in her mother's case records. The more she explained, though, the less it sounded like she had. She heard the panic in her voice, but made herself keep going.

'I know it's not much,' she said when she was done. 'And maybe you're right. Maybe it's not Blazer. But I have to look into it, and I need help if I'm going to find out more.' She held up her hands. 'I'm in over my head, Luke. That's why I'm here.'

The moonlight highlighted worry lines on Luke's forehead as he considered his reply.

'I know how much you want to get your mother's killer,' he told her carefully. 'But surely you know that signature's not proof of anything.'

'Of course I know it's not proof.' She bristled. 'For God's sake, Luke. Why do you think I texted you?'

He held up his hands. 'I don't know, Harper. Why *did* you text me?'

Stung, she drew back.

'Because I have these suspicions and I need someone on the

245

inside to prove me wrong,' she said, fighting to keep her voice even. 'Someone I trust. Someone smart.'

'Wait.' He squinted at her. 'You want me to prove you *wrong*?'

She nodded.

'I need someone with access to police records to find out if Blazer has an alibi for Whitney's murder,' she said. 'I'm not fixated on him, if that's what you're thinking.' She couldn't keep the hint of defensiveness out of her tone. 'I'm looking at a lot of possibilities. Whitney liked powerful men. It could have been one of the others. But I need to check Blazer out, too.' She paused. 'I'm running low on time. And I can't do everything.'

Luke rubbed his hand against his jaw.

'Harper, you sound like a cop. There's already a detective working this case.'

'Yeah, but it's *Blazer*,' she said, her voice rising. 'And he matches the description of a man who dated the victim.'

She drew a breath.

'Look,' she said, in more measured tones. 'I have to check this out. I don't want it to be him. If it wasn't Blazer – if I can prove he couldn't have killed her, and he didn't have a relationship with her – I'll take him off my list. He doesn't ever have to know I even considered him.' She took a step towards him, her eyes pleading for him to understand. 'But either way, I have to look into this. I have to understand why Whitney's murder looked so much like my mother's.'

He didn't agree right away, but she could sense he was wavering.

'Luke,' she said quietly, 'Blazer worked my Mom's murder. Even if he didn't kill her. He worked that case. He saw that crime scene.'

'So did half the detectives on the force,' he reminded her. 'Smith was there that day. And Ledbetter. The deputy chief was there.'

'I know.' She raised her chin, stubbornly. 'But they weren't dating Whitney three months before she died.'

'You don't know for certain Blazer was either,' he pointed out.

They were going in circles.

Harper's shoulders slumped. She'd told him everything she knew. If it wasn't enough to convince him to help, she had nothing else to offer him.

'I'm not trying to be unreasonable,' Luke said, his voice softening slightly. 'But you're asking me to find out if a homicide detective has an alibi. And not just any homicide detective. The one who hates my guts.'

Harper blinked.

'You and Blazer don't get along?'

His lips tightened. 'Hell no. The man's hated me since I was a rookie.'

This was news to her. Luke was the kind of guy who got along with everyone. Even when he was young, she'd seen how much the other cops liked and respected him. He did the work, followed the rules, played the game.

'Why does he hate you?'

'It's a long story,' he said.

It appeared, at first, he might leave it at that. But then, seeing her determined expression, he gave in with a resigned sigh.

'My first year in the detectives' squad, I caught a homicide case,' he said. 'Blazer was lead on it. He made a small mistake, nothing major. I spotted it. I was young enough and green enough to think it would be extremely helpful if I pointed it out to him.' He gave a short, humorless laugh. 'He spent seventy-two hours tearing me apart. Ridiculing my work, refusing to sign off on my report, hassling my sergeant to write me up. Trying to get me knocked back to uniform.'

His voice was flat, but Harper knew him well enough to see the anger that still burned at this memory.

'My sergeant could see what was happening, and he fought for me until Blazer finally gave up on getting me fired.' He gave a loose shrug. 'He's despised me ever since. To this day, he goes out of his way to try to damage my career.'

As she absorbed this, a sudden realization occurred to Harper.

'This is why you left the detectives unit,' she said. 'It's why you went undercover. You were getting away from Blazer.'

His expression told her she was right, even before he spoke.

'Once he got promoted to sergeant, he questioned every case I caught. Sent back every report. Wrote me up for minor infractions. I had to go. I didn't become a detective so I could fight Larry Blazer.' He met her eyes. 'But that doesn't make him a killer.'

'No, it doesn't,' she conceded. 'But consider this, Luke. If he was dating Whitney and he didn't tell anyone, he broke about fifty police codes. Even if he didn't kill her – we could take him down for that alone.'

Their eyes locked.

In the silence that followed, Harper heard a bird rustle in the trees at the edge of the clearing.

'What is it about you?' he asked then, with what seemed like genuine bewilderment. 'Why am I not walking away? I know this is nuts. But I'm still standing here. And I'm thinking about saying yes. Which makes me crazy, too.'

A flicker of hope leapt in Harper's chest.

'Are you saying you'll help me?'

Luke shoved his hands into the pockets of his jeans. He didn't look happy.

'Blazer won't find out,' she promised. 'We're not going to take any chances. If you hit any roadblocks on this – you walk away. You can't leave a paper trail or set off any alarms. I'll do the same.'

'Blazer's smart,' he warned her. 'He'll know.'

'We're smart too,' she said.

'Are we?' His tone darkened. 'What's smart about this?'

He held out his arms.

Caught off guard, Harper stared at him blankly. 'I don't understand.'

'Look at us.' His voice rose. 'We're sneaking around in parks after midnight. Spending the night together. Have you heard the rumors? I've been taking shit ever since Riley's party. Blazer's already gunning for me, and I keep giving him ammunition.' He dropped his hands. 'I'm not sure we're as smart as we think we are.'

Harper's lungs contracted. This was exactly what she'd feared.

'What are you saying?' she asked quietly.

Luke kicked a clump of dirt hard into the trees.

'Oh, hell, Harper. I don't know. It's not you. I don't understand myself, sometimes. I mean, what are we doing? And now this Blazer thing. Am I trying to get myself fired?'

An unfamiliar emotion made Harper's heart go cold.

She was afraid.

Afraid of losing something she almost hadn't had at all. She couldn't seem to find the words she needed to argue with him.

'Come on, Luke. I don't...'

There was a catch in her voice. He must have heard it, too – his head jerked up.

Across the darkness she could see the confusion in his eyes.

'I like you, Harper,' he said. 'I always have. But all this time we've never crossed the line. Why are we pushing our luck like this?'

'Because...'

Her voice trailed off.

So many things she wanted to say but couldn't, in case they were the wrong things.

When she didn't continue, Luke nodded, as if she'd confirmed his fears.

All of this was so horribly what Harper had feared would happen. That he didn't feel the same way. That it was all an awful mistake. That he didn't care enough. That she didn't deserve to be happy.

That she would be alone again.

But wouldn't that be for the best? Wasn't he right? They were pushing their luck.

The thing that had first drawn her to him was how much of her own ambition she could see in him. Being a cop was all he'd ever wanted. And he was risking that now, for her.

'We should stop,' she said.

Her voice was barely above a whisper but the night was still. He heard.

She felt him watching her, but she wouldn't look up.

'It's not safe,' she continued. 'You're right. As long as you're doing your job, and I'm doing mine. It's a mistake.'

He turned away, his broad shoulders hunching.

'If that's what you think… I guess you're right.'

She felt raw. The breeze she'd welcomed earlier was sandpaper against her skin. She wanted to go home.

Her only comfort was that, when she finally dared to glance at him, Luke looked as stunned as she felt.

Maybe he'd expected her to talk him out of it. Perhaps he'd thought she'd fight harder. But Harper couldn't ask him to risk his job for her more than once in a single night.

Could she?

When he spoke again, his tone was flat.

'I'll see what I can find out about Blazer. I think you're wrong. But I'll look into it as much as I can.'

He didn't meet her eyes.

'Great,' Harper said without enthusiasm.

'I'll be in touch.'

Turning away sharply, Luke headed for his car.

Harper didn't move as he pulled away, his engine a roar in the night, driving too fast on the bumpy road.

And just like that, as quickly and unexpectedly as it began, it was over.

Chapter Twenty-six

When she left The Watch, Harper drove straight home. Her hands were numb on the wheel.

The apartment was quieter and darker than she could ever remember it being before. It felt empty and stale – like no one really lived there. As she walked down the hallway, her footsteps echoed.

Zuzu meowed insistently, winding between her feet as she made her way to the kitchen.

In silence, she fed her. For a while, she leaned against the counter, watching the cat eat without really seeing her.

She knew she shouldn't feel this terrible. They'd only slept together once. It shouldn't matter this much.

It *mattered*.

Having him in her life for that brief time had changed everything.

Sometimes you don't know you're living in darkness until the first person switches on the light. When that light goes out again, the night is so much darker.

That was where she'd gone wrong, she told herself. Letting the light come on in the first place. Why had she ever let him turn on the light?

Forcing herself to move, she opened a cupboard, digging through it until she found an ancient bottle of Jameson's whiskey at the back. Grabbing it, she poured herself a large shot and drank it in one.

It set her throat on fire and that was fine. She wanted it to hurt.

Crossing the kitchen, she switched on her scanner to fill the silence but the familiar crackle of official voices was a wave of meaningless noise.

She turned it off again with an irritated flick of her wrist.

Picking up a book she knew she wouldn't be able to concentrate on, she headed towards the couch. She was almost there when someone knocked on her door.

She froze.

It was nearly two in the morning. No one ever came by this late – even Bonnie would call first.

The knock came again – insistent, but not loud.

Moving cautiously, she set the book down and made her way to the front door. She pressed her cheek against the cool wood to look through the peephole.

Luke stood on her doorstep.

Harper's heart began to race.

Despite herself – despite all she knew about loss and the darkness she could already see coming – she rushed to let him in, her fingers fumbling with the safety bolts, hands slipping clumsily as she yanked the door open.

'What…?' she began.

He didn't wait for her to finish the question.

'It's like this, Harper. I can't walk away from this. I thought I could, but I can't.'

His straight hair was wild, like he'd been raking his fingers through it, and there were spots of color high on his cheeks.

'I drove all the way home, and then I turned the car around and came back. Because I don't want to lose you.'

He sounded as breathless as she felt. She could see her own wild excitement in his eyes.

'I don't care if we're playing with fire,' he said. 'Do you?'

'No,' she said fiercely. 'I don't care.'

'I've given up so much for this goddamn job, I'm not giving you up, too.' He was talking fast. 'They can't have everything.'

He took a step inside, so close she could feel the heat of his skin. Her hands were reaching for him before she knew what she was doing.

'To hell with them,' he said.

Sweeping her into his arms, he stepped inside, kicking the door shut behind him. They stumbled backwards down the hallway, his mouth on hers, kissing her with a hunger that made her bones soften.

Nothing else mattered in this moment. All she cared about were his lips. His hands. The way he made her feel.

She parted her lips, running her tongue across his teeth, tasting the salt of him.

Grasping the hem of her top he pulled it over her head in one smooth move. His hands were warm and insistent as they slid up her shoulders to tug at her bra straps.

At the last second, her rational brain kicked in.

'Wait.' She pushed her hands against his chest, trying to catch her breath. 'Where did you park?'

'Five blocks away. Side street.' As he talked, his lips teased her throat, her jaw. His breath was maddening. 'I do this for a living, remember?'

She should have known he'd think of everything.

Harper tilted her head to catch his mouth with her own. And let her worries go.

This was what mattered. Only this.

In the morning, Harper woke up alone. The sheets next to her were cool and empty.

Reaching out one hand she smoothed the blanket, feeling suddenly hollow.

She'd been certain that, this time, he'd be here in the morning.

Slowly, she sat up, pushing her hair back out of her face.

Only then did she hear the unmistakable sound of the shower.

Pressing her chin to her knees, she let out a long breath.

He was still here.

Much had been decided during the night. They would be careful. They wouldn't be seen together in public. But they would not give each other up.

At four in the morning, her head tucked beneath Luke's chin, Harper told him she was sorry.

'I shouldn't have asked you to help,' she'd said, too sleepy to stop herself. 'It wasn't fair.'

She'd felt his lips brush the top of her head.

'You should be able to trust me.' His breath stirred her hair. 'I should be able to trust you.'

It had been an odd way of phrasing it. It struck her that he hadn't said that he did trust her. Only that he should. Still, she'd been too tired to dwell on it. To let doubt win. It was the last thing she remembered before falling asleep.

She wondered if he'd slept. Several times during the night, she'd half-woken and been hazily aware that he was awake. But perhaps she'd dreamed that. After all, she'd slept so hard, she'd never heard him get up.

Wrapping the sheet across her chest, she looked around her bedroom. Everything was as it always was. The fireplace with its Victorian mantelpiece. The old dresser she'd found at a flea market and painted white. The photo of her mother with an eleven-year-old Harper and Bonnie, skinny arms around each other, smiling at the camera – the only family photo she had in the apartment.

She knew Luke was trained to make quick assessments of people. Having seen where she lived in the light now, what would he think of her?

'You're up.' Luke walked into the room, a towel loose around his waist, hair damp and ruffled.

She hadn't noticed the shower stopping.

She watched him lazily as he moved. His muscles were well defined, his skin tawny but not tanned. He was perfect.

'So are you.' She stretched, faking a yawn. 'How long have you been up?'

'A while.' His eyes searched her face. 'I didn't wake you, did I?'

She shook her head. 'It's late. I just woke up.'

He didn't seem tense or nervous, in fact, he looked perfectly comfortable. Like he'd always been in her bedroom wearing only a towel.

The intimacy of the moment pushed back her doubts.

They could do this.

Still, they both moved carefully through the morning.

When she emerged from the shower a while later, she found him, dressed in the jeans and black T-shirt he'd worn the night before, standing in front of the fireplace looking up at Bonnie's painting of her.

A floorboard creaked under her foot, and he pivoted to peruse the bookshelves next to it. The movement was smooth, natural.

Turning toward the bedroom, Harper pretended not to notice.

It felt like they were cautiously discovering each other. Opening doors they'd been forbidden to unlock for years, and peeking inside.

They just had to be careful what doors they opened. Each of them had things they wanted to keep hidden.

Later, sitting across from each other at the kitchen table, they talked again about the Whitney case. Luke's long legs covered the distance between them; his bare feet rested lightly on top of hers.

'So, they're sure it's not the ex-husband?'

'According to Smith, he has a solid alibi.' Harper sipped her coffee. 'Clocked in at work before she was murdered. Was there all day. By the time he clocked out, she was dead.'

'You should check on him anyway,' Luke told her. 'Just in case.'

'I will.'

'What about the other men in her life?' He nudged her foot gently. 'You said she had a colorful history?'

Harper nodded. 'DJ said she made a lot of enemies. I have a list of her most recent partners.'

'You gonna check them out?' he asked.

'Of course.'

It came out sharper than she intended. He gave her a steady look.

'Come on, Harper.'

She didn't back down. 'I know what you're doing, Luke.'

'If that's the case, then you know you can't fixate on one suspect at the cost of all the others,' he reminded her. 'You have to look at every option.'

'That doesn't mean I'm not looking at Blazer, too,' she said stubbornly.

'Fine.' His voice was measured. 'I was getting to that. You're going to need proof Whitney really dated Blazer. You'll need evidence – photos or video. Something tangible. We have to prove it wasn't a coincidence that they were seen together. If you don't have that, no one will consider him a real suspect. So, that's your step one.'

It was good advice. Some of the tension left the air between them.

'I'll talk to Whitney's co-workers,' she said. 'See if I can reach her friends.'

'I'd talk to that receptionist you mentioned,' he said. 'The one that guy you work with spoke to. You might notice something he didn't. You're better at this than he is.'

Harper tilted her head. 'How can you be so sure I'm better?'

He smiled.

'Because you're the best, McClain.'

In the soft light, he looked younger. With his hair mussed and his shirt untucked, he seemed almost boyish. His eyes were bluer than she'd thought. An unusual deep lapis.

Catching her gaze, he lifted one eyebrow. 'What're you looking at?'

'You,' she said. 'I don't get to see you in daylight very often. You have pretty eyes.'

If she thought she could embarrass him, she was wrong.

Rising to the challenge, he leaned forward, eyes skimming her face, tracing the damp strands of hair lying against her shoulders.

'Actually, now that you mention it, your hair looks redder than I thought. And your eyes are almost pure green…'

'All right,' she said, squirming. 'That's enough.'

His smile broadening, he took a slow sip of coffee.

'I like the way you look, Harper. Day and night.'

Warmth rushed through her.

In that moment, it seemed to her they were falling into something real without ever meaning to. But then, falling accidentally is always easier than falling on purpose. You don't see the ground coming.

Glancing at his watch, Luke sighed.

'I've got to be in court in an hour. You better ask me all your questions fast. I know you want to know more about Blazer.'

Harper hated for the moment to end. But he was right. There was work to do.

She straightened in her seat. Her feet slid out from under his.

'What do you know about his personal life?' she asked. 'Is he married?'

Luke toyed with the spoon on the table.

'He's a confirmed bachelor,' he said after a brief pause. 'Lives in one of those modern apartments in the suburbs, with a swimming pool he never uses and a guard at the gate.'

'No kids?'

He shook his head.

'Does he date?'

'I wouldn't call it "dating",' he said dryly. 'As far as I can tell, he prefers a series of one-night stands with willing women who love a man with a badge.'

Harper made a face.

'Look, I never said Larry Blazer wasn't a bastard,' Luke said. 'But that doesn't make him a killer.'

Harper studied him curiously.

'You really don't think he did it, do you?'

'No, I don't.' The response came without hesitation.

'Why not?'

'He doesn't fit the profile. He's too controlled.' He said it with so little hesitation, Harper knew he'd thought it through. 'Blazer needs rules and regulations – he thrives on them. Uses them to his own ends. Killers are the opposite. They want to break the rules society sets out. Manipulate them. Damage them.' He met her eyes. 'Blazer's a tyrant, not a killer.'

'Anyone can kill if pushed hard enough, though. You're a cop – you should know that better than anyone,' she argued.

'I do know that,' he said, his voice sharpening. 'And I'm telling you I don't think you have enough on Blazer.'

Harper bit back an angry reply and took a long, calming sip of coffee. Every time they talked about Blazer they fought. They had to figure out a way not to do that.

As if he knew what she was thinking, Luke reached across the table for her hand.

'Harper, I don't want to fight with you. Not after last night,' he said, his tone softening. 'But… Do me a favor. Look into everyone she knew. Your killer's there somewhere. And you're going to find him.

'I just don't think it's Blazer.'

Chapter Twenty-seven

When Harper walked into the newsroom that afternoon, DJ was putting the finishing touches to an article about a new gym being built at a local high school.

'Wow,' she said, dropping her bag on her desk. 'That looks exciting.'

He spun his chair, stopping on a dime facing her.

'It's the *bomb*,' he announced, deadpan. 'Actually, I was offered a story about a drug-fueled supermodel orgy, but I said, No. I want to write about the gym. Please tell me all about your plans for basketball games and pep rallies.'

'Wise move,' Harper said. 'This town is crying out for pep rallies.'

She toyed with a pen, flipping it between her fingers.

Her talk with Luke had unsettled her. After he'd gone that morning, she'd spent the rest of the day going over her notes. She knew he was right, that she had to look at other possible suspects more seriously. She couldn't allow herself to fixate on Blazer.

This meant she needed to find out more about Whitney and the men she dated.

She had a pretty good idea where to start.

'Look. I know you're having the time of your life with that piece,' she said. 'But I've got a question only you can answer.'

'At last,' he said, brightening. 'My crime-solving skills are recognized.'

'If I wanted to talk to people at the college who knew Whitney,' she said, 'where would I go?'

'Development Department,' he said. 'That's where she worked.'

'Who would I talk to there?' Harper asked, like it was no big deal. 'That receptionist you mentioned. What was her name?'

DJ glanced over his shoulder at his computer, then turned back to her.

'You know what? Her office is open for another hour.' He tilted his head at his monitor. 'I'm through writing my Pulitzer submission. We could go to the campus, see what we can find.'

'You sure you don't mind?' she asked.

'For you?' he said. 'Anything.'

DJ's grin was endearingly crooked – his front two teeth crossed just a little, putting everything charmingly off-kilter.

Harper grabbed her bag. 'Did I ever tell you you're my hero?'

'Stick with me, kid,' he said as they headed for the door. 'I'll show you the ropes.'

When they pulled up at the university, the campus was quiet. The football field-sized parking lot held only a scattering of cars.

'Where is everyone?' Harper asked.

'It's nearly five o'clock,' DJ said as if this explained everything. Seeing the puzzled look on her face, he said, 'They're in a bar,

Harper. It's happy hour. Don't you remember being a college student?'

Harper shook her head. 'I've blocked it all out.'

The earlier sunshine was long gone now, the sky was overcast. The first drops of rain fell as they reached the administration building.

The nineteenth-century structure surrounded on all sides by rows of stone columns looked as colleges should – grand and eternal. Like most universities, though, the campus was largely modern, with mismatched buildings scattered across endless green acres.

Harper looked around, trying to remember the layout. It must be in her memory somewhere. After all, she'd studied here for more than two years before dropping out to work at the paper.

What she really recalled of her time here was feeling out of place. She'd been eighteen, like all the other freshmen. But she'd felt a century older.

The worst part was: Bonnie wasn't with her.

In her last years at high school, she'd more or less lived with the Larson family. Her grandmother had done all she could, but Bonnie lived much closer to school, so after a while, it made sense for Harper to stay with the Larsons during the week.

The two of them were always as close as sisters – closer in some ways, because they'd chosen each other. Naturally, Harper had always assumed they'd go to college together, too. They'd never really discussed it, but it seemed the obvious next step. Until Bonnie won a full scholarship to an art school in Boston.

When she announced her news, brimming with excitement, Harper hadn't been able to hide her shock.

Bonnie had always been there. Always.

Clocking her expression, Bonnie's own enthusiasm had evaporated.

'I won't go,' she'd said instantly. 'I… I'll turn it down.'

When she said it, though, Harper saw the joy go out of her eyes.

Seeing her deflated like that made Harper more aware of what she was asking.

After her divorce, Bonnie's mother had raised four kids on the small salary she earned working as a secretary. She couldn't begin to pay for college. Without the scholarship, Bonnie would have to take out student loans that could cripple her for the rest of her life. And she'd be giving up her dream school.

She couldn't ask her to do that.

'Don't be an idiot,' Harper had told her. 'We can't spend our whole lives together. You have to go to that school and suck up all the free learning. I'll be fine.'

Bonnie must have known she was lying – she always knew. But, this time, she let it go.

'I'll come back for Christmas and I'll be here every summer,' she promised. 'I'll email you constantly. You'll never notice I'm gone.'

That September, she'd loaded up her car and headed north. Harper said nothing, even as her heart fractured.

No matter what she told herself about how it was temporary, and it was only for school, in her soul she believed her best friend was deserting her.

Why shouldn't she? Everyone else already had.

Her mother was dead, and her father lived hundreds of miles away. She had no siblings, and her grandmother was, by then, in her seventies.

So, no. She couldn't relate to the other students, who had families back home, places to go on spring break, people to cheer them on when they did well. She had no idea what that was like.

Alone and unmoored, she'd floated into Savannah University in a dark cloud of misery. The other students took one look at her and veered away to the nearest sane alternative.

She didn't know what to study – she didn't care. Still, on the first day at registration, she was told she had to choose a major.

'You can change it later,' the uninterested woman on the desk said, adding, when Harper hesitated, 'Close your eyes and pick one, honey. There are a hundred people in line behind you.'

Under pressure, Harper selected journalism almost at random. It sounded interesting. It wasn't anything her parents would have chosen. It wasn't what Bonnie would choose.

No one was more surprised than her to find out she was a natural.

She chased the university president up the stairs to ask about racism in fraternities. She spent three weeks following candidates for student body president around as they campaigned.

Those anarchic, rough-and-ready days in the newspaper's tiny office, pounding out articles on old computers with a handful of other student volunteers were her only happy memories of that time.

In her second year, on the suggestion of one of her professors, Harper showed up at the Savannah newspaper with an article she'd written about a fracas between frat boys at a bar popular with students.

It wasn't Baxter she'd met with, but a junior editor. With an expression that indicated he was humoring her, he'd taken out his red pen and read the article.

When he finished, he'd removed his glasses to look at her more closely.

'How old did you say you were?'

The newspaper offered one internship each year. That year, they gave it to Harper.

She'd worked hard – showing up twice the number of hours required for the role. Without being asked, she made herself useful around the newsroom, writing obituaries and birth announcements, doing research for reporters. Making coffee runs.

Eventually, the editors gave her more challenging assignments, covering local meetings when the usual reporters were busy. The meetings often happened at night, so it was Baxter who edited her work on those occasions.

Harper absorbed everything with voracious hunger. Never questioning the editing. Never complaining about the hours.

Baxter rewarded her with more assignments.

When the next year began, the paper didn't choose a new intern. Harper stayed on. She signed up for fewer classes so she'd have more time to work.

On quiet nights, Baxter quizzed her about her work, her background. Harper evaded personal questions, but mentioned that, when she was in high school, she'd had a part-time job at the police station for three years.

When Baxter casually asked who she'd worked with, Harper reeled off the names she could think of, including Smith, the deputy chief, and several detectives.

The next evening, Baxter announced that Harper would begin shadowing the crime reporter, Tom Lane, on his rounds.

Lane objected virulently. He and Baxter had it out on the newsroom floor.

'This is ridiculous,' he complained, gesturing at Harper. 'I don't have time to babysit at a crime scene.'

'Tom, it's not optional,' Baxter informed him. 'This is part of your job. I think the girl has chops and I want to see what she's made of.'

'The girl has *chops*?' His voice rose. 'She's a teenager. She's not allowed to have chops.'

Harper, who was twenty, bristled, but knew better than to intervene. She kept her head down, pretending she wasn't listening to every word.

'Tom, she worked at the police station. She knows these guys. They'll share information with her they wouldn't share with someone else.' Baxter's voice had been measured but unyielding.

Tom's face reddened.

'What are you suggesting? That police don't share information with me? If you're not satisfied with my work, Emma, say the word.'

'Pull yourself together, Tom.' Turning her back on him, Baxter walked back to her desk. But he wasn't about to let it go, and he followed her, still complaining.

'She'll slow me down. She'll get in the way. I don't have time for this.'

'I don't know why you're still talking,' Baxter told him briskly. 'You won't win. Take McClain with you. Show her the ropes. I've got plans for her.'

Harper's heart leapt to her throat. Baxter had *plans* for her. This meant real reporting. No more obituaries and school-board meetings.

In the end, Lane gave in to the inevitable and allowed her to shadow him.

At crime scenes, they made an uncomfortable pair – Lane was several inches shorter than her and wiry, with thinning gray hair. Harper looked younger than her age, with auburn hair hanging nearly to her waist, usually wearing jeans and a T-shirt, clutching a reporter's notebook as if her life depended on it.

At first Lane barely spoke to her. He seemed to think if he ignored her eventually she'd go away.

He was overly protective of his beat – it drove him crazy when a detective at a scene recognized Harper and stopped to chat with her.

'If you want your quote in the paper,' he'd tell them, 'come to me.'

But the cops still looked out for her.

Once, after Lane drove off without her in a particularly dicey part of town, she hitched a ride back to the newspaper in Smith's car. As revenge against Lane's treatment of her, the lieutenant gave her insider information about a shooting that no one offered the older reporter.

After that, Lane finally seemed to realize there was no point in fighting anymore.

From then on, he was a useful if sometimes dour font of information.

It was Lane who explained what to look for in the crime reports each day.

'If it bleeds it leads, girl,' he told her one night at police headquarters. 'Murder, armed robbery, stabbing, shooting, interesting burglaries – that's it. The end. Anything else, it's a waste of your time writing it. Baxter doesn't want it and the public won't read it.'

'What's an interesting burglary?' Harper had asked, looking over his shoulder as he flew through the stack of crime reports so fast she barely had time to see what he was rejecting.

'Celebrities, athletes, politicians.' He ticked them off without looking up. 'Someone rips them off, readers care. Everyone else better get some insurance because I'm not going to write about them.'

This was precisely the system Harper employed today. She was so finely attuned to which crimes were news and which weren't, she could reject a case after reading the first line of the crime report.

At shooting scenes, she'd follow him closely – mostly because she didn't want him to drive off and leave her there, but also to see how he operated.

When the hour got late and the streets turned ugly, Tom was fascinating to watch, weaving through crowds of witnesses like a dancer, finding exactly the right person to talk to. The one who'd seen it all and had a pithy quote ready to tumble off his tongue.

Those nights, Harper absorbed the danger and excitement like oxygen. By the end of the first month working with Tom, she knew what she wanted to do with her life.

And it didn't involve college.

Over the course of the first year they spent working together, Harper showed up less and less at class, until she was so far behind she received a warning letter from the dean.

Baxter hadn't missed any of this. One day, without warning, she told Harper she was putting her on the regular payroll.

'Looks like you're part-time at college anyway,' she'd said. 'And you're useful.'

A short while later, Harper dropped out of school altogether.

The transition was easy. She worked a few day shifts, and on Tom's nights off she covered the police. It was a good system for everyone.

Harper, by then, had found the apartment on Jones Street. Her only furniture was a mattress and a bookshelf, but she felt like she'd finally found her place in the world. Everything seemed to be coming together.

So when, on his sixtieth birthday, Tom announced he'd decided to retire, she couldn't believe it.

'What are you going to do?' she'd asked him.

'I'm going to go live with my brother in Jacksonville.'

'That's it?'

Harper – then twenty-two – couldn't imagine giving up a job as a crime reporter for a boatload of nothing in Florida.

'Look,' Tom growled, 'the guy's an asshole, but he's an asshole with a condo and a fishing license. And I've had enough. I deserve to sit on my butt for a few years before I kick the bucket.'

Seeing the look on her face, he'd softened.

'Don't worry,' he told her. 'Baxter was right – you're a natural. You've already got half the PD wrapped around your little finger.'

It was the only compliment he ever gave her.

On the day he left, he gave her his scanner – the one she still used today.

'Don't listen to this thing too much,' he told her gruffly. 'It'll eat your life.'

'We're going over here.' DJ's voice was a lifeline, pulling her out of the past.

Blinking hard, Harper turned to see he was pointing towards a small, glass-and-steel building surrounded by azalea bushes.

Clearing her mind of memories, she followed him down a sidewalk that angled sharply between perfectly mowed lawns. In the distance some guys were throwing a Frisbee. She heard one of them laugh and shout something, but the words were lost on the breeze.

They were so young.

She'd never been that young.

DJ opened the glass door and she followed him into a small

modern lobby. It was icy cold inside – the air conditioning was set for a hotter day.

'*Hola*, Rosanna,' he called to the tiny, dark-haired woman at the desk.

She laughed, dimples deep in her round cheeks, and said something brief in Spanish that made him smile.

'Harper McClain,' DJ said, gesturing for her to step forward, 'this is Rosanna Salazar. She knows everyone who's anyone in fundraising.'

Rosanna giggled. 'Oh, David,' she said. 'You're such a sweet-talker.'

The two of them joked around but, from the way she was looking at DJ, Harper got the distinct impression Rosanna had a crush on him. She was probably five or six years older than him, but really cute.

She made a mental note to mention it to him later. It would be just like DJ not to notice.

'Harper is another reporter from the paper,' he explained. 'She's the one who wrote all the articles about Marie Whitney.'

'Oh.' The smile evaporated from Rosanna's face.

'It's very sad,' Harper kept her tone solicitous. 'Were you friends with her?'

Rosanna hesitated – her eyes darting to DJ, who nodded encouragingly.

'Not exactly,' she said. 'Marie... she kept to herself.'

Behind her desk, the office was modern and open-plan, with a scattering of desks and low file cabinets. The walls held arty black-and-white photographs of elegant people in ballgowns and tuxedoes that seemed out of place in such a workaday environment.

'Have you heard anything from the police?' Rosanna searched their faces. 'Do they have a suspect?'

DJ motioned to Harper, who shook her head.

'They're not saying much,' she confided. 'I know they're looking at people she knew. People she dated.'

She moved closer, closing the distance between herself and Rosanna. Inviting confidences.

'The police must have been here interviewing her co-workers?'

Rosanna glanced over her shoulder to make sure they wouldn't be overheard. But there was no one near.

'They went through her desk and took everything to the police station,' she whispered. 'Even her computer is gone.'

'That makes sense,' DJ assured her. 'They'll want to check absolutely everything.'

He leaned casually against the counter. The three of them were now a tight unit. Close together, sharing conspiratorial whispers.

'Did Marie have close friends?' Harper asked. 'People she went to lunch with?'

Rosanna pursed her lips. 'Can I be honest with you?'

'Of course,' Harper said.

'Marie was strange,' the receptionist said. 'You couldn't trust her. She'd be nice to your face, then you'd find out she was saying bad things about you behind your back. To your boss. She got ahead by knocking everyone else down. Does that make sense?'

She seemed almost relieved to be telling someone. As if she'd bottled it all up in the days right after the murder, when criticism of the dead would have been unforgivable.

'I know the type,' DJ said. 'Is that how she got promoted? She was young to be vice-chair.'

Harper had to admire how he was working Rosanna. He was patient and friendly, never intimidating. It felt like a normal chat among friends. It was working – Rosanna was bursting with secrets she wanted to share.

'OK, so, the woman who had the job before her?' Rosanna whispered confidentially. 'Marie told her boss she was lying about her expenses. She *was*. But when she left, she told me she only did it because Marie encouraged her to do it. She said everyone did it.' Her dark brown eyes were wide. 'She said I should never trust Marie. So I never did.'

Harper was increasingly fascinated by the two sides of the dead woman. Her perfect, polished exterior, and her hidden life of lies.

'What about her boyfriends?' Harper asked. 'You told DJ... I mean, David, she dated powerful men. Did you really see her with a cop?'

Rosanna nodded so hard her curls bounced.

'He came to meet her several times this spring. I'm sure he was police, although he didn't wear a uniform. He always waited for her outside. He wore a badge on his belt. And once, the wind blew his jacket open and I saw his gun, here.'

She gestured under her arm, where a shoulder holster would be.

Blazer had a shoulder holster. Most of the detectives did.

Harper and DJ exchanged a glance.

'Do you remember his name?' Harper asked.

Rosanna shook her head regretfully. 'He never actually came in to ask for Marie. He always stood outside and called her on his cell phone.'

'That's fine, Rosanna,' DJ said. 'Did you tell the police about this?'

'No.' She sounded surprised. 'They never asked.'

Harper had a sudden thought.

'Rosanna, when the police searched Marie's office, was that man – the one you saw outside – with them?'

'No.' Her answer was definite. 'In fact, I can tell you exactly who came.'

Opening a drawer, she dug around for a second, before pulling out a business card.

'It was this guy,' she said, handing it over. 'He said to call him if we thought of anything.'

The card read: 'Sergeant Frank Ledbetter, Savannah PD.'

Turning the card over in her hand, Harper frowned.

It was routine for detectives to divide the work on any case, but it didn't make sense that Blazer wouldn't personally oversee the search of the victim's place of work.

Why would he not want to be here?

Maybe because he knew his face might be recognized.

Handing the card back, she said, 'I know you've told us already, but would you mind describing the man again – the one Marie dated?'

'He was a big guy,' Rosanna said slowly. 'Tall. And, I think he had light hair, or maybe gray...' Her voice trailed off and she gave an apologetic wince. 'I'm sorry. I can't be certain now. It was months ago.'

Tall. Light hair. That described Blazer. But big? Blazer was tall and thin. Still, she could be misremembering. Or using the wrong word to describe him – some people use 'big' to mean tall.

'Are there any pictures of him?' Harper asked. 'Or is there CCTV here?'

'Nothing like that.' Rosanna said.

'Is there anything you can tell me about her other boyfriends?' Harper asked. 'Anyone you can remember?'

Rosanna bit her lip, thinking.

'She always had dates,' she said after a moment. 'She often changed here at work and then went straight out. But she didn't invite them to the office. It was like she kept them secret. That's why I remembered the cop. It was unusual for her to meet them here. There must have been something special about him, for her to let him come to the office.'

Harper was going to have to look elsewhere to find out more about Marie's ex-boyfriends.

She glanced at DJ, who gave an infinitesimal shrug. There was nothing more to get right now.

DJ smiled. 'Thank you so much, Rosanna.'

While he turned on the charm, Harper walked across the room to look at the black-and-white photos again. In each shot, everything looked so glamorous – long, silky dresses, sleek tuxedoes, crystal chandeliers, champagne flutes.

They could have been perfume ads for all the polish and glitz, except, occasionally she came across a face she recognized.

The town's former mayor was at the center of one, grinning broadly. In another, she spotted a well-known local business executive who starred in his own hilariously bad TV ads.

The face in the third picture on the wall, stopped her in her tracks.

'Hey,' she said, forgetting, in her excitement, to keep her voice down. 'Isn't that Marie?'

She pointed at an image of a beautiful blonde woman in a long white dress. The woman was slim, her shoulders pale and narrow. She was with a man who had his back to the camera.

Rosanna had to stand up to see the picture.

'Oh yeah,' she said. 'That's her. I forgot that picture was there.'

After a second, she and DJ resumed their conversation. Harper stayed where she was, staring at Marie Whitney's beautiful face.

Her hair glimmered in the light of the chandelier. Her smile was open and engaging, but it didn't reach her eyes. Those were dark and dangerous. And full of secrets.

Harper would have given anything to ask her one question.

The only person in the world who could tell her what happened that day, was in that picture. And she would never reveal her story to anyone.

Harper had never worked on a case where it was so hard to pin down even the most basic facts. Every clue she found slipped from her fingers before she could grasp it.

Once again, she thought about Camille Whitney and wondered if she was OK. If her mother had been kind to her. Or if she'd been as cruel to her daughter as she had been to everyone else.

It was as if there were multiple Marie Whitneys, and none of them could be trusted. Marie Whitney the single mother. Marie Whitney the victim. Marie Whitney the manipulative liar. And none of those women had any connection to Harper's mother. Except for how they died.

It felt like Whitney was playing her from the grave.

Harper was risking everything for this. Everything.

She had to find something tangible. Something real.

And she needed it soon.

Chapter Twenty-eight

The next morning, sitting at her kitchen table with her laptop and mug of coffee, Harper began working her way through the list of Marie Whitney's known ex-lovers. Without more to go on, it made sense to identify any potential suspects from the names they had already.

To start, she divided the list up into likely and unlikely.

The artists and grad-students she put in the unlikely column. There was almost no chance that they would know how to forensically clean a crime scene, as the murderer had done.

Of the names DJ had given her, that left the CEO, a prominent local lawyer, and a state senator.

She left vague messages for all of them with their offices, not mentioning the true reason for her call. They weren't the kind of men you got on the phone at the first try, or the kind to call you back if they knew for a second you suspected them of a crime.

Then she waited.

The lawyer called her first.

After a quick round of pleasantries, Harper got to the point.

'I'm writing a story for the newspaper about a woman named Marie Whitney,' she began.

The second the words were out of her mouth, he combusted.

'I know nothing about her. I haven't seen her in nearly a year,' he said, his voice rising an octave. 'I don't understand why you're even talking to me about her.'

'It's a routine call,' Harper said calmly. 'I'm trying to understand what your relationship was with her.'

'I had no relationship with her,' he insisted. 'Who told you I did?'

'A source,' she said.

'A *source*?' He half-shouted the word. 'You want to damage my reputation because of an unnamed source? That would be a very bad idea, I promise you. You do not want to mess with me, Miss McClain. I will slap your paper with an injunction so fast your head spins. Just try me.'

'I'm sorry,' she said, desperate to get something useful from him. 'Please, if I could have two minutes – I promise I won't use your name. If you could just tell me where you were the day she died.'

That set him off again. But somewhere, amid his rant, he managed to tell her he'd been in court that day – all day – and had the records to prove it. But he would not tell her anything about Whitney.

'There is no way I will talk to you about Marie Whitney. I have nothing to say about her. As I said, I've had no interaction with her in a long time, thank God. I suggest you find someone else to talk to. And leave me out of it.'

With that, he hung up.

Harper sat at her kitchen table, staring at the phone. The man had been furious but, it was more than that. He was scared – she could hear it in his voice.

Scared of what?

After that, she didn't expect to hear from the others at all.

To her surprise, though, the state senator returned her call within an hour. She'd expected to have to chase him for days. When she told him she was calling about the Whitney case, he sounded as nervous as a cat in a room full of pitbulls.

'I… I don't see why you called me,' he said anxiously. 'I haven't seen Marie Whitney in more than a year.' He paused. 'God. I can't believe what happened to her. I'm still in shock.'

'I'm only calling because I want to remove your name from my list.' After her experience with the lawyer, Harper kept her tone soothing. 'It would help me tremendously if you could account for your time.'

'How… How could I do that?'

'Well,' she said. 'Where were you the afternoon Marie Whitney died?'

His voice grew high-pitched. 'You don't think I had anything to do with what happened to her? My God, Miss McClain. I swear…'

'Not at all,' she assured him. 'I simply have to take you off my list. I'm doing this with everyone she knew. This is in no way an allegation and I will not put your name in my article. Please. Tell me where you were. It's that simple.'

'Oh God. This is a nightmare,' he said, unhappily. 'I don't… What day was… did it happen?'

Patiently, she gave him the day and the estimated time of the crime.

There was a pause – she heard the clicking of computer keys, presumably as he checked his calendar.

When he spoke again, the relief in his voice was palpable.

'The legislature was in session that day. I spoke on the floor at three o'clock precisely. I was there until seven that night.'

Harper made a note to check this, but she was inclined to believe him. He didn't seem smart enough or cold enough to commit such a perfect crime. At least he was calmer than the lawyer, though. She decided to push it further – see how much she could get.

'Senator,' she said, 'now that we've cleared that up, is there anything you can tell me about Whitney? I'm hearing that she was a... complicated woman.'

'That's a polite way of putting it.' There was a bitter edge to his voice. 'She tried to ruin me. She had no morals. No heart. She—'

He stopped suddenly, as if realizing who he was talking to.

'None of this is for attribution,' he said abruptly. 'I'll sue you if you print a single word.'

That was the second time someone had threatened to sue Harper that day.

'Senator, please,' she said, pressing her fingertips against her forehead. 'I won't mention any of this in print. Under any circumstances. This is deep background. Anything you can tell me would help me understand what I'm dealing with.'

This seemed to mollify him to a certain extent.

'There's not much to say. No one deserves to die like she did,' he said. 'But Marie Whitney came close. And that is all I'll tell you. I've got my career to think about.'

'Wait,' she said, 'isn't there something more you can tell me? Anything. People seemed afraid of her. Were you afraid of her?'

There was a long pause.

'I can't,' he said, and she could hear the conflict in his voice. He wanted to tell her something but wouldn't let himself take the risk. 'It's not possible. But I will say this: keep digging, Miss McClain. Someone braver than me will tell you the truth. I know I wasn't the only one.'

With that, he hung up.

Harper listened to the silence on the line for a long moment before setting the phone down.

I know I wasn't the only one.

What did that mean?

She felt increasingly confounded.

Why did the people in Whitney's life hate her so much? They all still sounded terrified.

She was dead. What could she do to them now?

The CEO was the last to respond to her call. He didn't get in touch with her for several days. She called every day, leaving polite messages that went unreturned.

Finally, late in the evening on the fourth day, she received a short, succinct email from him. It appeared to have been written personally, no secretary signed it.

> I suggest you stop calling my office. I know what you're working on, and I want no part of it. This is your final warning.

Harper stared at the email in stunned disbelief. She'd never told his secretary the reason for her call. Never mentioned Marie Whitney at all.

How did he know? And what if he didn't? He could be wrong.

Also, *This is your final warning*? That sounded like a threat.

She began to write a furious reply. But when she looked closer, she saw that he'd cc'd in another man – James Cohen, of Barrington Associates.

Barrington Associates was a local corporate law firm, specializing in protecting the privacy of high-wealth individuals. They were known to be vicious.

Harper let out a quick breath. And closed the email.

She couldn't take on a CEO and a prominent lawyer without Baxter and Dells finding out what she was up to. Those guys wouldn't sue her alone. They'd sue the paper, too.

And Baxter had strictly forbidden her to work on this story.

But there were other things she could do. If he thought he could scare her away, he was wrong. She wouldn't give up this easily.

Clearing her screen, she began to search for information about Sterling Robinson. Hundreds of articles appeared.

Frowning, she narrowed her search down to profiles, immediately honing in on a recent article from *The Wall Street Journal*.

Robinson was forty-six years old, the CEO of a media conglomerate called Sterling Enterprises. It owned websites, television stations and publishing houses throughout the world. Most of its websites were the click-bait kind, with pictures of beautiful movie stars and 'You'll never believe what they look like now!' as the link. Some, though, were thoroughly legitimate news sites, respected for their reporting.

In the photo at the top of the article, Robinson looked younger than his years, narrowly built, with thick dark hair and wire-framed glasses. The article said he was divorced, with no children. He lived in New York most of the year, but also had houses in San Francisco and Martha's Vineyard.

The only mention of Savannah, she noted, was that his company had opened an office in the city five years ago.

Most interesting, though, was the nugget that, along with the corporation, he ran a charitable foundation that gave millions of dollars to groups that supported the arts, and to universities for medical research.

Harper opened her notebook and wrote down the foundation's name, adding, 'This could be how he met Marie Whitney.'

She underlined the sentence three times.

She wondered if Robinson was in one of those pictures in Whitney's office. She would never have noticed – he would have been one more man in a tuxedo, smiling for the camera.

She couldn't see any obvious connection between him and her mother. Fifteen years earlier, he'd been building his company in New York. It seemed unlikely they'd ever have met. There was no indication he'd spent time in Savannah until recently.

Still, the possibility of a Whitney connection was enough to keep him interesting.

His charity work seemed to indicate he was not completely without merit, but his business enterprises showed clear ruthlessness. A few years ago, he'd intentionally put a newspaper in Tennessee out of business to boost the hits on his local news website. Hundreds of people lost their jobs.

The more she learned, the more Harper considered Robinson intriguing.

The fact was, someone as rich as him wouldn't have to kill Whitney himself. A man like Robinson could hire a hitman to do his dirty work for him.

A professional.

The thought chilled her.

All along she'd been convinced any suggestion that someone would have taken out a hit on a woman like Whitney was ridiculous.

Suddenly it was no longer absurd.

On the drive home that night, Harper's mind was tangled up in the case. The realization that Robinson was a potential suspect changed everything.

Luke's absolute conviction that Blazer couldn't be the killer had made her doubt her own judgment on the case. Now Robinson seemed a perfectly viable candidate, and she wasn't sure what to think.

But then, who was the man with a badge who visited Whitney at work? Was it Blazer?

If only she could find one person who really knew Whitney and was willing to talk.

As she turned off of brightly lit Bay Street, she found herself thinking about Camille Whitney. And wondering what she knew.

She must be with a relative now – probably her father. But where? And what had she told the police? Did she know who her mother was dating?

What had she seen that day?

Lost in thought, she barely noticed the black Mercedes as it pulled into traffic behind her.

When she turned onto Habersham Street, the black Mercedes turned, too.

Harper had eaten the last of the bread that afternoon, so she stopped in front of a 24-hour corner shop, and hurried in for bread, milk and eggs.

It was only when she pulled out into traffic again, and saw the Mercedes do the same, that warning signals went off in her mind.

There were no other cars on the street. It was always three car lengths behind her – never more, never less. She sped up, it sped up. She slowed down, it slowed down.

And she couldn't remember when it had first appeared.

She took a couple of unnecessary turns, making the block before heading back to Habersham. The Mercedes was always there – three car lengths behind – steady and purposeful.

The first tentacles of fear wrapped around Harper's chest.

She'd never seen the undercover cops drive a Mercedes – it was always sports cars and SUVs with them – and detectives used only American-made cars.

So, who was that?

Briefly, she considered driving straight to the police station. But then told herself she was being ridiculous.

If she was being followed, she wanted to know by whom.

Steeling herself, she turned onto Jones. A few seconds later, the Mercedes followed.

Harper flinched as its lights flashed across her rearview mirror.

'OK, you bastard,' she muttered, downshifting. 'Let's see what you've got planned.'

Smoothly, she pulled into her usual parking place under the oak, her eyes sweeping the sidewalk for anyone else who might be looking for her. But the street was empty.

Cutting the engine, she sat still, watching the Mercedes. It slowed as it passed – like it wanted to be seen.

The windows were darkly tinted. All she could see was the shadowy outline of a driver, staring straight ahead.

When it passed, she noticed the light above its license plate was out – the only part of it she could get in the darkness looked like 90K.

Her eyes still on the car, she dug in her bag for a pen and scribbled the partial plate on the back of her hand. Then she watched as it reached the corner, signaled left, and disappeared.

Chapter Twenty-nine

When the Mercedes was gone, Harper hurriedly opened the car door and vaulted out into the street, slamming the door behind her. Breathless, she ran into the middle of the road and stared into the shadows where the car had been, as if it might leave some trace behind. But there was nothing.

After a minute, she climbed the stairs to her apartment and unlocked the door, securing it behind her.

Leaving the lights off, she went to the window and peered out – but the street remained empty.

Harper didn't know what to make of this. Had the car really been following her? Maybe it was nothing more than a coincidence. The car happened to be going her way. Or maybe it wasn't the same Mercedes that had been behind her earlier.

Or maybe someone who knew what she was working on was trying to intimidate her.

Either way, she was going to have to keep a good eye out from now on. If someone was going so far as to actually follow her, things were getting serious.

Zuzu bounded into the room, her tail in the air, miaowing insistently.

'What about you?' she asked, stroking her hand across the soft fur. 'Did you see anything unusual today?'

She purred and rubbed against her ankle.

'Some guard cat you are.'

They walked together to the kitchen and she put some food out for her. As the cat ate, she opened the fridge looking for something for herself.

Only then did it strike her, she'd forgotten her groceries in the car.

With a sigh, she grabbed her keys and headed back across the dark apartment, right as someone knocked on the door.

Her heart kicked.

It was Luke's distinctive knock – three light taps.

Still, Harper checked through the peephole first. He stood in the glow of the porch light – his dark blue eyes watching the door as if he could see her through it.

She opened the door and reached for his hand, pulling him inside and checking the street behind him – empty again. No sign of the Mercedes.

'What's going on?' Luke asked, instantly alert. 'Why are you sitting in the dark?'

'It's probably nothing,' she said, closing and locking the door. 'But it might be something.'

They'd been seeing each other most nights, lately. Sometimes he texted first, sometimes he simply showed up. He always hid his car a few blocks away, usually on a quiet side street.

For Harper, it was almost scary how quickly this had become normal.

Trying not to sound like she was over-reacting, she told him about the Mercedes.

'I know it could have been a coincidence,' she said. 'But it made me jittery.'

'Coincidence or not, I don't like it.' There was real concern in his eyes. 'Give me those numbers and I'll see if I can run the plate tomorrow. A partial might be enough.'

Harper turned her hand over, letting him see what she'd written. Pulling out his phone, he tapped them in, and saved them.

'If it wasn't a coincidence,' he said, 'who do you think it could be?'

'I'm investigating at least three men, all of whom probably believe I'm going to ruin their lives,' she said. 'If one of them killed Whitney, now would be the time to get rid of me. Before I find out more.' She let out a long breath. 'Or it could have been someone who lives around the corner going home late. I don't know.'

For a second they looked at each other. Then Luke reached for her hand, pulling her close.

'I'll run those plates tomorrow, see if we can narrow it down,' he promised. 'I'm sure it's nothing.'

Some jittery, still buzzing part of Harper wanted to pace the room, analyzing all the possibilities. But she fought that urge and let herself lean into him.

She didn't want to rely on this – it was too easy having someone there for her. Someone who could fix things. Someone who cared.

But she couldn't help it. When Luke was with her, every punch life threw at her was easier to take.

Wrapping her wrists behind his neck, she raised her lips to his.

'You're so sexy when you offer to run plates for me,' she said. He smiled, his eyes crinkling.

'You are very easy to please,' he said, running his hands down her spine.

'I'm going to have to ask you to prove that,' Harper told him.

For a while after that, there was no more talking.

Much later, as they lay in her bed, she told him about the email from Robinson, and what her research had found.

'What are you thinking?' he asked, lazily running his fingers through her hair.

'I think Robinson just became a very interesting possibility,' she said.

'More interesting than Blazer?' His eyes held hers.

'At least as interesting,' she conceded. 'Maybe more.'

His fingers moved to the bare skin of her shoulder, where he traced soft figure eights.

'So, what are you going to do now? He doesn't sound willing to talk.'

Warm and comfortable, Harper burrowed closer to him.

'I'll dig deeper into his history,' she said, suppressing a yawn. 'See what I can find. Also, I think I need to find a way to talk to Camille Whitney.'

'Who's that?' he asked, his brow creasing.

'Marie Whitney's daughter,' she said.

There was a pause. 'Didn't you say she was twelve?' he asked.

Harper nodded. 'Yeah, it's going to be tricky.'

His hand dropped to the bed. 'You can't be serious.'

He stared at her. The look on his face told her she'd missed something.

'What?' she asked, genuinely puzzled.

'Come on, Harper.' His jaw jutted out. 'You cannot talk to a twelve-year-old girl whose mother was murdered. Have you lost your mind?'

'Hold on a minute.' Clutching the sheet tighter, Harper sat up. 'I'm not going to hurt her, Luke. I only want to see what she knows.'

'You can't.' He seemed genuinely horrified. 'She's a *child*, Harper. Wherever she is, the state is protecting her. The last thing she needs is some reporter digging around in her brain.'

Stung, Harper pulled back.

'I'm not *some reporter*,' she said tartly. 'I'm very good at what I do. I'm not going to dig in her brain.' Seeing the doubt on his face she said, 'I went through this same thing, remember? I have *been* Camille Whitney.'

He was treating her like a suspect, and suddenly Harper couldn't bear that. She had to make him understand.

'Luke, listen,' she said. 'I'm not going to do anything bad to that girl. I'm only going to talk to her. I know what not to ask her, and if she gets upset I'll stop.'

'*If* she gets upset.' Luke pressed his fingers against his temples.

'I've talked to traumatized kids before, you know,' she reminded him heatedly. 'I'm a crime reporter. I've talked to kids who've been shot. Who've seen people shot. I know how to talk to them.'

Luke sat up, too, the sheet falling to his waist. They stared each other down across the narrow expanse of white bedding.

'How will you even find her?' he asked. 'Her location hasn't been released.'

Harper opened her mouth to tell him, then closed it again.

Luke cared about her – she knew that. She'd seen the concern in his face tonight. But he was a cop. And what she had to do in order to find Camille wasn't legal.

'I don't know yet,' she said vaguely. 'I'm going to figure it out.'

It was the first lie she could remember telling him.

There was a long silence while he studied her.

When he spoke, his voice was serious.

'Harper, I want you to promise not to do anything illegal.'

She opened her mouth to argue, but he held up his hand, stopping her.

'I know what you're going to say. But can you at least promise me you won't break any laws, or do anything stupid before you talk to me or Smith first? Is that too much to ask?'

A long icy silence fell. Harper was the one to break it.

'I won't break any laws,' she said, reluctantly.

Something changed in his eyes. He'd gone very still.

'Why don't I believe you?' His tone was chilly.

'Luke, this is ridiculous,' she said, wondering how this night had gone so wrong. 'I don't tell you how to do your job, and you shouldn't tell me how to do mine.'

'It's not work if you're doing something stupid to try and get at this child,' he said, his voice rising. 'You've got people following you already. Do you have to keep pushing every button until someone kills you?'

'I'm not doing anything stupid,' she said, too angry to care that she wasn't certain this was true. 'For God's sake, Luke. Let it go.'

Neither of them slept much that night. Through the long dark hours, Harper lay still, listening to Luke's shallow breaths, wishing she could think of the words to fix this. And finding none.

The next morning, he left early, saying something about work.

Unable to sleep after he was gone, Harper got up and made a strong pot of coffee. Alone in the kitchen in the unfamiliar early morning light, she went over their argument in her mind.

Tracking down the girl would be on the edge, yes, but it wasn't completely insane.

The worst part, she decided, had been lying to him.

He knew she'd lied – of course he did. He was trained to detect deception. But he'd backed her into a corner.

Letting out a long, tired breath, she stared into the black heart of her mug of coffee.

Maybe this was crazy, after all. But over and over she came back to the same wistful question.

What if Camille knew something?

For weeks, Harper had been running in circles chasing Whitney's ex-lovers, putting herself in danger, to find any proof, any connection.

What if five minutes with that girl could lead her straight to the killer?

Anyway. She wouldn't hurt her. She'd be careful.

She was always careful.

When she drove to work that afternoon, she kept her eyes on her rearview mirror, but saw no sign of the Mercedes.

She heard nothing from Luke until after six that evening, when he sent her a terse, one-line text:

Plate fragment too short.

He didn't ask how she was – didn't ask if she was still being followed. Didn't mention seeing her tonight, or ever.

Despite herself, a thought entered her mind: what if she texted back that she wasn't going to track down Camille? Would he show up at her door at midnight, smiling and sexy? You did as I said, now all is forgiven?

Her remorse slipped away, replaced by cool determination. No one was going to control her. Not Luke. Not anyone.

She needed Camille's address, and she would get it. Tonight.

*

When she walked into the police station at ten o'clock that evening, Dwayne was sitting at the desk, heavy-lidded eyes focused on the TV in front of him.

He glanced up sleepily as she approached.

'Hey, Harper,' he said. 'How're you keeping?'

Harper could hear the sound of some sort of game coming from the TV – the mumble of announcers, the cheering of the crowds.

'I'm good, Dwayne,' she said. 'How about yourself?'

Her tone was relaxed. No hurry, no rush.

It was easier this time.

'It's the most boring night, if I'm honest,' he confided, leaning his head on his hand. 'I don't mind working when it's busy. But when it's quiet, every minute's got a whole day packed in it.' He shook his head. 'I don't like it slow.'

'Me neither,' she agreed. 'I was kind of hoping there'd be something happening here I could write about.'

'I wish that was the case, Harper. I truly do.'

'Oh well.' She shrugged. 'It doesn't matter.'

She prepared to leave, and then stopped, as if a thought had just occurred to her.

Her heart began to thud in her chest.

'Oh, hey, Dwayne,' she said, turning back. 'I think I left my umbrella in the back on Friday. Would you buzz me through so I can see if it's still there? The lieutenant told me he'd leave it outside his door.'

Dwayne frowned.

'I was back there a few minutes ago and I didn't see any umbrella.'

Harper forced a careless laugh.

'Oh, he probably forgot, knowing him.' She took a step away. 'Never mind. I'll ask him tomorrow.'

'No – you might as well go on back and check,' he said, with a loose shrug. 'I might have missed it. Ask the girls in dispatch if they know where he put it.'

Harper had a flash image of herself at sixteen, sitting next to Dwayne at the front desk as she waited for Smith to drive her home.

Her algebra homework was open in front of her, but she and Dwayne were talking while she handcuffed herself to the chair. She could viscerally remember the satisfying crunch of the lock as the cuffs closed.

'And Bonnie says I should go out with a boy named Larry,' she remembered saying, tightening the handcuff further.

'Never go out with a boy named Larry,' Dwayne had advised sternly.

He would only have been twenty-one then, barely out of his teens. But he'd seemed so old to her.

'Why not?' Harper reached for the tiny set of silver keys, which had been on the desk but had suddenly disappeared.

'Because boys named Larry cannot be trusted,' Dwayne informed her.

'Bonnie says he's nice.'

'Bonnie thinks every boy is nice.' His tone was dry.

'True.'

Harper frowned, leaning over as far as she could with her wrist chained to the chair back.

'Dwayne, I can't find the keys.'

Dwayne's lips twitched. He never could keep a secret.

He tapped her algebra book, open to some incomprehensible equation.

'Finish this, and I'll find those keys for you.'

She'd glowered at him.

'Dwayne! You can't force me to do homework.'

Grinning broadly, he'd leaned back in his chair, hands folded across his stomach.

'The sergeant gave me permission. He said to make you finish your math by any means necessary. This is any means.'

She'd begged and complained, but Dwayne held firm.

In the end, she'd had to solve all six equations before he unlocked her wrist. When she'd told Smith about it later in tones of outrage, he'd roared with laughter.

'Remind me to give Dwayne a raise.'

A needle-prick of guilt pierced Harper's conscience. If Dwayne were blamed for what she was about to do, she'd hate herself.

But she had to do it.

By any means necessary.

'Thanks,' she said cheerfully. 'I'll be right back.'

The buzzer sounded shrill in the empty lobby as Harper crossed through to the other side.

The heavy steel door slammed shut behind her with a prison clang.

The back corridor was empty.

Instead of heading down the hallway to the lieutenant's office, she turned down the shadowy stairs, taking the steps fast.

Her chest felt tight. Her heart fluttered a staccato beat.

When she reached the basement corridor, she made a quick right, half-running between concrete walls lined with posters in blue and green, urging officers to *Be safe out there*, and promising, *Your union is here to protect you.*

Breathless, she sped past the locker rooms. No showers ran at this hour. Shift-change was four hours away.

There were people upstairs – in the dispatch room, in the detectives' offices – but the building had a hollowed-out feel. She could hear only the muffled sound of her rubber-soled shoes against the concrete floor, and the too-loud rasp of her nervous breathing as she reached the archive room door.

The big storage room was cold and dark.

Harper felt blindly along the wall until she found the plastic light switches, flipping all three at once. The fluorescent strips buzzed, faltered and then sprang to life, flooding the room with harsh, clinical light.

Without hesitation, Harper dashed across the room to the computer. Switching it on without sitting down, she stood next to the desk, drumming her fingers impatiently on the metal top as the monitor churned and beeped.

The old computer took several minutes to wake up. The whole time, she barely breathed.

She'd gone over this in her mind again and again. She had to do this fast.

No mistakes.

At last, the login screen appeared. Relief flooded Harper's chest like oxygen.

Leaning over, she typed rapidly: 815NL52K1

The message welcoming Craig Johnson appeared as it had before.

Her heart thudding hard against her ribs, Harper navigated to the search box. She typed: 'Marie Whitney'.

The computer churned, before spitting out two file numbers. One from a few weeks ago. One from six months earlier.

Frowning, Harper made a note of the latter before clicking on the more recent file.

A series of files appeared.

Muttering, 'Hurry, hurry...' under her breath, Harper clicked on each one quickly, opening and closing them until she found the main investigation report.

Hurriedly, Harper scrolled through it, adrenaline helping her absorb the information it contained at sonic speed.

'Minimum twelve stab wounds', 'Most confined to torso', 'Attack occurred in kitchen', 'Defensive wounds to right hand', 'Finger severed'.

As Harper moved through it, suddenly a series of bloody photos appeared. Each portrayed Whitney's body from a different angle, some were close-up shots of the gaping wounds – raw and garish red against her pale skin.

Clicking through them hurriedly, Harper glanced at her watch. She'd been down here nearly ten minutes already. She had to go.

'Witness statements'. These were limited to neighbors saying they heard nothing, and to Camille Whitney.

Harper stopped on that one.

Witness was asked if anyone was in the house when she returned.
Response: I don't know (Witness is crying).
Witness was asked if her mother was afraid of anyone.
Response: My mother was never afraid. She said there was nothing to be scared of if you were strong. She was strong.

At the end of the statement, a note had been added in Smith's neat, right-slanted handwriting.

Camille Whitney will be living with her father, James Whitney, at 12057 Bromley Street, in the town of Vidalia. Social Services have been informed.

Harper scribbled the name and address in her notebook with her left hand, while frantically shutting the computer down with her right.

Shoving her notebook back into her pocket, she raced across to the door, turning off the light and reaching for the handle, just as the door opened on its own.

There was no time to hide. No chance to duck out of sight.

Detective Blazer stood in front of her, a cup of coffee in one hand, a chocolate cookie in the other, staring at her with a look of frank astonishment.

'McClain? What the hell are you doing in here?'

Chapter Thirty

When the worst thing that could possibly happen finally occurs, a kind of icy calm descends. Everything goes dangerously quiet. People who've been in car accidents talk about the sudden uncanny silence as the world spins and glass flies.

In the instant her eyes met Blazer's disbelieving stare, Harper understood that. She felt no fear at all. Only a distant dull surprise.

Instead of thinking up a reason for her presence in a secure area, she noticed odd details – his tie was off and the top buttons of his pale blue shirt were undone. His hair was rumpled. The lines on his forehead were carved deeper than usual, his chiseled features softened by fatigue. There was a file tucked under his arm, and it struck her with cool clarity that he must have come to the archive to return it before heading home.

'McClain?' Blazer's sharp voice jarred her, shaking her back to reality. 'An explanation, please?'

The room zoomed back into view – the seriousness of the moment rushing at her like a tornado bearing down on a trailer park.

The problem was, she had no good answer to give him.

Fleetingly she considered the umbrella story, but she knew it wouldn't fly. What would her umbrella be doing in the basement archive room?

She'd have to come up with something else.

Remembering something Tom Lane had told her long ago about lying – 'Hide the lie among the truth and no one will see it there' – she forced her expression into a look of surprised innocence. Eyes widening, breathing normal – slow and steady.

'I was looking for a file,' she explained, as if this made perfect sense. 'An old case file.'

Blazer's eyes narrowed.

'Nothing in this room is public record. Did you get permission?'

'Not exactly,' she admitted. 'But I've been allowed to look through cold case files before. And it's a very old case, so I didn't think anyone would mind. I could have waited until next week, but it was a quiet night so I thought I'd do it now and tell the lieutenant about it tomorrow.' She gave her shoulders an easy lift. 'Usually it's no big deal.'

His mouth twisted.

'It's ten o'clock at night. And you're in a secure area without permission. I can assure you, McClain, this is a big deal.'

Blazer's steady stare was unrelenting. She knew detectives well enough to know he was searching for minute signs of deception – looking for tells she didn't know she had.

She fought back the panic rising in her chest. Aside from the two of them, the corridor was silent and ghostly. No one knew she was down here.

She was certain if she talked too much he'd clock her nerves, so she said nothing – she just waited for him to ask a question.

'What case file were you looking for?' he asked after a long pause.

In an instant, Harper thought of other crimes she'd written about, images of bodies lying on concrete flashed through her mind, blood pooling on marble floors, walls riddled with bullet holes, guns lying forgotten in long grass.

So many cases. But the only name that came to mind was...

'I was looking for the files on my mother's murder.'

Blazer's hand jerked, sending coffee splashing onto his polished leather shoes.

'You were... *Why?*'

Now Harper began watching *him* closely. Had mention of her mother's case made him nervous?

'I have a theory that my mother's murder is connected to the Whitney case,' she explained. 'To know if I'm right, I need to see the records of my mother's case. There's not much going on tonight, so I thought I'd take advantage of that and check the files, but I forgot I'd need the case number and I don't have that. So I gave up.'

'You didn't see the file?'

She gestured at the long rows of metal shelves behind her, filled with stacks of cardboard boxes.

'How could I find it without the number?'

His eyes assessed her so coldly Harper fought the urge to shiver.

'What on earth makes you think the two cases are connected?' he asked brusquely.

Harper didn't blink. 'Same weapon, same MO, same clinical crime scenes, similar victims.'

If he noticed how easily those facts tripped off her tongue he didn't show it.

'That is extremely unlikely,' he said, 'your mother was killed over a decade ago.'

'I am well aware of that.' Her tone cooled. 'If the person who killed her was thirty-two years old, that would mean they're, what now? Forty-seven?'

At that moment, the lights in the corridor turned off, plunging Blazer into shadows. This happened regularly – the hallway lights were connected to motion detectors. All he had to do to get them to come on again was move. But he didn't move.

They stood facing each other in total darkness. Harper could barely see him.

'How would you know the age of your mother's killer? He's never been caught.'

There was a quiet menace to his voice.

He was standing too close. She didn't like this at all.

'I...' Her mouth went dry. 'I don't,' she said. 'It was only an example.'

Blazer took an abrupt step back. The small movement was enough to send light flooding through the corridor, illuminating the gray concrete walls. And the unexpected sympathy in Blazer's eyes.

'Look, McClain,' he said with a tired sigh. 'I don't know how you know as much as you know about the Whitney case but, given that you do, I can understand why you might think it could be tied to your mother's murder. There are enough superficial similarities that we noticed them, too.' He paused. 'You might not know that I worked on your mother's case as a junior detective. I remember it well.'

Harper was struck speechless by this. Blazer continued without waiting for her to respond.

'I can't explain why the killings look so similar,' he admitted. 'Sometimes you get two, unconnected crimes with the same MO. It happens. In the end, the simple fact is, there are critical differences that indicate to us it's not the same person.' He paused. 'I thought the lieutenant talked to you about this.'

'He did,' Harper said, recovering. 'But—'

'But you don't believe him,' he cut her off. 'And you don't believe me.' He took another step back, his expression flattening. 'You know what your problem is, McClain? You're not as smart as you think you are. And people who are half-smart like you get other people in trouble.'

'I'm not getting anyone in trouble,' she said.

But his patience had expired.

'Forget it,' he said, stepping back into the corridor. 'McClain, you're trespassing in a secure area without authorization. I intend to report this infraction to the head of the Information Unit and ask that your press credentials be revoked. I suggest you notify your editors.'

He gestured for her to walk in front of him.

'Let's go.'

Harper knew there was no point in arguing any further. She had no choice but to do as he said.

All the way down the cold, damp hallway and up the stairs he marched her, always unnervingly close behind, that coffee still clutched in one hand.

When they reached the security door, he slammed his fist against the green exit button, shoved the door open and stood to one side, pointing across the lobby at the front door.

'Get out now, McClain, before I arrest you.'

At the front desk, Dwayne stood up, a worried line above his eyes.

Harper shot him an apologetic look as she passed.

When she reached the front door, she looked back. Blazer still stood there, watching her every step. Making sure she was gone.

Chapter Thirty-one

When Harper's phone rang shortly after nine the next morning she was sitting on the living room sofa, waiting for it.

She pressed the answer button. 'Harper.'

'What the hell did you do?'

Baxter sounded incensed.

'Look, Baxter,' Harper began, 'I was only—'

But the question had clearly been rhetorical. Baxter spoke over her.

'The deputy chief of police called Paul Dells at *home* this morning. He gave him an earful about his reporter breaking into the police records room and digging through sensitive files. Paul had to endure a lecture about the Open Records Act without having a clue what was going on.'

She paused to take a furious breath.

'Baxter,' Harper tried again. 'It isn't as bad as he made it out to be.'

'Oh, isn't it?' Baxter's voice rose a decibel. 'For your information, I've just spent half an hour talking Dells out of firing you. I do not believe I've succeeded. I can't exactly blame him. Harper, what the hell were you thinking?'

The editor was incandescent. Harper decided she'd better withhold her defense for now.

'I made a mistake.'

'Damn straight you did,' Baxter snapped. 'Now you need to get your ass in here ASAP, and be prepared to apologize profusely. Dells is expecting you to be here in no more than twenty minutes. And I warn you – if you don't handle this right I'll be advertising your job by noon.'

The call ended so abruptly it took Harper a second to realize it was over.

The phone fell from her nerveless fingers onto the arm of the chair.

'Oh, hell.'

It had taken everything she had to sound calm on the phone, and now her stomach felt like it might leap out of her body and fly across the room. She'd spent most of the night working on her defense, and now that the time had arrived, she couldn't remember anything she'd come up with.

She was so screwed.

After leaving the police station last night, she'd gone back to the newspaper and sleepwalked through her shift. She'd said nothing to Baxter, who didn't seem to notice her subdued mood.

She'd thought about calling Smith to warn him, but that would have put him in a terrible position. He'd find out soon enough, anyway.

Now, of course, he knew.

Blazer must have called him as soon as he'd escorted her from the building.

In a daze, she left her apartment, locking the door without

looking at it. She climbed into the Camaro – already warm from the sun – and drove down leafy Jones Street, where Spanish moss swung gracefully in the morning breeze. Turning onto Broad Street, where the moss ended and the city grew grittier, the paint less fresh on the rambling Victorian buildings. To Bay Street, and her first glimpse of the river, gleaming in the blinding sun.

The short drive – one she'd made thousands of times over the last seven years – seemed interminable and foreign. As if she were looking at the long familiar landmarks for the first time.

The art students with their multi-colored hair, the expensive cars pouring into the downtown parking garages, the tourists in their baggy shorts – everything jumped out at her with painfully intense clarity. And then evaporated from her memory just as quickly, like a dream that fades when you wake.

What was she going to say? How was she going to convince them not to fire her?

Her normal parking space was taken at this hour – in fact, the entire newspaper parking lot was full and she was forced to park a few blocks away and feed the meter.

Nerves made her clumsy – the coins kept slipping through her fingers.

When she walked into the newsroom it was packed with the daytime crew. She hadn't been in at this hour since that first year at the paper. She'd forgotten what it was like when the morning sun poured through the big windows, highlighting the white columns and the rows of cluttered desks. It was a different place when it was full and night wasn't pressing its weight against the walls.

The noise of the room – half a dozen people talking on their phones at once, others typing furiously, laughter soaring down the hallway from the kitchen – was jarring.

Couldn't she get fired in peace?

There are no secrets in newsrooms. Whatever conversations Dells and Baxter had, they wouldn't have been quiet ones. And Harper was certain everyone in that room knew what was going on. The fact that they didn't look up now only indicated how serious the situation was.

They would all listen. But none of them relished seeing one of their own executed.

DJ was the only one to catch her eye. From across the room, he shot her a look of anguished sympathy. He'd texted her at least a dozen times so far today. Twelve variations on 'WTF?'

She hadn't replied. She was waiting for the call.

Now, holding his eyes, she shook her head very slightly.

'McClain.' Baxter barked the word from the doorway of Dells' glass cube of an office behind the city editor's desk. 'In here. Now.'

For a second the noise in the room diminished – a collective intake of breath.

Holding her head high, Harper made her way towards Baxter.

The editor's face was pale. She'd worn her best dark blazer and wool-blend skirt – too warm for today's sunny weather. But perfect, Harper thought, for a hanging.

Wordlessly, Baxter stood back and gestured at the open glass door.

Harper walked in.

Dells' head – brown hair perfectly blow-dried – was bent over a stack of papers on his desk. The cufflinks at his wrist gleamed, and the room smelled pleasantly of an unidentifiable but tasteful cologne.

Baxter closed the door. The noise of the newsroom faded to a low, distant rumble.

There were two modern leather-and-chrome chairs in front of Dells' sleek black desk, but Harper hadn't been invited to sit, so she stood awkwardly behind them, waiting for some indication of what she should do now.

Baxter was in the room behind her, her back to the door. She didn't sit either.

They stayed like that for what seemed like a very long time before Dells looked up. He wore frameless glasses with lenses so thin Harper couldn't imagine they served a purpose. All the professional friendliness she'd seen on his face the other day when he complimented her work was gone now, replaced by an equally professional disapproval.

'Miss McClain.' His voice was cool. 'I'm very sorry we have to meet under these circumstances.'

He laced his fingers together on the lacquered black top of his desk.

'A serious allegation has been made against you by the Deputy Chief of Police and I intend to get to the bottom of it. So, please, do me the courtesy of telling me the truth: did you or did you not break into the archive last night at the police station without permission?'

'I didn't break into anything,' Harper told him. 'I went into that room, but I've been in there before many times and I did not know it would be such an issue.'

This was the answer she'd come up with about three in the morning. Now it sounded hollow even to her own ears.

She couldn't tell what the editor thought – behind the thin lenses his pale eyes gave nothing away.

'Let's not indulge in wordplay here. The police consider this a break-in, because you went in without permission.'

His tone was still measured but she could sense the slight sheen of temper on the surface.

'Did you tamper with the files?'

She didn't blink. 'Absolutely not.'

'Then what did you do in that room?'

'I was going to look up a cold case file,' she explained. 'But I didn't know the case number, and without that I could do nothing.'

'Interesting.' His tone was cool. 'When you logged into the police computer, did it not give you the case file?'

A shard of pure crystalline fear pierced Harper's chest.

He knew.

He knew she'd logged in using her old pin number. The police knew. They knew everything.

She was finished.

'Excuse me?' Unable to summon the breath to speak normally, she whispered the question.

'My understanding,' he said steadily, 'is that you logged in to the police computer using an old identifying code, one issued to you when you were an intern years ago, and accessed a number of files. Is that not true?'

He enunciated each word with unhurried precision.

Harper could have denied it, but she had a feeling that would make it all worse. It was time to come clean, and see how much of her head they'd let her keep.

'Yes,' she said softly. 'It's true.'

Still standing by the door, Baxter let out a long breath. Harper didn't dare turn around to look at her.

Dells' fingers were steepled under his chin. He said nothing. He seemed to be waiting.

That was when she broke her own rule about talking too much when you're already in trouble.

'I've been investigating two murders.' Her words were quick and unemotional, like his. 'Fifteen years apart, but identical in every other way. One is the murder of Marie Whitney. The other is the murder of my mother.'

Dells' eyebrows winged up, but he let her continue without interruption.

'The files I looked at last night were related to the Whitney murder,' she said. 'I needed more information to understand if I was on the right track.'

When she paused for breath he finally spoke.

'Have you told the police about your suspicions?'

'I have.' She rested her hands on the chair back in front of her. 'I told the head of the homicide squad at the very start.'

'And what did he say?'

'He disagreed with me. Therefore, I've proceeded without police cooperation.'

A significant silence fell.

'Why on earth,' Dells asked dangerously, 'would you do that?'

'Because,' she said, 'I suspected the murderer was a cop.'

'Oh crap,' Baxter whispered behind her.

Harper kept her eyes on Dells, who was still observing her like a lab experiment. If he was surprised, or felt any emotion at all, he hid it damned well.

She never wanted to play cards against him.

'What made you think that?' he asked after a second.

Harper's heart skipped. She had no idea why but, for some reason, he was giving her a chance. She wished she'd slept at all last night so she could be certain her words made some kind of sense. She was almost dizzy with fatigue and stress.

Still, she stood straight as she made her case.

'In both cases, the method of murder was professional – the police themselves have used that term. Both murder sites were surgically cleaned. The killer wore crime-scene covers on his shoes in both cases. The clothing of both victims was removed posthumously. Whitney may have been in a relationship with a detective shortly before she died – no one would know more about how to keep a crime scene clean. This week, I've been trying to find out if the same might have been true of my mother, but so far, I haven't found the connection.'

Running out of breath, she stopped there. If that wasn't enough, more wouldn't help.

'You say "suspected",' Dells said. 'Why past tense?'

She had to give him credit. The man didn't miss a thing.

'Because,' Harper said, thinking of her conversation with Blazer last night, and the Mercedes following her through dark streets, 'there are other possibilities. Whitney hurt a lot of people.'

Dells considered this for a long moment. Through the glass walls, Harper could hear the buzz of conversation, distant laughter.

'Look, Miss McClain.' Dells leaned back in his chair, brushing something off the knee of his pants. 'You're an excellent reporter. Your work is the best I've seen in a long time. But you must know that there is a condition – a real psychological state – that happens even to the best reporters when they get too close to their work. It can become an obsession. It's not good for the writer and it's not good for the reader. I think this,' he pointed at her, 'is a textbook case.'

Harper wanted to argue – to explain that this wasn't what was happening here. She was keeping her distance from the case. She was *fine*.

When she drew a breath to speak, she saw his shoulders stiffen ever so slightly, and the delicate warning arch of his eyebrows.

Tightening her lips, she let him continue.

'You cannot and should not investigate your own mother's murder for this newspaper,' he continued, 'that's simply impossible.

I can't allow it. It stops now. As for the Whitney case, while I have great appreciation for the fine art of reporters' instinct, my understanding is that both Emma and the head of the homicide unit have told you you're on the wrong track, and I need you to drop that case, too. Let the police do their work.'

'But they won't.' The words burst out of her. 'Not if it's one of their own.'

'It's not your case, Miss McClain.' He'd raised his voice very slightly, but somehow that was intimidating enough to silence her. 'You are not the police. You are under no obligation to find out the truth in the matter, and I believe that if you continue to research the case you will so damage your relationship with the police as to render you no longer useful to me as a police reporter. Do you understand what I am saying to you?'

His eyes locked on hers and for an instant she saw the mercilessness there – the speed with which he could end her career, and how little he would care about what became of her after that.

Harper bit her lip so hard she tasted blood. The sting and the bitter copper of it helped her say what she had to say next.

'I understand,' she said.

'I am not firing you at this time,' he said after a moment. 'To be honest, I don't like being told what to do, and I didn't appreciate the deputy chief's tone this morning. The last time I checked the masthead, he didn't have a seat on the board of this newspaper. However, it's important to me that this sort of mistake never happens again. Therefore, I am suspending you for ten working days without pay, starting immediately. You will be on probation for six months. Any violation of the rules of your employment here will result in immediate termination without severance pay or notice. Do you understand these conditions?'

Harper tried to think of something to say – some further defense or explanation. But her mind had gone blank.

'I understand,' she said numbly.

Dells picked up the pen from atop the stack of papers on his desk and bent back to whatever task he'd been doing when she first arrived.

The meeting was over.

Chapter Thirty-two

Harper floated out of the newspaper building a few minutes later, her legs unsteady. The pavement felt soft and unstable beneath her shoes.

Baxter was right behind her.

Her assessment of the meeting was succinct.

'You're a lucky son of a bitch, McClain.'

They stood in the too-bright sunshine outside the newspaper's front door. The sun was just beginning to bake the sidewalk. People hurrying to work pushed by them, but Harper barely saw them.

'Look, Baxter…' she began.

The editor held up one thin hand to stop her.

'Don't bother.'

Reaching into her bag, she dug around. Pulling out a pack of Marlboro Lights, Baxter lit up, inhaling deeply.

'Dear God, I deserve this cigarette.' Each word emerged in a wispy puff of smoke. 'What a fucking morning.'

Holding a cigarette loosely between two fingers, she met Harper's eyes.

'You got a break, McClain,' she said crisply. 'You got off easy. I promise you, Dells won't give you another chance. This is it. Stop digging into the Whitney case or he'll fire you.'

She tightened her bag over one shoulder, took another hit on her smoke.

'If you keep digging, which I suspect is more likely, don't get caught. I don't have time to hire anyone.'

Holding out her free hand, she wriggled her fingers.

'Give me your scanner.'

'What?'

Not convinced she'd heard her right, Harper stared at her blankly.

Baxter sighed.

'You're off work for the next two weeks,' she explained. 'Someone has to take over your beat. I need your scanner.'

Harper pulled the scanner – which was turned off but with her all the time – from her bag. For a second, she looked at the device in her hand. It was virtually an antique. These days they made them smaller, less obtrusive.

But she'd used this one from the start. And Lane had given it to her.

With slow reluctance, she handed it to Baxter.

'Tell them not to drop it,' she said. 'It's old.'

Crushing her cigarette butt under the low heel of her shoe, the editor plucked the device from her fingers.

'They'll treat it like cut glass, McClain.' Her tone was dry. 'Now, go home, will you? And, for God's sake, stay out of trouble.'

With that, the editor strode back into the newspaper building, her brittle, blunt-cut hair swaying with each step.

When she was gone, Harper didn't know where to go. It felt

strange to be out at this hour. Bizarre to be standing in front of her workplace, where she was suddenly unwelcome.

In her pocket, her phone kept buzzing. She knew it was DJ, sending a hundred messages asking if she was fired.

She wasn't ready, yet, to explain.

She knew it made sense to go home. Instead, she walked in the opposite direction, across busy Bay Street, and down the sloping, cobblestone lane to the river.

It was quiet – most of the tourist restaurants weren't open yet. The air held the sticky sweet smell of last night's spilled beer. Underneath that, the cool scent of the wide river, glinting blue-brown in the hazy sun. In the distance, the high, white arches of the Talmadge Bridge soared like sails, unfurled into the breeze. On the water, a tugboat bustled by, its motor a rough purr. She could hear cars rumbling on the street behind her.

Life went on.

Finding a bench empty, save for an abandoned amber trio of beer bottles clustered neatly around its wrought-iron legs, Harper lowered herself onto the seat, warm from the sun, and took a deep breath.

How was she not fired?

She couldn't get her brain around it. During the seven years she'd worked at the paper, she'd seen at least a half-dozen people fired for much less.

Every reporter at a newspaper is as disposable as paper, and crime reporters the most expendable of all. Every class of college seniors held a potential two hundred replacements.

Still. She wasn't about to stop investigating the connection between the two murders.

A homeless man shuffled toward her down the waterfront, bleary-eyed and bear-like, coarse, dirty hair flowing loose over his collar. She could smell him long before he reached her – sun-ripened urine and unwashed sweat.

'Please,' he said, his voice hoarse and raw. 'Got a dollar for some food?'

The hand he held out was filthy. The sleeve's edge ragged.

On impulse, Harper dug in her pocket, pulled out some crumpled dollar bills and handed them to him without counting them.

He stared at the money with mute fascination – like if he looked at it long enough it would turn into the drugs or alcohol he really wanted.

'Good luck,' she said.

Her voice seemed to wake him from the money stupor and, clutching the bills, he scuttled away. Harper watched him disappear into the shadows behind Huey's restaurant.

That had been stupid of her.

Like most people, she was a month or two away from dead broke. Being a newspaper reporter in a town of this size did not pay well. She had, over the years, set aside a tiny amount of savings for car repairs or unexpected emergencies, but two weeks without pay was going to hurt. She'd get through it, but she'd feel it.

Maybe that guy once had a job and upset his boss. Maybe when it happened he didn't have two weeks' worth of savings sitting in the bank.

For the first time in her life, the possibility of losing everything seemed not at all farfetched.

That realization cleared the fog from her mind.

The deputy chief had actively tried to get her fired. There would be others in the police department who would want her gone once they found out what she'd done.

There was a code, and she'd broken it.

If she was going to get through this, she needed a plan, and if she was going to come up with one of those, she needed coffee.

Jumping off the bench, she headed back towards her car, her stride swift and resolute.

The town's eccentrics were out in full at this hour. As she made her way down the street next to the newspaper building she passed an old man in a tweed jacket and fedora walking a thug-faced bulldog wearing a University of Georgia T-shirt. The man tilted his hat politely as he passed her. The T-shirt-wearing dog, hopping along with its odd, mincing gait, didn't even glance at her.

This side of the city – its cheery, tourist-friendly, daytime side – was as foreign to Harper as Tokyo. Her Savannah was very different. Her Savannah was dark and dangerous nights in neighborhoods that would have sent these people running for their lives.

How had it come to pass that she felt happier and more at home in that Savannah than this one?

Something Dells had said flickered unwanted across her mind – the part about reporters getting too close to their stories. But that wasn't the case. She was, and always had been, in perfect control.

When she had the evidence together, he would see that.

That afternoon, Harper sat on the living room sofa, eating brown sugar Pop-Tarts straight from the package, staring at her notes on the Whitney case.

She thought about texting Luke, but she was afraid of what he'd say when he found out what she'd done.

On the other hand, he probably knew already. Everyone knew.

She sank further into the sofa, wishing the cushions would absorb her completely.

DJ had been sending her regular updates by text and email throughout the day, so she knew there'd been a staff meeting where

Baxter and Dells announced her banishment. She was also aware that Baxter had set up a rota for different reporters to handle the crime beat on various nights.

Mark Jansen, the city hall reporter, was taking the first night shift with his usual grace and team spirit.

> Jansen is losing his SHIT, DJ texted her. Says they should hire a replacement and he's not a substitute teacher. He and Baxter are going at it like two cats in a sack. Do you want me to video them? It's hilarious. She's destroying him.

Jansen was balding, with a pot-belly and a perpetually vexed expression. He was always the first one out the door at the stroke of five thirty each evening. Harper could imagine his fury at having to work late one night out of three hundred and sixty-five. The man was a living, breathing nap machine.

Typing fast, she replied:

> No videos. If you get caught, Baxter will kill you. But more updates please.

When this was all over, she was going to send DJ a fruit basket or a box of football tickets – whatever you send nice guys who did kind things for no reason.

When her phone beeped again, she grabbed it from the arm of the sofa to see DJ's latest update. But it wasn't from DJ. It was from Miles.

> Just heard. Coming over.

Harper winced.

She couldn't deal with another lecture. But there was no way Miles would take no for an answer.

Forcing herself up, she brushed away the crumbs and put the Pop-Tarts back in the cupboard. Then she hurried to her room and quickly ran a brush through her hair, and straightened her top. There was nothing she could do about the dark circles under her eyes.

Ten minutes later, Miles stood in the doorway, his crisp button-down shirt tucked into charcoal slacks.

She didn't like the new caution she could see in his expression.

'I don't even know what to say,' he began.

'You better come in before you start yelling.' Harper stepped aside.

'I'm not going to yell.'

They walked into the living room together.

She saw his gaze take in the notebooks scattered on the floor by the sofa before honing in on the scanner buzzing and chirping in the corner of the living room.

Baxter had taken her work scanner, but not the spare she kept at home.

'I'm only listening in case something happens and Jansen misses it,' she said with a touch of defensiveness. 'The guy's an idiot.'

'He is at that,' Miles agreed.

'Do you want something to drink?' Harper asked. 'Coffee?'

'I'm fine. Let's talk.' He sat down on the sofa without waiting to be invited. 'What happened?'

Her spine stiff, Harper sat across from him. Hesitantly at first, and then faster once she got going, she told him the basics, sticking to the high points. She told him about the Mercedes that followed her, the email from Sterling Robinson and her conversations with

Whitney's other panicked exes. And about how she decided to track down Camille Whitney.

When she finished, he leaned forward, hands resting on his knees.

'That Mercedes still following you?'

She shook her head. 'I haven't seen it again.'

There was a long pause while he seemed to process everything she'd told him. When he did speak, it wasn't what she'd expected.

'What's going on, Harper?' he asked gently. 'This isn't like you.'

There was no anger in his voice, only enough puzzlement and compassion to make her heart hurt.

'You push the limits all the time, but I've never seen you take the kind of chances you're taking lately,' he said. 'Why are you doing this?'

'I have to know,' she said. 'If it's related to my mom's murder, I have to know.' He tried to argue but she talked over him, her words coming out too fast. 'I don't trust Blazer to solve this. And I *have* to know, Miles. Can't you see that?'

She knew she sounded manic but she couldn't help it. She was pleading now. She'd give anything for him to say he truly understood.

But he looked away, his eyes stopping on Bonnie's portrait of her above the fireplace. In the butter yellow afternoon light, the red and orange of it appeared to be ablaze.

'I can't say I get it,' he said. 'Not completely. But I'm trying.'

He glanced at her.

'You still think it's the same guy killed Whitney and your mother?'

Harper hesitated.

'I'm not sure any more,' she said. 'But I don't see how it's a coincidence. And if it's a cop doing the killing, they're all going to protect him. Even Smith.'

'What if it's *not* a cop?' Miles asked. 'What if you're wrong? And you just put your whole career on the line for nothing.'

'Honestly? I hope it's not a cop. That's not the point of any of this. I'm not out to get anyone. But I have to know if the same person killed Whitney and my mother.'

'And you're willing to risk everything for it?' His eyes were cool, assessing.

'I already have,' Harper said.

Miles leaned back on the sofa.

'What're you going to do now?'

'I'm going to talk to Camille Whitney.' Her voice was resolute. 'Find out what she knows. She was there that day. No one was closer to Marie Whitney than her.'

Miles gave a slow, disapproving headshake.

'You talk to that child, Blazer will get your press pass pulled so fast your head'll spin. You won't be suspended. You'll be through.'

But Harper was ready for this.

'I'll use a fake name,' she told him. 'Dress differently. Do something with my hair. She's a kid. She'll never know who she talked to.'

Miles considered her gravely.

'It's a bad idea, Harper. You know that, right?'

Harper tried not to let him see how disappointed she felt. She knew she wasn't at her best – she'd had no sleep, and too many hours alone to go over and over her situation in her mind. Still, she was confident this was the only option she had left.

'I'm running out of leads,' she said. 'She's the last piece on the table. If she gives me nothing, I'm done.'

He looked down at his hands, thinking it over.

'You shouldn't do this, and I think you know that.' His voice was low. 'You have to stop before you've got nothing left to lose. You're *this close*, Harper.' He held his thumb and index finger an inch apart. 'This close to blowing up your whole career.'

She couldn't seem to tear her eyes away from that small empty space. She hated that some part of her believed Miles was right.

But the rest of her had to know if Camille Whitney knew who killed her mother.

Seeing that on her face, Miles shook his head in disgust.

'If that girl gives you nothing, you swear that's enough? You'll end this? Get back to normal work?'

In her heart, Harper didn't know if she could ever give up. Not as long as her mother was in the ground and the man who killed her was out there, somewhere. But if the Whitney child knew nothing, the simple truth was, she was out of ideas of where to go with her investigation.

'I promise.'

On the table across the room, Harper's scanner crackled a message.

'All available units: Code Twelve with multiple Code Fours. Intersection of Broad and White Streets. Four vehicles involved. One vehicle is Code Eleven. EMTs and Fire en route to the scene.'

Harper's brain translated each code into images of everything she was missing: A four-car accident with multiple injuries in the middle of rush hour. One car was on fire.

Miles stood up, his eyes taking on that hard focus they got when something big happened.

'Got to go.'

Harper followed him out.

On the front steps, he stopped and looked back at her.

'If you meet that little girl it will haunt you all your life, you know that, don't you?' he warned her. 'She's you, in a way. That's why you want to see her. This isn't about finding a killer cop. Or even solving your mother's murder. You're still trying to help your twelve-year-old self. But you can't, Harper. Not like this.'

He headed to his car, his last words hanging in the air.

'For God's sake, let this be the end of it.'

Chapter Thirty-three

With Miles' warning still ringing in her ears, Harper went back over everything she knew. Again, she came to the same conclusion – the two unplayed pieces on the board were Camille Whitney and Sterling Robinson. Whitney, she would get to but, in the meantime, she had to know more about Robinson to understand how he fit into this.

She'd already done basic research on him, but there had to be more. Grabbing her laptop, she began searching for every combination of words she could think of: 'Robinson and Whitney', 'Robinson and crime', 'Robinson and court'.

By the time night fell, she knew more about Robinson than she did about herself. She knew he grew up poor. Went to college on a scholarship. Got more scholarships. Went to an Ivy League grad school. Started his first publishing company with friends from school, and made his first fortune before he was thirty.

She'd found nothing to connect him to any crime. And no articles that featured both him and Whitney.

The Savannah branch of his empire was primarily charitable

– he employed twenty-five people in an office building downtown, and they oversaw his donations. She remained convinced that the charity was what connected him to Whitney. But there was no proof.

By midnight, the sofa was surrounded by her scattered notebooks, and her eyes stung from exhaustion. It had been several days since she'd last had a good night's sleep.

She felt light-headed. She'd eaten nothing but those Pop-Tarts all day and, when she forced herself off the sofa to feed Zuzu, she discovered there was only one can of cat food left in the cupboard.

She needed coffee. She needed fresh air. She needed sleep too, but that wasn't going to happen.

'I'm going out,' she announced.

Zuzu didn't look up from her bowl.

Grabbing her keys, Harper headed out the door.

The air outside was muggy and heavy – the humidity settled on her skin like a too-warm blanket.

The street was still. Nobody was out at all.

And yet the skin on the back of her neck prickled a warning.

Her instincts told her she was not alone.

Her brow furrowing, she stood at the top of the steps, scanning the street. The only movement came from insects darting through the glow of the streetlights.

She hurried to the Camaro and climbed inside, fumbling with the keys in her haste to start the car.

She didn't know what was wrong with her – there was nobody there. But she felt watched.

She kept her eyes on the rearview mirror as she pulled out on to the street. Nothing moved.

You're getting paranoid, she told herself.

She pulled to a stop in front of the 24-hour shop and ran inside, her bag bumping hard against her hip.

In the brightly lit store, she shoved cat food, coffee and random packages of food into the basket. She couldn't imagine cooking – or even eating real food. But she bought it anyway.

Talk radio poured unhappiness out of speakers she couldn't see, and the man at the register was so focused on it, he barely glanced at her as he rang up her purchases.

'That'll be thirty-two dollars and ninety-eight cents,' he said, pushing the card machine towards her without meeting her eyes.

After paying, Harper grabbed the bags and headed out to her car.

The street outside was empty when she dumped her purchases unceremoniously on the passenger seat, and started the engine.

As she pulled out smoothly, she saw the black Mercedes pulling out, too.

'Shit,' Harper breathed, staring at the dark reflection in the rearview mirror.

This was no coincidence. Someone actually was following her. And they didn't mind her knowing.

The car was keeping its distance – far enough behind that she couldn't read its plates. Whoever it was knew what they were doing.

Her gaze flickering between the mirror and the road, Harper turned left, then right again, then left, but her mind was racing. Where should she go? Home? The paper? The police station?

In the end, she decided she had no choice. There was no place else to go. She wasn't welcome at the paper or the police station. And she couldn't drive forever.

She'd go home. And she'd get that license plate.

Meticulously, she signaled before turning off of Habersham

Street. A few seconds after she made the corner, the Mercedes appeared behind her again.

She turned a few minutes later, and then once more, on to Jones Street.

The Mercedes did the same. Only, this time, it didn't follow her down Jones. Instead, it stopped at the corner.

Cutting the engine, Harper sat in the car for a second, staring at the headlights behind her. She still couldn't see the plates from here – the lights blinded her.

She had to have those numbers.

She unhooked her seatbelt and cracked the door, preparing herself. Then she leapt out of the Camaro and, in violation of every logical rule, ran straight towards the Mercedes as fast as she could.

At first, the driver didn't react – the lights and the tinted windows made his face impossible to see.

When she drew closer, though, the Mercedes suddenly began to back away from her, keeping enough distance so she couldn't make out the plates.

Frustration roiled Harper.

'Who are you?' she screamed, her voice splitting the quiet night. 'What do you want from me?'

There was no reply.

Instead, the car backed smoothly and quickly around the corner and then, just as she reached the intersection, sped away, tires screeching.

Harper ran after it for half a block before giving up, panting.

As she stood in the street, hands on her knees, trying to catch her breath, she was already narrowing down the list of suspects. Only two people in the Whitney case would have the wherewithal to have her followed – the lawyer and Sterling Robinson. She'd never heard from the lawyer again after that one phone call. There was no logical reason for him to suddenly decide to do this. He thought he'd scared her off.

That left the elusive millionaire Sterling Robinson.

And she had had enough of this.

Straightening, she stormed up the steps to her apartment.

Inside, she hurried to the kitchen, skidding into a seat at the table in front of her laptop.

Opening the email she'd received from Robinson several days ago, she hit reply and typed a rapid, furious message.

> Are you having me followed? Tell me yes or no so I know whose bastard I just chased down the street. You're a coward, Sterling Robinson. And cowards have something to hide. If you're hiding something, I will find it. I promise you that. You do not scare me.

Before she could change her mind, she hit send.

Harper didn't know when or how she fell asleep. After sending the email to Robinson, she'd paced the kitchen imagining what would happen when he got the message. Most likely, he'd go straight to Dells. Show him the threatening email and insist that she be fired.

She was too angry to care.

At some point, she'd worn herself out and ended up back on the sofa with her notes and a glass of whiskey. That was the last thing she remembered until she woke with a gasp.

At first, she was disoriented – trying to figure out what had woken her. A sense of movement – like someone was in the apartment.

It wasn't morning yet. Darkness still pressed against the windows.

Something hard had lodged itself under her shoulder. Reaching back, she pulled a rumpled notebook from behind her, open to the page with James Whitney's address.

She sat up slowly, dropping the notebook on the floor.

Something wasn't right.

The empty whiskey glass sat on the coffee table. The lamp by the couch was on, but the rest of the room was cast in shadows.

Stiffly, she rose from the sofa and took a step towards the door.

A blinding white light burst through the front window, pinioning her in its glare.

Bewildered, Harper froze, her heart pounding.

For a moment the light held her. Then it swung erratically across the room. First left, then right, in a slow smooth sweep.

Suddenly, her mind grasped what she was seeing.

She sprinted for the door.

Flipping open the locks, she rushed outside.

The air was cool and smelled of rain. No moon penetrated through the thick clouds. Streetlights sent ghostly shadows through the Spanish moss, which hung in the trees like small, limp corpses.

An unmarked police car was parked in front of her house. Luke stood by the open door, his hand resting on the searchlight mounted next to the side mirror.

Their eyes met, and he switched the light off.

Without pausing to put on shoes, Harper raced down the front steps in her bare feet. She hated how relieved she was to see him.

Then he spoke.

'I've been calling all night.' His voice was as cold as the ground. 'Your phone broken?'

Harper stopped a few feet away. Unable to bring herself to talk to him, she'd turned her phone off hours ago.

'Luke, I'm sorry.' She kept her voice low – the last thing she needed was for the neighbors to wake up. 'I … didn't know what to say.'

'Ten times,' he said. 'I called you *ten times*.'

'I'm sorry,' she said miserably. 'I couldn't face telling you.'

'I gathered that.'

Silence fell. His eyes held hers.

'Did you do it?'

Harper swallowed hard, hands tightening into fists at her sides.

'Yes.'

He closed his eyes.

'Harper…'

She'd expected him to be angry. Instead, he sounded hurt.

Panic gathered in her chest.

'I had to know what they knew.' Her eyes searched his stony face. 'You understand that, right?'

'How can I understand?' His voice rose. 'You *broke the law*. You did everything I asked you not to do.' He held up his hands. 'Why, Harper? Did you want to ruin everything? Was that your goal?'

'Of course not.' She took a step towards him, the sidewalk damp and rough beneath her toes. 'All I wanted was to see what they had on the Whitney case. That's all.'

'But you don't have that *right*.' He ran a tired hand across his jaw – he hadn't shaved. A shadow of whiskers covered his cheeks. 'You're not a cop. Sometimes, I honestly think you don't realize that.'

That stung.

'I know I'm not a cop,' Harper said. 'It's this case – this murder…'

He wouldn't listen.

'You keep blaming this case for your own actions. Like the

killer's making you do stupid things. Nobody made you break the law. You did that yourself.'

He sounded as tired as she felt.

'Luke,' she whispered. 'Don't be angry.'

She held out her hand. 'Come inside, OK? We can talk there.'

He shook his head slowly, like he hadn't heard what she said.

'You know what's funny?' he said. 'I always thought the rule about cops not dating the press was stupid. Now, I finally get it. We're different. We're on different sides.'

Harper's heart contracted.

'Stop this,' she said. 'That's not true.'

'Isn't it?' The look he gave her then was so wounded it was unbearable. 'I asked you not to go digging around. I practically begged you. And you did it anyway.'

'Luke…'

'Do you want to know why I asked you not to do that?' He didn't wait for her to answer. 'Because I knew if you did there could be danger. For both of us. And I didn't want to lose you.'

Harper's mouth went dry.

'*Luke.*' She breathed his name. 'What happened?'

'Funny you should ask.' His lips twisted into an angry interpretation of a smile. 'Today Smith called me into his office for a talk. He told me he knew we'd had an affair. Those were the words he used: "an affair". He threatened to have me knocked back out to uniform if I continued to see you. He told me you were using me to get information about official police work. He said there were suspicions I helped you break into the archive.' His voice thickened. 'He said I was a fool for letting myself be used.'

He pressed his fists against his forehead.

'Goddammit, Harper. Why did you have to go into that *room*?'

Harper was so stunned, she couldn't seem to form words.

Smith had always been on her side. Always. She couldn't picture one second of what Luke was describing.

'I didn't… Smith really said that?'

'Every word.' His voice was ragged. '*Now* do you realize what you've done? No one trusts you now. No one trusts *me*. I get seen with you ever again, my career is over. We're finished.'

'No.'

The word escaped Harper's lips against her will. But Luke wasn't listening.

'It's all messed up, Harper. We had something, but now it's over. Because of your obsession. Because you can't let go.'

He drew a ragged breath. And delivered the final blow.

'They're sending me back undercover.'

Harper froze.

'What… *Now*?'

He gave a curt nod.

'But you said you had to wait six weeks…'

'There's a case in play outside Atlanta.' He cut her off. 'State police. They're sending me on temporary transfer. Smith said…' He looked over her head at the open door of her house. 'He said he thought getting back to work would clear my head.'

Harper didn't like this at all. There was a reason they kept undercover officers off the street for large chunks of time after an operation – to keep them safe. There were people out there looking for them. Really terrible people.

'Wait. How can he do this?' Her voice quivered. 'It's too dangerous.'

Luke gave her a bitter look.

'It's all arranged,' he said. 'I'm heading out at dawn.'

For the first time since she'd started investigating the Whitney

333

case, Harper felt truly afraid. She was losing too much all at once. The police, Luke, Smith, maybe her job.

She wanted to hang onto something. Anything.

'Will I be able to reach you?' she asked. 'When you're gone? To make sure—'

'Hell, no, Harper,' he snapped. 'I'll be in a drug gang in some trailer doing God knows what.'

In that moment he looked so trapped. A chill shook her spine.

'Luke, please don't go,' she pleaded. 'I have a bad feeling about this.'

'Me, too,' he said. 'And I don't have any choice.'

He strode to his car, his back straight and stiff.

Harper felt rooted to the sidewalk. But she tried one last thing.

'In the morning, I'll call Smith. I'll try to explain.'

At this, he swung around so abruptly, she flinched.

'Don't talk to Smith. Don't talk to *anyone*.' He held up his hands. 'Every time you move you break something. You're so destructive, Harper, can't you see that? You destroy everything you touch.'

Climbing into the car, he slammed the door hard. A second later, the engine roared into life. The car peeled away from the curb.

Harper stood still as the sound of the engine faded into the darkness, until the night seeped from the ground into her bones and she began to tremble.

Chapter Thirty-four

The next morning, Sterling Robinson replied to her email.

His message wasted no words:

> I will be in the area Sunday night. If you complete
> the attached affidavit and return it to me by this
> evening, I will meet with you.

Harper, who had spent the morning in a state of despair, read it three times before her brain would accept what he'd said.

After that, she sat back in her chair and stared out the kitchen window, thinking it through.

Of course, it could be a trap. If Robinson was the killer, this could all be a set-up to get rid of her.

She knew she should be afraid, but she felt no fear at all.

She had to know the truth. And she would pay almost any price to have it.

The attached affidavit was as straightforward as the email – a basic promise from her not to write about him in any way for any publication. It was one paragraph long.

Harper signed and dated it, and dropped it off at his Savannah office that afternoon herself.

A polished and manicured receptionist plucked the envelope from her hand without raising an eyebrow.

'This is very important,' Harper told her. 'He must see it.'

'I'll get it to him,' the woman said crisply, dropping it in a tray and turning back to her work.

There wasn't anything else Harper could do. She went home and waited.

The next day was Saturday, and Robinson did not contact her.

By Sunday afternoon, she'd given up hope. But then, at 5 o'clock, her phone buzzed.

It was a text from an unrecognized number.

All it said was 27 Officer's Row, Tybee Island. 9pm. SR.

Harper's stomach tightened.

Tybee Island was twenty minutes' drive outside Savannah, on the coast.

She'd expected him to want to meet at his offices, or perhaps an anonymous hotel bar. But this was a residential address.

He wanted her to meet him late at night in a house miles outside of town.

Harper wasn't afraid of much, but the idea of going to meet a strange millionaire, who might or might not be a murderer, set off all her warning signals.

But it was too late to get scared now.

She thought about it for a long minute. And then she replied.

I'll be there.

*

If you haven't got a boat, there's only one way to get to Tybee Island – down a long, gently winding two-lane highway through dense Georgia marshes, heading due east. It's an isolated road – all you can see in any direction is smooth, high marsh grass and sky. At night, it feels endless and empty.

Harper had always thought it looked like a great place to dump a body.

As she headed out to meet Robinson, the Camaro's headlights seemed to sink into opaque darkness.

There were few cars on the road – all the day trippers had gone home long ago. There was no reason to go to the coast at this hour.

Her hands were tight on the wheel as the Tybee town limits sign flashed by.

She'd been out there many times, of course, to go to the beach with Bonnie. Still, the island's tangle of streets was confusing – she hit two dead-ends before she found the road she wanted – a narrow, smooth track that hugged the northern coastline.

The road was lined with beach houses. She kept getting brief glances of dark ocean before another tall structure would veer up, blocking the view.

She was nearly to the end when, with little warning, a white wooden gate appeared in front of her.

Harper stopped the car, straining to read the sign on the high stone wall near the gatehouse.

Officer's Row, it said, in elegant font.

This was the place.

The gatehouse door swung open, and a man in a dark uniform walked out, talking into a walkie-talkie.

He motioned for her to roll down her window.

'Who are you here to see, ma'am?' he asked politely.

'Sterling Robinson,' Harper said.

'Your name?'

'Harper McClain.'

'One moment, please.'

He stepped away, talking quietly into the device.

A moment passed.

Without another word, he strolled back to the gatehouse. A second later, the gate rose with smooth silence.

The guard motioned for her to drive on.

The houses behind the gate were enormous, sprawling, faux-Victorian mansions, with perfect, manicured lawns.

The only car Harper passed as she made her way down the lane was a security van, driving slowly in the opposite direction.

The people who lived on Officer's Row cared a lot about safety.

Number 27 was at the end of the lane – a turreted white house with wraparound balconies on the first and second floors. It had a gorgeous view of the Atlantic Ocean, which stretched out behind it, glistening bluish black in the moonlight.

Harper parked in the empty driveway and killed the engine. All the houses were set far back from the street, separated by tall hedges and enormous, landscaped yards. It wasn't completely isolated, but it sure wasn't cosy.

For the first time in her life, she wished she had a gun.

Shoving her phone into her pocket, she got out of the car and closed the door.

A stone path, illuminated by ankle-high lights, cut through the lush, tropical garden to the front stairs.

The air was much cooler out here than in the city; a steady breeze blew off the sea carrying with it a heady scent of sea salt and sweet, night-blooming jasmine.

She climbed ten steps to the ostentatious front door and, bracing her shoulders, rang the doorbell.

Long seconds passed and nothing happened, then she heard locks being turned. The door opened.

In person, Sterling Robinson was taller and thinner than he appeared in pictures. He wore chinos and a blue pullover. His dark hair was wavy. His wire-framed glasses gave him a professorial look, but behind the lenses his eyes were alert – predatory.

'Harper McClain.' His tone was weary resignation. 'I suppose you better come in.'

Inside, the house seemed even larger than outside, like some sort of fairytale castle. Fans spun dizzyingly from soaring ceilings, the floors were marble. There were few pieces of furniture. It was cool but not cold.

It felt empty. Harper had the distinct impression they were alone in the house.

'Follow me.' Robinson led her across the vast, airy entrance to a wide hallway, and then on to a spacious living room with soft white sofas and matching chairs clustered around beige rugs.

Motioning for her to sit, he said, 'Would you like a drink?'

'I'll have whatever you're having,' she said.

He arched one eyebrow.

'I'm having club soda,' he said.

'That's fine.'

He disappeared for a second. Harper gazed around her – there was no art on the walls. Nothing personal.

When he returned, he handed her a chilled glass and sat across from her.

'Now,' he said, 'would you kindly tell me what this is all about? I'm not used to getting calls about dead women.'

'I'm looking into the murder of Marie Whitney...' she began.

'Why? You're not the police.'

The way he cut her off was brusque but not outright rude. It

339

seemed more as if he was in a hurry to know everything. Harper decided to respond in kind.

'No,' she said. 'I'm not the police. But I think the police are doing a bad job.'

'So do I.'

He leaned back, watchful.

'So you've decided to investigate the investigators,' he guessed.

'Yes.' Before he could speak again, she added quickly, 'Did you have me followed?'

'I'm a careful man, Miss McClain,' he said. 'I got all your messages, and I wanted to know more about you before I decided how to proceed. I'm sorry if I scared you.'

'Like I told you in my email,' she said coolly, 'I don't scare easy. But I don't like being watched.'

'Me neither,' he said. 'And yet here you are.'

'I take your point,' she said. 'But I am investigating a murder.'

'And thus you are in my living room.' Robinson crossed his legs, leaning back. 'Crime is your beat, but you don't usually do investigative pieces. Why now?'

Harper was impressed. He'd done his research.

'This case is different,' she said simply.

'How?'

She hesitated, deciding how much to share. So far, he wasn't at all what she'd expected. He was calm and cool, but also curious and interested.

He didn't act like he was guilty of anything.

'Why don't you trust them to deal with this case?'

His questions were so rapid-fire, Harper didn't have time to get ready, or even recover from the last one.

It was a great technique. It threw her off her game and kept her there. The only option was to tell the truth.

'I think it's possible Marie Whitney was dating a detective shortly before she died,' she said. 'And I'm trying to find out who killed her – him or you.'

Robinson paused for a fraction of a second.

'Have you got proof of who she was dating?' he said, ignoring the allegation about himself.

'I'm looking for it.' Buying time, Harper took a sip of the water. The bubbles tickled her throat. 'At this time, all I have is the word of people who knew her.'

'What makes you think I might have killed her?'

'I'm told you dated her, too,' Harper said. 'I've been contacting everyone who had a relationship with her to try and find out who she really was. So far, the picture I'm getting is not a pretty one.'

His mouth twisted. 'That doesn't surprise me.'

'I've had two incredibly powerful men threaten me already because they were so frightened to even talk about Whitney,' Harper told him. 'I need to know why they're afraid. And why someone wanted her dead.'

'I can answer that,' Robinson said. 'Because she was a monster.'

Harper tried not to betray her excitement.

'What does that mean?' she asked.

He paused, looking out at the ocean.

'You've seen pictures of her, I assume?'

Harper nodded.

'Then, you know she was beautiful. But the pictures don't tell you everything. She was intelligent, witty, charming...' He glanced at her. 'I've never met anyone like her. She had this way of finding out what you wanted and giving it to you. In return, you gave her things. Money, confidences, information, access to your life. You didn't even notice you were doing it. You simply did it. You wanted her to have it.'

He took a sip of his drink – the ice clattered against the glass.

'And then she used all of that to blackmail you.'

Harper stared. 'She blackmailed you?'

'Oh yes.' He sounded bitterly amused. 'Me and many other people. Not only men, either – women, too. She was very good at it.'

'But…' Harper's mind was racing, thinking of the lawyer's anger, the senator's fearfulness, the things Rosanna had said.

The puzzle pieces clicked into place.

'Holy shit,' she whispered.

Robinson tilted his glass at her. 'My thoughts exactly.'

It took Harper a second to gather herself.

'Do you mind if I ask how she blackmailed you?'

For the first time, Robinson hesitated. She could see him debating internally how to respond.

'I suppose you did sign that affidavit,' he said, after a moment. 'You understand what would happen to your career if you printed any of this?'

'Of course,' she said. 'You have my word.'

'I have your signature,' he corrected her. 'I have your oath.'

Then he let out a breath, as if readying himself for something painful.

'I met Marie at a fundraiser two years ago,' he said. 'I oversee a charitable foundation.'

'I know,' Harper said. 'You do good work.'

'You researched me.'

'Of course.'

Another half-smile.

'As I was saying,' he said. 'I worked with Marie on a project raising money for scientific research into malaria and other tropical diseases at the university. She was…' he rolled his hand, '… all

342

the things I said. Beautiful. Alluring. We began a relationship.' He paused. 'The only problem was, I was still married at the time.'

He stood abruptly. 'Would you mind if we went outside? I could use the fresh air. Bring your glass.'

Without waiting for her response, he crossed the room to a glass door Harper hadn't noticed before. When he opened it, a warm breeze blew through.

Grabbing her drink, she hurried after him out onto a spacious veranda, where a low, dark sofa set was arranged around a glass coffee table.

Once again, they sat across from each other. Ocean breezes ruffled her hair.

There was that scent of jasmine again. It must grow everywhere around here. She wished she could see it, but the moon had gone behind a cloud and the darkness hid even the sea. She wouldn't have known it was there, had she not been able to hear its low, powerful rumble.

'Where was I?' Robinson asked.

But she knew he didn't expect an answer. He was staring beyond her – through her.

'Anyway, we started an affair, and I think you can see where this is going. She threatened to tell my wife. Demanded more than a million dollars. She had pictures taken of us.' He waved his glass. 'The usual tawdry thing.'

His voice was emotionless, and yet Harper could see how much this affected him. For someone so skilled at hiding his emotions, there was still a kind of transparency to him on this subject.

'Around that time, my wife found out she was pregnant,' he said.

Harper's breath caught. She had an awful feeling she knew where this was going.

'The problem Marie didn't understand – couldn't possibly have seen – was that I couldn't be blackmailed,' he explained. 'If you're blackmailed once, you're blackmailed for life. They can drain you dry. So, I went on the offensive. I had Marie investigated. Every facet of her existence. That's when I found out she'd done this before. Many times. To many people.

'I got sworn affidavits from numerous people about her offenses. I threatened to expose her. To have her fired. She agreed to back off.'

He fell silent.

In the darkness overhead, something flew by, quick and deadly. A bat, perhaps.

'Something happened,' Harper prodded gently.

He nodded, and reached for his glass.

'Everything seemed fine for a few weeks, and then someone sent my wife a series of pictures of Marie and I making love. Different locations. Different positions.'

He emptied his glass.

When he spoke his voice was steady, and somehow that made it worse.

'My wife left me,' he said. 'And then she got rid of the baby.'

For a second, Harper searched for the right words to say to that. But there weren't any.

'I'm sorry,' she said.

He didn't seem to hear it.

'As it turned out, Marie didn't want money any more. She wanted blood,' he said. 'She got it.'

Harper let that sentence hang there.

Then, ever so gently, she said, 'Mr Robinson. Did you kill Marie Whitney?'

To her surprise, he gave her a dry smile.

'Call me Sterling, please. I insist everyone who accuses me of murder uses my first name. And no, I didn't kill her. The day Marie Whitney died, I was in New York. I was photographed many times that afternoon at a function at the Metropolitan Museum of Art. I have plane tickets and proof of my travel. I can provide you with all of the evidence of my innocence you would like.'

'Did you have her killed?' Harper persisted.

'Don't you see, Miss McClain?' He turned over his hands. His long, artistic fingers reminded her of her mother's. 'That's not how I work. My wife broke my heart. But that wasn't Marie Whitney's fault. It was my fault. Because I broke my wife's heart first.'

His eyes were steady; earnest.

'Marie Whitney was like a brown recluse spider. You don't blame the spider because it bites. It's what it was born to do. Marie was born to destroy. I should have seen it. I pride myself on my ability to see through people to their core. Her, I misjudged. And it cost me.'

Harper thought she'd never met anyone quite like Sterling Robinson. He was smart. He was ruthless. And, to her own surprise, she believed him.

He stood up.

'I'm going to get another drink. Something considerably stronger. Would you like one, Miss McClain?'

'Do you have any whiskey?' she asked. 'And please. Call me Harper.'

On the way back to Savannah across the marshes later that night, Harper thought of what Sterling had said. About his wife. And Marie Whitney.

She kept thinking about how he compared her to a poisonous

345

spider. The more she learned about the murder victim, the more she agreed.

In the end, she'd stayed at the beach house for another hour, drinking whiskey sodas and dissecting Marie Whitney. She told Robinson her theories, leaving out the part about her mother.

At her request, he produced the private investigator's reports, and spread them out on the coffee table. In them, she found the senator's name, and the lawyer's, along with the names of several other powerful Savannah glitterati.

But no Larry Blazer. In fact, no police at all.

'Are you certain she was involved with a detective?' Sterling asked, seeing the disappointment in her face.

'I'm not certain of anything any more,' she replied.

Kneeling on the floor next to the over-sized coffee table, her hands filled with papers, Harper looked down at the names of all the people Whitney had damaged in her short, dangerous life.

How was she going to figure out which one of them had killed her? And what, if anything, connected them to her mother?

Every day seemed to throw another of her theories out the window. Now, she felt like she was flailing blindly for some idea of what happened. Some clue as to why Whitney's murder looked so much like her mother's.

Sterling shook his empty glass, watching the clear ice cubes dance.

'Marie was very intelligent. Extremely adept at judging the men she went after,' he said, thoughtfully. 'She would have known a detective could see through her more easily. Maybe after the first thrill of it, she realized he could threaten her meal ticket. Police officers don't have much money to spare. She'd have little to gain from that relationship. As soon as she figured that out, she'd have walked away. If he did kill her, the key is what he had to lose. What could she threaten him with?'

Taking off his glasses, he rubbed the bridge of his nose. Harper noticed his eyes were an unusual gray – clear as water.

'Why did you never try to ruin her?' Harper asked. 'After what she did to you?'

'I always thought that, one day, I would,' he said, with disarming frankness. 'I intended to build a relationship with the university president and have her fired, her career demolished.' He straightened the papers. 'But she had a child, who she was raising alone, and I didn't want to harm the child. I wanted to be better than her. So, I decided to wait.

'But then,' he leaned back against the sofa cushions, 'someone killed her first.'

At the mention of Whitney's daughter, Harper saw Camille's face in her mind. Stricken brown eyes filled with tears. Clinging to Smith.

'I'm going to see her,' she announced. 'Camille Whitney. Find out what she knows.'

He cocked his head. 'You know where she is?'

She nodded. 'With family. Not far out of Savannah.'

'She probably doesn't know much,' he told her. 'Whitney didn't introduce most of her lovers to Camille. I only met her once at a charity function for children. She never knew about her mother and me, as far as I know.'

Somehow this didn't come as a surprise.

'I'm all out of options,' Harper had confessed then. 'I've got this one last shot. If nothing comes of it...' She pushed the papers back to him. 'I'm in trouble.'

Now she thought about his cautioning words. Whitney had

introduced him to her daughter, but not as a lover. Just another man at a charity party.

The odds of Camille having met Marie's cop boyfriend – if there ever really was a cop boyfriend – were slim.

Worse still, tonight had made Harper even more doubtful of the whole idea of Blazer as someone Whitney would have dated. Blazer's bachelor apartment in the suburbs wasn't in the same league as Sterling Robinson's palatial home. What would Whitney have seen in him? What could he have that she wanted?

Still, there was nowhere to go but forward. Camille Whitney might know something. And she was going to arrange to meet her.

Soon.

Chapter Thirty-five

Vidalia, Georgia, is one of those country towns you've driven through a thousand times without ever paying much attention.

Main Street was also Highway 280, and it rumbled fast past the chain restaurants, pawn shops and big box superstores that fill most farm towns these days.

The old downtown, though, was nicer – lined with neatly pruned trees, it still had some charming 1940s shopfronts, but Harper didn't notice them at all.

Because she was lost.

'Stupid, damned redneck town,' she muttered, as she U-turned for the third time.

Pulling abruptly into the parking lot at the Dairy Queen, she parked and punched numbers into her GPS harder than necessary, grumbling under her breath. Soft rain misted the car windows, turning the town gray.

Why couldn't she find this house?

It had been five days since her meeting with Robinson.

Five days without work. Five days of isolation and self-doubt.

Day after day, with nothing to do, she'd talked herself into, and out of, this trip a million times.

In the end, though, she honestly felt she had no choice. She couldn't walk away from the Whitney case without trying absolutely everything.

With all that had happened, though, she couldn't show up at the Whitney house as Harper McClain, currently suspended newspaper reporter.

When she called James Whitney to arrange a visit, she introduced herself as a state-appointed counselor.

It had been surprisingly simple to get him to accept this, and then to agree that she should visit his daughter.

In fact, he'd seemed almost eager for her to come.

'I'm worried sick about Camille,' he'd said on the phone. 'She's lost in her own head. Won't do anything at all. She stares into space. I sure do hope you can help her.'

Behind his soft, Georgia accent she could hear the undertone of fear, a shiver in his breath. It was, she suspected, the only hint he'd give of the pain he was dealing with, and his worries for his daughter.

'I'll do all I can,' she promised him.

At the time, she'd felt a stab of guilt. After all, she had no professional skills in dealing with traumatized children.

Now that she was here, though, her inability to find the place was, if nothing else, tempering her other emotions. She was already ten minutes late, and *why* hadn't she thought to ask if he'd hidden his house in a tree, or buried it in a culvert?

She'd driven up and down the wide, flat streets that crisscrossed the town, and still couldn't find the number she was looking for. Each house was virtually the same – low-slung, post-war houses with sprawling unfenced yards, grass turning brown as summer burned the green away, and a pickup truck in the driveway.

Maybe she hadn't gone far enough. She would try again, this time going all the way to the end of Bromley Street.

As she prepared to pull out onto the highway again, she caught a glimpse of herself in the rearview mirror and recoiled. The dark brown wig, cut smooth and straight so the hair brushed the tops of her shoulders, completely altered her appearance.

It was Bonnie, of course, who'd loaned it to her. She had a closet full of cosplay gear and preferred 'real hair' wigs, which she usually bought, horribly, on eBay. God only knew where they came from.

'This one, I think,' she'd mused, plucking the glossy brunette option from atop a disturbingly blank Styrofoam head.

By then, Harper had already tried a long blonde wig (disaster), and refused blue and pink (Bonnie's preferences).

She'd known she needed to hide her auburn hair – it was the most distinctive thing about her. But she had her doubts about a wig. It seemed so obvious – like everyone would know it wasn't her real hair.

When she'd slipped on the brown wig, though, the transformation was so thorough, she scarcely recognized herself. Her face looked paler and her eyes looked darker.

It was astonishing how such a small change could alter her so completely. And how convincingly real it looked.

Bonnie – who knew only that she needed to change her appearance for undercover work, and who thought this was the most brilliant thing she'd ever heard – had stepped back to study her handiwork.

'You look like a spy,' she declared approvingly. 'A pale spy. You're going to have to change your makeup. Luckily…' she waved a long, slim brush at her, 'I went to art school.'

Now Harper's eyes were lined with a trace of dark pencil, and her cheekbones highlighted with a touch of pink. The light freckles that dusted the bridge of her nose were all but invisible.

She'd intentionally dressed the way she thought a counselor might – in a conservative over-the-knee skirt and baggy blazer. She looked like a combination of Baxter and a high school teacher.

She looked like a lot of people – but she looked nothing like Harper McClain.

There was no way for Bonnie not to notice she wasn't working. When she asked what was going on, Harper told her the truth – that she'd gotten into trouble for a story she was working on, and she was suspended for two weeks.

Holding the makeup brush in the air, Bonnie tilted her head.

'But why are you investigating if you're suspended?'

'It's the thing I was working on when this all kicked off,' Harper had told her vaguely. 'I want to know how it ends.'

Bonnie shrugged and dabbed the brush in creamy powder.

'Your life is so weird,' she said.

'Tell me about it,' Harper had agreed.

Now, spinning the wheel, she turned the rented black Ford back onto Bromley Street. She'd decided the Camaro was too recognizable, and she didn't want to take any chances, so she'd leased the most anonymous car she could find, and then spent the first half hour trying not to slam the brakes so hard she went through the windshield.

By now, though, she had the hang of it. She was frustrated by the lack of power when she pressed the accelerator, but she also felt pleasantly invisible.

The one-story houses, most white or gray, rolled past again. But when she reached the 12000 block, once again the houses ran out. It was like the town just ended. Fields stretched out beyond that point – the soil rich, dark brown, turned in neat straight lines.

This time, though, she persevered, continuing on as Bromley turned from a residential street into a farm road. After five minutes' drive through the fields, to her relief, a house appeared in the distance – it was an older, two-story farmhouse, not unlike her grandmother's place had been, albeit in worse condition.

The yard was a bit overgrown, and the farm tools and implements scattered around outside the barn gave it something of a disreputable look.

Harper slowed as she neared the driveway, checking the number on the mailbox: 12057. This was the place.

Carefully, she pulled in, parking next to a battered Chevy truck with a riding lawnmower in the back.

Taking a steadying breath, she climbed out of the car and shut the door. Carefully, she picked her way through the tools and flat tires to the wooden steps leading up to a wide porch.

Everything could use a lick of paint, but it was a lovely old building. The columns holding up the porch roof were original, hewn of solid oak.

Once upon a time, a farmer would have lived here with a family of six or seven kids and an exhausted wife, and the place would have been alive with noise and life.

Now it was uncomfortably quiet.

Setting her face in lines of professional neutrality, she rapped her knuckles crisply against the door.

For a moment, there was no reaction. Then she heard the soft sighing sound of movement, like the house warning her. A second later, the recognizable clump of cowboy boots on wood floors.

The door swung open.

The craggy face looking out at her had spent time in every kind of weather, but it wasn't old – maybe mid-thirties. Large, warm brown eyes met hers.

'Miss Watson?'

She'd borrowed the pseudonym from a great-grandmother. It hung as loosely on her shoulders as the blazer.

'Yes,' she said. 'Are you Mr Whitney?'

She kept her voice low and warm, adding what she hoped was a soothing timbre to her words. She remembered counselors with voices like that from her own childhood.

'Yes, indeed.' He held the door open for her. 'Please come in. And call me Jim. We've been waitin' for you.'

His voice was uncertain but cautiously friendly as he led the way down a long, brightly lit hallway, past one of those old staircases wide enough for a hoop skirt, with a handrail begging for children to slide down it.

The house was as she'd expected – high ceilings and wood floors, a bit dinged up, but still the kind of comfortable place where you could easily imagine relaxing in the battered window seat with a good book.

It had the faint, warm smell of toast that Harper suspected might somehow be permanent – soaked into the wood over the years.

The rugs thrown here and there were cheap and worn, but clean. Everything was serviceable and solid, a description that applied to James Whitney himself.

He wore faded jeans with a big leather belt, and a checked shirt tucked in neatly. His brown hair could have used a cut, but the shagginess of it suited his face.

There was a sadness to him – not only in his expression, but in his whole being. He was easily six feet tall, but stood slightly hunched, like he was bracing himself for the next blow.

'Would you like a cup of coffee?' Jim swung his hands in an awkward gesture. 'Maybe we could talk a while before I go get Cammy.'

'Sure. That's a great idea.' Harper followed him through the living room – soft, sagging sofa, covered in a hand-knitted throw – to a dining room that was clearly rarely used, with its display of china that in no way belonged to this man, and into a big, country house kitchen.

This was the best room in the house, with tall, 1940s glass-front cabinets and big sash windows, bringing in a view of soft gray sky and a cluttered yard.

Jim gestured at the scrubbed oak table that looked like it might have been in this house since the day it was built. Harper took a seat in a wooden chair.

'Coffee?' He held up a coffee pot enquiringly.

She nodded. 'Black.'

He brought it over in two mismatched mugs in yellow and blue, and sat down heavily in the chair across from hers.

They both took contemplative sips. The coffee was good – fresh. He must have made a new pot shortly before she arrived.

Jim looked uncomfortable but hopeful – like he wanted to talk but didn't know what to say.

'So... Camille,' Harper said, in her pretend-counselor voice. 'Tell me more about her. How is she?'

He shook his head.

'Not good, Miss Watson. There's no progress.'

'Please,' Harper said. 'Call me Julie.'

With a shy smile, he ducked his head.

'Julie.'

Guilt tightened itself around Harper's ribcage. He was so *nice*. She felt like a sociopath, tearing through his life for information.

She heard Luke's voice in her head. *You're so destructive, Harper, you know that?*

Stiffening her spine, she pushed that voice away. She'd come too far to stop now.

'You call her Cammy? Is that your nickname for her? What should I call her?'

'Oh,' he said, surprised. 'You can call her Camille. Cammy was her baby name. I still call her that because...' He stopped, trying to think. 'I just do.'

Harper smiled. 'I understand.'

There was another awkward pause.

She glanced around the kitchen. There were touches to this house – the china, the floral tea towels hanging from the rail, the cheery cups – that indicated the presence of a woman. But he wore no wedding ring.

'Is it only you and Camille living here?'

He nodded, his face reddening.

'Yeah. It's me and her now.' He took a sip of coffee. 'Her mother and me, we met young. Got pregnant by mistake. Broke up when Cammy was still a baby.'

He gave a sad, unconvincing chuckle. 'It was never going to last. Marie got a job in the city and, *whew*.' He made a flying gesture with one hand – a plane taking off. 'She was out of here.'

His eyes glanced off of Harper's.

'Can't say as I blame her. Not much around here for a girl like her. She liked the finer things. I couldn't give her that.'

Harper kept the surprise out of her expression.

Marie Whitney had grown up *here* in Vidalia. Had lived in this house.

This was so far from the Marie Whitney she'd been discovering – the manipulative, sophisticated blackmailer, with her silky ballgowns, champagne and millionaires. It was impossible to imagine her in this kitchen, making supper.

How she must have hated her life here. Resented this quiet, well-meaning man.

She sipped her coffee.

'Did she take Camille with her, when she left?'

Jim shook his head.

'Not at first.' Another short, humorless laugh. 'That girl. She took her clothes in a suitcase and left me a note saying she was gone. Left Camille with my mother for the day and never come back.'

He drained the rest of his coffee without, Harper suspected, tasting it.

'Yep,' he said, mostly to himself. 'It was a couple years later she got in touch, saying she was sorry and could she see Camille? So...' He shrugged. 'A girl needs her mother. The rest is history.'

Everything was falling into place. Marie had run away and started over without the baggage of a child and husband. Then, when she was ready, she came back for the one thing she'd left her husband – their daughter.

It was breathtakingly cruel.

'What about you?' she asked. 'What happened to you after they both left?'

He shot her a quick look she couldn't read.

'What about me?' He asked it as if the question made no sense to him. 'Well, I'm a hired hand on one of the farms you drove past on the way here, and I do other odd jobs. I'm not married.' He gestured at the kitchen around them. 'I reckon that's obvious. I had a girlfriend for a while but...' His voice trailed off. 'Didn't work out.'

The last three words were almost unintelligible, and suddenly all Harper wanted to do was give this man a hug. She wanted to do it so much she had to clutch her coffee cup to stop herself from running around the table to tell him everything would be all right. Not just because it would be insane, but also because it was entirely possible that it wasn't true.

Everything wouldn't be all right.

The world didn't like men like him anymore. Men with strong hands and no education. Sometimes it felt like life was trying to push them out altogether.

'I understand,' she said quietly. She pushed her coffee cup aside. 'Now. Tell me about Camille. Is she talking to you at all?'

This was safer ground, and Jim sat up straighter.

'She's so quiet,' he said. 'I try and talk to her, and she'll answer, but only a bit, you know? Not yes or no, but almost. She has nightmares every single night – wakes up screaming for her mother.' He looked away. 'That's the worst part of it.'

Harper's heart twisted. How well she remembered those nightmares.

Every so often she still had them.

'And school? I take it she's not back at school yet?'

'Oh no.' He shook his head. 'She's not ready for that. I've got her books and papers here, and I'm doing my best to get her to read, but her concentration ain't so good these days.'

'I understand.' Harper picked up her teaspoon and turned it in her hands. 'Is there anything else you want me to know before I talk to her?'

'I just… I want her to be able to sleep without crying,' he said softly. 'I want her to know it's going to get better. That someday, she'll forget what she saw.'

No, she won't, Harper thought.

There was a pause.

'Well.' Jim stood up. 'I guess that's it. I'll go get her. You can stay right here.'

He left the room, boots clomping on the floor.

Harper listened, following his progress easily in the old house, down the hallway, up the stairs. She envisioned a wide, breezy upstairs landing, lined with sturdy doors. She heard him knock on one of them, and then the faint rumble of his voice.

A minute later he walked back into the kitchen, holding the hand of the girl Harper remembered from the murder scene.

She looked paler now, and thinner. A cloud of long, dark hair seemed to envelop her slim body. She was small for her age. And the huge, brown eyes she remembered from that day studied her warily.

It was all so horribly familiar, for a second, Harper couldn't breathe.

She was seeing herself at twelve, huddled behind the living room door, long skinny legs, unbrushed hair loose around her face, pressing her ear to the wall, trying to hear the adult conversation inside. Trying so hard to understand what had happened to her whole world.

In an instant, she felt again the raw, salted-wound pain of that time.

Shoving her chair back, Harper stood.

She'd waited so long, and risked so much for this moment. She had to keep her head together. She needed to play this right. Not for herself. But for everyone in this room.

'Hello, Camille,' she said calmly. 'My name is Julie. I'm so happy to meet you.'

Chapter Thirty-six

Camille kept her eyes fixed on the worn wood floor.

'I'd like to talk to you, if you don't mind?' Harper said in her new, soothing voice.

Camille hunched her shoulders in a noncommittal shrug.

When it was clear she didn't intend to reply, her father directed her to a seat across the table from Harper. The child didn't seem to care where she sat. She let him arrange her in the seat like a doll.

'Would you like some juice, honey?' he asked.

Camille stared mutely down at her hands, resting on top of the scarred table.

In a flash Harper saw her grandmother standing in the kitchen, long silver hair wound into a heavy bun on the back of her head. She had a delicate, dancer's neck, and narrow shoulders and she was holding a pitcher filled with fresh lemonade.

'Would you like a glass, Harper?'

Condensation ran down the sides of the pitcher and Harper was so thirsty. But she wouldn't admit it. She wouldn't say anything.

She hadn't spoken in days, and she didn't intend to start now. In a world without her mother, what was the point of talking?

Without waiting for a reply that clearly wasn't coming, Jim walked over to the fridge and took out a bottle of apple juice.

After pouring her a glass, and refilling Harper's mug, he backed away from the table.

'I reckon I'll leave you two to talk in private.'

His eyes sought reassurance from Harper. She gave him an encouraging nod.

He closed the kitchen door. She waited until the sound of his footsteps told her he'd headed to the living room.

Camille stared at the amber liquid in her glass. Her shoulders were hunched, her hands gripped the table edge until her knuckles turned white.

'Camille,' Harper said softly, 'do you know why I'm here?'

The girl didn't react.

'I'm here to talk. That's all.'

Still nothing.

'Have a lot of people been talking to you?' Harper guessed.

Still looking at her glass, Camille nodded, and a curtain of hair fell into her eyes. She pushed it back impatiently, like it bothered her.

Her hair was such a tangle.

Harper knew that traumatized children often regressed to a younger age. They wouldn't brush their teeth or comb their hair. Sometimes, for a while, they couldn't remember how to dress.

She could imagine Jim not knowing how to help Camille brush that mass of hair into a neat braid, or pull it back into a smooth ponytail. He'd want to, but his big hands would struggle not to pull or to hurt.

Harper had decided Julie would carry a handbag, so she had one

361

with her – black, with a snap-top – she'd borrowed from Bonnie. It contained a brush she was supposed to use to smooth her wig.

'Is your hair bothering you?'

For the first time, Camille looked up. She regarded Harper with new interest. Fine, dark brows drew together.

After a long moment, she inclined her head in a nod so slight it was almost imperceptible.

Reaching down, Harper pulled out the brush, digging around until she found an elastic hair band – her own hair often bothered her, so she always had extras around.

She held both up so the girl could see them.

'Want me to braid it?'

Camille hesitated. Her eyes studied Harper with a look that was surprisingly savvy.

A flash of her mother's intellect – quick and telling.

'I know you can brush your own hair,' Harper said. 'But braids are a pain to do, aren't they?'

This time, Camille's nod was stronger.

Harper smiled. 'Come stand here.'

She gestured at the space in front of her chair.

There was a long pause, when she thought the girl had changed her mind. Then, cautiously, Camille got up and walked over until she stood in front of her.

'Now, turn around.' Gently, Harper placed her hands on the girl's shoulders – bones delicate as birds' wings – and guided her until her back was to her.

Starting at the ends, she brushed the tangles out of her thick dark hair. She knew how to do it so it didn't hurt. After all, she'd once been a girl with long, tangled hair herself. Still, she checked.

'Am I pulling?'

Camille shook her head, hair swinging.

Harper kept waiting for her to walk away – to decide this was too weird – but Camille seemed content to stand as she worked the brush through her tangles with light but determined strokes.

Harper waited until she was sure she was relaxed before asking the first question.

'Your dad tells me you have nightmares.'

Camille said nothing.

'Are they bad?'

The girl's head bobbed once.

Harper lifted the brush until she stopped moving. Then resumed the slow, meditative process.

'About your mom?'

Another slight nod.

'And that day.'

Camille's stillness was her answer.

'You know what?' Harper untangled the last of the knots in her hair. 'I used to have nightmares exactly like those.'

Camille said nothing, but the slight tilt of her head and the hitch in her breathing told Harper she was listening.

'I had a trick that made them stop.' Carefully, she separated the girl's hair into three sections. 'When I went to bed every night, I would think of things I wanted to do. Places I wanted to go. I would think of sailing on the sea, or playing in a beautiful park. I would imagine I had a big dog with me, one that was fierce to everyone else, but loyal to me. And I would have these adventures at night with my dog to protect me.'

Her voice was light and lilting, a gentle calming sound, as her fingers began weaving Camille's hair into a dark, glossy rope, the way it had been the first time she'd seen her.

'After a while, whenever I started to have one of those night-mares, my dream guard dog would come get me and take me

363

away somewhere safe. He protected me every single night. I was never alone.'

She was nearly to the end now, the braid was almost finished. Camille was still listening.

'Would you try that? Make your own dream guard dog to protect you?'

Camille nodded so fiercely, Harper had to let the braid go for a second to avoid hurting her.

'Good.'

She wrapped the band around the end of the braid three times, then patted Camille on the shoulder.

'All finished!' she said brightly.

Without warning, the girl spun around and threw her arms around Harper's shoulders so hard, she thought her wig would fall off.

'Thank you,' Camille whispered.

It was the first thing she'd said.

Harper, who had never in all her life told anyone about the dream dog that had helped her survive the aftermath of her mother's murder, hugged her body gently.

Her heart ached for all that was about to happen to her. All she would go through over the coming years. It would get worse. Things always get worse.

'I promise,' she told her with quiet fierceness. 'You will get through this. Your mother would want you to get through this.'

Hearing the words Harper had told herself many times, Camille nodded hard. Wiping tears from her eyes, she then returned to her chair, and picked up her juice, as if everything that had happened were perfectly normal.

Harper surreptitiously checked her wig – but Bonnie's pins had held. Everything was in place.

When she resumed her seat, Camille had stopped staring into her drink; she seemed more interested in Harper. Her dark eyes roved across her face with open curiosity.

'Where are you from?' Her voice was steady – it sounded older than she looked.

'Augusta,' Harper said, without missing a beat. Her own social workers had sometimes come from there, so she'd chosen it for Julie.

'I've never been there.'

'It's nice.' Harper had never been to Augusta either.

They sat for a moment in companionable silence, Camille took a sip of her juice.

Harper stirred her coffee thoughtfully, judging whether the time was right. But Camille seemed calm now.

'Can we talk about your mother?'

Camille set her drink down hard, spilling a drop of the liquid.

'Don't worry.' Grabbing her napkin, Harper reached over and wiped the spill. 'I've got it.'

When her hand withdrew, Camille was still staring at the empty spot where the spill had been.

'We can talk about her,' she said.

Harper paused.

She needed to play this right. If she pushed her too hard, she'd lose her. If she didn't push hard enough, she'd get nothing. She decided to start easy.

'What was she like?'

There was a long silence – so long, Harper thought perhaps the girl wouldn't talk after all. But then, Camille raised her eyes from the table.

'She was beautiful,' Camille said. 'All of my friends thought so.'

How interesting, Harper thought, that the first thing she'd

thought of was her mother's appearance. If someone had asked the same thing about her mother, she would have said, 'She was an artist. I loved her.'

'I've seen pictures of her,' Harper said. 'She was very pretty. Did she have a lot of friends?'

Brightening, the girl nodded so hard her braid swung.

'She was very popular. She went on lots of dates.'

This was precisely the opening Harper had hoped for.

'Did she?' She smiled. 'I'm not surprised. Did she have a boy-friend?'

Camille gave her a secretive look. 'She had lots of boyfriends.'

Now that sounded like the Marie Whitney Harper was getting to know.

'Have you seen any of your mom's boyfriends since you came to live here?'

Her smile fading, Camille shook her head.

She'd gone suddenly quiet.

She hadn't seen the boyfriend. But surely she'd seen Blazer. The notes in the Whitney file indicated he'd interviewed her. On the other hand, maybe he sent someone else to do that, and signed off on their notes. She needed to be sure.

She took a slow sip of coffee, buying time. When she spoke again, her tone was casual.

'Have the police been checking on you?'

Camille nodded. 'They're here all the time. And social workers.' She made a vague gesture. 'Everyone.'

'Have you met Detective Blazer?'

Harper watched her closely.

Camille thought for a second, and then nodded.

'He's trying to find the killer.' She said it with sudden fierceness.

'Exactly,' Harper agreed. 'Has he talked with you? Made sure you're OK?'

'Yes,' Camille said. 'He's nice. He brought me some books to read.'

They'd clearly met more than once, and there was nothing in Camille's face to indicate she saw him as anything other than a kind cop.

Harper was no closer to knowing who killed her mother and Camille's mother than she'd been weeks ago.

The realization was crushing. All that work – everything she'd risked. For nothing.

Camille was watching her curiously.

'Can I ask you a question?' Camille asked.

'Of course.'

'Will the police catch the person who hurt my mom?'

Instantly, Harper had a flash memory of Smith, standing in her grandmother's living room, clutching a glass of iced tea.

'We're going to find him, Harper, I swear it.'

And she remembered the faint warmth of hope thawing the ice under her skin, just for a minute.

For a child, false hope trumped no hope every time.

She leaned forward, stretching out her hand to press Camille's fingers. The girl didn't pull her hand away.

'I know the police are working very hard,' she said. 'I'm sure they'll find whoever did this. They are looking for him day and night.'

Camille's huge eyes held hers.

'I would like to catch him.' Her voice was low and razor sharp. Suddenly she sounded much older than twelve. 'I want to catch him and make him *pay*.'

Her eyes blazed with rage.

This was why she wasn't talking to the grown-ups around her – this anger. She was so furious she couldn't find words to express her wrath.

Everyone around her was telling her everything would be fine, and only she, still young enough to see the truth right in front of her, knew there was no such thing as fine any more. There was only vengeance.

For an instant, Harper could have sworn she saw her younger self on the other side of the table, not Camille. A curtain of auburn hair, hazel eyes filled with pain. Looking, with desperate hunger, for answers. Answers no one could give her.

Panic rose in her throat like bile.

Dear God, what was she doing here? This was madness.

It was as if she could really see herself for the first time – an imposter in the middle of someone else's tragedy. In her eBay wig and baggy blazer, pretending she could help.

She couldn't help anyone. She couldn't even help herself.

She'd roped Bonnie into this deception, pushed Luke away, probably lost Smith forever.

And all for what?

She was sitting in a broken-hearted child's kitchen, trying to trick information out of her so she could staunch her own bleeding. Heal her own pain.

Miles and Luke were right. She had to let this go. At least for now. Not to save her job.

To save her soul.

Chapter Thirty-seven

On the long drive home, Harper kept seeing Camille's expressive face.

They'd talked for only a while longer. The emotions of the conversation were taxing for the girl, and Harper was desperate to leave before she did more damage.

But as she prepared to leave, guilt had gnawed at her, sharp and painful.

She couldn't walk away from her. Leave her to climb out of this hell alone.

In violation of everything that made sense, she'd written her cell phone number down on a scrap of paper and pressed it into Camille's small hands.

'If those nightmares don't stop,' she said. 'You call me, OK?'

'OK.'

Camille had carefully folded the paper and put it in her pocket.

When they walked out of the dining room together, Jim Whitney hurried out into the hallway to meet them. His eyes settled on Camille's smooth hair.

'Don't you look pretty, honey,' he told his daughter, before turning to Harper apologetically. 'I can't seem to get the hang of how to help her with things like that.'

'You'll figure it out,' Harper assured him. 'Camille will show you how.'

When she left, they'd both stood on the porch together. Jim waving. Camille standing straight, watching her go.

Those huge eyes stayed with her all the way down the highway.

Harper got stuck behind a tractor outside of Vidalia, and later a two-car accident slowed traffic to a crawl, so it was more than two hours before she reached the outskirts of Savannah.

Her cell phone rang as she sat at a red light, and she fumbled with it, answering without looking at it first.

'Harper,' she said. The light turned green.

'Harper, it's Billy.' Her landlord's normally jovial voice was unusually serious. 'I need you to come home. There's been a break-in.'

Harper was so stunned she nearly slammed into the back of the car ahead of her, which had braked abruptly.

When she screeched to a stop inches from its back bumper, her heart was in her throat. She saw the driver frown at her in his rearview mirror.

'A break-in? At my *apartment*?'

'I'm afraid so, honey.' Stress made his Louisiana accent thicker than ever. 'Them kids upstairs, they called and told me your door was hangin' open when they got back. Already called the cops, but you need to get on home now.'

'Thanks, Billy,' Harper said grimly. 'I'm on my way.'

When the light turned green, she floored it, but traffic slowed her down.

At every red light, she kept thinking, *Get home. Get home. Get home...*

It took twenty long minutes to make her way through the rush-hour traffic to the graceful oaks and tall, old buildings of Jones Street.

When she pulled up, Billy was standing on the porch with a worried frown. When she climbed out of the rental car, he stared at the Ford.

'Y'all got a new car?'

'It's a rental,' she explained. 'Mine's been acting up.'

She'd taken off her wig at a truck stop an hour ago, where she'd stopped for gas and a cup of nuclear-powered trucker coffee, so at least she didn't have to explain her appearance.

'How bad is it?' she asked, hurrying up the front steps.

'It's bad.' Billy patted her awkwardly on the shoulder. 'But don't you worry. We can fix it.'

Harper stepped numbly through the front door. A quick glance at the locks told her they were undamaged.

'How'd they get in?' She glanced back at her landlord.

'Kitchen window's broke.' He pointed towards the back where afternoon light was flooding down the hallway. 'Looks like they used a crowbar.'

The window. Why hadn't she insisted on bulletproof glass?

The front hallway was exactly as she'd left it. Even the light was still on. It was only when she turned into the living room that she could see the damage.

The television was smashed – the screen a cobweb of broken glass – and the stereo had been ripped loose from the speakers, leaving wires trailing uselessly across the floor. Papers were flung everywhere – pages had been torn from her notebooks and scattered like confetti.

Harper saw the plastic pieces of her police scanner in a corner – the gash in the wall above indicating someone had hurled it there with great force.

Through the haze of shock, she had one very clear thought – this damage looked vindictive.

The sofa and chair had been knocked onto their backs, cushions sliced open so foam spilled out like intestines.

It was such a mess, the last thing she noticed was the worst thing they'd done.

The portrait Bonnie had painted of her seven summers ago – someone had taken a knife to it. Two deep, crisscrossing gouges had been carved across her face.

Next to it was a single word, painted on the wall in some dark substance.

RUN.

Harper made a small, involuntary sound. She pressed her fingers against her lips.

The warning had been scrawled with a brush, with fast, furious strokes. The paint dripped down the wall like blood.

This was no ordinary burglary.

Harper had moved beyond fear now, and into a kind of icy calm.

Careful not to touch anything, she picked her way through the chaos to the kitchen. Here there was more evidence of destructive fury – glasses broken on the floor, contents of the refrigerator had been hurled around until ketchup and salad dressing ran down the walls she'd so carefully painted last summer.

There was no sign of Zuzu anywhere.

She felt a cold distance between herself and the scene in front of her as she turned down the hallway.

The bedroom had received most of the invaders' attention. Sheets had been ripped off, clothes emptied from drawers, the mattress had been sliced in several places and the filling torn out. The bedside drawers lay on the floor, with the contents hurled everywhere.

'You said the police already came?' Her voice was devoid of emotion.

'About twenty minutes ago.' Billy's voice was tight with suppressed anger. 'Policeman barely got out of the car. Walked up the front steps, said something like, "Boy they sure made a mess of this place. Guess she should've got better locks." Then he got back in his car and drove away. Said he'd write up a report.' He scratched his cheek, eyeing her dolefully. 'Question I got is, how'd that policeman know it was a woman who lived here? I sure as hell didn't tell him.'

Billy grew up with nothing. And if there's one thing anyone who grew up poor knows, it's what it looks like when the cops are messing with you.

'The cops know me,' Harper said numbly.

'They know you so much they don't come in to make sure you're all right? What's going on, Harper? Why'd they write that on your wall?'

She looked at him bleakly.

'I don't know.'

She was tired of feeling lost and confused. And she was so grateful she'd put her few remaining boxes of family belongings back in the attic a few days ago. At least they didn't get that.

Billy crossed his arms, lips pursed like they held an invisible cigarette.

'I'm worried about you, sweetheart,' he said. 'What're you gonna do?'

It was a good question.

Already the apartment was fading into a twilight gloaming.

As Harper looked around at the ruins of everything she owned in the world, she thought of Camille Whitney and her father.

Maybe this was karma. Maybe she deserved this.

Billy was still waiting for a response, but she didn't know what to tell him. He should be worried. Everyone should worry.

'Would you stick around a few minutes while I gather some things?' Her voice was thin but horribly steady. 'I don't want to be alone.'

Billy looked affronted.

'I ain't leavin' you here alone for some criminal to come finish his job. I got a .45 caliber semi-automatic says nobody hurts you, Harper.' He patted the gun in the waistband of his baggy jeans. 'You take your time. I'm gonna go out back and secure that window. You need anything, you holler.'

Harper cast him a grateful look.

'Thank you, Billy.'

He waved that away.

'Don't you be thanking me. They break into my house and get at my people, it's on me.'

As he walked out, Harper called after him, 'Keep an eye out for my cat, will you?'

His reply was faint as he disappeared out the back door: 'Cat'll run a mile from this craziness.'

Once he was gone, Harper moved quickly. She didn't want to be here. Every instinct she had was screaming at her to get out.

Crossing the room, she pulled the damaged painting from above the fireplace and leaned it by the door, trying not to look at the gashes across her younger face. Moving faster now, she gathered her mother's paintings as well. She loaded them all carefully into the trunk of the rental car.

Running back up the steps, she dug through the chaos in the

bedroom until she found her suitcase. She threw it on top of the damaged mattress and rifled hastily through the clothes on the floor, taking anything that looked remotely wearable.

As she placed a top in her bag she noticed, as if from a distance, that her hands were trembling.

When the bag was full, she zipped it shut and lugged it to the door.

By then, Billy was nearly done sealing the window – the plywood cover blocked the last of the day's light from the kitchen, casting the apartment in shadow.

He came in through the back door, whistling a tune she didn't recognize.

'That'll do it,' he said with satisfaction. 'Ain't nobody else getting in here tonight.'

With his hammer dangling from one hand, he walked out the front door.

Harper lingered, taking in the destruction of her home. Committing to memory what had been done to her. She never wanted to forget this moment. She wanted it seared on her skin.

It would never happen again. She wouldn't allow it.

Squaring her shoulders, she followed Billy out.

After he locked up, they stood together on the front stoop.

'You got somewhere to go, darlin'?' Billy asked. 'You won't be able to live here for a week or so.'

The concern in his voice made Harper's heart twist.

'I'll be fine,' she assured him.

He didn't look convinced, but he knew her well enough not to push it.

'Well, don't you worry about a thing here,' he said. 'I'll get my cleaning service to come clear up the mess. I'll have that window replaced this week. It'll all be back to normal in no time.'

But Harper knew it would never be normal. Someone had invaded the only safe place she had – a place she'd worked so hard to protect. And now it was ruined.

The things she hadn't told Billy swirled in her mind. She'd been a police reporter long enough to know this was no ordinary burglary. Whoever did this *hated* her.

They wanted her to know they were coming for her.

She wasn't safe anywhere now.

Chapter Thirty-eight

Bonnie lived in a small Victorian duplex on 26th Street, near the railroad tracks.

It was cute – with bay front windows and a porch with an old-fashioned swing – but the neighborhood was right at the edge of Harper's tolerance. She'd covered a shooting five blocks away a few years ago.

Still, Bonnie loved it and refused to move.

'You're obsessed,' she always said when Harper harassed her about safety. 'I'm perfectly fine here.'

As it turned out, she was right – it wasn't her place that got broken into.

Now as Harper lugged her suitcase through the gate and up the front steps, she was glad Bonnie had never moved.

She could hear music playing inside as she rang the doorbell.

When she opened the door, Bonnie's wavy blonde hair was pulled back in a messy ponytail. She wore an oversized white button-down shirt and cut off shorts. She must have been working

– pale blue paint was smeared on her fingers. There was a smudge of it on her cheek.

'Harper!'

Bonnie's surprised eyes took in her crumpled expression, the suitcase at her feet. Her welcoming smile faded.

'I'm so sorry, Bonnie,' Harper said helplessly. 'I didn't know where else to go.'

While she unpacked the car, dumping her suitcase in the crowded spare room, where filmy pink curtains were draped haphazardly over the window and a sequined throw gave the bed a disco sheen, Bonnie poured them both glasses of wine.

Later, sitting on the front porch swing with a glass of Chardonnay, slapping at mosquitoes as the sun set, Harper told her about the burglary.

She tried to make it sound like no big deal, but Bonnie wasn't fooled.

'First your job, now this.' Her eyes searched Harper's face. 'Something's going on.' She swung her wine glass at the empty street on the other side of the low fence. 'And, by the way, where's your hot cop? Why isn't he protecting you?'

'Oh, yeah. I forgot to tell you that part.' Harper took a long drink – the wine was cold and sharp on her tongue. 'He broke up with me.'

Bonnie's jaw dropped.

'Well, shit,' she said. 'What happened?'

'It's no big deal,' Harper said unconvincingly. 'We haven't been together long. Better to find out now.'

Bonnie fixed her with a steady look.

'Harper, stop it.' There was no anger in her voice; only gentle determination. 'You're lying about the burglary, and you're lying about your guy. You're scared and sad – I can see it on your face. You might as well tell me the rest.'

Clutching her wine glass to her chest, Harper slumped on the wooden seat.

'I'm sorry,' she said, miserably. 'I didn't want to ruin your whole day with my messed-up life.'

'Don't be an idiot,' Bonnie said. 'Tell me everything. I can take it.'

The thing was, Harper couldn't tell her everything.

So she told her some of it. She told her about Marie Whitney and the murder scene so like her mother's. She told her about Luke, and how he thought she was obsessed. And she confessed that she was starting to believe he was right. She told her about Blazer's cold fury that night in the archive room – how sure she'd been that he was the killer. And then she told her that she thought she'd been wrong about that.

'All I can do is go back to the beginning,' Harper said helplessly. 'Look at all of Whitney's boyfriends again. There's a lawyer who freaked out when I called him, but I don't know how to investigate him without being sued. And then there's every other man she ever dated.' She held up her hands, wine splashing from her glass onto her skirt. 'That could take weeks, and by then I think I will have gone insane.'

Throughout it all, Bonnie listened, filling her wine glass and holding her hand as she talked and talked, until the sun went down and the air began to cool.

Finally, her tongue loosened by wine, Harper told her the thing she hadn't really let herself think about until now.

'Whoever broke into my place...' she said brokenly. 'I think it could have been cops. Getting revenge for what I did. It was

379

personal. Things they did… that message… it wasn't an ordinary theft. They were trying to intimidate me.'

Bonnie frowned. 'You really think the police would go that far?'

'It happens.'

It was hard to explain to someone not steeped in the culture that police are slow to love, and quick to take offense. That they react viscerally and viciously to suspected betrayal.

She'd seen it in action. She just never thought it would be directed at her.

She hadn't been back to the police station since she broke into the archive, but Luke had made it clear she wasn't welcome there.

'What are you going to do?' Bonnie poured the last of the wine into their glasses, setting the empty bottle on the porch beneath their feet. 'If the cops broke into your apartment, that's serious. You can't let that go.'

'I'll call Smith,' Harper told her reluctantly. 'Tomorrow.'

'Oh, the lieutenant.' Bonnie brightened. 'He'll help.'

'I'm not so sure,' Harper said.

She told her what Smith said to Luke – about how she couldn't be trusted.

'I betrayed his trust,' she said. 'I let him down.'

'Come on, Harper,' Bonnie said, unconvinced. 'He blusters, but he loves you. If you tell him you're sorry, he'll fix things. He always does.'

She made it sound so easy.

'What about Luke?' Bonnie nudged her shoulder. 'You have to get in touch with him.'

Harper shook her head.

'I can't.' She sank down on the wooden swing. 'He doesn't want me any more. I can tell. Besides. He left town.'

'He'll come back,' Bonnie assured her confidently.

With lithe ease, she hopped to her bare feet, sending the swing swaying.

'Come on.' She held open the front door. 'Enough sadness. I'm drunk. Let's eat some food while I finish fixing your life.'

The next day, Harper woke up to find herself in a bewildering sea of pink. It took her a second to realize what she was seeing was sunlight, streaming through Bonnie's vivid pink curtains.

She closed her eyes again.

Her head ached, and her mouth was dry. She desperately needed to pee.

There was no point in trying to get back to sleep.

She rolled out of bed, sending the sequined throw to the floor with a metallic jangle, and headed downstairs.

Bonnie wasn't up yet, so Harper put some coffee on and perused the limited food options. Aside from skim milk, yogurt and peanut butter, there wasn't much to choose from.

She sniffed the milk suspiciously before pouring it into her coffee, and gave up on breakfast.

After the wine ran out, the two of them had found the vodka in the back of Bonnie's freezer, ordered Chinese food, and talked late into the night. They'd finally gone to bed at around two.

Harper had been certain she'd never sleep, but the booze and exhaustion did their work, and she remembered no dreams.

This morning, though, she felt adrift. Cut free from all her moorings.

No job. No boyfriend. No home.

All she had was the Whitney murder. Did she still want to go on with that?

She'd promised Miles she'd stop if she learned nothing from

Camille Whitney. But that was before someone destroyed her home. Before they slashed her face.

When she'd gone to Vidalia, she'd taken her notes and her laptop with her.

If she wanted to, she could dive in right where she left off.

But did she want to?

Flopping back on Bonnie's sofa, she gave a low groan of misery.

'Oh my God.' Bonnie's husky voice floated down the stairs. 'You sound like I feel. Please tell me there's coffee.'

After Bonnie left to teach a workshop at the art school ('My students will all be more hungover than me,' she assured her as she put on her darkest sunglasses), Harper tried to keep herself busy.

First, she called a locksmith and made an urgent appointment to replace the cheap locks on Bonnie's doors and windows.

Then she extended the lease on the anonymous Ford.

Until she knew who broke into her apartment, she had to stay out of the Camaro. Too many people would know that car from a mile away.

A low-simmering sense of panic still told her she'd made a mistake coming here – that she was putting Bonnie in danger. But nobody knew where she was.

It should be fine. So, why didn't it feel fine?

Not for the first time she thought longingly about calling Luke. Begging him to come back.

But he'd told her once, during those long nights of confessions, that when he worked undercover he couldn't keep his phone with him.

'The most identifying thing you've got on you is your phone,' he'd said. 'I could track you across the country, find out everything about you, know your job, your family, your friends – all by looking at your phone.'

Because of this, he always left his phone at a safe drop, miles from wherever he was working. He tried to check it every couple of days, he said. But sometimes that wasn't possible.

If everything he told her was true, then his phone wasn't with him now. If she did break down and call him, who knew when he'd get the message? And even then, why would he care what happened to her now?

She had to sort this out herself.

That afternoon, she sat on the sofa in Bonnie's living room, which, with colorful fabrics draped everywhere, Bonnie's vivid paintings on the wall and candles filling the fireplace, had the appearance of an artistic harem, and stared at her phone.

Slowly – her fingers moving unwillingly – she scrolled to Smith's cell phone number.

Maybe he wasn't as angry as she feared. Maybe he would listen to her.

The phone rang five times. She was about to hang up when he finally answered.

'Smith.'

The word was a terse growl.

It wasn't a promising start.

'Lieutenant,' Harper's voice was small. 'It's me.'

There was a pause.

'What do you want, Harper?'

She'd never heard him sound so distant.

'I ... I wanted to apologize for what happened. The archive room. I shouldn't have gone in there.'

'No, you shouldn't have.'

'I'm very sorry,' she said. 'I feel terrible. And I want you to know it wasn't Dwayne's fault. I lied to him. And that was wrong, too.'

She couldn't hear anything on the line. The silence lasted so long she wondered if he'd hung up.

'Hello?' she said, tentatively.

'Dwayne was written up for what happened,' Smith told her. 'He offered to resign but I refused. He will receive no pay increase this year, thanks to you.'

Harper dropped her head into her hands.

'Don't punish Dwayne,' she pleaded, her voice muffled. 'You know it wasn't his fault.'

'No, it wasn't his fault. I've made it clear to him that he has you to thank for this situation.'

Harper tried to stay calm. She had to fix this.

'I know you're angry with me, and I hope you will find a way to forgive me,' she said.

But when he spoke again, his tone was, if anything, more forbidding.

'What you did, Harper, was unforgivable. Your behavior has been outrageous. And now two of my officers have suffered because of it.'

Two.

'Luke had nothing to do with any of it,' Harper told him.

'Didn't he?' His voice was ice. 'You got him tangled up in this obsession of yours, and now you've left him in a position where he can't properly function as a detective. You've put both him and Dwayne in terrible positions with your childish behavior. And me, too, actually. The deputy chief is aware of our friendship. And I've been put on notice that I may be investigated by internal affairs. Which could ruin my career.'

Harper let out a long breath.

'I am truly sorry,' she said again, her voice trembling. 'I didn't mean to hurt anyone.'

'Sorry doesn't cut it this time,' he said. 'This is bigger than sorry.'

Harper pressed her fingertips against her forehead. All she wanted to do was to end this painful call, but she had to talk to him about the burglary. She had nobody else left.

'Lieutenant – did you know my house was broken into?'

There was a pause.

'I heard something about that.'

'It wasn't a normal break-in,' she told him. 'They slashed Bonnie's painting – you know the one. They slashed my *face*. They didn't take much of anything. Lieutenant... Please tell me your guys didn't do it.'

An arctic pause followed.

'Harper, there's something I want you to know.' He spoke slowly. Enunciating every syllable. 'You have violated my trust, and the trust of everyone here who considered you their friend. And now you dare suggest to me that sworn public servants broke into your house and stole your television. Do you have any idea how unstable you sound?'

Harper went numb.

'I understand that you have been suspended from the newspaper,' he said. 'Please, use this time to get the help you need.'

The phone dropped from Harper's fingers, hitting the floor with a thud.

Smith knew all her pressure points, but he'd never used them like that before. He'd always been willing to forgive her. This time, she'd gone too far, even for him.

She really was on her own now.

*

That evening, Harper drove back to her apartment.

She didn't want to go – didn't want to see it in its damaged state again.

But she had to find Zuzu.

The sun was beginning to set when she reached Jones Street. The sky above the tall old townhouses flamed red and amber.

Finding a parking space half a block away, she pulled in and cut the engine.

Everything looked the same. The Camaro was still under the oak tree, right where she'd left it. Anyone looking at the apartment from outside might think she was in there already.

She had to force herself to get out of the car.

The short walk down the block seemed endless. Her hands were clammy as she slid the key into the lock.

When the door swung open the apartment was swathed in shadows.

Plywood still covered the back window – Billy hadn't had a chance to fix it yet.

Gingerly closing the door behind her, she stepped inside, reaching instinctively for the light switch, before pulling back her hand.

All her nerves were alert.

It was hot – Billy must have turned off the air conditioning – and uncannily quiet.

Her cautious footsteps seemed too loud, her breathing amplified, as she tiptoed down the hall.

When she reached the living room, she stopped mid-step.

Everything had been moved.

The damaged sofas had been righted, and left in different places than they'd been before. Someone had removed the broken pieces of the scanner and the television. Wires no longer trailed from the stereo speakers.

It took her a second to process. The cleaning service – they must have come today.

The vinegar smell of spilled food was gone – replaced by the astringent chemical scent of cleaning products.

Someone had scrubbed at the threat painted on the wall but failed to remove it. The word was fainter now, but still there, stark and threatening.

RUN.

Wrenching her gaze away, she moved through the apartment that now felt as if it belonged to someone else. She had to step carefully to avoid running into things.

She was nearly to the kitchen when she heard a soft shuffling sound.

Harper froze.

The sound seemed to come from the bedroom.

Looking for anything that could be used as a weapon, she pivoted hard in that direction.

Everything was quiet again.

It's nothing, she assured herself, although her pounding heart didn't believe. *It's someone walking upstairs.*

Then, she heard a distinct, soft *thud.*

There was no question that sound had come from inside this apartment.

Someone else was here.

Her chest tightened around her lungs.

She took a stumbling, panicked step back. She had to get out now.

She was scrambling for the door when a small shadow shot into the hallway from the bedroom.

'Oh, holy shit, Zuzu,' Harper gasped, doubling over. 'I think you killed me.'

Her voice echoed off the empty walls.

The tabby rubbed against Harper's ankle.

Scooping her up, Harper buried her face in her warm, soft fur, feeling the rumble of her purr.

'I'm so glad you're alive,' she whispered.

When her heart returned to normal, she carried her to the kitchen. Someone had washed the cat's food and water bowls and left them in the dish drainer.

She filled them both and set them on the floor.

For a while, she stood quietly, staring at the wood covering the window.

Then, slowly, as if losing her balance, she slid down to the floor.

Pressing her back against Billy's hand-made cabinet, she stared down the shadowy hallway at her ruined apartment.

She had no Luke. No Smith. No home. No job.

And yet. Whoever did this didn't understand her at all.

They were trying to scare her away but they'd invaded her *home*. The only safe place she knew.

Now, she couldn't ever give up.

One way or another, she had to get to the truth.

Chapter Thirty-nine

The next morning Harper was up early. She'd hardly slept, and yet she felt wide awake.

She'd spent much of the night going through her notes, over and over again, looking for anything she might have missed. Going through Sterling's list of Whitney's lovers – crossing out those who had alibis, running basic checks on everyone else.

It had been late when she came across words she'd scrawled that day with DJ at the college. Something she'd thought then, but had forgotten amid all the chaos that followed.

Find out more about that picture of Whitney.

The glossy black-and-white picture on the wall in the Development Office.

She'd meant to go back and see it again – ask Rosanna if there were more.

Everyone had told her she needed proof of who Whitney was dating. Well, there was a picture of her with a man. It wasn't much, but it was a start.

As she brushed the tangles from her hair, she studied her face in the mirror. Her cheekbones looked too sharp. Her eyes looked harder than she remembered. These last weeks had changed her.

Good. She'd thought she was tough before. She was tougher now.

Bonnie was still asleep when she slipped down the stairs, her rubber-soled shoes nearly silent on the wood floors.

Clutching the shiny new keys the locksmith had given her the day before, she headed for the door. It had rained in the night, and the morning was damp, so she borrowed one of Bonnie's less flamboyant jackets from the hall closet.

Then she climbed into the anonymous Ford and drove out towards the suburbs.

The college was very different at this hour than it had been at her last visit. The guest parking lot was packed, and she drove around for ten minutes before finding a free space.

The last time she'd been here, DJ had led the way, but it was easy enough to retrace their steps. Past the administration building with its columns and marble halls, down the sidewalk beyond the modern library and coffee kiosk, until she saw the glass-and-steel building she remembered from her previous visit.

It was shortly after nine o'clock when she stepped inside the fundraising office. Rosanna was once again at the front desk, but this time she was not alone – the room bustled with activity. All the desks behind her were full, phones were ringing, staff hard at work raising money.

Busy talking to a woman in a suit, Rosanna at first didn't notice Harper. When she did, her brow furrowed.

Harper hung back, her focus on the black-and-white image of Marie Whitney. There was no sign of a country girl from Vidalia in that picture of an elegant woman in a sleeveless silk dress, a glittering necklace around her long, slim throat. She was laughing at something the man next to her had said, her head thrown back.

Pulling her phone out, she took a quick photo of the picture. She wanted to look at it more closely on her own.

When she turned back, the woman in the suit was gone. Rosanna was watching her anxiously.

Harper kept her expression reassuring.

'Hi,' she said casually. 'Do you remember me?'

'You work with David.'

Rosanna glanced over her shoulder, as if she feared they might be overheard. But everyone was too busy to notice.

'Is there something you need?'

'I'm sorry to bother you again,' Harper said, keeping her voice low. 'I only have one quick question.'

'I don't know if I can help you.' Rosanna's hands toyed nervously with a pen. 'I told David everything I know.'

'It's about that picture of Marie Whitney.' She pointed at the image on the wall. 'When was it taken?'

'It was the spring fundraiser, in May, at City Hall,' Rosanna said, some of the tension leaving her shoulders. 'I remember because the governor was there. It was a big deal.'

'Do you know who took it?'

'There's a local photographer who does all these things. What's his name again?' Rosanna's face screwed up with thought. 'Hold on a second. I'll have it here somewhere.'

She typed something into her computer. A second later, she looked up brightly.

'Yes, here it is. His name is Jackson. Miles Jackson.'

All the blood drained from Harper's face.

She was sure she hadn't heard her right.

'Are you... Did you say, Jackson?'

Rosanna nodded, a puzzled frown shadowing her face.

'Yes. He shoots most of our events. I'm sorry – is something wrong?'

Of course, now that Harper thought about it, it made perfect sense – Miles was often hired to shoot events like this. It was his bread and butter.

So why had he never mentioned that he'd met and photographed Marie Whitney? How had this never come up in all of their conversations?

Why would he hide that?

'Miss McClain?'

Gradually Harper became aware that Rosanna was talking to her.

'I... I'm fine. Thank you,' she said, backing away. 'That's all.'

She rushed from the building, pushing the door so hard it thumped against the wall.

In a daze, she half-ran for the car.

Her mind was racing.

Miles made a terrible suspect. He had been unaware of her mother's murder until she told him. There was no reason to think he was covering anything up.

But still. Why hadn't he said anything?

She had to understand how this was possible.

When she reached the car, she realized she was still clutching her phone in her hand. Numbly, she scrolled to his number and dialed.

Miles answered on the third ring.

'Hello?' He sounded rough. It was early for him – he must still be in bed.

'It's Harper,' she said. 'We need to talk. Can I come over?'

'What's happened?' He sounded suddenly awake.

'I need to talk to you about something.'

Her voice was so taut, he had to notice.

There was a long pause.

'Give me fifteen minutes,' he said.

When Harper buzzed Miles' loft apartment, the front door clicked open instantly.

All the way over she'd been trying to think of an obvious explanation for that photo, and coming up blank.

The photo was a close-up – he'd zoomed in on her face. He would have had to ask her permission for that. He and Whitney would have had a conversation – however brief.

And he never thought, in all these weeks, to mention that?

As the faux-industrial elevator rose soundlessly, she grew increasingly angry.

She kept thinking about all the times he'd warned her off the case, told her she was wrong, implied that she was being irrational – and all the while he was hiding this from her.

When she reached the fourth floor, his door was propped open. She strode down the hallway, fighting the urge to punch the wall.

In his apartment, watery gray light filtered in through the huge, warehouse windows.

Miles was in the kitchen making coffee.

Everything she was feeling must have shown on her face because, when his dark brown eyes met hers, his brow creased.

'What's going on?'

'Why didn't you tell me you knew Marie Whitney?'

Her voice was strident, filled with the frustration and fury of the last few awful days.

'What?' He looked stunned. 'Because I don't.'

She held up her phone, open to the picture she'd taken twenty minutes earlier.

'Did you or did you not take this picture, Miles?'

Setting his coffee down carefully, he walked over and took the phone from her hand.

Puzzlement flickered across his face.

'I don't remember this,' he said, but he sounded uncertain.

'According to the Development Office at the university,' she said, 'you took it. And it looks exactly like your style. Open aperture. No flash.'

'I shoot a lot of events. You know that, Harper. Maybe I took that. Maybe I didn't.'

Harper stared at him in disbelief.

'I have spent the last few weeks of my life – and lost everything I have – investigating this woman.' Her voice was low and ominous. 'And you don't *remember*?'

'Now, hold on.' Miles held up his hands. 'Let's do this one step at a time. When was that taken?'

'May.' She spat the word out.

'Wait here,' he told her. 'We're going to figure this out.'

He disappeared behind a screening wall, returning a moment later with his laptop.

Setting it on the long oak table, he flipped it open and started it up.

'Tell me more about the party. Where was it?'

Harper watched him narrowly.

'All I know is it was at City Hall. Spring fundraiser.' She thought back to what Rosanna had told her. 'The governor was there.'

He paused – his fingers hovering above the keyboard.

'I remember that night,' he said slowly. 'There was a champagne fountain. And a pretty good jazz band.'

He typed something fast, peering at the files.

'May, you say?'

Looking over his shoulder she saw hundreds of folders, organized by month. May had been busy for him – it was packed.

'Wait a second,' he said suddenly, 'I think I found it.'

He'd opened a folder dated May twenty-second. It held hundreds of images – one-inch black-and-white squares of elegance and candlelight.

He opened one at random and they both squinted at it. It was clearly a grand party – but there was nobody in it she recognized.

'Hard to tell,' Miles added.

Sliding into the chair next to him, Harper leaned closer to see the screen.

He opened another picture, and another, and then Harper saw Marie in that recognizable white dress, at the back of one of the images.

'There,' she said, pointing. 'That's her. That's the dress.'

Now she could see why Miles might not have remembered Whitney was at the party. It had been a crowded event – everyone dressed to the nines. Everyone wearing jewels. Everyone holding champagne flutes.

Miles had taken hundreds of pictures that night of many glamorous women.

'Good,' he murmured.

His attention was on the image, searching the background, looking at faces.

'I want to see if she's with a man.' Harper's anger had ebbed. She was utterly focused on the images on the screen. 'In the image I showed you, she's laughing with a man but you can't see his face. I need to see if you took any pictures of her with him, or with any other men who might be our guy.'

Nodding, Miles began clicking through the pictures – opening and closing them one after another. Almost all of them were of local dignitaries – people Harper could vaguely remember seeing on the news, or in the paper.

Their smiles, fixed and fake, or relaxed and happy, blurred together.

Over and over again, Marie flitted across the lens, sometimes at the edge of the picture, sometimes at the center of the action.

Each time, Harper's heart jumped. But there was never one with a good image of the man.

They were both beginning to lose hope when Miles opened a familiar-looking shot.

Harper's hand jerked up.

'That's him. The man she's with in the picture I showed you.'

They both leaned closer.

The picture had been taken toward the end of the night. The crowd was growing sparse. Marie was dancing with a broad-shouldered man. The way he held her was intimate – a hand brushing the side of her breast, another resting on the curve of her hip. She was smiling up into his eyes.

'There's something familiar about him,' Harper murmured, looking at the picture. 'Something about the posture... I can't place it. But I feel like I know him.'

Miles zoomed in on the two of them.

'I can't see his face,' he said. 'But you're right. There is something about him.'

Closing the picture, he looked back at the folder. 'I think I took more shots of them dancing. Let me see.'

Clicking fast, he opened eight pictures at once. They appeared to have been taken in sequence.

The man was spinning Marie slowly. Neither of them seemed to have noticed the photographer shooting them from a few feet away.

They were too into each other.

In the first image, they saw the back of his head.

In the next, he'd turned more towards the camera, Harper could make out a square jaw, and sturdy but not prominent nose.

In the third, he was sideways to the camera, smiling down at Marie.

Harper stared in disbelief at the craggy face she knew so well, the solid jaw, thick, salt-and-pepper hair. The broad shoulders she'd always relied on.

'I'll be damned,' Miles said, stunned. 'That's Lieutenant Smith.'

Chapter Forty

Harper couldn't seem to breathe. Miles was huddled over the computer, his jaw set, grimly opening one image after another, while she kept staring at that single incriminating photo.

Yesterday, Smith accused her of betraying him. He told her she'd ruined his career.

And there he was, dancing with the murder victim in his arms.

None of it made sense.

Maybe they met that one night, she told herself. Maybe, like Miles, he didn't remember her. After all, they were only dancing.

Only they weren't. It was much worse than that.

Working in near silence, she and Miles searched for more images of Smith from that elegant party in May. In the end, there were so many of them that, using the time-stamps, they could piece together most of the night.

Smith first appeared on camera shortly after nine o'clock in the back of a shot of some local dignitary. He appeared to be walking in the door of the ballroom, his eyes searching the room.

A shot taken fifteen minutes later had him in a shadowy corner, talking with Whitney, their heads bent close together, backs to the camera.

An hour later, they found him in the back of another shot. He was whispering in her ear, each of them holding champagne flutes. Whitney was smiling.

They kept to the corners, at the back of the room. They were hiding, even then.

A photo Miles had taken twenty minutes later, of a waiter carrying a tray laden with glasses, captured a shadowy image of the two of them in a dark corner near the kitchen, wrapped in a passionate embrace.

Miles' lips were drawn tight as he placed all the incriminating photos in one folder.

Harper couldn't seem to process what she was seeing. She felt no fear. No anger. Just a curious, awful emptiness.

When they'd gone through everything, Miles stood without a word. Gathering a handful of papers off the end of the table, he hurled them hard into the trash.

'Goddammit.'

Harper stared at nothing as he crossed the apartment to stand in front of the windows looking out at the river. The sky had remained gray all day – the water looked dark and turbid.

She felt empty.

'This is dynamite,' Miles said, and he didn't sound happy about it. 'We are sitting on a stack of dynamite here, and we're playing with matches.'

Harper didn't reply. Her thoughts felt as muddy and slow as the river.

What were they looking at in those photos?

Harper had seen Whitney's entire file – there wasn't one word in there about Smith knowing her. The law required him to reveal any relationship, and to recuse himself from any investigation in which he had a relationship, however minor, with either the victim or the suspect.

But he hadn't done that. Why not?

The obvious answer was he was protecting Pat and the boys from his infidelity. But if that were the case, all he had to say was that he and Whitney were friends. That would be sufficient.

But he hadn't even done that.

She pressed her fingers against her temples.

'Marie Whitney was a serial blackmailer,' she said. 'Smith's married. He's got kids. What if Whitney was blackmailing him?'

'He cheated,' Miles snapped. 'Men cheat. They don't kill their mistresses. Even if she did blackmail him, it doesn't mean he killed her.'

'Men kill their mistresses,' Harper said evenly. 'All the time.'

She was seeing how it might have worked, and she didn't like how plausible it was.

'Here's what we do know,' she said. 'Smith hid a close relationship with the murder victim. The murder victim blackmailed at least three of her previous lovers. Whitney died just a few short weeks after this picture was taken. Her murder looked exactly like my mother's murder. Smith worked my mother's murder. He had motive. He had means.' Her heart hurt so much she had to force herself to say the last three words. 'He had opportunity.'

Miles looked at her, his eyes bleak.

She inhaled, a quick gasp for oxygen. 'Please tell me I'm wrong, Miles. Please, I'm begging you. Tell me this is an insane theory.'

Miles ran his hand across the top of his head.

'He has questions to answer,' he said. 'But that is all right now.'

Harper was still trying to understand.

'How can we only be seeing this now, Miles?' Pain put an edge on her voice. 'First you didn't remember seeing Whitney at that party, then it turns out you forgot seeing Smith, too? He's in all your photos. You took pictures of them *kissing*. And you didn't know?'

Miles held up his hands. He looked shaken.

'Everyone was at that party, Harper. The police chief was there. The mayor. The governor. It would have made perfect sense to me that the head of the detective squad was there. The only picture of them kissing, they're in a dark corner – I never even noticed them when I shot that picture. I was looking at the mayor, who was right in front of me.' He ran a hand across his jaw, his whiskers rasped. 'There was nothing memorable about any of it. Marie Whitney was nobody then. She was still alive.'

A heavy silence fell.

'Oh God, Miles,' Harper whispered. 'I think he did it.'

Their eyes met.

'I do, too,' he said.

Harper felt like the ground had given way, and they were both sinking into it.

How could it be Smith?

Smith, who'd cradled her in his arms when she cried about her mother.

Smith, who'd taught her about honesty and integrity.

Dropping onto the leather sofa, Miles lowered his head to his hands.

'We don't have enough,' he said, after a moment. 'You take this to Baxter, or the chief of police, and Smith will cover his ass and tell them you're crazy. He'll say you're obsessed, and you're dragging me down with you. You and I will argue our side until the cows come home, but they'll believe him.'

Harper thought of what Smith had told her the day before. *Use this time to get the help you need.*

'I think that's his plan,' she said.

'OK then,' he said, lifting his head. 'Before we go to anyone else with this, we need to get more information.'

'How do we do that, Miles?' she asked helplessly. 'It's taken weeks to get what we have.'

He shot her a look.

'You're a reporter. The simplest way to get information is to ask.'

'What?' Her voice rose. 'You want me to ask *Smith*?'

'It's not as crazy as it sounds. You know him better than almost anyone,' he reminded her. 'Given everything that's happened, if you were, say, to get in touch. Tell him you want to talk. Ask him to meet you after hours, I reckon he'd say yes. Then you give him the evidence, see how he reacts.'

The idea of confronting Smith made Harper feel physically ill.

'He won't want to meet me,' she said. 'We talked on the phone yesterday and it went badly.'

'You can use that in your favor.'

Harper hesitated, thinking about Smith. How he worked.

He liked to think of himself as in charge – handling everything. No detail missed. The only time he'd lost his temper was when she'd suggested police officers might have been behind the break-in.

'I guess I could tell him I've got proof his guys broke into my place,' she said. 'I'll say one of them dropped something personal, and that I know who it is. I'll threaten to go public.'

Miles bobbed his head.

'That could work.'

Jumping to his feet, he began pacing the floor in front of the window.

'Arrange to meet him somewhere quiet,' he said. 'I'll wire you up to record the whole thing. Then you show him these pictures.' He gestured at the laptop, still open to a picture of Smith and Whitney looking into each other's eyes. 'See if surprise scares the truth out of him.'

It was a good plan. Smith wouldn't have a clue that she knew about his relationship. She'd catch him off guard.

He thought she was powerless – out of work. Out of friends. Alone in the world. He'd never suspect her of wearing a wire.

She suppressed the voice in her head that asked why, if Smith had killed Whitney, he wouldn't kill her, too.

He wouldn't, though. He couldn't. This was *Smith*.

When she spoke, her voice was steady. 'When do we do it?'

'Sooner would be better than later,' Miles said. 'But I don't think we should do this on our own. We need some backup here. Where's that boyfriend of yours?'

When Harper gave him a blank look, he swirled one hand impatiently.

'Where's Luke? He's the best undercover guy in the business. We need him on this.'

There was no point in asking how he knew – word got around.

'Smith sent him to Atlanta on a job,' she said.

'Well, wherever Luke is and, whatever he's doing, get in touch with him.' His voice was tense. 'Get him back here. We need him.'

'He's in the middle of a job,' Harper repeated.

'What we're about to do is very dangerous.' Miles held her eyes. 'You tell him, if he wants you to live, he needs to get his ass back to town. Fast.'

They spent the rest of the day working out the details.

As they talked over cup after cup of coffee, Miles kept his hands busy adapting a wireless microphone transmitter to enhance its signal.

Tiny black and chrome electronic parts scattered across the white sheet of paper he'd spread on the table. His tools lay among snaking strands of wire and metal as they discussed how this would go. What she should say, how she should approach it. Where it should all happen.

They barely noticed as the sky outside the apartment's windows turned dark gold, then pink, before darkness descended.

All evening, the two of them stayed in Miles' apartment, going over the plan from every angle, his scanner grumbling in the background, John Lee Hooker growling ominously over the top of it.

Very late that night, as Miles dug in his storage closet for spare parts, Harper slipped into the bathroom with her phone and called Luke.

When his voicemail message started, she closed her eyes, letting that deep, familiar voice flow over her.

When the time came, she was glad she sounded calm. Talking quickly, her low voice reverberating off the cool, tiled walls, she told him what was happening. And what she and Miles had planned.

'I don't think we can do this alone,' she said. 'Please, if you can, come back.

'And, Luke – I'm scared.'

Chapter Forty-one

When Harper woke on the sofa the next morning, a soft gray light illuminated the room. She sat up, kicking her legs out from under the blanket that covered her.

Hearing a rustling sound, she twisted around to look over the back of the sofa. Miles was at the kitchen table where he'd been when she fell asleep.

'Test test test,' he said quietly.

He pushed some buttons on a black metal device in front of him. After a second, his recorded voice played back to him, clear and crisp: 'Test test test.'

'It's working?' she asked hoarsely.

He glanced at her over the top of his glasses.

'So far,' he replied, adjusting something with a tiny screwdriver, 'so good.'

The shadows under his eyes indicated that, while she might have had a few hours' rest, he hadn't.

Throughout the day, they tested the device at different distances.

First, Harper stood in the bedroom whispering as Miles recorded her. Then out in the corridor. And finally downstairs.

The system needed minute adjustments, but each time, it transmitted and recorded at impressive distances.

After that, they raised the stakes – moving outside his apartment. Harper stood in the rain at the far edge of the building's parking lot while Miles stayed inside with his receiver, recording her talking quietly.

'Hello hello. I'm getting drenched,' she said. 'Over.'

It recorded perfectly.

Later, when the weather worsened, they tried the device in wind. That was less successful – the wind cut out her voice enough to cast doubt on what she was saying.

There was only so much Miles could do about this. They would need a still night if they wanted a decent recording – clear and unambiguous enough to stand up in court.

After endless discussion, they'd chosen a location – Harper would meet Smith at The Watch.

Miles had been dead set against it at first – too isolated. But Harper had insisted.

'Smith will know he's safe there – he'll think nobody could ever hear what he's saying,' she said.

Of course, there was more to her thinking than she let on to him.

She knew The Watch. She felt safe there.

It rained all afternoon. Harper sat near the windows, her phone in her hand, gloomily watching the water run down the pane. The storm front was due to pass in the early evening, and a dry night was forecast, but it was hard to imagine at this moment.

'If the wind's not blowing, we can still do this even if it's raining,' Miles told her as they sat on his sofa rehashing the plan for the umpteenth time. 'If there's a bit of light, I could even film the whole thing.'

'I don't know,' Harper said doubtfully. 'It's pretty dark at The Watch.'

'It is at that.' Miles rubbed a hand across his jaw. 'Still, there might be a way. I could go down there early, set up a camera with a night-vision lens in the trees. It would give you more protection. And I've been thinking more about the logistics. If I park down below the bluffs, you'd be right above me. Close enough to operate the camera by remote control.'

Without waiting for her response, he jumped to his feet and flung open a closet filled with boxes of equipment. Mumbling to himself, he rummaged through it and then emerged, holding a box with both hands triumphantly.

'I knew it was in there somewhere.'

He carried the box to the table and pulled out a small camera.

'This'll work, Harper,' he said, reaching for his glasses.

As he began tinkering again, Harper checked her phone.

Still no message from Luke.

But she could do this. She'd be fine. The worst part of it, she'd decided, would be calling Smith. Tricking him into meeting her. If she could get through that, she could do the rest.

All day long, the idea of that call lying ahead of her like a wolf waiting around the next bend turned her stomach to acid. It was a relief when five o'clock finally came and they agreed it was late enough to leave Smith with little room to maneuver, while still giving Miles time to set up.

Outside, the rain was finally ending. Weak evening sun was forcing its light through the clouds when Miles picked up the phone and dialed the main police number. They suspected Smith would refuse a call from her, so they'd decided to get Miles to make the call.

'Lieutenant Smith, please,' he told the receptionist. 'Tell him it's Miles Jackson.'

Harper sat on the sofa watching him, anxiously biting her thumbnail.

After a moment, he held out the phone.

'They're putting me through.'

Letting out a long breath, Harper took it from him.

The hold music was a cheerful cover of some fifteen-year-old pop song she probably would have recognized if she weren't so terrified.

A click interrupted the song, mid-chorus.

'Smith.' The lieutenant's gravel voice sent her stomach plummeting to her shoes.

She swallowed hard.

'Lieutenant,' she said faintly. 'It's Harper.'

Silence.

She could imagine Smith in his office – the one he'd wanted so badly – picking up that heavy Montblanc pen, and toying with it as he decided what to say.

'I'm not entirely certain we should be talking,' he said at last.

'Me neither,' Harper told him. 'But I'm afraid we have to.'

'And why is that?' His tone turned suspicious.

'My landlord found something at my house – a police ID. I have proof your guys did this.' She made her voice just angry enough. But not so fierce that he might hang up. 'Now, I don't want to take this to Baxter – we both know what she'll do with it. I don't want to go to war with your guys. I want to end this. Let's meet, you and me, and work this out.'

On the sofa across from her, Miles was very still, his eyes fixed on her face.

'I don't know what you're talking about, Harper.' Smith sounded frosty. 'I told you the police had nothing to do with the break-in. I believe your imagination's gotten out of hand this time.'

Harper pressed her fingertips against her forehead. This time, when she spoke, the emotion was real.

'Oh, Lieutenant. Can we not do this?'

Another long silence followed.

She imagined him sitting in his chair, the cool stream of air conditioning from the vent above his office door. The muffled voices in the busy corridor.

'Fine.' Smith sounded curious now, and less prickly. 'What exactly do you want?'

'I want to meet,' Harper said. 'Tonight. You and me. Let's see if we can work this out in a way that helps both of us.'

His chair creaked – she guessed he was leaning forward, resting his elbows on his desk.

'How is that possible?'

'You want me to stop investigating the Whitney case. I want to put an end to this situation with the break-in so we can both get back to our lives,' she said. 'I want to talk about how we can exchange what you want for what I want.'

She held her breath. If he was going to refuse, now was the time when he would tell her he didn't know what she was talking about. When he accused her of being dramatic.

He did none of that.

'Where do you want to meet?'

Her heart kicked hard. He was going for it.

She looked at Miles and nodded. His shoulders sank.

'Meet me at The Watch,' she said. 'At midnight.'

'Midnight?' Irritation gave an edge to Smith's tone. 'Can't we do it earlier?'

'It has to be midnight,' she said firmly.

He was quiet for so long she was sure he was going to refuse. When he spoke again, it was so abrupt she jumped.

'Fine,' he snapped. 'Midnight. The Watch. This is it, though, Harper. No more.'

The dial tone buzzed loud in her ear. He'd hung up.

She looked at Miles.

'We're on.'

Chapter Forty-two

The forecasts proved correct, and by the time Harper drove the rented Ford into The Watch a few minutes before midnight, the rain was a distant memory. The night was clear and cool. A nearly full moon hung overhead, illuminating the park with an ethereal shade of blue.

Earlier, Miles had spent an hour out here, setting up a remote-control camera in the oak branches that arched over the crescent-shaped viewpoint.

He'd returned to the loft apartment at eleven, covered in mud up to his knees, looking grimly pleased.

'Whatever happens,' he assured her, 'we'll get it.'

Now, the Ford bumped and juddered down the rough lane, tires spinning in the mud left behind after two long days of rain.

Putting the brights on, Harper leaned forward peering into the shadows. She was looking for the mark Miles had left her. When she saw the tattered pizza box held in place with a fist-sized rock, she turned toward it.

'I'm parking on the box,' she told the empty car.

The cameras had been set up to capture the area immediately around the pizza box. Wherever she stood, she should be on film.

She was wearing Bonnie's black cotton jacket again. It smelled of her familiar floral perfume. Somehow that made her feel less alone.

There'd been no word from Luke.

She'd called him again this morning, and texted him a few hours ago with the time and the place.

Some part of her knew he wasn't coming.

Maybe he didn't have his phone. Maybe he simply didn't care any more.

Either way, she and Miles were going to have to do this on their own.

Miles had connected a microphone the size of a pencil tip to the jacket's top buttonhole. The breast pocket held a transmitter no bigger than a deck of cards.

Her phone buzzed as she turned the engine off. It was a text from Miles:

Coming through loud and clear.

Well. At least there was that.

Her hands felt like ice and she rubbed them together, trying to get the blood flowing. When she looked down, her knees were shaking.

Abruptly, she yanked the keys out of the ignition and shoved the door open, jumping out, and slamming the door behind her.

She just wanted to get on with this. Get it over with.

Rain had left the night with a crystalline sheen. Everything seemed to sparkle in the moonlight – the wild length of the tree branches, the broad curve of the river, the graceful metal sails of the bridge in the distance.

All of it looked more beautiful than she could ever remember.

In her heart, she hoped Smith had an explanation. Something simple and honest – *I made a mistake. It was only that once…*

But no matter how she tried to spin it, no explanation made sense.

In the late-night hush, she heard the car long before it pulled in.

The mechanical purr of the engine grew louder until the head-lights danced on the trees, and the silver SUV swung into view, bouncing down the rutted drive.

It was Smith's personal car, she noted, not the city-issue four-door all the detectives drove. He wasn't here as the head of the detectives squad. He was here as Robert Smith.

Whoever that was.

She squared her shoulders.

'He's here,' she told the air.

The vehicle pulled up next to hers and the engine cut out.

In the sudden silence, Harper could hear her heart hammering against her ribs and the sandpaper rasp of her nervous breathing.

She was irrationally convinced Smith would hear it, too, as he opened the door and climbed out, and she tried to calm herself.

'Harper,' he growled, shutting the door with a thud that echoed off the trees. 'Whatever you've got to tell me, it better be good.'

He picked his way carefully across the mud, his familiar, lived-in face and intuitive eyes passing in and out of shadow. At his wrists, gold cufflinks glittered in the moonlight. His shirt, of an expensive white fabric, gleamed.

His Italian leather shoes skidded in the muck. Cursing, he stopped to knock a clump of mud off against a tire.

Back when he was on the street, mud wouldn't have bothered

him, Harper thought. Back then he wore cheap shoes, and he believed in his job.

Things were different now.

Straightening, Smith dusted his hands on the legs of his suit with a look of distaste, and met her eyes.

'What the hell is so important I had to leave my house at midnight and come out here to the back end of beyond?'

'I told you on the phone, we found something – incriminating evidence.' Harper was surprised to find her voice was steady. Her hands were trembling so violently she had to shove them in her pockets. 'But I lied about what we found.'

Smith's eyes darted up to hers.

'Explain.'

'No,' Harper said flatly. 'I want *you* to explain. Explain your relationship with Marie Whitney.'

'Who?' Smith's frown was blank, as if he'd never heard of her. 'Oh, the murdered woman.' He gave a small disinterested shrug. 'I don't know much about that case, Harper. Talk to Blazer.'

His tone was elaborately unworried, but Harper saw the first signs of uncertainty. His hands clenched and released at his sides. His breathing had gone shallow the second she mentioned Marie's name. In the moonlight, a fine sheen of sweat glittered on his forehead.

Whatever he'd expected from this meeting, he hadn't been tense until now.

'Well, I was going to ask Blazer, but I decided it would be better if I talked to you first.'

With effort, Harper kept her tone casual, unthreatening. She took a step toward him, careful to stay inside the camera shot.

'I've been up at the college lately, talking to her co-workers. They all describe a man she was dating. They thought he was an undercover police officer, but I believe from their description he's a detective.' She held Smith's eyes steadily. 'They say he's tall, broad-shouldered, with graying hair.'

'That's a pretty vague description.' Smith gave a dry, sardonic laugh but his eyes darted around, as if he was looking for something in the shadows.

'Yes, that's what I thought, too,' she said. 'At first.'

In the distance, a car was passing slow and near on the road outside The Watch. Harper froze, instantly alert. She saw Smith look toward the sound.

Had he asked someone to meet him here?

But the car kept going; the sound of its engine fading away.

Smith turned back to her, his jaw set.

'Look, Harper. I'm not handling the Whitney case,' he said. 'I know you're obsessed with it. But if you want to talk about it, you have to talk to Blazer.'

His tone was dismissive, amused.

'You keep saying that,' she snapped. 'Be careful, or I will.'

Smith went still.

'What exactly is going on here, Harper?'

She paused, ordering herself to stay calm. She couldn't get angry and overplay her hand.

Slow and steady – it was all she had.

'Like I said,' she continued calmly, 'I was curious about this man. This detective who dated Whitney. Because there was nothing about him in her file.'

Smith's eyes darted up to hers.

'Of course,' Harper continued, 'if a detective had been in a relationship with Whitney and did not reveal that to the investigating officers, that is a fairly serious breach of ethics. So, I couldn't stop wondering who that detective might have been. At first, I thought it was Blazer. But I was wrong.'

She pulled her phone out of her pocket.

'Lieutenant, I want you to look at something.'

She opened the black-and-white photo of Smith and Whitney on the dance floor at the gala, Whitney laughing up at Smith, his hand easy in the small of her back.

She held her phone up so he could see.

'Do you recognize the man in this picture?'

The light from the screen of her phone turned his face ghostly white as he leaned forward to look at himself. He stared at the image for a long time before straightening slowly.

'Lay it out for me, Harper. What are you suggesting?'

His expression was unchanged, but his voice held a new note of icy menace that sent a chill down Harper's spine.

But now that it was all happening, Harper wasn't afraid any more. She was hurt. And she was angry.

'I'm suggesting that you knew Marie Whitney,' she said. 'That you had a romantic affair with her. I'm suggesting that she blackmailed you – threatened your job and your marriage. I'm suggesting that you stabbed her to death on her kitchen floor. I'm also suggesting that, when you thought I was getting too close to finding out, you got rid of me.'

She drew a breath.

'That, Lieutenant, is what I'm suggesting.'

Although her heart was racing, her voice was rock steady. She stood square-shouldered, her eyes locked on his.

Smith blinked before she did.

'This is insane,' he growled. 'Listen to yourself. Are you out of your mind?'

But his voice lacked conviction, and there was a distant, pan-icked look in his eyes.

All the breath left Harper's lungs.

Until that moment some part of her had clung to the hope that she was wrong. Now, though, she could see the truth in his face.

Desolation swept her anger away, leaving only loss.

'Why did you do it, Lieutenant?' she asked, bewildered. 'What was she going to take from you? How much was it really worth? You took a life, Lieutenant. You took a *life*.'

At first he didn't reply. He stood still, shoulders hunched.

Somewhere on the river below, a chain jangled – a boat shifting with the water. A breeze worried the leaves overhead.

Suddenly, Smith laughed, a cold and desperately unfunny sound.

'I never thought you'd sink to this,' he said bitterly. 'You've got no loyalty, Harper McClain. You, of all people.'

He pulled his hands from his pockets. In his right hand he held a 9 mm semi-automatic.

He pointed it squarely at her chest.

Harper recoiled, pressing herself back against the rented Ford.

'I cared for you.' His voice rose. 'I took you into my *home*. This is how you thank me? You want to destroy everything I've built? Everything I've fought for? And, for what? For what, Harper?'

She couldn't take her eyes off the gun. It gleamed black and oily in the moonlight.

'Lieutenant.' It came out faintly – a wisp of a word. 'Please. Put the gun away. I'm not armed.'

'That was a mistake on your part.' He twitched the gun.

Harper flinched.

'You betrayed me,' he said, and his voice quivered. 'I should have listened to the others. I should have known not to trust you.'

Harper could hardly hear him. Her eyes were fixed on the pistol.

'Lieutenant,' she said. 'Please.'

'You pushed and pushed,' he growled. 'I gave you so many opportunities to let this go, but you would not stop. And I will never understand why.'

Harper's mouth was so dry she had to swallow hard before she could form words.

'That murder scene looked exactly like my mom's.' Her voice broke. 'That was it. That's all it ever was. I had to understand why.'

She looked at him imploringly. 'It wasn't supposed to be you.'

Smith's face crumpled.

'You were never supposed to see that murder scene, Harper. Reporters don't get to see murder scenes. There are *rules*. Dear God, why don't you obey the rules? If, just this once, you'd done as you were told, none of this would have happened.'

He sounded desperate. And desperate men with guns are the most dangerous force on earth.

Harper knew she should run, scream… Do something to defuse this situation. But she stood there, her back pressed against the hard metal of the car, eyes burning with unshed tears.

'Oh, Lieutenant,' she whispered. 'You didn't kill her, did you? You wouldn't do something like that. I don't believe it. I don't.'

This seemed to throw him off balance. For a second the gun went slack.

'Harper…'

His voice trailed off. Then he straightened and pointed the gun at her again.

'You should have let go of the case, Harper. You should have walked away. But you didn't. I'll regret that fact for the rest of my life.'

Harper stared at the man she'd thought of as a surrogate father, pointing a gun at her chest. In that instant she saw her mother's body, lying still in a spreading puddle of blood on her kitchen floor. She saw her own blood-covered hands struggling to grasp the phone. She saw Camille Whitney's tormented brown eyes.

She saw all that they'd lost.

Her heart stopped pounding.

Straightening, she flung out her arms to either side.

'Just *do it*,' she challenged him, her voice ringing out in the quiet. 'Shoot me and get it over with. If that's what you want.'

He raised the gun.

That was when a voice rang out from behind her.

'Drop the gun, Lieutenant.'

Harper knew that voice.

Luke stepped out from the sheltering trees to the right of the car. His gun was trained on Smith, steady as steel. He didn't look at her. His eyes stayed on Smith.

'I mean it, Lieutenant,' he said. 'Drop it. Or I will take you out.'

Smith shifted his gun to point at Luke, who kept himself far enough from Harper to make it impossible to cover both of them.

'Walker, put that gun away,' Smith growled. 'I'll have your badge.'

Luke's gun didn't waver. 'No, you won't, sir. I'll have yours.'

In the distance, Harper heard the faint, shrill cry of sirens. Not one or two of them – but dozens. A chorus of urgency, far away, but growing closer.

She saw Smith's face change as he heard it, too.

'They're coming for you, Lieutenant.' Luke took another step toward him. 'Put down your weapon. It's over.'

Smith had gone white as paper. His desperate eyes skittered from Harper to Luke as the sirens closed in – their mournful wail becoming deafening. Harper could already see faint blue lights through the trees, scattering drops of color across The Watch.

The lieutenant's hand trembled. In the shadows, the lines on his face seemed deeply carved. Suddenly, he looked old.

He turned to Harper.

'I'm sorry,' he said. 'I never wanted to hurt you. I didn't mean...' His voice trailed off.

A tear streaked down Harper's face – hot and unexpected.

'Lieutenant...' she whispered.

For a moment it looked as if he would do as Luke said – the gun moved shakily down. But then he seemed to change his mind. In one practiced move, his arm swung up again, and he pointed the gun at his own head.

Something inside Harper fractured. She couldn't lose another one.

Not again.

'No!'

She heard herself scream, and then she was running towards him, feet sliding on the mud.

'Harper, stop!' Luke shouted behind her.

But she was already grabbing Smith's arm with all her strength. The first police cars were roaring through the trees toward them, sirens shrieking, blue lights blinding.

Smith struggled with her – she could smell his aftershave, the acrid scent of fear sweat.

Then the gun went off with a tremendous, deafening retort that split the night like thunder.

Something burned Harper's shoulder – a sharp, unbearable flame. Her feet left the ground.

She was suddenly weightless – airborne.

Falling light as a feather through the darkness into nothing.

Chapter Forty-three

Harper lay on her back in the mud staring up at a dark sky, lit by flashes of blue. She felt strange – her mind seemed disjointed. Broken free of its moorings.

What happened?

Luke dropped to his knees next to her, whispering her name, hands searching her body.

'Are you hit?' he kept asking, his voice breathless and thin. 'Harper, *are you hit*?'

She tried to answer him, but her mouth had gone numb.

When he found the blood, pulsing warm and thick from her shoulder, his breath hissed between his teeth.

'Oh, fuck, Harper,' he whispered. And then loudly, over his shoulder, voice cracking, 'She's hit. Get an ambulance out here. *Now.*'

Harper couldn't breathe.

'Help...' she gasped, trying to reach for him with hands suddenly so heavy and uncooperative they wouldn't leave the ground.

Luke ripped off his shirt, wadding it into a ball and pressing it hard against the wound at the front of her left shoulder. She could see others gathering behind him, dark shadows against the flickering blue.

In the distance, she thought she saw Smith being led away. She wanted to ask if he was OK but the words wouldn't form.

'Ambulance is en route,' someone said.

Luke didn't look away. His eyes held hers.

'Stay with me, baby,' he kept saying, his voice low and pleading. 'Stay with me.'

It struck Harper that she was shivering with such violence her teeth chattered, and yet she felt oddly warm. The ground was soft and comforting beneath her.

Nothing hurt. Nothing felt real.

'Where's that fucking *ambulance*?' he shouted.

Someone said something to him, but Harper didn't hear it.

She was so tired. So very, very tired.

Her eyes felt weighted down. It would be so good to rest.

Her eyes drifted shut.

'No!' Luke cried, shaking her. 'Don't you close your eyes, Harper McClain. Don't you dare give up.'

The fear in his voice pierced the fog clouding her mind.

It took everything in her to blink – to see again that flashing blue-and-black world. And Luke's determined face.

'That's it,' he whispered, pressing hard against the wound. 'That's it. You stay awake.'

When the ambulance arrived seconds later, it was Toby who jumped out first, running across to kneel in the mud next to Luke.

Beneath that shock of hair, his face was more serious than she'd ever seen it.

'Oh crap, Harper,' he said gently. 'What have you done to yourself now?'

She tried to smile but nothing was working.

Luke talked fast. 'It was a nine-millimeter bullet to the shoulder. Point-blank range.'

Toby absorbed this information calmly. 'Any other wounds?'

Luke shook his head. 'None that I can find.'

Now that help was here, he seemed more panicked, hands gripping too hard on the fabric shoved against her shoulder.

'OK, buddy.' Toby reached for the wadded-up shirt, gently placing his hand on Luke's. 'You did good. I'm going to need you to step back now, and let us work.'

For a second, Harper thought Luke would refuse – every muscle in his body tensed. Then, with visible effort, he lifted his hand. And stepped away.

Instantly, two other paramedics swooped in where he'd been.

Something cool and metal sliced her shirt away from her skin. Low voices gave orders. Someone – Toby? – rolled up her sleeve. Harper felt a sting, and flinched.

'It's an IV, Harper,' Toby reassured her, taping the needle into place.

'Don't you let her die, Toby,' she heard Luke say from somewhere. His voice was thick.

'Don't worry.' Toby leaned in, blue-gloved hands strapping an oxygen mask over her face. Sweet, fresh air filled her lungs. 'Harper isn't going to die today.'

He sounded so certain.

It was the last thing she remembered.

Chapter Forty-four

The trial of Lieutenant Robert Smith lasted fifteen days. It would have taken longer, but he refused to defend himself.

Without his cooperation, his lawyer struggled, and the process was brief and merciless.

The case was followed in breathless detail by the *Daily News* courthouse reporter, Ed Lasterson, who did, everyone agreed, a pretty good job, given the newspaper's own involvement in the story.

On the stand, Smith looked smaller and grayer – as if jail were diminishing him day by day.

His wife, Pat, gaunt and tight-lipped, was in the courtroom on the first day with Kyle. They sat on the front row. Pat wept quietly. Kyle did not. He sat straight, his shoulders square and stiff, braced to take the punch as prosecutors accused his father of the worst crimes.

After that they never came back again. So they weren't there when Harper took the stand, one arm and shoulder still encased in a stiff medical sling.

She was glad of that, at least.

When she told the court how she'd unraveled the case – deciding it had to be a detective, and eventually stumbling across that photo – she remained controlled.

The only time her voice broke was when she described what she remembered from The Watch.

'I don't think he meant to shoot me,' she said, looking at Smith. 'I think he meant to shoot himself.'

Sitting with his lawyers, Smith kept his gaze lowered throughout her testimony, but in that one moment their eyes met, and she saw only emptiness there.

The video Miles made was played during the trial, although the audio was found inadmissible by the judge. So the jury watched a silent film of Harper and Smith – turned an otherworldly green by the night-vision lens – arguing. They saw Smith point a gun at her. Watched her stand up to him. And saw Luke appear from the trees like a vengeful hero from a western, gun already in his hand.

The camera was behind Smith when he raised his gun to his head, so his expression couldn't be seen as Harper flew across the mud to knock the weapon from his hand.

Only when she watched that video did Harper see the sheer terror on Luke's face when she ran to Smith. And only then did she know that he was running right behind her the whole way.

She watched herself grab Smith's arm. Saw his hand jerk back from the force of the gun's recoil.

Saw her own body twist and fall backward to the ground.

She watched as Luke punched Smith so hard the lieutenant spun sideways, the gun flying from his fingers.

Luke was handcuffing him as the first uniformed officers ran into view.

That was when the film ended.

But Harper knew what happened next.

The ambulance rushed her to the hospital and straight into surgery.

When she woke from the anesthesia, Luke was asleep on the chair next to her bed, clad in incongruously bright turquoise scrubs he must have borrowed to replace his blood-soaked clothing.

Even in sleep his face was creased and tense.

Groggy from drugs, she lay still, watching him for a long time, waiting for him to wake so she could thank him. At some point, she drifted off.

When she woke up that afternoon, the chair next to her bed was empty.

She moved to sit up, to look around for him – but every motion sent burning pain slicing through the left side of her body.

Sweating, she lay still again.

That was when the surgeon appeared in her doorway, along with a cluster of medical students who stared at her with worrying interest.

'Oh good,' the surgeon said, grabbing her chart. 'You're up. How are you feeling?'

'Like someone shot me in the shoulder.' Harper's voice was hoarse.

'Well, it turns out that's exactly what happened,' the surgeon agreed jovially.

He checked the dressing on her wound, studied the numbers on the heart monitor with interest, while keeping up a solid line of patter for the students. When he'd finished, he set the chart down.

'You know, Miss McClain, you didn't make it easy for me. The bullet missed your heart by three inches.' He glanced at the students with a modest smile. 'Luckily that's plenty of room.'

When they were gone, Harper located her phone on the bedside table. Gritting her teeth against the pain, she reached over to pick it up.

When she called Luke, though, the call went straight to voice-mail.

The same thing happened that night. And the next day.

After a while, she stopped calling.

She thought she knew why he didn't want to talk. The fact that he'd saved her life didn't make their problems disappear. He believed she'd betrayed him by breaking into the records room over his objections. He'd asked her not to take that chance and she did it anyway.

The trust between them was still damaged.

She would always have her job, and he would always have his. And their jobs were designed to conflict. He was making a decision for both of them.

Still, she had to fix this. Somehow. She would make this better.

Because in her mind she still heard his voice, that night out at The Watch.

Don't you dare give up.

On her last day in the hospital she received a text from Sterling Robinson. All it said was:

You have rare gumption. I insist you survive. S

When she was taken down to the bill payment department later that day, the woman at the counter told her, 'Someone's covered all your medical costs. In cash.'

She knew it was him.

Smith's lawyers fought valiantly, trying to get him off on grounds

427

of mental incompetence. Pleading guilty to murder, it seemed, made you crazy.

But Smith undermined this at every turn.

He insisted on testifying against himself. After a legal struggle, he took the stand and told the court he had indeed been Marie Whitney's lover.

They'd met after she was mugged – that earlier crime report Harper had glimpsed in the police files. Within weeks, they were sleeping together.

He'd given her money and expensive gifts until she became too demanding. Then things went sour between them. When he broke it off, she blackmailed him. She had photos of the two of them in compromising positions, proof of everything he'd given her. She threatened to present this evidence to the chief of police and Smith's wife.

Afraid of what the news would do to his family and his career, Smith had continued to pay her for months, until his retirement account was drained. Even then, he said, Whitney wouldn't back down. Her demands grew increasingly strident.

Losing control of the situation, and desperate to protect himself, Smith stole money from the police department – redirecting payments of public funds to give to her, until someone in his office started wondering what was going on.

When Whitney renewed her threats of exposure if she didn't get more money, he'd panicked.

'I think I had a complete breakdown,' he'd told the jury, head bowed, shoulders hunched, 'I cannot otherwise explain how I allowed myself to do what I did.' He'd stared down at his hands, knotted together on the polished wood of the witness stand. 'I can almost not remember that day at all. I don't want to remember.'

From then on, the outcome of the trial was preordained. It was purely a matter of going through the legal paces.

When the jury went out to deliberate their decision, Harper offered Ed twenty dollars to call her the second they returned. He refused the cash.

After four hours of silence, he called her at six o'clock that night.

'They're coming back.'

She was there, sitting in the last row, her good hand gripping the wooden seatback in front of her, when Smith was found guilty of the murder of Marie Whitney, and sentenced to life in prison.

Only when he was handcuffed and led from the courtroom did Harper finally let herself cry. Sitting on the wooden pew, her face buried in her hands.

She cried for Camille Whitney. For both their mothers. And for herself.

Chapter Forty-five

After his conviction, Smith was processed and transferred to the state prison outside Reidsville, a nowhere town an hour's drive from Savannah.

He wasn't allowed visitors for the first month, in order – the prison spokesperson told Harper – that he'd have a chance to settle.

On his first visitors' day, Harper was there, sitting in a cheap plastic chair in the bunker-like visitors' room, having left her phone, keys and scanner in a numbered plastic tub in reception.

She'd been to jails before for interviews, but never like this – never for someone she cared about. Someone who had betrayed her trust.

The prison was a vast, intimidating high-security building hidden away behind a twenty-foot steel fence topped with barbed wire. As she pulled up to the gate, she saw sharpshooters with binoculars and rifles positioned atop towers at every corner.

The guard checked her driver's license against a list on a clip-board, and then waved her through.

'Have a nice day,' he told her.

Inside was a concrete hell of echoing voices, crying babies, repeated cold-blooded announcements about drugs, guns and threats of arrest. It smelled of disinfectant, sweat and a bitter residue of fear.

Harper sat stiffly in her chair, conscious of every single person around her, eyes on the door through which the prisoners appeared, one at a time. When Smith finally walked through, her heart twisted.

His hands were cuffed to a chain connected to his ankles. Like all the other convicts, he wore a plain white jumpsuit with a number on the back. He looked thinner and much older, but there was some color in his cheeks.

He shuffled behind the guard, his eyes sweeping the room anxiously. When his eyes met Harper's, his shoulders sagged.

Slowly, he made his way toward her, his chains jangling with each step. When he neared, a guard bristling with weaponry appeared next to him to unlock the handcuffs.

The guard recited the words he'd already said dozens of times today.

'No touching. No exchanging of belongings. Hands on the table. Don't make me yell at you. Enjoy your visit.'

With that, he walked away. Leaving the two of them alone.

Rubbing his wrists, Smith lowered himself into the seat, swinging his chained ankles under the table, with effort.

Harper had waited a long time for this moment. Now that it had arrived, all the words she'd planned to say disappeared from her mind.

She hadn't told anyone she was coming here today. Not even Bonnie. No one would understand. But there were things she had to know. Things only Smith could tell her.

She'd told herself it would be hard, but she could get through it. She was prepared to cry, to scream.

Now that she was here, though, she felt curiously empty. As if her real emotions were far away.

Smith eyed her cautiously. When she said nothing, he gave a long sigh.

'Dammit, McClain,' he growled. 'Don't you *ever* give up?'

'No, sir,' she said. 'I do not.'

She rested her hands on the scarred table. She didn't know where to start – or what to say.

'You look thin,' she told him. 'Don't they feed you here?'

'They do. But the food is terrible.'

'Well,' she said. 'I guess losing weight is good for you.'

'That is what they say.' He glanced at her shoulder, clad in a loose, dark top. 'You got that cast off.'

Harper shifted her shoulder experimentally, feeling the familiar twinge of damaged muscles and scar tissue.

'They took it off a month ago,' she said. 'A bit of physical therapy and I'll be able to throw a punch again.'

Suddenly grief shadowed his face.

'I am truly sorry, Harper.' His voice grew unsteady. 'You know that bullet wasn't meant for you, don't you?'

'I know.'

She did know. She'd always known. She'd felt the resistance when she tried to pull his arm down. The way he'd fought to keep the gun pointed at himself.

Nonetheless. It felt good to hear him say it.

Harper took a breath.

'Lieutenant...' she began.

He shook his head in disbelief.

'Are you really going to call me that?'

She tilted her shoulder. 'It's what you are to me. What do you want me to call you? Robert? Mr Smith?'

'I guess that does sound strange coming from you,' he conceded gruffly.

'Lieutenant,' she began again, 'I hate that it ended like this. I think I never believed, in my heart, this was possible.'

'I hate it, too, Harper.' His voice carried more feeling than he'd ever shown during the trial. 'More than I could ever begin to tell you.'

Someone across the room started to cry. The guards migrated closer to that table, looking for trouble.

Harper braced herself.

'I have some questions.'

Smith almost smiled.

'Why am I not surprised?' He shifted in the plastic chair, his ankle chains rattling. 'Ask away. I've got nothing but time.'

'Well.' She cleared her throat. 'Obviously, I understand the Whitney case. I was in the courthouse every day. You didn't contest the charges. What I don't get, is why the murder looked exactly like my mother's.'

She leaned toward him, her eyes fixed on his.

'I need to know the truth – did you kill my mother?'

The mingled surprise and horror on his face gave her the answer she sought even before he spoke.

'My God, Harper. No.' He leaned forward urgently, chains clanging. 'Please don't think that. I am not the man you're looking for. I killed Marie Whitney. I am a murderer. I accept the jury's verdict. But not your mother. I swear it.'

Harper held his gaze for a long moment, then, finding no sign of deception, leaned back.

There was so much she wanted to say to him. She wanted to

tell him how much he'd destroyed. She wanted to tell him about Pat and Kyle and Scott, whose lives would be tainted forever by his actions. She wanted him to know that he'd taken away the last of her trust.

And then, there was Camille Whitney.

But she hadn't come here to tell him things he knew already.

She'd come here for answers.

'If you didn't kill my mother, why did you use exactly the same method?' she asked.

At that moment, a new visitor walked in and Smith looked across the room at the door leading out of the prison – one he'd never walk through again.

'Did you know I've solved nearly every murder I've ever investigated?' he asked. 'Thirty years as a detective and I can count on one hand the number of murders that went unsolved. A few of those really got to me. Your mother's case.' He turned back to her, his eyes like steel. 'That was one of those.'

Around them the noise of the room receded. The smells, the guns – all of it faded into the background. All Harper heard was Smith's familiar baritone.

'I think every major crime that goes unsolved chips away at your soul,' he said. 'Mostly they're small dings – you barely notice them. But your mother's case... that was different. That one was a break right down the middle. Because of you.' His eyes swept her face. 'I promised you I'd get him. And every day I didn't solve that crime, I thought about the look on your face when I first walked up to you that afternoon.'

Harper bit her lip, hard, but didn't interrupt him.

'Sometimes I think my whole life might have been different if I hadn't pulled that case,' he said. 'Choices I made would have gone the other way if I hadn't made a promise to you I couldn't keep.'

A guard walked by their table, nightstick swinging, gun heavy on his hip. Harper saw Smith assess his posture, his weapon. It was so automatic – she wasn't sure he even knew he'd done it.

When he spoke again he sounded tired.

'I worked so hard on that case – we all did. Day and night. We never got a break. Whoever did it was good. He was a pro. We found nothing we could work with. *Nothing.* We called him the invisible man.'

He paused, remembering.

'When Marie threatened me that last time…' Hands turning over on the table – rugged palms. '… I never planned to kill her. She told me she was going to Pat – that she'd make my boys hate me. She'd take away my job – my family. It all happened too fast – my reactions were inhuman. They were horrible.' His voice dripped self-loathing. 'But when it was over, I remembered the invisible man. I thought about how he did it. And I decided I needed to be him.'

He gave a sad nod.

'That's why the scenes look alike. I designed the second one to look like the first. A direct replication. If he got away with it, I thought I could, too.' He exhaled. 'Turns out I was wrong.'

It wasn't the answer Harper wanted but, still, there was a hollow satisfaction as the last missing piece finally fell into place.

It would have been simple, in a way. Every detective has all the tools for covering up a murder in the trunk of their car. Gloves and alcohol wipes, bags for removing evidence, shoe covers.

'I'm so sorry you're still looking for your murderer,' Smith concluded with real regret. 'I wish I could at least give you that.'

Something he said triggered a sudden image in Harper's mind of fierce brown eyes staring at her across a scarred kitchen table.

And make him pay.

'Camille Whitney,' she said, cutting him off abruptly. 'I don't understand. She had the same experience as me. How could you let that happen to her?'

Smith had been so composed. Now, though, his face crumpled. He buried his face in his hands. A long moment passed before he could speak.

'That, I believe, was God reminding me he was watching.' He wiped his cheek with the back of his hand. 'I thought I had it all figured out. I knew her dad was going to pick her up that day after summer school. He always did on Thursdays. Every single time. That was why I chose that day. I knew Camille wouldn't be there. But, that morning, her dad got called into work.'

He met her gaze with eyes that suddenly looked ancient.

'What I did to that girl will haunt me the rest of my days. I took a life, which was unforgivable. But I also ruined a child's future. And I know from watching you what that means.'

She couldn't think of anything to say to that. If he wanted absolution he wasn't going to get it from her. But at least, now, she understood.

There was one more thing she needed explained. Then she'd be done here.

'Lieutenant,' she said. 'The break-in at my house. Why did you order that?'

The sadness left his face, replaced by something else – something more urgent.

'Harper,' he said, 'you have to believe me. I had nothing to do with that burglary.'

He leaned towards her, reaching out across the table as if to take her hands.

A guard barked an angry warning across the room. Smith pulled back. But his face was passionate.

'You must believe me,' he said again. 'That wasn't the police. It did not come from our ranks. I swear it.'

Harper thought of the word left on her wall in black, stark letters, paint dripping down like blood: *RUN*.

A shard of fear pierced her heart.

'If it wasn't you...' she said. 'Who was it?'

'I don't know, but I don't like it,' he said. 'The things you told me – slashing the face of your portrait, leaving a message on the wall – that indicates a personal relationship. It's someone close to you. Whoever it is, if they're willing to take chances like this, they are incredibly dangerous.' He held her eyes. 'You need to be careful.'

The air felt suddenly clammy and dank.

Since the break-in, Harper had replaced the windows with bulletproof glass and added an alarm system. The threat left on the wall had long ago been painted over.

Nonetheless, she didn't feel safe there any more.

She'd told herself it was the sense of invasion that had pushed her away from her home. Now, though, she wondered if it wasn't her instincts warning her things were not as they seemed.

A forlorn hopelessness swept over her. What was she going to do? She needed help.

The problem was, the person she'd always gone to for advice was sitting across from her in chains.

Who was she going to turn to now?

She'd come here today to get what she wanted and walk away for good.

Now, all of a sudden, she couldn't imagine her world without Smith in it.

She'd lost so much already, she had precious few people left to hold on to.

There was no way she could forgive Smith for what he'd done, but the truth was, she *needed* him.

Once upon a time, long ago, he'd saved her sanity. In some way, he'd been doing that ever since. Without him, what would become of her?

Grief hit her like a fist, knocking the wind out of her.

How could he do this? He was supposed to protect her.

He had to protect her.

Tears burned her eyes, and she blinked them back hard. She wasn't going to wail like that woman across the room. That wouldn't get her anywhere.

She was going to make him help.

Squaring her shoulders, she drew a breath and raised her eyes to his.

'So,' she said, 'what kind of person are we dealing with here? Someone with an obsession? Maybe someone I've written about?'

For an instant, she thought she saw a hint of understanding in his expression. As if he knew everything she was thinking.

Then that cool, professional mask descended, and she could never be certain whether that look had been real, or all in her imagination.

'It's hard to say.' His voice was thoughtful. 'I don't think so. This is bigger than that. This is someone you've personally inter-acted with. Someone who's met you. You might have no memory of this meeting – but somehow it became meaningful to him. Now, tell me again, everything you can remember about the break-in. From the start.'

Forgetting the crowded room and the patrolling guards, they broke the case down into its smallest pieces so Smith could study each one, like he used to in the comfortable, smoke-filled study in that big suburban house.

As the day stretched on, and the autumn sun drifted across the blue Georgia sky, Harper could almost fool herself that everything was the way it had been.

And that she wasn't a little more alone out there than she used to be.

Acknowledgments

I would like to start with a huge thank you and a tiny apology to the gorgeous city of Savannah, Georgia, because I have taken a few liberties with it. Among other things, I've invented a newspaper that doesn't exist, and I have created a police department that suited my needs. Most of the restaurants and bars in the book are not real. There is no Library Bar in Savannah. There is no place that I know of in Savannah precisely like The Watch.

Finally, all the people in this book are fully invented. The police officers and the murders are all fictional.

Still, I have tried very hard to be true to the feel of Savannah. And to treat it with respect. I have very fond memories of my years working as a reporter in that city, and of the people I knew there. It was the best first job a girl could have.

Many, many thanks go to my brilliant editor, Sarah Hodgson, and the entire team at HarperCollins. I am thrilled to be working with such amazing and talented people. I hope we make many beautiful crimes together.

In a lot of ways, this book was a leap of faith for me. My

wonderful agent and friend, Madeleine Milburn, knew it was the book of my heart and, despite my nervousness (Should I write it now, or later? Should I write something else instead? Should I...?), calmly told me to just go write it. I am grateful to her for believing in me. She, Hayley Steed, Alice Sutherland-Hawes, and Giles Milburn – the whole agency helped make all of this happen.

Enormous thanks also to my brilliant partners-in-crime who read the first draft of this book and helped me make it better: Ruth Ware, Lee Weatherly, Sam Smith, Holly Bourne, Melinda Salisbury, Alexia Casale – what in the world would I do without you?

Finally, thank you to my husband, Jack, for insisting for as long as I have known him that I should write this book. But I was always busy, and there were other things to write, and I wasn't ready and I wasn't ready and I wasn't ready.

Now, I'm ready. I love you.

Can't wait to continue the
Harper McClain series?
Read on for a sneak peek of the next
instalment, coming April 2019...

Chapter One

'Eight ball in the corner pocket.'

Leaning over the edge of the pool table, Harper McClain stared across the long expanse of empty green felt. The cue in her hands was smooth and cool. She'd had four of Bonnie's super-strength margaritas already tonight, but her grip was steady.

There was a delicate, transient point somewhere between too much alcohol and too little, where her pool skills absolutely peaked. This was it.

Exhaling slowly, she took the shot. The cue ball flew straight and true, slamming into the eight, sending it rolling to the pocket. There was never any question, it hit the polished wood edge of the table only lightly, and dropped like a stone.

'*Yes*.' Harper raised her fist. 'Three in a row.'

But the cue ball was still rolling.

'No, no, no,' she pleaded.

As she watched in dismay, the scuffed white cue headed after the eight ball like a faithful hound.

'Come on cue ball,' Bonnie cajoled from the other side of the table. 'Mama needs a new pair of shoes.'

Reaching the pocket lip, the ball trembled for an instant as if making up its mind and then, with a decisive clunk, disappeared into the table's insides, taking the game with it.

'At last.' Bonnie raised her cue above her head, triumphantly. 'Victory is mine.'

Harper glared. 'Have you been waiting all night to say that?'

'Oh my God, yes,' Bonnie replied.

It was very late. Aside from the two of them, the Library Bar was empty. Tuesdays were always quiet, and the crowds had thinned early. Carlo, who worked the late shift with Bonnie, had finished wiping down the bar an hour ago and gone home.

All the lights were on in the rambling bar, illuminating the battered books that filled the shelves covering the old walls. It was familiar – even cosy, in its way, with Tom Waits growling from the jukebox about love gone wrong.

Despite the hour, Harper was in no hurry to leave. All she had at home was a cat, a bottle of whiskey and a lot of bad memories.

'Rematch?' Harper glanced at Bonnie. 'Winner takes all?'

Propping her cue against a wall already scuffed with blue chalk, Bonnie walked around the table. The blue streaks in her long, blonde hair caught the light when she held out her hand.

'Loser pays,' she said, adding, 'Also, I'm all out of change.'

'I thought bartenders always had change,' Harper complained, pulling the last coins from her pocket.

'Bartenders are smart enough to put their money away before they start playing pool with you,' Bonnie said.

There was a break in the music as the jukebox switched songs. In the sudden silence, the shrill ring of Harper's phone made them both jump.

Grabbing the device off the table next to her, Harper glanced at the screen.

'Hang on,' she said, hitting the answer button. 'It's Miles.'

Miles Jackson was the crime photographer at the Savannah *Daily News*. He wouldn't call at three in the morning without a good reason.

'What's up?' Harper said, by way of hello.

'Get yourself downtown. We've got ourselves a murder on River Street,' he announced.

Miles had her on speaker phone – in the background she could hear the rumble of his engine and the insistent crackle of his police scanners.

'You're kidding me.' Harper stood up, the pool game instantly forgotten. 'Are you at the scene?'

'Just pulling up now,' he said. 'Looks like every cop in the city is here.'

'On my way.' Harper hung up without saying goodbye.

Bonnie looked at her enquiringly.

'Got to go,' Harper said. 'Someone just got murdered on River Street.'

Bonnie's jaw dropped. 'River Street? Holy crap.'

'I know.' Grabbing her bag off the battered wooden chair, Harper made sure her reporters' notebook was inside. 'If it's a tourist, the mayor will absolutely lose her shit.'

Setting down her cue, Bonnie ran after her as she raced out of the small pool room into the main bar.

The music was louder in here, echoing off the old walls of a building that had once been a library and that, even now, held bookshelves on every wall, stacked with paperbacks.

'Give me a second to lock up,' she said. 'I'm coming with you.'

Harper blinked. 'You're coming to a crime scene?'

447

'You've had four margaritas,' Bonnie reminded her in a voice that brooked no opposition. 'I made them strong. You'll be over the limit. I've only had two beers tonight.'

Behind the bar, she opened a wall panel and flipped some switches – the music fell silent. A second later, the lights began to turn off one by one, until only the red glow of the entrance sign remained.

Grabbing her keys, Bonnie ran back to join Harper, the heels of her cowboy boots clicking against the concrete floor in the sudden quiet, short skirt swirling around her thighs.

Harper gave her a sceptical look.

'You know there'll be dead people there, right?'

Shrugging, Bonnie unlocked the front door and pulled it open. Steamy southern night air poured in.

'I'm a grown-up. I can take it.'

She glanced over her shoulder with a look Harper had known better than to argue with since she was six years old.

'Let's go.'

* * *

At the edge of the city, overlooking the Savannah River, Bay Street ran parallel to River Street, but about twelve feet higher. Below lay the old wharves and warehouses that had once serviced tall ships, sailing for Europe, but which now served the city's massive tourist industry.

The street was virtually empty when Bonnie swung her pink pickup, with 'Mavis' painted on the back in bright yellow, into a parking spot and killed the engine.

From her window, Harper could see flashing blue lights down at the water's edge.

'Come on,' she said, throwing up the door and jumping out.

She landed hard on the curb, and the bullet wound in her shoulder throbbed a sharp warning. She winced, pressing her hand against the scar.

It had been a year since she'd been shot. It was rare for the wound to twinge like that these days. It usually only acted up when the weather changed.

'You'll be a walking barometer now,' her surgeon had remarked jovially at one of her check-ups. 'Always be able to tell when rain is coming.'

'That is not the superpower I was hoping for,' she'd responded.

Secretly, she was glad the pain was still there. The wound – which she'd sustained while exposing former Lieutenant Robert Smith for murder – served as a reminder to be careful who she trusted.

Bonnie, who had missed her pained expression as she walked around the truck to join her, looked down at the line of police cars below and whistled.

'Damn,' she said, 'It really is right in the middle of everything. That's just a couple of blocks from Huey's.'

Huey's Bar and Restaurant was one of the most popular tourist joints in the city.

Harper had already noticed the proximity. She needed to get down there.

'They'll close the street,' she said, pointing to her left. 'Let's go down that way.'

They strode down the cobbled incline towards the river. Harper's rubber-soled boots struggled to find grip on the rounded stones. Bonnie swore as her boots skidded.

River Street was the oldest lane in the city. It was undeniably atmospheric, with the old docks converted into artfully landscaped plazas where visitors gathered and buskers performed. Warehouses that once stored cotton and indigo had been repurposed as pubs, restaurants and shops selling pralines and T-shirts with slogans like 'MADE IN THE SOUTH'. During the day, a brightly painted streetcar rumbled up and down the water's edge, dinging its cheerful bell.

Harper usually avoided it. It was packed with tourist traps and no interesting crimes happened here.

Tonight, though, was different.

Crime tape had been strung from light pole to light pole, blocking the narrow street. Flashing blue lights lit up the night.

Harper scanned the scene – the road was packed with police cars but she could see no trucks bearing the hallmarks of the local TV news stations.

She smiled to herself. Bless Miles for staying up all night listening to his scanner. They'd have an exclusive on this.

About thirty yards beyond the tape, a cluster of uniformed cops and plain-clothed detectives gathered at the foot of the old, stone staircase that led back up to Bay Street. They were all looking down at something.

'Look, there's Miles.' Bonnie pointed. 'Hey Miles!'

The photographer was on the far side of the street. Hearing her voice, he looked up, and waved them over.

As always, he looked dapper in slacks and a button-down shirt – as if he'd been dressed early and waiting for this crime to happen.

'Well, well, well,' he said, as they walked up. 'Is it two-for-one night? I didn't bring my coupon.'

'Hi Miles.' Bonnie beamed at him. 'Fancy running into you at a murder scene.'

'The night is full of surprises,' he agreed.

'What'd we miss?' Harper gestured to the crowd of cops. 'Any ID on the victim? Is it a tourist?'

'Nobody's saying anything.' He gave her a significant look. 'The tape was up when I got here. They've kept it quiet on the radio – there's no chatter. I almost missed it myself. I heard some chit-chat about the coroner which let me know something was up, otherwise I'd still be home.'

Keeping it quiet – that meant the police were trying to buy themselves time. They knew this story was going to be big.

Their editor would want to know about this as soon as possible.

'You called Baxter yet?' she asked.

He shook his head.

'Don't have enough to tell her,' he said. 'I've got nothing but instincts right now says this isn't a normal crime.'

Harper didn't reply, but they both knew his instincts were good. Still, better to wait until they knew more for certain.

Bonnie listened to all of this, but said nothing. Harper wondered how she and Miles must look to an outsider. After years of working together, the two of them had a kind of complex shorthand that included no platitudes for the dead. When it came to a crime scene, they were pure business.

In the distance, the crowd of officers shifted. Near the foot of the steps, Harper saw several figures in plain clothes, crouching low. She squinted into the shadows but couldn't make them out.

'Who's lead detective?' she asked Miles, who stepped over to join her.

'Daltrey.' He raised his camera to take a speculative shot, then checked the image on the screen.

Harper's shoulders relaxed just a little. She could work with

Julie Daltrey. The same wasn't true of all the detectives these days.

A rumble broke the stillness, and they all turned to see a white van with the words FORENSICS UNIT on the side rolling slowly past them, its tires stuttering on the cobblestones.

A uniformed cop ran over to untie the crime tape and let it through. As the van pulled in, its cold, bright headlights swung to the cluster of investigators, lighting up the scene like a film set.

They all saw the body on the staircase in the same instant. The young woman lay face up across the lowest steps, wide eyes staring at the black sky. Her fingers still clung to the metal railings, slim legs sprawling at an unnatural angle. She wore a knee-length skirt and boots.

The hairs on the back of Harper's neck rose.

This was no gangbanger crime. She could tell that from here.

The woman's green T-shirt looked familiar, although she couldn't make out the writing on it.

Miles gave a low whistle and, lifting his camera, fired off a rapid series of shots.

Harper stood on her toes to get a better look.

Beside her, Bonnie made a stifled shocked sound.

'Don't look at the body,' Harper advised. 'Take a walk if you feel sick.'

But Bonnie didn't look away. Instead, she leaned against the crime tape, straining to see the woman, pushing hard enough to make it bow.

One of the uniforms flashed a light on her disapprovingly. 'Hey you – get back.'

Harper turned to ask her what the hell she was doing. The last thing she needed was for Bonnie to piss off the cops. But when she looked at her face, the complaint died on her lips.

Bonnie looked stricken.

'Oh my God, Harper,' she said, staring at the body on the stairs. 'I know her.'

Don't miss the next book in the Harper McClain series, coming in April 2019